'Dizzying and exciting and unsettling, and beautifully told'
Reverend Richard Coles,
'Big Writers on Their Best Reads of 2022', *Daily Mail*

'This is a novel full of suspense and surprise. It made me
laugh and brought back memories of a time in my own life. I
missed the characters as soon as I'd finished'
Sarah Lucas

'The musings of the book's protagonist on the radical power
of art to act as a catalyst for personal change make it an
exhilarating, erudite read'
Liam Hess, *Vogue.com*

'I travelled on the exquisite vessel of James Cahill's prose,
unable to disembark. The journey is sensual, treacherous and
elegiac. The final landing, breathtaking'
Maggi Hambling

'[An] arresting debut novel . . . a masterly attention to detail
and an irresistibly propulsive, almost swaggering style'
Michael Delgado, *Literary Review*

'[A] simmering debut novel'
Esquire.com

'Wow. It is magnificent. Simply magnificent . . . *Tiepolo Blue*
really has blown me away: the gorgeous phrase-making; the
sure-footed pacing; the (re-)immersion in a world I know, or
knew, in a way that is both hard-edged with historical detail
and almost hallucinatory'
Robert Douglas-Fairhurst

Tiepolo Blue

James Cahill

sceptre

First published in Great Britain in 2022 by Sceptre
An imprint of Hodder & Stoughton
An Hachette UK company

This paperback edition published in 2023

1

A CIP catalogue record for this title is available from the British Library

Paperback ISBN 9781529369427
eBook ISBN 9781529369403

Typeset in Sabon MT by
Palimpsest Book Production Ltd, Falkirk, Stirlingshire

Printed and bound in Great Britain by Clays Ltd, Elcograf S.p.A.

Hodder & Stoughton policy is to use papers that are natural, renewable and
recyclable products and made from wood grown in sustainable forests. The
logging and manufacturing processes are expected to conform to the
environmental regulations of the country of origin.

Hodder & Stoughton Ltd
Carmelite House
50 Victoria Embankment
London EC4Y 0DZ

www.sceptrebooks.co.uk

For my parents, Frances and Joe,
and for Alexander Caplan

You say to the boy open your eyes
When he opens his eyes and sees the light
You make him cry out. Saying
O Blue come forth
O Blue arise
O Blue ascend
O Blue come in

Derek Jarman

PART I

I

It is late September – and a new term. Don Lamb has spent the afternoon in Jesus College library, reading letters from the eighteenth century. It has been raining – the air is still damp – but as he cycles back to Peterhouse, the sun comes out and catches the world off guard. The paths and trees of Christ's Pieces look naked in its glare. The houses across the park glow like bronze.

It is one of those moments when summer and autumn creep into one another, each uncertain of its territory. The breeze is mild, like liquid, and the trees – still in full leaf – quiver and bristle. Slowing to a stop, Don screws up his eyes. The sky is breaking. A rush of exhilaration passes over him, mixed with sadness. It's inexplicable. He knows what the term will bring, his life isn't chequered by surprises or excitements, and yet – he can't explain the feeling.

There is a smell of wet nature in the air – a leafy, muddy, mulchy aroma, underscored by something dank. He pedals along the path – slowly, like a man less busy than himself – crossing islands of shadow. Cambridge is still quiet from the long summer break, but students are beginning to return. Two of them are suddenly in his way: young men absorbed in animated talk, walking towards him, their faces enlarged by mirth. Their words reach him as blunt fragments of sound. With a swivel of his handlebars, he veers off the path.

The change of course sends him straight into a stone bird bath, hitting it hard with his knee. Don slides off his bike and grips his leg; the pain subsides and leaves him in a tranquil stupor. Rainwater has risen to the rim of the basin, and the clouds overhead are visible through a debris of leaves, petals and insects – dead and living – on the surface of the little pool. A cigarette butt floats in the confetti. The edge of his face is there too in the water, a slice of brow and cheekbone and one dark eye.

A sign at the end of the park marks the boundary of Christ's Pieces. It's a strange name, as if the son of God lay dismembered beneath university land. Steering the bike around a coil of dog shit, he kicks one leg across the saddle and cycles past the bus station, into the benign heart of Cambridge.

The sunlight is retreating as he turns into the gate of Peterhouse. Beyond the porter's lodge, in the middle of the front court, is something odd – a pile of rubbish on the lawn. It looks as if a skip has been emptied.

Affecting indifference, he asks the porter when it will be cleared away.

'Not for some time, Professor Lamb.'

The porter's smile makes Don reluctant to ask more. Amid the latticework of pigeonholes, oak-walled inlets stuffed with envelopes and newspapers, fat wads of paper and stray sheets, his own niche (*Professor D. Lamb*) is empty.

The pile of rubbish is more than it seemed. The skeleton of a bed lies at the centre of the grass – an iron frame packed with coil springs. It is propped up at one end by a mound of empty liquor bottles, crushed beer cans and snarled-up clothes. On the grass beneath is an industrial lamp that rotates with slow, robotic gyrations. A black cable snakes across the lawn and disappears underneath a door at the perimeter of Old Court.

There is a sign near the path.

Angela Cannon
SICK BED

4

Don looks back with fascination at the objects. Intermittently, the lamp shines through the wire innards of the bed with a blinding flash and spidery shadows race over the quadrangle.

Someone – the thought comes to him as he stands there – might see him. Colleagues might be watching from the windows of Old Court – watching this very second, squinting to register the verdict of the art historian. And so he assumes a look of cool disdain. The lamp changes angle and blazes through the pile of bottles, illuminating their glass surfaces – green, brown, the electric blue of a spent litre of Bombay Sapphire. The colours induce a fit of blinking.

Walking around the court to the staircase that leads to his rooms, he resists the temptation to look back. But the view from the window of his study allows him another glance at the junk on the grass below, so peculiarly arranged. It's more contrived than a heap of refuse. More knowing. He tugs the curtains closed, and the thin fabric pulses with an alien glare. Lighting a cigarette, he looks around him, as if to reassure himself that the rest of his surroundings are unchanged – just as they have ever been.

The tautology of his name has always pleased him. Donnish, serious, dignified – that is how his life has been. He came to Cambridge aged seventeen, and over the years his consciousness has fused, like ivy eating into stone, with the town. He turned forty-three this summer. Sometimes the span of time seems like nothing. His memories are entwined with the foliage of Peterhouse, with the gardens and meadows and surreptitious river. His thoughts are the mirror image of Cambridge's unchanging vistas, his mind sustained by the rituals of academic life.

His rooms are two of the oldest in the college. The larger room, his study, contains his collection of prints and drawings, most of them by masters of the Rococo – a modest collection, modestly arranged. In the centre of the room is a scale model of the Pantheon, carved from cork and mounted on an oak console. Between the windows, resting on two brass hooks, is a small ornamental sword. All around the walls, books fill the shelves. On his desk is a framed photograph of a greyhound, black and white and fading.

In one corner is a column of cardboard boxes, each filled with paper and labelled meticulously in marker pen – *Palazzo Sandi*, *Residenz Würzburg*, *Santa Maria del Rosario*: the divisions of his private archive. From the age of seventeen, Don has collected reproductions of the frescoes of Giambattista Tiepolo – hundreds of postcards, prints and pages from books.

Tiepolo is his enduring love. All this time he has been readying himself to write a book – *the* book – on that genius of eighteenth-century Venice: the last of the Old Masters, the first of the moderns. Other art historians have described Tiepolo as a painter of sweetness and light, a divine choreographer. Not Don. With every picture he keeps, the ghost of the artist beckons him a little further, demanding the scholarly treatment that only Don can give. 'No more sweetness and light,' he hears Tiepolo say. 'Show them how *classical* I am.' The book is still in its earliest stages, a swirling suspension of ideas. The task will be difficult – the most complex yet.

The adjoining room, Don's bedroom, is bare apart from a single bed, a sink and a cracked mirror.

Changing his leather shoes for slippers, he turns on the radio to hear a succession of pips:

'And now the news at six o'clock. There is no end in sight to the war in the Balkans – Sarajevo remains under siege. The Prime Minister, John Major, faces fresh allegations of sleaze within his government. Madonna, queen of pop—'

He switches it off. There is nothing of interest in the day's news.

There is a scent of antique paper on his fingers. Tiepolo's correspondence from Milan – the cache of letters he was reading earlier – steals back to him. He removes his notes from his briefcase and pores over them at his desk.

Not until he left Venice, his known universe, did life begin.

Milan – Mediolanum to the ancients – saw the blossoming of Tiepolo's early maturity. It took a classical city to raise him to greatness.

Hours pass and he forgets to go down to dinner. His mind is closed to the distant clatter and drone from the Hall, interrupted just once by the saying of grace; it fizzes with the small quandaries of the 1730s.

Late in the evening, he reads through his script for the Fitzwilliam Lecture. It is an early teaser of his book on Tiepolo. He tries sections out loud. There is one passage, a description of the *Allegory of the Power of Eloquence*, which he plans to deliver from memory. He will step away from the lectern, relinquish his notes – as if the words have come to him in a rush of inspiration. Standing in front of the bedroom mirror, lit from behind by the glow of his study, he delivers the phrases perfectly, gracing his diction with careful motions of the hands – a single raised finger. He repeats the section, over and over, until half the night has passed.

*

For the Fitzwilliam Lecture, Don wears his best suit of midnight-blue silk, with a white shirt and a blue silk tie.

Passing out of the college at seven o'clock, he is too busy rehearsing his speech in his head to take notice of the rubbish piled on the grass, although the lamp is strafing the dark court with garish light. Nothing matters, tonight, but the lecture. He sweeps down Trumpington Street with a growing sense of occasion, feeling his mental powers enlarge. As he arrives at the Fitzwilliam Museum, crossing from the cold night into the crowded lobby, he is conscious of heads turning – a momentary lull.

He shoulders off his overcoat and hands it to an attendant.

The girl's nervous smile makes him aware, for a moment, of his own simmering anticipation. Is it nervousness? Dismissing the thought, he smiles back at her and prepares to scale the stairs. But just then, fingers close around his forearm. He turns.

It is Val – Valentine Black – the Head of Department.

A familiar scent, of cologne mixed with cigarettes, closes in. Val ushers him into an empty gallery.

'No need for apprehension,' Val murmurs as they cross the darkened room. 'You'll rise to the event. You always do.'

'I'm not apprehensive. The thesis is the thesis. Haven't I always said so?'

Val halts and laughs – an easy, elegant, enrapturing laugh. Don watches him. Val is in his sixties, but he could pass for a decade younger – a tall, slender man with a mass of black hair swept off his tanned forehead. His teeth are white and gapless, and they replicate – in the half-light of the gallery – the excited shine of his eyes. He is wearing a dark blue suit similar to Don's, but in place of a tie, a silver-grey cravat nestles inside the collar of his shirt.

'Very good, Don. Didn't I give you that line? Anyway, you'll be superb. They'll love you – or hate you – for your brilliance! This way – the back stairs lead straight to the stage.'

The stage is a temporary platform, stapled with a pelmet of maroon linen, erected at one end of the grandest gallery in the museum. At its centre is a lectern, isolated in a pool of light. Beyond, four hundred empty seats extend across the room – two vast banks of green plush, parted by an aisle. A hum of voices is audible through the closed double doors at the far end.

Val shows Don to a seat at the back of the stage, directly beneath Edward Lear's painting of a Greek ruin in flowery English countryside.

'We'll start at eight,' he says, standing at the lectern and surveying the vacant chairs. 'I'll introduce you first, of course.'

'Nothing too long, I hope.'

Val swings round and gives a conspiratorial grin. 'Just a few simple words, Don. No introduction is needed, really, but you know the format of these things.'

Just after eight o'clock, with four hundred eminences waiting in their seats, Val ascends the platform, passes into the spotlight and raises his hands. Seated close behind him, Don watches his friend with a controlled expression.

'We have as our speaker tonight a world-renowned scholar,' Val begins, skimming the room with eager eyes and bringing his lips close to the microphone that rises like a black poppy from the lectern. 'A celebrated authority on the art of the Rococo period. And,' he turns to Don and lowers his voice, 'a dear friend of mine.'

Val's cut-glass accent is so clipped and precise, Don thinks, that it suggests a trace of German, perhaps the result of his proficiency in multiple languages. Silence intercedes on his words like a deft blade. Don bows his head.

'The audience will forgive me if I indulge in a short – how to say it? – a *peregrination*, yes, through the achievements of Professor Lamb. Don himself will perhaps not forgive me so readily.'

Polite laughter rolls through the room, and Val chuckles into the microphone.

'Professor Lamb is no ordinary art historian. He is, let me be quite clear, the embodiment of art history in Cambridge. I can barely recollect a time when he wasn't a shining light in our academic pantheon. And yet, once upon a time, he was my doctoral student – the best I ever had.' Val flashes another glance in Don's direction. 'He arrived in Cambridge at the end of the 1960s – a time of insurrection for some, but for Don a moment of intellectual genesis, a first flowering. Classical forms, not Marxist credos, were his guiding precepts.'

Someone in the audience begins to mutter – the faint, familiar sound of academic dissent. Val draws breath.

'By the age of twenty-five he was a fellow of Peterhouse. At thirty he was a professor. His first book, *Classical Allusion in the Venetian Seicento*, was a path-breaking feat – a divine marriage of classical philology and aesthetic acumen.' Val adjusts the microphone on its stalk, sending out a loud bolt. 'There followed a succession of masterly publications, each book a dazzling opus. The villas of Andrea Palladio, the origins of the northern Italian Baroque, the minor works of Nicolas Lancret – a brief Francophile detour, shall we say?' Val's hands spray the audience with invisible confetti; his eyes are alight. 'Many of you will remember his radio programme, *A Venetian Odyssey* – how he sailed through Venice on a gondola, pronouncing on the churches and *palazzi* with bone-dry wit!'

Another vibration of laughter, stronger than the last.

'Here is a man for whom scholarship is a compulsion and a duty' – Val slaps the lectern, causing it to wobble – 'but a duty he loves. He has ennobled the role of the art historian in Cambridge – and quite possibly beyond.'

The applause is tentative at first, then vigorous, urgent, filling the room. Val raises one hand like a conductor marking a significant rest.

'Ladies and gentlemen, I give you Professor Donald Lamb.'

With a balletic sideways movement, Val vacates the stage. Don rises amid another explosion of claps and walks the few steps to the lectern.

Before him is his script, sprinkled with last night's annotations. The microphone casts an elongated shadow across the page. He raises his eyes, smiles at the sea of dimmed faces, and fixes his attention on the opening line.

'I wish to dwell' – his voice swells through the room – 'on the immensity of Tiepolo's skies. The *depth of field*.'

He lifts the remote control for the projector – a sliver of black

Bakelite – and ratchets the first slide into view. A screen hanging diagonally behind him beams out the image of two deities – a beautiful goddess and an old bearded god, embracing in front of a luminous sky.

The speech proceeds just as he planned. In phrases that build and redouble like music, he explains the arrangement of gods and men in Tiepolo's frescoes – the complex spatial hierarchies that underlie those apparently carefree scatterings of figures. He explains how each arrangement was exquisitely planned – mapped and measured according to the Golden Ratio – how every cloud and pocket of sky has its place in the classically proportioned system . . .

From time to time, he scans the audience and sees his colleagues from the department, clustered in a single row. Many other faces are familiar.

Twenty minutes into the lecture, just as he begins a digression on Euclidean geometry, he senses motion at the back of the room. He glances up, motoring along on memory, and sees that a woman has arrived late. She is moving along the back row, past a line of seated figures, to an empty chair. The light in that quarter of the room is stronger; it seems to pick her out. She is black, an uncommon sight in Cambridge, and probably in her early forties. She wears a sleeveless top of mottled gold.

Don's eyes return to the woman as he guides his audience through the ethereal spaces of the frescoes. By some reflex, he seeks her out each time he looks up. Her face is solemn and handsome. With a pang of alarm, he finds that she is looking straight back at him with a quizzical, questioning expression – not quite a smile, although her lips are curling in that direction.

He reaches a minor climax – wryly reminding his audience that man has always had the gift of flight, at least in Rococo art – and he raises his eyes to see the same look of bemusement, stronger now than before. She watches him with concentrated intensity. Just where his points are strongest, his propositions boldest, she appears – by a contraction of the brows – to debate, to disagree.

He crunches the slide carousel into its next sequence, carried on a tide of adrenaline, and wills himself to ignore the worm of doubt that has entered him. An image of shimmering sky flashes up behind him – the cosmos painted over the span of a ceiling, peopled by mythic characters, receding into a whirlpool of golden light. *The Allegory of the Power of Eloquence*. The moment has arrived.

He steps away from the lectern and raises one hand in a leisurely fashion.

'This marvellous scene,' he hears himself say, 'graces the Palazzo Sandi in Venice. You will observe how Cupid flies blindfolded over the heads of the doomed lovers, Orpheus and Eurydice.' He listens to the cadence of his voice. From within his own head, he admires its tone, its resonance. With his non-gesticulating hand, he tries to find his jacket pocket.

Then his eyes betray him. They fly across to the face of silent dissent, to see that dissent is mixed, now, with open amusement. His heart beats hard.

'The *sanctity*,' he declares, and flings out his hands, before realising that his voice has stopped like a recording suddenly cut off. What sanctity? His brain is a brilliant white void. Before him lies an army of expectant faces – just a few of them beginning to detect an unintended pause, and one of them wearing its irony openly.

'The sanctity—' he blurts, clutching the last words he remembers. Then he repeats them more quietly, almost to himself, his voice stifled by horror.

They know he is lost. Frantically stroking his jacket, he bows slightly and feels a sharp, hot prickling across his forehead. He clasps his hands together. They are soaking wet.

'Prompt!' comes a shout from the audience. It is Gene Caskill – of course. Don sees the man's teeth framed by his bushy beard. A ruffle of laughter spreads among his other colleagues from the department. He fights to regain himself. With willed dignity he steps back to the lectern, brings a shaking finger to his notes, and finds his place. The seconds are long and torturous.

'Yes, indeed, the sanctity of the upper air,' he begins, and takes a deep, vitalising breath.

In a moment, he has recovered his momentum. He tells them of the allegoric connections between mythic episodes, the zones of the heavens, the paradoxical effects of sunlight – how it sharpens and dissolves! He is back on track. The sweat grows cold on his face and around his chest. He stays at the lectern and his eyes stay faithful. They avoid the back of the room.

It is close to nine o'clock when Don delivers his final sentence.

'The flat adornment conceals an orderly firmament.'

He stands back from the lectern and allows a smile to spread across his lips. A smile of closure that sings out with wordless significance: *The End*.

Silence reigns for several seconds, before the audience breaks into grateful applause. He allows himself to look across the room and sees that the woman in the back row has gone – her seat is an empty green space.

An attendant strides up to the lectern, bearing an oversize bouquet. The flowers glide towards Don, obscuring their bearer from view – all he sees is a rainstorm of ivory petals and greens. The misery that has been lurking inside him subsides. He will repent again later – tomorrow, for weeks after. But for now, shielded by petals, he is safe from regret.

As the bouquet sways and bounces into his arms, sheathed in cellophane, the scent hits him; it wraps around him and drowns him. The sound of clapping is like a downpour on the roof.

As he walks back to Peterhouse, shortly before eleven, he thinks over Val's extraordinary hymn of praise. None of it was untrue, and yet, in recollection, the praise seems excessive. It somehow presaged that devastating embarrassment onstage.

In Old Court, the lamp beneath the bedframe overtakes him on its lurching course, spins around the quadrangle and catches up with him again as he turns onto his staircase.

Sitting at his desk, he remembers how his colleagues from the department crept up to him at the drinks reception with qualified words of acclaim, and how Val then appeared as if from nowhere, arms stretched wide, overflowing with sparkling energy.

'Wonderful, Don, just scintillating. The Venetian sky – not a screen but a threshold! A triumph of reasoning. And you recovered superbly from that little pause.'

The words made him feel desolate in what should have been – what so nearly had been – his moment of triumph.

He crosses to the window and pushes aside the curtain. Old Court is dark and deserted – the flashing light of *SICK BED* has now ceased. By standing at the edge of the window, he is able to eliminate the pile of metal and glass from view. From this angle, the court is the same as it was in the 1960s – and for a long time before. The chessboard pattern of the grass is powdery grey in the moonlight, sombre as a mezzotint. Time seems to disappear from the courts and walkways of Cambridge at night. Just now, Old Court seems as old as the universe.

The static scene transforms his mood, stills his rueful thoughts. A rallying voice takes their place: the lecture was a success, *a triumph*, just as Val said. Never mind those seconds of forgetfulness. He recalls how Roman generals, on their victory parades, were accompanied by a slave who whispered to them in the blaze of their success: *remember, you are mortal. Memento mori.*

He withdraws to his bedroom, passing from room to room with the refined, measured gait of a successful man. As he climbs into bed, he realises how tired he is – so tired that thought and regret have disappeared, leaving behind a monumental peace. As he sleeps, he feels elevated. His simple iron bed is like a plinth.

*

Don wakes refreshed by sleep. Too refreshed. It is already seven o'clock.

He rushes out of his room, down the staircase to the bathroom, and twists on the taps. The pipes screech and water explodes into the tub. Behind the frosted glass window, the light is harsh – Cambridge light.

Afterwards, before dressing, he examines himself in the bedroom mirror. His face looks etiolated, older than it is. His skin is pale and lustreless, and his dark hair – still thick, at least – is threaded with grey. Shadows hang about his eyes. Stray black hairs spread erratically across his chest. The crack in the mirror slices diagonally from his left nipple to his right shoulder, making a pale bust of his upper body. He takes a step back and notices a bruise on his knee, a crescent of bright purple and blue where he hit the bird bath. His stomach is flat, and a spindly column of hair leads from his navel to the thicket above his penis, which rests meekly against the slung weights of his testicles; unlike the rest of him, it seems hardly to have aged.

Occasionally, when he surveys himself in the nude, he sees the lithe body of his younger self, and as he catches sight of the lost youth in the older man, that soft sagging pendulum twitches into sly wakefulness.

His lecture for the morning is on Tintoretto's depictions of Roman ruins. He reviews the topic as he walks through Old Court. SICK BED is hideous in the autumn light – the tangle of rusty springs, the mound of bottles and cans and clothes, that dronelike swivelling light.

As the chapel bell chimes, Bruce Day plods through the college gate, filling the stone portal with his giant frame. Bruce is a scholar of medieval history for whom academic life has been a steady descent into lethargy. He has been at Peterhouse for forty years. Rumour has it that he was handsome once, and imaginative – but then the college lives on myths of past greatness.

Following Bruce through the gate, pacing on one side of him and then the other like an agitated flunky, is a boy in his late teens – an undergraduate, asking about the Treaty of Brétigny. Bruce ignores him. The boy gives up and drifts away, just as Bruce sees Don and indicates by a tilt of the head the assemblage on the lawn.

'Contemporary art comes to Peterhouse!' he shouts with a grin that is meant, perhaps, to be ironic. His eyes bulge in their fleshy sockets, beneath the wild flicks of his eyebrows.

Don doesn't reply. He maintains an expression of cool dignity as he turns onto Trumpington Street.

The monstrosity on the lawn plays on his mind, though, as the day passes.

Val will know the meaning of it, he says to himself. Val will be able to explain.

Val is the figurehead of a group of fellows who virtually rule the college, wielding as much power as the Master. 'Not a sparrow can fall to the ground within Peterhouse,' Val likes to say, 'without my knowing it.' His moods, his whims, his worship of tradition and disdain for new trends, his meticulous manners and occasional lack of manners – all express the character of the college. He refers to himself as the Queen of Peterhouse.

'What is this disfigurement, this act of vandalism on the lawn?' Don demands, taking Val aside in the Senior Common Room in the late afternoon. 'How did it happen?'

'It's the new Master,' says Val with airy resignation. 'The new Master commissioned it.'

'It's a disgrace.'

'It's contemporary art. And it's staying for a year – possibly longer. Believe me, Don, I'm as sorry as you are.'

'It's an intolerable insult,' Don bursts out. 'An affront to our intellects, to our knowledge – to *my* knowledge.'

'A monumental edifice.' Val smiles a mordant smile. Taking Don by the arm, he guides him towards a pair of sagging leather armchairs.

'Why weren't you consulted? Why wasn't I consulted? As an art historian, I mean. I could have advised – we could have stopped—'

'As an expert on contemporary art?' Val starts to laugh. 'Come on, Don. The Master knew what your reaction would be. And he knows a thing or two about new art.'

'Is it some kind of joke?'

'Far from it. It's by an artist called Andrea somebody. Or Angela. Ah yes, *Angela Cannon*. Very modish, apparently. Very edgy. A star of Goldsmiths College, I'm told.'

It's the new Master. Don hears the words every day, despite the fact that the Master and his wife Briony arrived five years ago. Frank Davis was previously the Director of Channel 4 Television. He is the first Master of Peterhouse, in seven hundred years, from outside of academia – and the change has not gone down well. Frank's appointment was an experiment by the ruling group of fellows, only vaguely conscious of the content of Channel 4 and hopeful of moulding this easy-going man in their own image. But Frank and Briony are political, and they don't share the politics of the Peterhouse elite.

Don skirts on the edges of that elite, relying on Val for his knowledge of college power struggles. Politics in general hold little interest. Why should he care about the European parliament elections any more than Napoleon's invasion of Venice? Politicians, he likes to say, are creatures of a day. Ideology has become passé, Soviet Russia has crumbled, the old polarities are turning into poses. He senses a shift among his students away from the fierce principles of earlier times towards a hollower rhetoric. The twentieth century is in its decadent phase, without long to run. What is there left to say?

As for religion, it interests him only inasmuch as it has produced great works of art.

His mind circles back to Val, who is now leaning back in his chair, pointing a lit cigarette towards the ceiling, professing with sarcasm on the current state of British art. Val pronounces the words *conceptualism* and *abjection* as if they were sticky, unhygienic specimens between his fingers. His eyes sparkle as they register Don's renewed attention. He holds out his cigarette pack and waits for Don to take one.

'The will to *shock* transcends any other impulse,' he is saying. 'As for questions of iconography, or form, or even representation . . .'

Don settles back and floats on the unstoppable tide of Val's words. He feels some of his outrage subsiding into fatigue. Val, he reflects, is his only friend. Don has always struggled to relate to people, to create those easy cordial bonds (inflections of the voice, quick empathic glances) that friendships demand – except with Val, who took him up before his professional carapace existed.

'Theory has no place in the lexicon, any longer,' Val continues. 'Decorum is out. Playing dumb, shouting *arse*, has become an attractive critical position.'

Don feels his eyes widen in a reflex. He can't repress a smile. He has always been in thrall to Val's wit. At a deeper level, he has always been gratified by Val's affection. Val is a man of restless mind, alert and energetic, sometimes irritable and sardonic, but unwavering in his loyalty to Don. Even so, they are different. Val has charm and sociability, and an ability to quench inhibition at will. In matters of sex, he is fearless. *I'm just an old poof*, he likes to say, when people ask – however obliquely – about his private life.

'But who am I to talk?' Val says with a sigh, and he leans towards Don. 'The new Master's ideas – his beliefs – are going to change this place beyond recognition. Wait and see.'

'We can't allow it,' Don says, with a desperate sigh.

Val smiles ruefully and shrugs. Don reflects that his friend has a strange gift for unconcern. Perhaps Val has no need to fight. He is twenty years older than Don and his reputation was sealed long ago. His first book, *The Neoclassical Pose*, was published in 1960. Concise but brilliant, it was already a classic by the time Don became his student – a vigorous defence of classical aesthetics, expressed in stripped, staccato prose. Pretenders, revisionists, detractors have all come along – challenging Val's principles, dismissing his tranquil certainties. And yet those certainties have endured, like monuments.

'And do you know what else?' Val says. 'The Master has appointed a poet in residence. No, a *poetess*.' He looks out of the window at the Fellows' Garden, at the russet leaves and the cropped lawns – vacant apart from a darting squirrel.

Don's thoughts have returned to SICK BED – unhappily, involuntarily. The bedsprings, the bottles, the paranoid flashing.

'Erica Jay is her name,' Val continues. 'The Master has sent me a copy of her collected verse. Never heard of her. But what do I know?' He speaks with levity but also bitterness. 'I'm just an old fossil who *happened* to be friends with Auden.'

2

Michaelmas term rolls by. *SICK BED* remains. When the low sun glances across the bedframe, scratches in its charred surface glister like silver hairs. In the evening, the object creeps beyond its physical outline. The lamp, turning incessantly beneath the coil springs, throws haywire shadows across the lawn and buildings. Most of the academics of Peterhouse are baffled. Many are openly hostile. A rumour has begun that the sculpture wasn't the Master's idea at all, but that of his wife. Briony Davis is an artist in her own right, a sculptor of busts. Her portrait of Harold Pinter, an emaciated likeness in the style of Giacometti, stands in the lobby of the National Theatre. Some say she created *SICK BED* herself, Angela Cannon being a pseudonym.

One of the college fellows, an ecclesiastical historian, claims that Angela – or the Master's wife – has been commissioned to design a new cenotaph in Whitehall. It will consist of a burnt-out shipping container standing endways on a mountain of tyres.

Don's hostility is deeper. As the weeks pass, it takes on an intensity that makes it impossible for him to talk about or even look at *SICK BED*. When he passes through Old Court, he fixes his eyes on the chapel clock or the repeating arches of the cloisters. But the spinning lamp has a way of breaking into his field of view. Like a street musician he once encountered in Venice – strumming and screeching, leering at him, baying for liras – it refuses to be ignored.

To his dismay, he hears undergraduates marvelling in front of the sculpture with languid words of praise. That is forgivable;

they're young and naïve, eager to see radicalism in any kind of ugliness. But one of the celebrants is the college chaplain, a man well into his sixties.

'The more I look at it,' he remarks to Don, 'the more it reminds me of Constructivist art. Those qualities of angularity and torsion.'

They are passing simultaneously through the college gate. *SICK BED* flashes ahead of them.

'I'll take your word for it,' says Don.

'And the sculptures of Mariam Schwarz – that same brutal sincerity.' The chaplain pants slightly as he keeps pace. He is a small, plump man with clouds of white hair and a face as smooth as a young woman's. 'Or Barbara Hepworth. That bedframe calls to mind Hepworth's use of a string mesh inside a bronze armature.'

Where, Don thinks, has the chaplain learned to speak like this? He smiles bleakly and sets his eyes on the doorway to his staircase, halfway round the court.

'I met her once, Hepworth,' the older man carries on. 'Down in St Ives in the summer of '67. I remember the date because Joe Orton had just been murdered.'

Don walks faster.

'Such a shock, I'll never forget it. Bludgeoned to death by his boyfriend with a clawhammer. A case of jealousy, the master turning on his protégé . . .'

With an effort, Don outpaces him and hurries up the stairs to his rooms.

As he enters, he has the impression that his study is somehow different. He sees it from a disengaged angle, as if he were a stranger to his own life. The place is tidy and sedate – almost oppressively orderly: hundreds of books packed in systematic order around the walls, two identical sofas covered in faded red linen, the cork Pantheon rising between them, and the small replica sword, coated in a film of dust.

Arranged across his desk are reproductions of frescoes by Tiepolo, printed on differently sized sheets of paper. Some are as small as postcards, others as large as a tabloid newspaper. They show the painted ceilings of European churches and palaces. Each one produces the illusion of a roof opening to reveal a sky filled with figures – flocks of bodies, soaring and tumbling, spelling out a breezy allegory: a glorious nation, the continents of the world, a triumphant god.

These are the objects of Don's research – the focus of his unwritten book. For hundreds of hours he has bent over the images, often late into the night, drilling into them with his eyes. He has laid rulers and protractors over the pages, aligning his tools with the architectural details that skirt the edges of each picture – the steps, pillars and cornices that mark a boundary between the real architecture of the fresco's setting and the illusion of the painted sky. With fine ruled lines, he has dissected each scene into geometric segments.

Also on his desk is a notepad, thick with minuscule writing. He has noted the direction and quality of light in every picture (*westerly gleam*, *matutinal radiance*, *crepuscular tints*). He has analysed the distribution of clouds and air, assessing the depth of field with fanatical precision. Long columns of measurements indicate the probable distances between objects – from the sharpened points of Neptune's trident to the tip of Pegasus's wing, to the wisplike birds overhead . . .

Slowly and painstakingly, Don is revealing the celestial realm of Tiepolo's frescoes to be a compendium of classical rules. He feels rising excitement as the gods in heaven fall within his discriminating net. He has decided that the book, when it is published, will be called *The Skies of Tiepolo*.

Standing in the doorway and mentally itemising the contents of the room, he sees the reproductions on his desk, for a moment, as a grid of blue panels – blocks of pure, milky light. But when he crosses the room, the pictures are restored to their normal aspect. Complexity returns. His sense of dislocation – that flicker of *jamais vu* alienation – passes.

*

Mariam Schwarz. The name has been loitering in his thoughts. He scans the library shelf. Schultze, Schuyff, Schwarzkogler, Schwitters . . . Nothing on Schwarz.

He has come to the History of Art library to verify some references for his paper on Vitruvius, but the name of the sculptor mentioned by the chaplain – supposedly the inspiration behind Angela Cannon's *SICK BED* – has crept back into his head, prompting him to stray across to the modern sculpture section.

'Do you have anything,' he asks the librarian – a neat, astute New Yorker named Judy Cummings – 'on Mariam Schwarz? A sculptor, apparently. I can't see anything in the monographs.'

'Ah yes,' says Judy, recognising the name at once. 'Post-war, found objects. Let me see.' She rifles through miniature drawers packed with cards, humming as she searches. Then she withdraws a card and holds it above her head, reading its contents through the gap above her glasses. She leads Don to another part of the library, an unlit corner where exhibition catalogues are held.

Judy traces the book spines with her finger. 'Here we are.' She slides a slim hardback book off the shelf. The words *Women Sculptors of Today* are printed on its hessian cover. 'You'll find something about her in this.'

Don flicks through the book as Judy turns to a trolley crammed with oversize volumes and wheels it away with determined force. It is a catalogue from an exhibition held at the South London Art Gallery in 1952 – a survey of female sculptors in Europe and America. The pages are foxed and faded.

Mariam Schwarz's entry consists of a black and white photograph alongside a paragraph headed 'A Pioneer of the Found

Object'. The words are printed in bold, unornamented typeface. The picture is grainy and shows a metal framework – a children's climbing frame, possibly, or a scaffold for adverts – silhouetted against a white sky. The structure is black, mangled and clogged with objects. It looks like the aftermath of a freak storm. Clothes hang forlornly from the bars and a wooden chair has been jammed crossways through the framework. There's an ironing board – or a canoe, it's hard to tell – and what looks like the branch of a tree, bristling with twigs.

The text is a short biography.

Mariam S. Schwarz arrived in London in 1941, an émigré from Berlin. In 1949, she made a tour of the United States, where she met Marcel Duchamp and the abstract sculptor David Smith. Her sculptures have begun to feature welded metal and objets trouvés in rebarbative compositions that bear witness to the traumas of our present century. Mrs Schwarz is married to a distinguished lecturer at the Warburg Institute, London, where she recently unveiled a relief in beaten aluminium to coincide with the Festival of Britain.

Don snaps the book closed. It amazes him to think that this is already the stuff of art history. Not his art history, however. He notes approvingly that the creation in the photograph has been captioned '*Destroyed*'.

The art of Tiepolo and the other great Venetians will last longer than hers, whoever she was. The classical spirit in art is timeless, and Tiepolo was the last truly classical artist, the inheritor of a golden thread. If only the rest of his colleagues could see. But many in his department are caught up in the philosophy of the 1970s – they have eaten the apple of cultural theory.

For Don, the role of the art historian is to distil Beauty into her component parts. It is a long time since he bothered with questions of society, politics or psychology – fashionable irrelevances. He writes instead about the fundamental things: form, proportion, light, balance.

With a light and balanced step, he makes his way back to the familiar shelves, intent on tracing his references.

*

Every night at seven o'clock, the bachelor fellows take their places – in subtly changing configurations – at a long table at the end of the Hall. Raised on a platform, they sit beneath oil portraits of men very like themselves in attitude and expression. Sometimes they are interleaved by guests – passers-by in their otherwise changeless realm. The students occupy three rows of tables running the length of the room – a noisy counterpoint to the faces of age and wisdom around High Table.

Don has arrived late for pre-dinner drinks. The fellows are already moving from the Old Combination Room into the Hall, and as they take their seats for dinner, he finds himself next to Ferdinand Fernandez. Ferdinand is the youngest fellow in Peterhouse – not quite twenty-seven, from an aristocratic family in Argentina, with glossy black sideburns and needle-sharp eyes set too close together.

As they sit through a starter of onion soup, Ferdinand tells Don of his research into an antique statue of Pompey the Great.

'Scholars have got it wrong,' he declares between slurps. 'To see that statue as a *portrait* is to misread it.'

'Indeed,' Don says. He casts a surreptitious eye around the table. The chair to his right is empty. On the other side of Ferdinand is Val – holding a spoonful of soup to his lips with eucharistic solemnity – and beyond Val, a woman he doesn't know. She is black. He catches a glimpse of her face in profile. Its contours express a beauty that has outlived – outgrown – youth. Next to her, at the head of the table, is the Master, Frank Davis – broodingly aware of his unpopularity. His wife, Briony, never comes to High Table.

'A colossus,' Ferdinand says, 'but so fraught with ambiguity!

Pompey, Julius Caesar – no one knows the real subject. The head doesn't even belong to the body. Just consider the discrepancies in the carving of the marble – the hair on the head, quite different in technique from the hair below . . .'

Don holds tepid strings of onion in his mouth, afflicted by a momentary inability to swallow. Where has he seen her before? He raises his napkin to his lips and releases the slivers invisibly into its folds. Pretending to listen to Ferdinand, he leans forward and allows his attention to drift along the table.

Val is speaking to her, telling a story. He emotes with his hands and rounds off his anecdote with an obsequious laugh. Don sees her react with a doubtful, amused parting of the lips.

And then he remembers. She is the woman who arrived late at the Fitzwilliam Lecture and regarded him with that same expression, subtler than a smirk – and more devastating.

'And the process of viewing,' persists Ferdinand. 'So riddled with contradictions! The naked man versus the imperial pose, the mortal body beside the emblems of status, that giant orb in the left hand . . .'

Don leans further into the table. The woman is saying something about oral poetry – memories transmitted from place to place, like the chain of beacons on the hilltops around Mycenae, carrying news of victory from Troy. Her intonation, now that he thinks about it, is low and lyrical – a performance poet's.

He rests his spoon inside his bowl. Of course – she is the new poet in residence Val spoke about, Erica Jay. The memory of the Fitzwilliam Lecture returns to him with a sting, and he decides that the most dignified course of action will be never to speak to her.

Her conversation with Val has shifted from Mycenae to Peterhouse.

'There aren't many other people of colour here,' she says, circumnavigating the table with her eyes. 'Am I the only one?'

Don can't make out Val's answer – only its imploring tone and the velvety laughter that quickly envelops it.

She doesn't seem satisfied.

'Do you all live here in the college?' he hears her say. 'All of you men together?' That delicate smile has reappeared.

'A clerisy of bachelor dons . . .' Val begins, before again becoming silkily inaudible.

Don looks down the length of the hall and imagines, for a moment, that he sees the place through a visitor's eyes. A medieval room, dressed in nineteenth-century panelling and furniture, soaked in history and tradition and candlelight. He feels irritated by Erica Jay's persistent questioning, by the amused disdain which lies beneath it. Disdain for their way of life – his way of life. But he feels a deeper irritation at the thought that she might have a point, that they *are* ridiculous, he and Val and Ferdinand and the rest.

'And where are you from, Miss Jay?' Val ventures. 'Originally, I mean.'

'Brixton.'

'Ah, well then, we are two peas in a pod. Yes, two peas in a pod!'

Yes, Val can be ridiculous.

'The statue is as complex as any Cubist abstraction,' Ferdinand maintains. 'The iconography refuses to cohere into a unified system. Instead – *radical* multivalence. The image is at once man and god—'

Don turns to face him. 'And what about that ugly stump of tree, chasing the statue's leg? What does *that* have to do with multivalence?'

Ferdinand looks at him in stern amazement. 'It's a prop, Lamb. That's all. A formula for adding stability to the marble.'

Conversations break and reform with the change of courses. Ferdinand turns to Val and starts to declaim on Hadrian's Villa at Tivoli. Don sits back and his eyes float over the objects on the table – a cut-glass pitcher of water, a trident of candles in a sculpted silver holder. Relieved at being left alone, he directs his thoughts back to his unfinished paper on Vitruvius. It is so nearly complete, except that he can't quite decide how to conclude. What should be his culminating point?

He becomes aware that the place on his right is now occupied. He turns fractionally. A woman faces him with a relaxed, confidential smile. His own smile flickers and dies. It is Erica Jay. She has moved from her seat between Val and the Master; perhaps one of them suggested she come and sit beside him.

He finds himself nodding dumbly at her, as if to acknowledge some wordless compact between them.

'I'm sorry, I don't know who you are,' he says at last. A lie, and not what he meant to say.

She ponders his words. 'Call me Erica.'

He drinks a mouthful of wine. 'Professor Don Lamb.'

'Yes, yes of course. I heard you the other night.'

In his discomfort, he wonders whether she occupies a room close to his own. Has he been talking in his sleep? Then he understands – the lecture; and he relives the moment when his eloquence disintegrated. At speed, he tries to think of some way of alluding to the occasion, a sly reference to her presence there. But to say anything on that topic would make him seem absurd, and so he asks in his politest tone what she is doing in Cambridge.

'Right now, I'm researching a new poem. A narrative poem.' Her words are strong and rounded.

'Research? Which libraries will you be using?'

There is something intolerable about her tranquil gaze. He breaks away from it and rearranges the contents of his plate – pork, potatoes, *haricots verts*.

'It's more about a sense of place,' she replies after a pause. 'Did you know there was once a riot in the hotel next door to this college, back in 1970? That's what my poem's about.'

The Garden House riot. He remembers it well. A protest

against the military dictatorship in Greece, directed at a local hotel that happened to be hosting a dinner in celebration of the country. It quickly descended into mayhem. Socialist students set up a loudspeaker in a room at Peterhouse, just over the wall from the hotel. Some broke into the event and threw bricks. He was kept awake all night by the blare of dissident Greek music and the distant smashing of glass, and by a more immediate sound: banging on his bedroom door.

'I remember it vaguely. I think I was an undergraduate at the time.'

She retells the story, every stage of the miniature battle. As she talks, Don notices that several of the fellows around the table have run out of conversation. They are drinking in morose silence. Bruce Day's voice is just audible from the far end. He has placed his hand over that of a young male friend. Don hears the words 'a chivalric alliance'. Some pearl of medieval history.

'Eight students were convicted,' Erica says. 'They went to prison. My poem gives the story in their voices, like a chorus. Their accounts of the night, their hopes for a world revolution, their *what ifs*.'

'A world revolution – the outcome you would have wanted?' The question was meant to be droll, but it sounds arid and prickly.

She reflects for a moment. Her eyes are large, unperturbed. 'It's not about what I would have wanted. I wasn't there. It's more a case of bearing witness. That's what a poem does. It's what *art* does. It brings back what's real – lays it bare.'

'Art', he echoes, while in an unthinking motion he draws a circle on the table with his finger, 'conjures other realities. It describes worlds that resemble our own only in part. It translates life into higher forms – *dignifies* life – through the refractory glass of allegory. Art, I believe, is a sequence of confirmations. Yes, confirmations of what is good and true.'

His finger has ceased its motion. He sits back. His words have given way to an unexpected rush of feeling – a flushing pride. The image of the *Allegory of the Power of Eloquence* glows in his brain.

'Confirmations,' she says. 'I like that. But I don't know about your – what was it? – allegoric glass. Sounds kind of like a smokescreen.' Her smiling incredulity has returned. 'What I think about art is this. It confirms – sure – but it also refuses to confirm. It takes what's there in the world and repeats it, reuses it, throws it back at you. And it makes you question what you know, what you *believe*. To hell with dignifying life, art *destabilises*. I mean, what *is* good and true?'

He stares at her, convinced that she's making no sense, and yet flummoxed – stumped for a reply.

'I'm not waiting for an answer,' she says. 'All I'm saying is, art is the same thing as life – and life is dangerous and uncertain.' Suddenly her smile is simpler, without its former challenge. 'Tell me about yourself.'

Reticence closes tighter around him. 'There's precious little to tell. I arrived here in 1968, and I never left.'

'Did you ever think of stepping out, into the world?'

The question is casual and candid. But it provokes a familiar pang of annoyance.

'Academia,' he replies, 'is as much a part of the world as politics, or art, or writing poems.' There is a long silence before he speaks again. 'I suppose you mean the world of popular appeal. You may not remember my radio programme, *A Venetian Odyssey*. A concise history of the city's art and architecture. It was reviewed in the newspapers' – he touches together his finger-tips – 'not unfavourably.'

Erica's expression is a mixture of acuity and distance, as if two minds were operating in tandem within her.

'I guess we're only as real – any of us – as we allow ourselves to be.' She has ignored him, slipped into abstraction, and yet her words are like sparkling foam on top of a deep sea of meaning.

For the short remainder of their conversation, he is distracted by thoughts of his public image. He tries to imagine how his obituary in *The Times* will read. *Professor Donald Lamb, art historian, a fearless defender of the classical tradition.* It will fill many columns, of that he is certain.

While pudding is being served, Erica excuses herself. She has to go back to her room to write. In the dying minutes of dinner, he is left alone. Ferdinand Fernandez has returned to the library. The Master too has escaped. The Hall is almost empty. Only a handful of dons remain at High Table, lapping port, breaking the silence with sporadic mutterings, ending the evening as they end every evening. He feels desolate.

Val comes and sits next to him.

'I think her poetry is very bad,' he says in a near-whisper.

'Poetry? Whose poetry?'

'What do you mean, *whose*? Erica Jay's! Our poet in residence. The great *artiste*. Didn't you see the way I had to pay court to her under the Master's eye? Such insolent questions.'

'I haven't read her work,' Don says, unwilling for some reason to betray his own misgivings. 'I'm sure I ought to have done, but you know how busy I've been – my paper on Vitruvius.'

'You only need to read a page,' hisses Val, 'to know that it's horrific. No cadence, no lyricism, no structure! It's nothing but bare prose chopped into half-lines. And so *worthy*. Race and empire – yes, empire, but not as Auden had it.'

'And how was that? How did Auden have it?'

Val seems not to have heard. He is looking at himself in the convex face of his spoon. He often finds reason to mention that he once knew W. H. Auden. They moved in similar circles. Val is proud of his literary connections, and he knows good poetry – and bad poetry – when he sees it.

'It's *bad* poetry.' He hammers down the spoon. 'Politically correct. That, I believe, is the term. Politically correct.'

'Politically correct. Ha. Yes, that's very good. Who coined it?'

'Oh, I don't know, it's doing the rounds.' Val's sigh carries the trace of a whimper. 'Why is she *here*? Why?'

'It's the new Master,' Don murmurs.

When he retreats to his study, he stands at the window, angling himself to hide *SICK BED*, and looks at the cobbles and stonework and the black panes of the windows opposite. His eyes refocus and he examines himself in the window's dark mirror. The lines fanning out from the corners of his eyes are horribly noticeable. But when he moves again by the smallest degree, he is a boy of nineteen.

He thinks back to the Cambridge of his youth. A gay sort of place. Peterhouse especially. But there was a discreetness and innocence about the whole matter. Erotic impulses were transformed into something as safe and stylised as a Noël Coward play, a pretty Cantabrigian drama whose costumes were stripy blazers and pastel-coloured trousers. Sex was buried in the unspeakable night – and it passed Don by. Romantic possibilities were like the indistinct sounds of a distant party, overheard from his library desk on a hot day.

All except one. Anders Andersson, an undergraduate at Peterhouse, lived on the same staircase as Don. They passed on the stairs numerous times with barely a word, until one evening: Don was going up to his room, a pile of books under one arm, and Anders was heading out. The young man, dreamily drunk, caught Don's eye and smiled and began to speak, then tripped and fell straight into Don's arms, helplessly, gently (the books clattered down the stairs), and kissed Don on the lips. Then he pulled back and laughed – Don remembers the sweet alcoholic smell of his breath – and disappeared into the night.

Love fell into Don. The kiss lasted a second, maybe two. But the event set off a dynamo in his heart and head, waves of feeling he couldn't control. He avoided Anders for days, not knowing how to face him, and yet his thoughts circled him obsessively. Wherever he went, he imagined them together – speaking freely, electrified by each other's nearness.

When they finally saw one another again, Anders looked straight through him with a vague, unconcerned smile.

Don wrote a letter confessing his love. A long letter, burning with sincerity – it took the best part of a night to write. At dawn, he carried the letter to the porter's lodge and left it in Anders's pigeonhole. He waited for a day, for two days, driven almost mad with anticipation, but terrified also of seeing Anders, of having to explain. Then came the response. A letter in his pigeonhole: *his own letter*. It had been opened, read – and returned.

He recalls how he stood there with the pages in his hands. He searched for a scribbled note, a fingerprint, any sign of a reaction. But all he saw was his own streaming handwriting, mocking in its fluency.

He saw Anders just once after that. It was several weeks later, as he crossed Magdalene Bridge on a muggy spring afternoon. Men were strolling around on the grass of the riverbank, some of them in swimming trunks. Kneeling at the edge of the water was a young man with his shirt hanging out and his sleeves rolled up; his blond hair fell forward to conceal his face. He gestured to another man who stood waist-deep in the water, hunching his shoulders against a surprise breeze. Then the kneeling figure sat back and Don saw that it was Anders, speaking with a cryptic smile to his friend. He remembers how the trees over the river were lopped, and how two swans glided past, leaving deep, fluted wakes; and how he stood there on the bridge, fused to the iron railing, and gazed.

Not long after, Anders went away on a year abroad that never came to an end. Don kept the letter but could never bring himself to read it again. He tucked it into the pages of a book – a red volume with gold lettering – and put it on a shelf. Soon enough, the dynamo slowed and died – never to restart. And the book disappeared, he doesn't remember how. Perhaps he threw it away.

Occasionally he wonders where Anders went, what he became. But his imagination returns a blank. The boy who fell into his arms only existed at a point in time.

He shifts a little and SICK BED edges into view. With the light off, it looks like a burnt-out wreck. He draws the curtains and seals himself inside the dim golden glow of his room.

He never married. That is how his *Times* obituary will conclude, the way that obituaries do for men like him. It's a singular existence, this one, he thinks. Just as Erica Jay observed, Peterhouse is a colony of bachelors – no women, a monastic sort of place. And as for romance, that Noël Coward drama ended a long time ago, or moved elsewhere, to an unknown place.

*

Peterhouse is changing. Don alone senses it. SICK BED has beamed its glare into every corner; its light has skimmed every blade of grass. It's as if an old friend has been replaced by an imposter in flawless disguise.

Late one afternoon as he passes through Old Court, he sees the chaplain standing beside the grass with a cluster of young people. They are too young to be undergraduates. They must be sixth formers up in Cambridge for an open day.

'Don't you think,' the chaplain is saying, 'that it has the character of Naum Gabo's constructions of the 1920s? The same starkness, the same linearity?'

Don walks by. The shadows cast by the revolving lamp chase him around the margins of the court – he can feel the lines like a whip on his back.

'There goes Don Lamb,' he hears the chaplain cry out. 'The great art historian of Peterhouse.'

In the sanctuary of his study, he finds that he is breathing fast. He leans on the arm of the sofa. His heart feels tight. The room around him, his old familiar room, radiates a fakeness that he can't put his finger on. The wallpaper, a William Morris carnival of flowers, becomes, in a flash, opaque and stifling. In the next moment it seems like a mirage he might step through.

The final victorious line of his lecture at the Fitzwilliam, several weeks ago now, returns to him as a singsong refrain.

The flat adornment conceals an orderly firmament!

It repeats in his head like a nursery rhyme – sonorous, insistent, growing vacuous with repetition. A perverse impulse makes him cross to the window and look down at *SICK BED*. The lamp tilts up in his direction.

An orderly firmament!

There is brandy in his cupboard. He pours some into a dusty glass and carries it to the sofa. Passing the window again, he notices the chaplain and his teenage disciples on the path below. They have all begun to laugh.

He settles onto the sofa and relishes the burn of alcohol in his throat. A mental picture looms into focus: himself as a twenty-year-old, standing between his parents on graduation day in front of the gleaming façade of the Senate House. The actual photograph exists somewhere, in one of his boxes or drawers. In the black and white snapshot, Don looks younger than he was, no more than a frowning boy with a scroll balanced between his fingers, and his parents seem older – already white-haired and frail, coaxed out of the protective shell of their life in Dorset.

He remembers how his father, at a loss for words that day, pointed to the scroll and asked Don if he needed him to sign it, like a legal witness. A moment later, Antony Lamb realised that the scroll was nothing more than a plastic tube – a prop

35

for the photograph. Don recalls how his father laughed to hide his embarrassment.

Val was there, too, performing some minor yet essential ceremonial role, basking in the reflected glow of that year's crop of students, and one student in particular. As Don stood on the lawn of the Senate House with his parents, Val glided over in his black gown and shook their hands – chatted with Paula and conferred (in graver, manlier style) with Antony. He won the Lambs' trust and affection in minutes.

The photograph was taken by a hired man in a hood – Don is sure of this, but somehow, thinking about it again, he has the strange fictitious impression that Val took the picture. He can see Val there, beaming at him and his parents, activating the shutter with a squeeze of the rubber bulb. But that isn't how it was. Val must have been standing near the photographer, watching the Lamb family from a discreet but close remove.

He slumps down a little on the sofa. That was the beginning – and at forty-three he is still young, at least in academic terms. How strange that his mind should leap back now to that point of origin. He drifts in and out of consciousness, wondering if things were easier back then, when the future was pure potential.

When he wakes, it is almost time for dinner.

It is past ten o'clock as Don walks from the Hall back through Old Court, contemplating an hour's writing before bed. The lamp of *SICK BED* is still whirring. They seem not to switch it off any more.

But for some reason – maybe it's the soft touch of the night air – he turns around and walks to the college gate. Outside in the street, undergraduates are sauntering along. Somewhere in the distance a choir is rehearsing.

He glances across the road and sees that the gates to the

Master's Lodge are open. The Queen Anne house is so familiar that he rarely examines it. He crosses the road to look more closely, and the thought passes through his mind – not for the first time – that the house might one day be his. The new Master won't stay forever, and the senior fellows will never again risk an external appointment. Val is the obvious candidate, as the longest-serving fellow. But Don would be a safer option – less political, less theatrical. It's not impossible.

He wanders over the dark forecourt and creeps along the front of the house. A window on the ground floor is open. The drawn curtains glow red and he can hear voices inside. The Master is hosting a private dinner. He recognises the low, earnest voice of Frank Davis, and that of his wife.

An abrupt laugh behind the curtains causes his heart to thud. Val's laugh – a unique, silvery noise. Val is dining in secret with the Master, consorting with the enemy. Don tries to make out the words of their conversation. The tone is convivial. Conspiratorial.

There is a crunch of gravel behind him. He turns to see Bruce Day, Distinguished Professor of History, watching him from a few feet away.

'Taking in the night air, Lamb?'

'Indeed,' he answers.

But Bruce's grey eyes phrase another question.

Don bows his head and walks away. As he leaves, he hears another eruption of laughter from inside the house and then Val's voice – clearly this time:

'Oh, he'll do it! He'll do it all right!'

Don ponders the words. They mean something but they make no sense.

There are hidden sides to Valentine Black. Semi-hidden. He is known to have another life in London. Stories circulate about his early years, his associations with artists and poets. He was painted in the nude by Patrick Procktor, although no one can claim to have seen the picture. At some time in the distant past, he came into money – he owns a house in Dulwich to which he retreats during the vacations. He has often invited Don to stay, but Don has regarded the invitations as symbolic gestures to be graciously deflected.

'You'll take me up in the end,' Val always says with a patient smile. 'My house will be your house, whenever you decide you want it.'

Is it possible, Don now wonders, that Val and the hated Master are friends? He dismisses the thought. Probably this is just the latest scheme – the newest plot – in a steady sequence of schemes and plots whose one object is to keep Peterhouse as it has always been. The plotting is part of the life of the place, as indelible as the stonework or the walnut tree in the Fellows' Garden, hundreds of years old, propped up now by a timber contrivance – a kind of tree calliper.

When he returns to his study, he sits at his desk and adds fifty-seven new measurements to Tiepolo's skies. The chapel clock has struck two when he finally lies on the sofa, but he still doesn't feel like sleeping. His eyes follow the line of mottled plasterwork that divides the ceiling from the walls. As he lies there, a scribble of light cavorts across the room, and he makes out the silhouette of a bedspring.

3

In early November, Don receives a letter from BBC Radio 4. It is an invitation to contribute to the weekly cultural programme *Shifting Perspectives*. The topic, the producer writes, will be Angela Cannon's provocative and powerful installation at Peterhouse College.

He is standing at the window of his study as he reads the letter, with a direct view of its subject.

Our listeners would welcome your insights into this ground-breaking work of art, not only as a fellow of Peterhouse College but also as an art historian of renown.

Memories of his radio series *A Venetian Odyssey* haven't faded, it seems, at the BBC. Someone has recommended him as a dissenting voice – or the voice of sanity. For a minute or two, he nods slowly at the framed photograph that sits on his desk, searching for guidance in the dog's sparrow eyes.

Iris, the family greyhound, was put to sleep on his parents' orders after he went away to Cambridge. It was an act of convenience, not mercy. The Lambs were too spent to walk the dog any longer; she had become a burden. The first Don knew of it was when he returned to find her ashes on the mantelpiece. He buried them himself, under a pine tree in Sandbanks, shovelling the earth with hoarse gasps. It was the hardest physical effort of his life, digging that deep hole and throwing in the heavy little urn.

He folds the letter and places it in a drawer.

But its words return to him throughout the day. Like tiny

spurs, they prick his insides. *Provocative. Powerful. Groundbreaking.*

That evening, he sits with Val at High Table. Val's private dinner with the Master has been preying on his mind, but he doesn't know how to raise it. To admit that he knows about it will reveal that he was spying.

Instead, he tells Val about the invitation he has received from the BBC.

'Of course I won't do it,' he says, after reciting the letter from memory.

Val has been nodding at the details, chuckling at the overblown words, but at this last remark he raises his eyebrows.

'Why not?' There is a gleam in his eyes, almost of amusement.

'Why not?' Don lets out a sharp laugh. 'What a question. And from you of all people. I have a paper to finish, a book to write. The idea that I would waste time and energy speaking about that diabolical creation—'

'It's just a trip to London – an hour at Broadcasting House.'

Don looks hard at Val. 'We're in the middle of Michaelmas term. I'm lecturing five hours a week, not to mention the teaching, the marking, the committee meetings. It's nonstop – I barely sleep.'

'Forget all that, Don. Just think of your public profile. *Shifting Perspectives* would give you a national platform. You'd be the envy of our department.' Val lowers his voice slightly. 'And more than that, don't you think you have a duty?'

A duty. Surprise and anger dispel the words that are striving to form.

'If you feel this strongly about *SICK BED*,' Val continues, 'shouldn't you explain? Shouldn't you defend what is good and true in art?' The gleam has intensified.

'I'll think about it.'

'You'll be excellent. A beacon of clarity!'

'I said I'll think about it. And it's highly unlikely.' Don's words are defensive, verging on fierce. A powerful, unplaceable unease has risen in him.

Val makes a humming sound. 'This wine is remarkable. Have some more.'

'I have a two-glass rule on weeknights.'

'Forget that. This wine is worth it.' Val picks up the bottle and floods Don's glass. 'Beaujolais supérieur, 1989.' He utters the vintage as if he's revealing a magic formula.

As they drink, Val nimbly redirects the conversation to a favourite non-Cambridge subject – the affairs of the Brockwell Collection.

'Such goings-on there. I must fill you in.'

The Brockwell is a small museum in south London where Val serves as chairman of the trustees. Don hasn't been there in years, but he knows that it houses an outstanding collection of the smaller paintings of Tiepolo.

'You remember Maurice Forster?' Val goes on. 'I'm afraid to say that dementia has completely destroyed him.'

'I'm sorry to hear it,' Don replies, as plates of lamb and polenta are laid before them. 'A great man, in his prime.'

'Yes, yes, it's terrible. Forster has been Director of the Brockwell since the Blitz.' Val sighs. 'It came to a head when he was discovered with one of the marble busts, *deep* in conversation.' Val's teeth gleam. They are long and well preserved. 'Apparently it was Roubiliac's portrait of Alexander Pope.'

'Ah yes, a fine piece.'

'But that's hardly the point, Don. The man was talking to a statue. Gabbling about the museum finances and God knows what else. His mind has completely gone.'

Don bows his head solemnly.

'The stuff of comedy,' Val continues, shaving the fat off his lamb cutlet, 'if it weren't so pitiful. I'm glad to say that we've found a home for him in the City of London – a foundation for geriatric freemasons. But it does leave a new problem for the trustees – the vacant directorship.'

'Thaddeus Knight is the obvious choice,' says Don. He is thinking still of Maurice Forster, confiding dementedly in the marble Pope. Who witnessed the incident – who reported it?

'Knight? He's Forster's age, near enough. Too old.'

Don considers. 'Why not Chris Courtney? I've heard they find him too – well, too English, too Anglo-Saxon, at the Louvre.'

'That man has been a disgrace since he was a boy. Anglo-Saxon? That's the least of his crimes.' Val sucks a wisp of creamed polenta from his fork and swallows. 'No, we're after a heavyweight academic for the Brockwell.' He fixes his pupils on Don and there is a long silence.

'But Val, that's ridiculous. I haven't set foot in the place in ten years. And I'm an art historian, not a museum professional.'

'Exactly. You'd be perfect – just the change the Brockwell needs. A man of acumen. An intellectual weathervane.'

Don starts to laugh. 'It's impossible. You said yourself that scholarship is a compulsion and a duty. It's my life.'

'Perhaps it's a duty you're ready to be released from.'

Don can't believe Val is being serious. He averts his eyes from his friend's expectant stare; they alight on the tattoo snaking across the forearm of the girl who – just at that moment – is pouring wine into Val's glass. He finds that he can't make sense of the image spreading across the arm's smooth underside – a snake, a twisting vine, a scroll: it slips from his mental grip every time he thinks he has it. He raises his eyes to see that the girl is looking back at him, registering his curiosity. With a spasm of surprise, he finds that he is looking at a young man – pale and femininely pretty, easy to mistake as female.

The bottle slips and wine splashes across Val's wrist, onto his white cuff. Val mutters and dabs with his napkin. The young man recedes, and it is only later that Don thinks it odd that he didn't apologise or react, withdrawing without a word.

Don and Val speak for more than an hour about the future of the classical tradition, forgetting all else.

After dinner, as he walks around Old Court towards his staircase, studiously ignoring the assemblage on the lawn, Don comes face to face with Erica Jay. They are a few feet from one another when he sees her. Their eyes meet and she smiles. A steady smile that gives nothing away. For a moment, she seems about to speak. Then she walks on.

Perspiration breaks out on his forehead. That throwaway smile has made him feel peculiar – ignorant and spent. It's as if his knowledge – the stockpile of his credentials – has been exposed, dragged out of the safe confines of his persona and left on the grass like some vain and ridiculous relic. He squirms in the grip of the new feeling.

*

A few days later, he and Val are sitting in the Fellows' Garden, side by side on a bench, wrapped in their overcoats. It is a cold, bright November morning.

'I hope you've given thought to appearing on Radio 4,' Val says.

Don watches his breath condense on the air. He doesn't reply.

'And to that other matter.'

'The Brockwell Collection?'

'Yes.'

He has given thought to it. Unserious thought. A change of career would be drastic. Impetuous. Still, it does no harm to imagine . . .

'Why would I make that kind of move? Academia is all I know.'

Val gives him a rueful look. 'I want to help you. I don't want you to end up like *them*.' He indicates, by a roll of the eyes, two ageing academics treading the path in front of them. 'Your dynamism will only fade the longer you stay here. Your *dunamis*.' He pronounces the Greek with finesse. 'Don't lose that, Don. It's a rare thing. Perhaps I had it once myself, but—'

Don tries to interrupt but Val halts him. 'I accept it. Look at me, I've been in this university all my life.'

'That's not true. You disappear to London all the time.'

'Less and less. I've shrivelled, shrunk into, into . . .' Val tries to draw the right word out of the cold air, then suddenly he laughs and shows the backs of his hands. 'Walnuts!'

Don looks at the mottled topsides of Val's long fingers, one of them studded by a signet ring, another by an oval ruby, then looks up.

In the same instant, Val reaches out and holds Don's shoulder. His face is serious as he says, 'I love you.'

His hand drops away.

The utterance is so unexpected that Don wonders if he's imagined it. His mind stalls, incapable of reaction, and he finds himself staring dumbly at his friend. In the face, Val looks younger than he has for years, almost as he looked when Don first knew him.

They both turn towards the garden, streaked with pale shadows. Whether through Val's sudden declaration, or by some agency of the garden itself – the sight of a distant patch of grass beneath a tree – his mind is transported back.

He had walked out here on his first morning at Peterhouse in 1968, eager to escape the crowd of new faces in Old Court. The first-year undergraduates were massing on the lawn, ready for the matriculation photograph. Flightless crows in matching black gowns – boys whose smirking expressions he remembers even now, long after their names eluded memory. Walking among them that day, he realised with sinking horror that they all knew one another from school. Their voices were leisurely and commanding.

'Who's *he*?' one of them said, indicating Don (mute and standing apart) without looking at him. Don's brain and body recoiled. He walked away, through the nearest archway and along a stone passageway. As he went, he met his own reflection in the diamond facets of a leaded window – and he noticed, for the first time, how sculpted and delicate his features were, solemn to the point of mournfulness, like a boy from Picasso's Blue Period, only neater: his hair was brushed and parted for the photograph. What did they know, he thought – the crowers back there in the court – about art?

With that, he passed into the serene emptiness of the Fellows' Garden and wandered along the path. His suit and gown, and the tight white bowtie, felt starchy around his body.

As he walked, a man rounded a bend in the path, coming face to face with him. A slim, suited man with dark hair, perhaps in his mid-thirties. Don stopped. The man stopped. They faced each other across a few feet of gravel, before the man broke into a smile that struck Don as strange – an intimate smile, as if they were already acquainted.

'Where are you going?' the man said, in a tone more curious than challenging. 'Won't you miss the photograph?' His accent was unusual – crisp English edged with foreignness.

Don looked back at the stranger. They were the same height, he noticed – and the same build.

'The matriculation photo? It's at twelve o'clock. I have time.'

The man's smile changed – became more circumspect. 'Time for what?'

'Time to explore.' Don held his eye by an act of will.

'Weren't there enough diversions among the milling crowd?'

Before Don could answer, the man had wheeled around and was walking beside him, spiriting him along, glancing sideways at him. They continued in silence, their sleeves skimming once or twice. Don noticed that the man's suit was actually a velvet jacket – dark blue but intermittently bright – offset by dark moleskin trousers (cut just above the ankle) and leather shoes without laces. A precise, stylised outfit – neater than what an academic would wear. The velvet jacket matched the blue of his narrow knitted tie.

'They're not all like that, you know,' the man suddenly said. '*We're* not all like that, in this college. Public school, I mean. Oh, I know that Peterhouse has a reputation for it. But it has other reputations too – you'll see.'

The sun had broken through the clouds, rinsing the garden in glassy brightness. Abruptly, the man swerved off the path, striding over the grass, as if he had a destination in mind. Don followed, remaining a few steps behind.

'Are you a student here?' Don asked, feeling silly the moment he had spoken. The man was older than any undergraduate. And yet, for a fraction of a moment, the idea had seemed rational. There was something about his trim clothes and swept-back hair – and that easy candour.

'I'm a Fellow.' The man was fiddling with his jacket. He extracted a cigarette, encased in charcoal-dark paper, and lit it. 'Don't worry about them,' he said, blowing smoke, and he pointed his cigarette back in the direction of Old Court. 'The aristocrats. The young masters. They feed off their own complacency – I've seen it ten years in a row. They'll eat themselves to death.'

'I'm Don Lamb,' Don said, in a rush of eagerness that he couldn't have explained.

'Yes,' said the Fellow. 'Yes, I know. You're an art historian, aren't you?' With practised aim, he threw the unsmoked remainder of his cigarette in an arc across the lawn (how decadent, thought Don, to discard it after a single puff). It struck the edge of a stone bird bath, its intended landing place, and rebounded into the air. 'My name is Valentine. Or Val.'

They had arrived at a pool of sunlight beneath a tree, encircled by spindly shadows – summer hadn't quite disappeared from this spot. Val crouched down, bouncing gently on his heels, and beckoned to Don. In the stronger light, his velvet jacket was a brilliant mid-blue that seemed like an affront to the stone buildings and skeletal trees. Don sat on the dry grass.

'You'll be seeing more of me, here and there. I lecture on neoclassical sculpture in the eighteenth century – the tranquil exterior, the baroque inner life – if that's your kind of thing.'

'It is. Or' – Don surprised himself by laughing – 'it *could* be.'

Val grinned and nodded. 'I hope so.'

Now, more than a quarter of a century later, Val is gazing out at the garden. He hasn't spoken for a long time.

Don has the fleeting feeling – like a quiver of nostalgia – that all of his years, hours and seconds in this place have collapsed into a singularity. Then background sounds rush into his head – Bruce Day's voice booming through an open window, the shouts of undergraduates in the next court.

What does Val mean, *I love you*?

Don quickly rationalises it. His friend is given to theatrical flourishes. It was a rush of sentiment, a burst of fondness. Besides, *love* can have so many meanings: they both know their Greek.

'There's no need for you to say that,' he says at last.

Val doesn't reply for a while. Then he turns to Don and presses his hands on the edge of the bench. 'Yes there is. I never have, and soon you'll be gone.'

Don looks away, fixing his eyes on the gravel path, and thinks that this is ridiculous. He searches the garden and the buildings for any way of changing the subject.

Then, in an instant, Val reverts to his usual breezy style. 'Your *dunamis* must be protected! A formidable scholar, but surely a man of action too. Yes, a museum career beckons – I've never been so sure of anything.'

Hundreds of dead leaves, shrivelled and curled, flutter over the grass like an advancing army.

*

The prospect began as a pinprick of light. It seemed absurd at first. Don Lamb presiding over one of London's smaller but most prestigious museums. And yet the pinprick is gradually widening – turning into a porthole through which the Brockwell Collection looms as a picturesque vista. Could he start over – begin a new life? His heart turns light and giddy at the question, as if an illicit desire has erupted.

He begins to contemplate the lives lived outside of academia. Cambridge is his world, but now, more than ever, he is troubled by an awareness of the world beyond Cambridge. Apart from lecture theatres and hotels, he has rarely stepped into foreign places. Venice is no more than an ornate memory: he relies on pictures of the buildings and works of art that once entranced him. And London is as foreign as anywhere.

As the aperture widens, his resentment about *SICK BED* shades into obsession. The letter from the BBC is still in his drawer. Still unanswered.

Val is waging a campaign of persuasion. Don knows his friend; he recognises that old persistence, delicate but unflagging. When their conversations break, Val returns with calculated casualness to the subject of the Brockwell Collection and its vacant directorship.

*

'Suppose,' Val says, 'that all these years in Cambridge have merely been a beginning. The prelude to some bigger existence.'

It is late on Friday evening, and they are sitting together in the Old Combination Room.

'It would be the longest prelude to any career in history,' Don replies.

'Cambridge would turn out to have been your chrysalis. Years of routine and restraint preparing you for *life*.' This last word comes out as a shout. A few other dons, embedded around the lamplit room, turn nonchalantly in their armchairs.

'I've always dreamed,' Val continues, 'of defecting to a museum. Cambridge is so stifling! A little market town. And such gossiping, such snobbery . . .' He drinks from the glistering orb of his brandy glass. 'The trustees of the Brockwell once invited me to stand in, you know, as Director. Back in the '60s. Maurice Forster was in trouble with the police. Benighted times – I won't bore you with the details. But I didn't go, I couldn't do it. I wasn't brave enough to leave academia, Don, even for a short while.' He smiles desolately. Don wonders if he has had his teeth whitened. 'I'm too old now, of course. I'll die in Peterhouse. Gosh, this brandy is like purifying fire.'

They sit in silence for a while, then Val starts up again, like a boxer circling back.

'I've told you before, Don, and I'll say it again. The academic life fails its most loyal devotees. A rot sets in. Your own successes become pleasureless, and other people's successes' – he laughs bitterly and sluices his brandy – 'are a kind of death. Just look.' Bruce Day and Ferdinand Fernandez have walked into the room, engrossed in talk. 'They'll be bitching about Howard Crow's essay on the decline of Classics, you can be sure of it.'

Bruce Day creeps towards them. 'Black, Lamb,' he says in an urgent tone. 'Have you read Howard Crow in the *New York Review*? Pulitzer populism. Disgraceful.'

Don leans back in his chair and drinks. He shuts his senses. The brandy cleanses his throat and numbs his head. He glances through the aperture. Why, he asks himself, hasn't he visited the Brockwell Collection for so many years? Why, for that matter, has he gone so rarely to London – or those parts of London that lie outside the enclaves of academia? The other parts. He reflects on the other parts of himself – whether there are any, or could be.

'He presents himself as a historian,' Bruce is saying, 'when he's no more than a sociologist of education.'

'I was invited to write in his festschrift, you know,' murmurs Val. 'I refused, of course.'

Don looks at the men around him. Cambridge holds them in its orbit, just as it holds him. He feels that old insurrectionist desire to step outside of himself – break loose.

'By the way,' Val suddenly says to him, leaning forwards and seizing his arm. 'Have you thought any more about that invitation from Radio 4? *Shifting Perspectives*?'

'Yes, I'll do it,' Don hears himself say.

*

He armours himself in a blazer of grey wool and a Peterhouse tie.

In the dark of the early morning, he cycles to Cambridge station and catches the train to London. Through the window, the mist-blanketed fields are touched by intimations of dawn. The beautiful view bounces off his retinas.

He takes a cab from Liverpool Street to the doors of Broadcasting House, where he is met by a junior producer. She looks as young as one of his students – younger.

'We're thrilled you could make it, Don,' she says, ushering him through the bronze portals into a lobby of striped stone and backlit glass.

Don follows her along a sequence of corridors, each more

drab than the last. They come to a waiting room where the etched glass windows emit a dull, urban light.

'Do have a seat,' says the producer with a reassuring smile. 'We won't be long.' In an instant she has disappeared.

For five minutes, he wanders around the waiting room, hearing his leather shoes squeaking on the lino floor. Through a vent in the glass, he sees a light-well clogged with rubbish – broken bottles and cigarette ends, the top layer of decades' worth of accretions.

The producer returns with two strangers – a woman with a shaved head and a young man with earrings in both ears.

'Okay,' she announces. 'We're going live in ten minutes. This way, guys.'

Don follows the girl and her two companions out of the room, along another passageway. She throws open a door and ushers them into a small cubicle. It is windowless apart from a glass panel in one wall, on the other side of which a shadowy figure sits at a sloping desk bristling with switches. She manipulates the controls with agile, unhesitating movements, a pair of headphones clamped around her head.

'Take a seat,' the producer says. 'Robin's on his way.'

Since he left Cambridge, Don's brain has been empty of anything apart from his prepared words of critique. Now, for the first time, he begins to feel nervous. He hasn't been in a recording studio for years. The room is claustrophobic. It feels like the centre of a hostile world. And who are these two other characters, standing apart, chatting inanely? He had expected to be the sole interviewee.

He sits in front of a microphone and waits. The producer offers him coffee; he declines. Silent and tense, he peers at the Marconi microphone, sheathed in a metal grill and anchored like a trophy to a square base. It makes him think in a vague way of the Second World War – ominous broadcasts, new forms of weaponry.

A man breezes into the studio. He seems, to Don's tautened senses, like a sudden burlesque interlude – a montage of tanned skin, bleached teeth, pressed linen and corrugated hair. He greets Don with debonair haste, introducing himself as Robin Hands, the presenter of *Shifting Perspectives*. 'Please don't stand!' he says, then turns and kisses the bald woman on both cheeks – 'Well look at you!' – and does the same to the man.

Don recalls having met Robin Hands before in a Cambridge situation. He stands up, clears his throat and attempts to remind him.

'Well yes, that's *right*!' says the presenter, receiving a pile of notes from an assistant. 'I'm so glad you could join us today, Professor Lamb – or may I call you Don? Representing Peterhouse!'

Has he noticed the tie?

'Representing reason, truth and scholarship,' says Don, trying – and failing – to inject his words with levity. 'But I shall save my verdict for your listeners.' His voice sounds odd to him, as if he's primed it already for the live broadcast.

Robin Hands gives another crinkling grin, then settles in a chair and waves his guests into theirs. He slides a pair of headphones over his rippling hair and communicates with the woman through the window in rapid radio jargon. A lamp on the wall flashes red.

Robin Hands lights a cigarette and reads from a typewritten page: 'Hello!' (His voice is suddenly different – richer in tone, proclamatory.) 'I'm joined today by three expert witnesses from the world of the visual arts. Celia Ellsworth is chief art critic for the *New Statesman*. Jason Long is an artist and filmmaker who has been nominated for this year's Turner Prize for a mesmerising installation exploring' – he traces the text with his little finger – 'selfhood and subculture in 1970s Liverpool. And finally' – he shoots Don an ingratiating smile – 'Don Lamb is Professor in the History of Art at Peterhouse College, Cambridge, and a world authority on eighteenth-century Venetian painting. Now, how many of those can there be?'

Don's heart starts to pound in his ribcage. He hears his seat creak as he sits up even straighter.

'It's to Peterhouse, the most ancient of Cambridge's colleges, that we turn first. A new artwork has disturbed the cloistered calm of the place. It's called *SICK BED*, it's the creation of British artist Angela Cannon, and it's made entirely from rubbish – or to be precise, clothes and bottles and an oxidised bedframe.' The presenter's words are like long strands of silk, and the blue smoke of his cigarette tumbles upwards in arabesques. 'The sculpture has found a permanent home in Old Court, one of the loveliest quadrangles in England. Many are excited by the new arrival, but it's not – it's fair to say – to everybody's taste.'

Leaning over his microphone, Robin Hands shines his eyes around the table like a referee. Don's words are ready, like loaded ammunition. But the host turns first to Celia Ellsworth. She declares *SICK BED* the latest iteration of the avant-garde spirit, a radical feminist deployment of the idiom of the found object. Domestic cast-offs have been fashioned, she explains, into a meditation on gender, loneliness and mental illness.

'By the 1960s, anything could be art,' she says, concluding a digression on the sculptural readymade. 'Anything at all. That was revolutionary. And I guess' – she glances at Hands, then at Don – 'still too much for some people.'

Hands smiles and strokes his fingers. Don sits erect and expressionless.

Then it is the turn of the artist, Jason Long. He starts by claiming that Angela Cannon is a demiurge, endowed with the powers of a shaman. In rhapsodising sentences that unravel like streamers, he speaks of grids and cages and crucibles; the expression 'the prison of the hangover' develops into a pulsing refrain. Every so often, Robin Hands interjects with a question or remark that propels him into another hyper-eloquent torrent. He refers finally to the influence – the profound, osmotic influence – of the sculptor Mariam Schwarz.

'Schwarz, yes of course,' says Robin Hands. 'A clear influence.' Celia Ellsworth nods vigorously.

Mariam Schwarz – it's the same name that the chaplain of Peterhouse came out with. As Don speculates whether there's a conspiracy at work, his moment arrives.

'As a Peterhouse man, Don Lamb, what has been your reaction to *SICK BED*?' Robin Hands makes a pitched roof out of his fingers.

Don has been silent for so long that his voice has dried up. The sound that comes out is withered and ravenous.

'You were correct, Robin, when you said that this *thing* is not to everybody's taste,' he says, straining to jumpstart his vocal cords. 'It is not to my taste, I must confess, nor to the taste of many others in Cambridge who have dedicated their lives to questions of beauty and aesthetics.'

Robin chuckles politely and draws on his cigarette. He indicates with his eyes a glass of water that sits untouched near Don's microphone. Don ignores him.

'You say that it is made of rubbish. But a, a – a midden of urban refuse has more dignity than the so-called *SICK BED*. To call it a sculpture at all is laughable.'

'Midden,' repeats Celia Ellsworth with a sarcastic tut.

Don suddenly feels cold and unwell. He struggles to retrieve the words he came prepared with. But anger is surging to the surface, annihilating memory. He leaps into the void.

'Rubbish speaks, at least, of lowly cycles of existence – of earth's diurnal course. But this concoction represents nothing more than its own grotesque idiocy. It is a silly, superfluous spectacle – spectacle being the crucial word, for it cajoles our attention, it hijacks our senses, like the worst kind of brattish child. To be sure, it lacks the simple honesty of rubbish. It is closer to the jabbering of a tramp in a train carriage, importuning for cash and charity, or the abject mess he leaves when he defecates for provocation's sake on the well-paved street.'

'Oh, come on,' says Celia Ellsworth with a roll of the eyes. 'It's supposed to be provocative. That's the beauty of it – the power.'

'Have you actually looked at it?' demands Jason Long with narrowed eyes. 'Except from the top of your ivory tower?'

Looking down at his notes, Robin Hands raises a finger. 'How does it make you feel, Professor?' he asks. 'Forget about thought – what do you *feel* when you look at *SICK BED*?'

Don's lips tremor. 'It is devoid of grace, proportion, craft or technique – devoid of anything that might pass for representational content or spiritual depth.'

'Answer the question!' shouts Jason Long with a scathing smile.

Robin Hands crushes his cigarette to death in a glass ashtray. 'Is the problem that it's non-representational?' he ventures. 'Does art have to be representational?'

'The problem is that it's *base*,' says Don, amazed by his own anger. 'A base creation and an affront to the sanctity of the college. A cynical and witless contrivance.'

'Well, I think that's what you'd call a difference of opinion,' says Robin Hands – smoothly, coolly – as he signals through the window. 'And if your curiosity has been piqued, you can see Angela Cannon's *SICK BED* at Peterhouse College.' Without looking back at Don, he turns to a new page in his pile. 'Now, when Kylie Minogue and Jason Donovan first met, they were young actors on a daytime soap . . .'

Robin Hands recedes into genial commentary. The young producer appears from nowhere, and silently she ushers Don back to the waiting room. He observes, as he leaves, that the other guests are staying for the next segment.

Outside, it has started to rain. He is forced to walk for a mile before a taxi appears. Regent Street has never looked so grey.

* * *

When he reaches Cambridge in the early afternoon, his bike is missing from the station car park. The D-lock lies in two sections on the pavement, sawn through. Taxis are queuing at the rank, their engines dribbling exhaust fumes, but he decides to walk back to Peterhouse.

Cambridge, as ever, feels several degrees colder than London. He fastens the buttons of his Crombie overcoat and stoops against the oncoming wind.

At the end of Lensfield Road, as he's about to cross into Trumpington Street, he spots his bike – or the remains of it – in the gutter. The tyres have been punctured. One of them has become detached and lies limply across the spokes. Both wheels are twisted out of shape, and the large basket where Don usually keeps his briefcase has been torn off, as if savaged by an animal: a husk of wicker still clings to the handlebars.

He stands over the wreck and looks around him. The road junction is quiet. An old Volvo spins gracelessly around the roundabout. A woman is watching him from the steps of the Royal Cambridge Hotel, smoking a cigarette. She has frizzy red hair and wears a leather skirt.

Picking up the bike and resting it against railings, he feels an overpowering misery. It's a deeper feeling than any event of the day can justify. He abandons the wreck and wanders onto the Fen Causeway, the broad tract of road that crosses the wild meadows around the river. After crossing the bridge over the Cam, he turns into Coe Fen. He veers from the path into the meadow, over wet, boggy grass. The mist of the morning hasn't quite lifted; it is thickening now into fog. The wind stings his hands. A cyclist races along the towpath – relentless as an ancient messenger – but otherwise the place is deserted. *Shifting Perspectives* replays in his mind, and he thinks of everything he forgot to say.

For a second it's as if the earth has dissolved. He looks down.

His leather shoe is embedded in a cowpat – a large medallion left by one of the roaming cattle of Cambridge. A rank rural smell rises from its broken surface. His foot sinks deeper into the boggy ground, and wetness closes around his ankle.

With an effort he unglues his shoe and cleans it on the grass as he trudges across the meadow in the direction of Peterhouse.

*

Shifting Perspectives is broadcast the following morning. Don doesn't bother to listen. Shut in his study, he turns his thoughts to Tiepolo's chalk sketches. Few people in the college are likely to hear the programme. Soon it will be nothing but a memory. On his way to his morning's lectures, passing through the college gateway, he notices a group of students giggling.

It is only when he returns to Peterhouse at midday that he begins to detect an altered mood. The other fellows fall into groups when he walks past. Sometimes a head turns – eyes fix rapidly on Don – and then the spy returns to the furtive cluster. More than usual, colleagues are evading him – all except for Bruce Day, who emits a jubilant laugh when he sees Don in the court. The sound ricochets off the buildings and leaps into the grey sky.

'A base creation!' he wheezes. His eyes look ready to burst with pleasure.

At the end of the afternoon, Don sits alone in the Senior Common Room and drinks black coffee. The room is deserted. Something is wrong – some petty objection, he suspects, to the fact that he has appeared on national radio. Val warned him that people would be jealous. But he feels a growing nervousness as those words repeated by Bruce, *a base creation*, echo through his mind.

He is trying to read the *Times* letters page, running his finger-tips up and down his knitted tie, when the door opens and Val walks into the room. Don looks up. Val closes the door behind him – a firm, purposeful action – and crosses straight to Don's armchair.

'What were you thinking, Don? That was madness.'

Don notices an unfamiliar tightness in his friend's face. He closes the newspaper.

'Madness? That I should dedicate my time and mental reserves to defending the college?'

Val studies him with sharp, enquiring eyes. 'What were you thinking?' he repeats.

Don swallows the remainder of his coffee and rests his head in the cradle of his outspread fingers. He feels suddenly deflated. Defeated.

'I had words ready. A judgement. But it was like a dream, or a nightmare – you know the one, where you go onstage and can't remember your lines.'

'You didn't exactly seem lost for words.' Val adjusts the positioning of his rings, finger by finger.

'I spoke from the heart. Was that a crime?'

'I was expecting scepticism, your usual black wit and wisdom – not a diatribe. What was that about tramps in the street, for God's sake? You've caused terrible upset, I hardly need say.'

'Frank Davis, you mean?'

'Many people, not just Frank. And yes – Frank is incandescent. But what did you expect? Erica is his protégé – his great experiment. He's very protective of her.'

'Erica Jay? What does she have to do with this?'

Slowly, Val's face loses its tightness – slackens into an incredulous smile. 'Don't tell me you didn't know.'

'Know what?'

'You must be the last person.'

'I don't understand, Val.' Agitation is creeping over him.

Val's smile breaks now into dismayed laughter. 'And I was *sure* I'd told you. Erica Jay *is* Angela Cannon. Oh Don, how could you not have realised? They're the same woman: she writes under a pseudonym.' Val sits down in the armchair opposite and stretches back with feline languor, raising his face to the ceiling. 'She likes to keep her art and poetry apart – don't ask me why. One is just as outrageous as the other, to my mind.' He sits forward again, disbelief returning to his face. 'How could you not have known?'

Don feels as if his chair, the entire edifice of padded leather, is floating on deep water.

'You never told me. You know you never told me.'

'Oh, that's not true,' Val says, in a gentler voice. 'I forget what you don't know, the way you insulate yourself, bury yourself in work. There's no use getting upset about it. You should have known – and you didn't.'

Don's agitation is turning to cold, sickening despair. 'What shall I do?'

Val watches him with detached intrigue. 'I don't know, Don. I really don't.'

4

At dinner, Erica Jay is nowhere to be seen. Frank Davis is absent too. Other than Don and Val, six fellows are dining at High Table, together with a couple of guests. Not one of them has met Don's eye. He feels nauseous.

Halfway through the main course, Frank Davis appears. He is accompanied by a visitor and doesn't appear to notice Don or anyone else as he passes to the head of the table. Don glances swiftly to his left. Like most of the Master's guests, this one has the look of an urbane outsider – a jovial character in a white suit (odd for the time of year), with a strident laugh. For a frightful second, Don thinks it is Robin Hands of *Shifting Perspectives*. But no. Just some other personality.

'The minister of culture,' Val says in a hushed voice.

Don has no idea if this is the truth. He resists the impulse to look back.

Val tries to distract him with talk of other – trivial – things, but his eyes and brain are adrift. He looks at the bottles and glasses in front of him, the rows of students at the tables beyond, the stone tracery of the window in the far corner of the hall, and senses that an invisible membrane has dropped between him and the world he has inhabited for so long.

The laughter of the Master's guest repeats in his ear like a raven's screech.

He recognises people, but without conviction. The man diagonally opposite him might be Bruce Day's imposter. Ferdinand Fernandez is performing a rote version of himself.

As his plate is cleared away, Don looks up the table again. Frank

Davis is sitting alone in contemplation. Now that Don thinks about it, the call of the raven ceased some minutes ago – the man probably left early to return to London. Frank glances back at him across the gap of empty seats. He looks tired. Don's mind changes gear and he considers some form of reserved greeting – life must, after all, go on . . . But the Master speaks first.

'I don't have anything to say to you tonight, Don.' His voice is calm and even – the voice of an arch diplomat, or a television executive. 'I've written.'

Don's lips work away silently. He becomes aware of the constricting tightness of his tweed jacket: it wraps around his chest like a net.

Frank's eyes have wandered over to the students' tables as he loses himself again in private reverie. On Don's other side, Val comes out with some chattering irrelevance. Don raises a hand to stall him.

'I suppose you expect me to apologise,' he declares, loud enough to recall Frank from his meditations. There is silence around the table.

Frank's pale eyes settle on him. 'That's the very least I expect.'

The Master's face – that unassuming, middle-aged, managerial face – has a muted intensity about it. A steel that Don has never perceived. He feels wrongfooted. Maybe there was more to the man all along.

'Angela was amazed by what you said,' Frank continues. 'Horrified, actually. And so was I.'

Erica, Angela . . . It still seems like a joke, or a fantasy. Don wants to explain that he had no idea. But some internal hand of restraint – together with Val's silent, accusing presence – checks him. He clears his throat.

'I was asked onto the radio to give my views as an art historian.' His measured tone belies the thudding of his heart.

'And not just any art historian,' Val interjects, with jarring cheerfulness.

'I duly expressed my views, in robust words.' Don meets the Master's emotionless gaze. 'What do I have to apologise for?'

'I have a duty of care towards everyone in Peterhouse,' says Frank. 'We're a community, not an amphitheatre of egos. I'm extremely concerned that Angela will leave because of this. She was doubtful enough about whether she wanted to be in this place.'

Tension rifles through the air. The college fellows unite in silent defence of Peterhouse. But Frank remains unaware – seems, in fact, to have forgotten that anybody else is present.

'An apology would be a start, Don. And not just for your robust choice of words, as you call it, but for the despicable manner in which you spoke them.' A heat of feeling is breaking through the diplomatic carapace. 'Since we're now talking about it, I might as well tell you what I have in mind. I want to convene a conference here in the college – a day-long festival, let's call it – in celebration of *SICK BED*. I'm thinking that several of the fellows could give talks on the sculpture.'

'An interdisciplinary colloquium,' Val quips. 'Very trendy.'

'I'll say some words of introduction,' Frank goes on. 'The chaplain has already agreed to speak on the liturgical aspects of the coloured glass and discarded clothes.' His eyes brighten fractionally. 'After that, I would like you, Don, to give an address – a more sober reflection this time. Perhaps you might consider some of the parallels between *SICK BED* and your own research on skies and light.'

Keeping the angle of his head locked, Don feels the rapt attention of his colleagues like a searing heat. At the edge of his vision, he sees Val pick up a glass and sluice the contents. He feels like the victim of a grotesque show trial. He stares back at the Master and tries to chuckle, but his voice breaks into a jangle of shrill and baritone noises.

'I've outlined the plan in my letter to you,' Frank says. 'The festival will be on the last Friday of term, right before Christmas. I've just been speaking with a producer from *The South Bank Show*, perhaps you saw him? They're going to film the whole thing.' He manages a thin smile. 'Your involvement would go a long way to building bridges with Angela – and with me.'

Building bridges . . . Don foresees the abject act of penitence, a travesty of his academic principles. He would never recover in the eyes of his colleagues, and Frank knows it.

'You would sooner receive my resignation than see me mock myself in that way.'

There is a flash of bafflement in Frank's face – the bafflement of someone whose outstretched olive branch has been taken, inspected, and snapped in half.

'Then I await your resignation.'

The room seems to be changing colour. The air has acquired an oily, yellowish hue. Don watches Frank through the varnished medium, feeling as if reality is decelerating as the substance of the atmosphere dries and hardens.

'You know I don't want it to come to that,' Frank says.

Don's lips have been stunned into twitching paralysis. Before he can reply, Frank has walked from the room.

'Davis has signed his own death warrant,' Val whispers.

Don ignores him. The show of solidarity has come too late. Furiously, he looks around the table at the other fellows. But they have already taken cover – broken into various small conversations. Ferdinand Fernandez is busy pouring his store of knowledge into the ear of an elderly scholar. Bruce Day is ogling a young friend.

'What people forget,' Bruce says, 'is that Enoch was a very fine classicist.'

The boy indulges him with dancing movements of the head.

Involuntarily, Don rests his head in his hands. He is overcome by a sense of absolute, irreversible alienation. Is it simply the shock of the Master's challenge? He insists to himself that this is just another Cambridge quarrel. Nothing has to change. And yet . . .

In a gentle voice, almost as quiet as thought itself, Val says, 'You need a new life, Don. A new start.' He places a hand on Don's wrist – Don feels the warmth of his fingers, the hardness of a ring. 'The Brockwell Collection! No, wait a moment – just listen. Think of it as a period of indefinite leave in London. Just the stimulus you need to finish *The Skies of Tiepolo*.' As Val grows excited, he speaks with the strange German lilt that sometimes tinges his speech. 'And best of all, the museum has just been bequeathed a painting by Tiepolo. The oil sketch for *The Martyrdom of Saint Sebastian*.'

At this, Don looks up. 'That's been lost for two hundred years.'

'It's just been found.' Val smiles serenely.

'When? Where?'

'Last month, at a castle in the Black Forest. Do you remember my old friend, Klaus von Löwenstein?'

'The crown prince? Vaguely, yes. Hasn't he just died?'

Val nods. 'In the summer – liver cancer. The picture turned up in his attic, wedged in a fireplace! Poor Klaus, he probably had no idea it was there.'

'That's extraordinary.'

'Isn't it? Anyway, Klaus's family – cousins, a silly little nephew – asked me to inspect the estate and advise on the art and antiques. This was while I was over for the funeral.' Val's voice is low, as if he's taking care not to be overheard, and yet his eyes blaze with triumph. 'Most of it is middling stuff. Hordes of slimy landscapes, a few decent Goltzius etchings. Imagine my amazement when I found the Tiepolo.'

'And you never said a thing.' Don stares at him, astonishment giving way to exasperation.

'I couldn't, Don. Not until I was sure it was real. You must understand that. But there's no doubt in my mind. And it's taken time, but – well – I've managed to persuade the family to donate the picture to the Brockwell.'

Don sits back and regards the length of the hall. 'I've always wanted to organise an exhibition of Tiepolo's oil sketches,' he murmurs. '*The Martyrdom of Saint Sebastian* could be the centrepiece.'

For a minute or two, the excitement of the news eclipses everything else. Then the painful residues of the confrontation with Frank seep back. He realises that tears are pooling in his eyes. As Val reminisces about the Prince of Löwenstein, Don stands abruptly and strides from the room, between the tables of laughing undergraduates. That blithe, unending laughter – what is it ever about?

Outside in the court, in the cold dark night, feelings flow out of him like blood from a fresh cut. He stands in front of *SICK BED*, in the path of the circulating light. The lamp blazes through the heap of bottles, dazzling him with synthetic blue. He lifts his head slightly and sees a softer light behind the tall window of the chapel. Singing is audible – a resonant contralto. He hardly ever steps inside the chapel, but the sound tempts him around the path. He pushes open the chapel door, just wide enough to slip inside.

What he sees causes him to stop, motionless.

The chapel is bathed in light. Every candle is aflame. His eyes travel up the black and white paving of the nave, between the empty choir stalls, and he sees Briony Davis – the Master's wife – standing before the altar in a long black gown that leaves her shoulders and arms naked in the golden glow. Her grey-brown hair has been gathered in a complex design around the crown of her head, and her face seems transfigured by an ecstasy of concentration. She is singing a melodic, discordant aria.

As Don holds open the door, a high vibrato note rings through the air. To one side of Briony, in the corner of the chapel, the chaplain sits at a grand piano, swaying gently as he plays with closed eyes. Next to him, standing at the piano and watching Briony with a dark, liquid gaze, is Erica Jay. Angela Cannon. Artist and poet in one. Don steps back and closes the door.

*

The decision – which for weeks has been a matter of indecision – is easy to make. He wakes up and sees a clear winter sky through his window, and he knows that his time in Cambridge is over. He is still filled with rage at the Master, and still riddled with a deep, crawling unease about Erica Jay: what will he say to her if they meet again? But most of all, the revelation of the rediscovered Tiepolo – a promised gift to the museum – has soared up like a portent that he can't ignore.

Val sets about making arrangements at once. In a matter of days, the board of the Brockwell Collection has unanimously approved Professor Lamb's appointment as the new director. Val insists that Don will stay at his house in Dulwich for as long as he needs – everything is ready and waiting. Don sends a short, handwritten letter to the Master, devoid of reference to their discussion at High Table. He receives a surprisingly warm reply.

The following week, Don's resignation is announced by letter to the fellowship. The announcement produces waves of unrest and speculation, but these do their best to remain subterranean and undetected. The shock of the news is rapidly absorbed, and in the end, the day is much like any other at Peterhouse.

'We'll have a leaving party for you when I'm back,' says Val as they perform a circuit of Gisborne Court that evening. 'A proper send-off.'

'Back from where?'

'I'm leaving for Marrakech this Saturday.'

Don nods in morose silence, remembering. Val goes to

Marrakech every year for a month's break. *December is the loveliest month in Morocco*, he likes to say. Don has listened to countless tales of Christmases in the gardens of La Mamounia, of New Year's parties in the house of an obscure English painter – a maze of arches and lanterns.

'I'd rather not have one,' he says. 'A party, I mean. I've never been one for farewells. In any case, I'm not going yet. I'll have to serve a term's notice. Maybe two.'

Val seems on the brink of laughter. 'Impossible! The museum needs you in a few weeks.'

'That soon?'

'The Master will release you from your college duties. And I suggest that we hand your PhD students over to Igor Kaveckis.'

They stroll through an archway into the Fellows' Garden, where the grass is brittle with frost. A full moon is rising.

'I'm still amazed,' Val says.

'Amazed about what?'

'Amazed that you're going.'

'But it was your idea, Val.'

'My suggestion, yes, but your decision.' Val stops and raises his eyes to the night sky. 'I suppose I never thought you'd actually do it – break free from Peterhouse. I underestimated your resolve.' He walks on. 'But it's the right thing. I'm sure of it. This preposterous festival was just a signal sent by fate.'

The festival is happening next week. Don has already seen bright green posters around the college: a day of lectures, debates and happenings in honour of *SICK BED*. Gene Caskill is among the speakers – something about breaking apart the canon (spelled *Cannon*). Briony Davis will give an opera recital at midnight . . . There will be no escape.

Val is watching him. Perhaps he can read Don's thoughts.

'Why don't you come with me to Marrakech?'

They have wandered off their usual course, along a narrowing avenue of leafless hawthorn bushes.

'I mean it,' Val continues. 'Peterhouse is melancholic at this time of year.'

Don has always wanted to see the minbar of the Kutubiyya Mosque, that marvellous stepped pulpit carved in the twelfth century, replete with geometric marquetry. His senses are already expanding at the prospect . . . But he knows he can't go. He has decided to ignore Christmas and the vacation around it, to ignore everything except for *The Skies of Tiepolo*.

'I'll book you a room at La Mamounia,' Val is saying. 'You can think of it as a going-away present.'

'I can't, Val. I'm sorry. It's my book – I'm at a critical point.'

But is it really just the book, he wonders, as he tries to pinpoint his aversion? He has a sense of the world, and the future, opening around him in concentric circles. London is an uncharted dimension, just beyond the horizon. Morocco would be like leaping into wonderland. And besides, what would he and Val become – together – in such a place? In the rooted geography of Peterhouse, they live in a perennial present tense, outside of deep time. This is where they belong, where they have always belonged.

For the first time, Don tries to imagine what it will be like between the two of them once he has left.

Val walks a little ahead of him, into the gloom. They have ventured into the furthest reaches of the garden, the part known as the Deer Park. There haven't been any deer for decades.

'I knew you wouldn't, really.' Val turns to Don. His face is serious, and as pale as bone. Then he breaks into a resigned smile. 'But I'll write to you. December is the loveliest month in Morocco.'

*

On the day of the *SICK BED* festival, Don goes into hiding.

He retreats to the university library, and then for several dull hours to The Eagle pub, where he sits hunched over a glass of bitter ale. He returns to Peterhouse just before midnight to find a party in full swing in Old Court. The lamp at the centre of the sculpture is moving at triple its usual speed – a wild, flashing centrifuge. A haze of cigarette smoke swirls in the light. Music pounds out of speakers stationed around the court.

In a daze, Don sifts his way through the revellers. Halfway up the staircase to his rooms is a lavatory, external to his quarters but used by no one apart from him. He rinses his face in the sink and stands at the metal urinal. The music in the court outside ceases abruptly. In its place is a vast, unreal silence. He feels a growing calm, as if the tension of recent days is draining away, down the plughole . . .

He hears footsteps and becomes aware of someone alongside him at the urinal. Almost at once he knows that it is Gene Caskill, his nemesis in the History of Art department. He remembers how Caskill heckled him during the Fitzwilliam Lecture, at that moment of devastating silence – 'Prompt!' – rousing their colleagues to laughter.

'Good morrow, Lamb!' sings Caskill in an affected, Shakespearean manner. His voice is sonorous in the tinny echo of the room. 'What a day. How come I haven't seen you until now?'

Don ignores him. There is a hard, spattering sound as Caskill urinates. Then a different sound reaches his ears from the window – Briony Davis's aria in the chapel, rising to that soaring high note. He feels transfixed, as if the sustained climax has resonated with a deep inward frequency.

'How goes the pursuit of truth and beauty?' demands Caskill. 'And what's this about you leaving?'

Don zips up his fly and turns to look into the face of the man beside him, that beaming, bullying face he knows so well.

'Oh, fuck off,' he says in a near whisper.

His private mental vocabulary has sprung into the world. He

is shocked by its escape. Caskill looks shocked too, and vaguely delighted. As his urine continues to clatter against the metal, he releases a loud cackle.

For days afterwards, Don barely leaves his rooms. He stays inside, bent over his notes and pictures. The world beyond his windows – the chanting of carols, the panning light of *SICK BED* – recedes to the limits of his consciousness. Instead, he thinks regularly of the oil sketch of *The Martyrdom of Saint Sebastian*, just discovered and soon to travel to the Brockwell Collection. Perhaps his own arrival will coincide with that of the picture.

Just occasionally, the knowledge of Erica Jay's presence in the college returns to him, and he feels a piercing fear at the thought that he might see her again.

On Christmas Eve, he receives a postcard from Val. It contains nothing more than a few lines about a trip to a hammam (*I left a transformed man*). He spends the following day in the deep fictive space of *Apollo and the Continents*. In previous years, he has dined at the Master's Lodge on Christmas Day, along with the few other fellows who remain in the college. This year, the invitation arrived as usual – a gilt-edged card embossed with florid script – and he tore it into pieces. The flakes of white and gold are still at the bottom of his wastepaper bin.

He forgets about food until the small hours of the night, when he creeps outside and walks to the all-night kebab van on King's Parade.

*

Val returns from Morocco a couple of weeks into the new year, tanned from the hot weather – and just in time for Don's departure.

'I'll drive you to London,' he says, taking Don by surprise as he breaks off from an account of the pink stone of Marrakech, the bewitching chaos of the Jemaa el-Fnaa and the beauty of a minaret rising above orange trees – images of impossible beauty in the dimness of the Senior Common Room. They are in their usual spot, sunk in the leather armchairs that have become their static doubles. 'I insist on it. I still recall your first day at Peterhouse. I want to be with you on your last.'

'My first day,' Don echoes. 'God. It feels like another era.' He picks up his near-empty cup of coffee and crosses to the window.

'It was another era, Don.'

'I remember . . .' Don falters for a moment, checked by a pang of embarrassment, then pushes himself on. 'I remember you appearing out of nowhere when I was in the Fellows' Garden. Like a messenger in a Greek play. You said something about the aristocracy, those boys who thought they ruled this place – that they'd choke on their own complacency, eat themselves to death.'

'Well, isn't that what happened – in a manner of speaking? Where are they now?'

Don turns with a grin. 'A fair few of them are friends of yours, I believe.'

Val stands and laughs, coming to join Don at the window. 'It depends on what you mean by friends. I have connections. But as for friends . . .' His voice has quietened. He reaches for Don's elbow, that familiar gesture – but perhaps Don is standing a fraction further away than he thought: he fails to make contact, and his arm swings back. 'I didn't appear from nowhere, you know. I'd seen you. I'd been watching.'

Early on the following Sunday, Val drives over to Peterhouse in the old Mercedes that he keeps in a rented garage on the outskirts of town. It is a low-slung raft of a car – black as a hearse and trimmed with flawless chromium. Don's possessions are carried by the college porters through the gate, piled in the boot and spread across the back seats – folded clothes, cardboard boxes, framed prints and drawings, and the cork model of the Pantheon, which suffers a disfiguring chip to its dome as Val loads it into the car. It is agreed that Don's books will follow by van at a future date.

It feels like a ritual, this phased and sedulous removal of his effects. He stands for a moment at the window of his study and wonders what any of it means. The person who he was seems to have exited along with the contents of the room: it's as if he has been evacuated from himself.

In the court below, the bottles of *SICK BED* rise on the grass like a fungal growth. Just as Don turns away from the window, a porter carries the final cardboard box through Old Court. The lid blows off in a gust of wind, and a handful of small pictures fly out, fluttering across the path and the lawn – little cut-out scenes from the Archepiscopal Palace in Udine and the Palacio Real in Madrid. The porter puts down the box and scurries about, trapping the errant frescoes with his feet and grabbing the lid. Only one picture escapes his grasp, or his notice. It darts through the bedframe of *SICK BED* and lodges beneath an empty rum bottle.

Church bells ring through the streets as they wind their way out of the city centre in Val's car. It is brightening into a beautiful January day.

How strange, he thinks, to be returning to London so soon after the last unhappy visit. For a while, he feels a nagging doubt. The journey seems like a performance – he can't believe he is really leaving. But as Cambridge recedes, he relaxes into the cracked leather seat, basking in its ingrained aroma of tobacco and cologne, and feels himself merge with the soft suspension of the Mercedes.

Val turns on the radio. Sir Ernst Gombrich is the guest on *Desert Island Discs*.

'That old bore!' Val cries out. 'How could they think to invite him on?'

Don is sure that the programme is a repeat – that he heard it three years ago or more; but he doesn't say. He watches his friend from the corner of his eye. Val steadies the car with one hand, his concentration switching between the road and the rear-view mirror. The steering wheel is a Mercedes star – three steel arms diverging from a central dial, inside a ring of dimpled mahogany. He is familiar with Val's expression – lips slightly parted, eyes alive with concentration. A handsome face, refined without being delicate. The face is so familiar to him, so automatic in his memory, that he has stopped seeing it. He finds himself looking at his friend, really looking, for the first time in months – maybe years.

'My mother knew Gustav Mahler extremely well,' says Gombrich out of the grill of the radio. 'She was a member of that circle.' His German accent is still heavy after half a century in England.

Clavichord music starts up.

'I remember,' Val says, 'that Ernst always used to be the first to ask a question in seminars. And usually it was the same question. There would be a long and tortuous paper from a young researcher on some *microscopic* aspect of Renaissance painting' – he changes gear forcefully – 'and then he would say, in that thick accent of his, "So what?"'

Val pronounces the 'v' of *what* with vehemence. His own German accent is uncannily convincing. They both laugh.

'So what, so what indeed.' Val switches back to his own voice and coasts into the fast lane.

Don knows that for a man of his age, Val is good-looking, not to mention vain. But as he sits beside him now, he is struck once more by how well preserved he is. The lean, angular face, lightly tanned, is that of a younger man. The hair is dark and abundant, in spite of Val's advancing years.

Val senses Don's attention and turns with curiosity. Embarrassed, Don looks the other way – at the long unchanging stretch of embankment through the passenger window.

A Mozart piano concerto begins to play. Don sinks into a doze. It is a state too shallow and sunlit to be called sleep, but powerful enough to erase thought.

When he opens his eyes again, they're close to London. Warehouses skim past, along with used-car dealerships and stray terraces of shops, mattress and sofa superstores – their windows thronging with promises – and pair after pair of semi-detached houses from the interwar years, losing the veneer of newness and neatness they once had. He looks down at his hands. They are white and sallow against his flannel trousers. But a trace of pink – drawn out by the sun – is beginning to show through the waxy surface.

Val is fiddling with the radio, resting two fingers on the base of the wheel. A blast of sound invades the car – manic thudding and an electronic squeal. At once, Don is wide awake. The noise is sharp-edged, deranging; it breaks into his head, scrambles his nerves. Strangest of all, Val seems to be laughing.

'What a bacchanal!' he cries, and reaches again for the dial. Suddenly the sound is doubled, trebled, as he twists the volume to full.

'Make it stop!' Don shouts. 'Jesus, Val, make it stop!'

'This is Kiss 100,' yells a voice across the blare.

'Please, God.'

With a swift movement, Val has restored Radio 4.

'Really, Don,' he says with a sigh. 'There's a lot you'll have to get used to, living in south London.'

They speak little for the rest of the journey. London envelops them like an incoming tide. Don has never travelled through the city by car. He stares out of the window and tries to sort the districts one from another, but somehow fails to notice when they cross the river. South London, the region that Val seems to regard as separate and special, arrives as a slow deluge of traffic, heat and noise.

They creep along the Brixton Road. A Jamaican man with a striped woollen hat crosses the road, cutting in front of the car and causing Val to brake. The man glances at them and strums the car bonnet with his fingers as he passes.

They turn into a side road. In the distance, a radio mast rises like a gigantic spire.

'I meant to tell you,' Val says, breaking the silence. 'Erica Jay gave a performance of her poetry the other night in the college bar.' He turns to Don with a broad grin. 'Do you know what? Her stuff is much better when she reads it aloud. Mesmerising, actually.'

They pass a neoclassical church, grey as poured concrete. On the other side of the road is a run-down cinema, painted in peeling white, with the word *FRIDGE* spelt across the façade in cavorting letters. Dulwich, however, is different. An oasis of parks and trees and well-kept Victorian villas in Tudor or Gothic dress, strung out along grass-fringed roads. Dotted along the pavements are little white posts threaded by chains. It doesn't feel like London at all.

5

Number eleven Montcalm Road is a detached house – not large, but not small – partly obscured from the road by hedges and a giant horse chestnut.

Val pulls into the driveway and the house rolls into full view. Don assesses the Georgian design – an asymmetric stack of pediments and pilasters, balustrades and swelling bay windows. A brocade of ivy spreads across the dull yellow brickwork.

'The House Beautiful!' Val grinds the car to a halt and ratchets up the handbrake.

'It's a bit more than a pied-à-terre.'

'It was my London base once – on those occasions when I stayed in London. They became fewer, but I kept the place as a . . .' Val thinks for a moment as he opens the car door, then turns back to Don with a smile full of intent. 'As a boarding house for friends. Come inside – we'll come back for your things.'

Val leads him up the front steps and presses a button at the centre of a brass panel. Don stands alongside him, feeling as if he's being dropped off at school.

Almost at once, a woman answers the door. She is tall, in the prime of middle age and wears yellow corduroys and a T-shirt printed with the Olympic rings. *Los Angeles 1984.*

'Ina!' cries Val.

'Val!' says Ina with stern warmth. Her hair is short and greying, and her eyes are bright blue. She has a handsome, mannish face.

'Don, please meet Miss Ina Stables, my devoted housekeeper.'

Ina's smile is confined to her eyes. She leads them along a

hall bathed in a golden half-light. Against one wall is a console table (a rare type – Roman, eighteenth-century) topped by an alabaster slab and propped up by three gilded, grinning cherubs. On top is a small statue of Hercules manhandling a bull – gilt bronze. Further down the hall is a marble bust of a Roman nymph – Don tries to examine it, but Val hurries him along – then a line of Regency-era portraits, serene countenances enclosed by powder-coated wigs. The place smells like a church. Blooming flowers in vases add a sweeter tinge. Everywhere there are pictures, objects, patterns.

They pass into a kitchen at the back of the house. It is bright and simply equipped, an antidote to the hall. Its décor is that of a recently passed era – plastic cupboards in a pale shade of turquoise, cork tiles, a table covered in a gingham cloth. This, Don senses, is Ina's domain.

'I live through there,' she says, answering his thoughts, and indicates a frosted glass door in the corner of the room. It leads to a bungalow extension, visible through the window, that runs along one side of the garden.

'Built as an artist's studio in the war years,' Val explains, leading Don to the window. 'And now Ina's annex.'

The annex is an ugly addition to – subtraction from – the main house. But then the garden, too, is a mess – as shambolic as the interior of the house is ordered. A blanket of brambles, ivy and weeds extends, knee-deep, to the back of the annex, where it rises into a solid wall of shrubs – honeysuckle, hydrangeas, laurels, all defiantly evergreen on this January morning.

'*Il giardino povero*,' says Val, as if to excuse the garden's wasted state. 'There's a statue somewhere out there, would you believe, by John Gibson.'

'Are you here alone, Miss Stables?' Don asks.

'Mamma lives with me,' she says. *Mamma* – she pronounces it strangely, like *hammer*. 'She's old and very weak. You won't hear much from her. Or from me – I'm out a lot.' She switches on the kettle and it gives out a spurting sigh, like a patient on a respirator. 'I'm going to the cinema tonight. *The Quick and the Dead*. Would you like a cup of tea, Professor Lamb?'

'Thank you, yes. And please – call me Don.'

'Poor old Ma,' Val murmurs, turning away from the window. 'I'd say hello, but I know how it unsettles her. How many years young is she now?'

'Eighty-five this summer.'

'*Eighty-five!* I can't believe it.'

'Yes, a great age, all things considered. But not much of a life any more. I often think she's dying more than she's living.'

'Oh, say it ain't so,' Val protests in a Deep Southern drawl that seems oddly facetious.

Don stands there and wonders what to say. He wasn't expecting a housekeeper and her elderly mother – but then what *was* he expecting? Life beyond Cambridge has been a blank until today. Detail by detail, that life is now materialising like an improbable story.

'Perhaps, Ina,' Val begins after a moment, 'you might give the garden a trim when the weather's milder.'

'Not without Mamma's say-so.' She pours water into a yellow teapot. 'You know that she loves the wildness of it.'

Val beckons. 'Come, Don. Let me show you to your room. That tea needs to infuse.' He leads the way upstairs, past a small clay vessel – Minoan, Don suspects – that sits on one side of the bottom step. The carpet is clamped in place by brass bars. On a half-landing, where the staircase turns, is a black lacquered cabinet. It squats on four stout feet. Flecks of turtle shell and brass marquetry spread across its surface.

'Do make sure you sample the delights of Dulwich,' Val exhorts in the style of a tour guide. 'The Horniman Museum, Belair House, the park. *Dulwich* Park, I mean. Don't go to Brockwell Park – an unlovely place, full of thugs and drunks.

Best avoided.' He strokes the dust off another urn. 'It's a pity that the museum has to share its name.'

The first-floor landing is coated with green silk and boasts another collection of painted faces from the days of the Grand Tour, interspersed by small Italian landscapes. Val opens the door to a bedroom overlooking the driveway and road.

The space appears sparse after the aesthetic overload of the hallways – a large, airy room with peach-coloured wallpaper, a wardrobe and a double bed. The one concession to theatricality is a desk in the bay window, a black mahogany edifice fringed with gold leaf and studded with panels and scrolls.

'I've cleared the room out for you, removed everything. It can be your study – just like in Cambridge.'

'You mean this was your room?'

Val waves a hand dismissively. 'I'm here less and less. Don't think of it as mine or yours.' He is next to the desk, looking out of the window. Don hangs back. 'I hope you'll stay here, Don. For as long as you want.'

Val's eyes have lost their knowing glint. His façade appears to tremble – the wise, alert countenance falters into vacancy. Then he strides across the room and ushers Don out, back down the stairs.

They drink tea in the sitting room and Val discourses on the many roles of a museum director – appeals for funds, the chairing of meetings, expressions of sincerest gratitude. Don nods and listens, and contemplates his plan for an exhibition of Tiepolo's oil studies with *The Martyrdom of Saint Sebastian* at its centre. Then they begin the grim job of transferring his possessions from the car into the hallway. Ina helps, carrying stacks of boxes with ease. His things accrue in a pile at the foot of the stairs.

'Most of it will have to go in the cupboard,' Val says as he deposits a pile of framed pictures. 'You won't have room for all your bric-a-brac upstairs.'

Don notices, at the top of the pile, the framed photograph that sat on his desk at Peterhouse – Iris, the monochrome greyhound.

In less than an hour – before Don realises they have finished unloading the car – Val is shouldering on his overcoat and saying goodbye.

'Good luck, Don. Call me soon.' He makes a phone gesture with his hand, then brings his fingers momentarily to his lips.

Don watches him from the front door. 'Can't you stay a while longer?'

From the bottom of the steps, Val looks at Don, then up at the house, then back at his friend, as if he is calibrating the two. His face takes on the same strange blankness as before. He checks his watch.

'No. Sadly not. I'm having dinner with Liza – you remember, Willie Maugham's daughter. Then the opera – Donizetti, *La fille du régiment*.'

Val clasps his chest, dumbstruck by the music he hasn't yet heard.

Liza Maugham, Donizetti, a sumptuous hoard of art and furniture . . . Don has always regarded Val's other life with awed reticence. He knows that Val was a society figure in the 1960s, that he associated with gay poets and artists, and that when he was still in his twenties, he testified before the Wolfenden Committee. There are stories of parties, holidays in Tangier, trips to Somerset Maugham's villa on the Riviera. But they have always been stories and nothing more.

Val clambers into the car, stabs the key into the ignition and winds down the window.

'I'll be back, Don,' he calls out. 'The week after next, in fact. There's a private view at Leighton House.' He gives a knowing smile. 'The great and the good will be there!'

He waves and drives away, hooting as he pulls onto the road.

That afternoon, Don feels acutely, farcically alone – like an actor on a stage, watched by an audience of hundreds.

He organises his notes, typewriter and a few other possessions in the bedroom. There is a shallow shelf on one wall where his sword fits perfectly. Afterwards, he unpacks his boxes of pictures, rifling back through the years of his life. At the bottom of one, he finds a postcard from the Residenz, Würzburg – Tiepolo's allegory of the planets and continents, with its vast arena of sky. He thinks back to the first time he went there, aged twenty-seven, and wonders if he really remembers it at all – or if the spectacle of his younger self, staring up at the vaulted ceiling, is itself just a picture in his imagination.

Oblivious to the sunny day outside, he lays pictures across the desk and the floor, crawling on his hands and knees like a man searching for a dropped jewel. Hours pass. The yawning canopies of palaces and cathedrals multiply across the room – apertures of colour broken up by lines of carpet and the cracked leather surface of the desk.

In the middle of the afternoon, Ina appears in the doorway.

'Gosh – what a constellation.'

Don stands up, his knees clicking as he straightens.

'The ceiling frescoes of Giambattista Tiepolo,' he says, giving careful inflection to the Italian. He feels awkward, apologetic – like a guest who has already outstayed his welcome.

'How beautiful. Except I won't be able to hoover with all that paper on the floor.'

Afterwards, he wonders about opening the window, but worries that a breeze will dislodge his pictures from their assigned places.

* * *

Under the rosy light of the desk lamp he makes corrections to his opening chapter, but it feels like work for work's sake. Every so often, he stands and looks out of the window at the driveway and the road below. It is so unlike Old Court – so suburban. Not a don in sight. A yellow Citroën is parked at an angle on the gravel.

Night is falling. He turns on the radio and listens to the final minutes of a documentary about the mysterious death of a media tycoon. The man's body was recovered from the sea off Tenerife some years ago. A heart attack, most likely, but conspiracies persist. Another programme starts – something about art and Modernism. The jaunty music, Stravinsky or similar, should have been a warning. Robin Hands is the host.

'Ezra Pound', he drawls, 'dismissed the art of the ancient Greeks as *caressible*. For Pound, modern art was the opposite – wild and dangerous.'

Don switches the radio off and goes downstairs. The fluorescent light of the kitchen hums awake. He remembers that Ina has gone to the cinema. Her infirm mother exists somewhere beyond the frosted glass door leading to the annex. The lights behind the glass are out. He listens for a sound. The old woman must be sleeping – probably spends most of her time in bed.

He isn't hungry but decides to open a bottle of something. Behind the kitchen door is a rack filled with Beaujolais supérieur, 1989 – at least thirty bottles, all the same. He finds a corkscrew and fills a glass, then wanders through the house. He drifts up and down the stairs, in and out of the unused rooms.

Val's house is like a fantasy – soft-lit, lined with silk, filled with French furniture and small masterpieces of Italian mannerism. Don walks in a kind of trance past fragments of ancient statuary – Egyptian, Greek, Roman, Syrian – and tapestries woven with chivalric tales. The place throbs with taste and cultivation. The glut of periods and styles is topped off by references to Val's adopted faith, a portrait of Cardinal Newman, a silver crucifix spread-eagled on a panel of blood-red velour, a rosary that has been draped like a necklace around a plaster cast of Antinous.

Strangest of all are the copious flowers – vases of carnations, violas and chrysanthemums (watered and replenished, presumably, by Ina) which breathe their perfume into every empty room, affronting the winter.

The House Beautiful. Yes, Val has done well to keep his London life apart from Peterhouse. Sipping wine, Don begins to speculate on what is to come – on life at the Brockwell Collection. Still unsettled by the newness of everything around him, he allows a flicker of curiosity – something like excitement – to pass through him.

He sleeps lightly and wakes before dawn. When he opens his eyes and sees the peach-coloured room, he forgets where he is for a moment.

He slides from bed and treads around the room in his maroon cotton pyjamas – lightly, as if he were afraid of being detected. He is reassured by the sight of his pictures, an atlas of imaginary skies.

Downstairs, the kitchen is empty. He finds ground coffee and a cafetiere, then sits at the table while he sips black coffee and thinks. He forgot to ask Val about *The Martyrdom of Saint Sebastian* and when it will arrive at the museum. Perhaps the staff will know. He climbs the stairs again, cup in hand, and tries to write for an hour.

While his bath runs, he lays out his clothes on the bed, changing the tie several times – red, then blue, then a pale silvery lilac.

As he comes back down the stairs, Ina is standing in the hallway. She is wearing a powder-blue tracksuit and white trainers. Her face is flushed.

'Hello Don. Help yourself to breakfast. There are eggs—'

'Ah, thank you Ina, but I'm due at the Brockwell Collection in less than an hour. Do you know the best route?'

Her eyes convey the same reserved amusement that he noticed the previous day, when she first opened the door.

'There's only one route. Straight up Montcalm Road, through Dulwich Village, past the Crown and Greyhound pub.'

*

The Brockwell Collection stands back from a road so thick with bushes and trees that it might be a country lane. It is a single-storey building, long and windowless from the front, raised on a shallow elevation of lawns. It is a mixture of scenic and austere, not unlike a mausoleum.

Don walks through a pair of stone gateposts and passes between velvet expanses of grass. He thinks of Tiepolo's first journey to Milan.

To one side of the path stands a man in a green apron, holding a rake.

'Good morning,' he says. His face is somehow familiar – slender, willowy, crossing from youth into middle age. His hair is light, almost blond.

'Don Lamb,' says Don, and watches the man from the path.

The man raises his rake off the ground in friendly salutation.

'What a handsome garden,' Don murmurs with contrived airiness. 'Those crocuses. So bright! So – abundant.'

Swiftly he continues up the path. The façade of the museum, he now sees, is punctuated by shallow alcoves with curved tops. Rising from the centre of the building is a green dome that wasn't visible from the road.

His approach through the garden has been observed. Standing by the door is a small, solemn woman dressed in a wool skirt and a matching jacket – dark blue, tightly knit.

'Welcome, Professor Lamb,' she says. 'Welcome to the Brockwell Collection.'

She introduces herself as Maud Berenson, the Chief Curator.

Her eyes are grey and clever behind large glasses, from which beaded strings hang in swaying arcs.

Her greying hair is drawn back and fastened with a tortoise-shell clip, and the smell of her perfume – rose musk – comes in bursts, as if mechanically released. Pearls circle her neck in two tiers. Her teeth, when she smiles, are gigantic.

'I see you met Paul – our groundsman. He keeps a watchful eye over things here.'

She ushers him through mahogany doors into a high-ceilinged foyer where the parquet glistens like water. They pass a portrait of John Ruskin – Millais's painting of the eminent Victorian in front of a waterfall. It hangs opposite a reception desk where a young woman – as pensive, in her way, as Ruskin – is seated behind carousels of postcards.

'This,' says Maud as they walk into the first gallery, 'is the Octagon.' Don looks around the eight-sided room, at the floor of black and white marble tiles, at the emerald walls crowded with portraits – Van Dyck, Lely, Dobson, Reynolds – then up to the glass dome, a rosette of green panes. Large thresholds on either side of the gallery permit access to the rest of the museum.

'It will all be rehung, of course, for our next exhibition, "Caravaggio's Muses",' Maud carries on. 'Visitors will walk straight into the exhibition the moment they arrive. Accessibility, you see, is our watchword here at the Brockwell.' Her teeth flash full beam at him.

'Accessibility? I'm not sure I understand.'

Maud nods and doesn't reply.

Turning round, Don sees two marble sculptures placed on either side of the doorway through which they entered. They are ancient Roman statuettes of Venus, each resting on a cylindrical plinth of salami-red porphyry. The nude figures mirror one another, bending forwards in the same swivelling movement with one hand placed over the region of the vulva.

'The guardians of the museum,' says Maud. 'Montague

Brockwell, our founder, picked them up in Rome in the 1730s – along with quite a lot else.'

Don's eyes wander ahead, along the interconnected chambers that lead in both directions from the Octagon, allowing a view of the length of the museum. Gilt-framed paintings, marbles and bronzes stretch into the distance both ways.

Maud guides him through the building, announcing the names of the galleries. Most of the rooms are named after benefactors – the Van Hoogstraten Hall, the Arpels Annex, the Robilliard Room for Prints and Drawings.

At the end of the parade of galleries they arrive at a door marked *Private*. It leads into a wood-panelled corridor running back along the length of the building. Open doors admit lazy oblongs of light into the narrow space. Particles of dust stream through the shafts.

'The staff quarters,' she announces with a flourish of the hand. '*This* is the Desenfans Reading Room' – she points into a small cubicle, clearly never used, containing a bare table and metal filing cabinets. 'And *this* is the Summer Refectory.' She takes him into a long room dominated by a giant oval table. In the polished surface he sees the metal tracery of the skylight overhead, and beyond, the milky sky – carved into hard, bright shapes by the ironwork. Around the walls are portraits of men – once eminent, now forgotten – not noteworthy enough for public display.

'What a curious name,' Don says. 'Was it a dining room once?'

'No – no it wasn't. We've only ever used it for staff meetings.' She has a habit of nodding at her own pronouncements, as if she's responding to a second self who steers her from within, tugging away at the cables of her frontal lobe. 'The senior staff meet every Wednesday at ten o'clock. You will chair our sessions from now on, of course. Right – this way.'

Next door is another spacious room with windows over-looking the gardens at the back of the museum. Through the glass, he catches sight of the gardener, Paul.

'This we call the Communal Office.'

The space is drab and steeped in a smell of mouldy paper crossed with cigarette smoke. A handful of employees sit at ill-matching desks crowded with typewriters and telephones, between columns of filing boxes and towers of exhibition catalogues.

'No computers,' says Don approvingly.

Maud hesitates before replying. 'Not quite yet. Maurice Forster was an arch traditionalist, in some ways.'

One of the staff is writing in an immense ledger. He is a broad, baggy man with blunt features and scant hair, aged around sixty. Swathes of dull green tweed hang around his limbs and belly. As Don and Maud approach, he stands and treads towards them with an eager, wading movement.

'So good to meet you, Professor Lamb,' he says, glowing red. 'We're glad – very glad – that you're here.' His loud voice has a trace of the East End.

Don takes his hand. 'Good,' he says, and laughs drily.

The man makes a variety of high-pitched sounds that don't cohere into words. On his upper lip is a moustache of sweat which he licks with quick upthrusts of the tongue.

'Bill Hoare is our Keeper of Pictures and Head of Conservation,' Maud says. 'He's overseeing the restoration of Poussin's *Triumph of David* and Boucher's *Two Nymphs of Diana resting after their Return from the Hunt*.'

Bill rubs his hands. 'Restoring life and light to those lovely nymphs, layer by layer. Such careful work!'

'It seems to me that a number of the paintings here need cleaning,' Don responds. 'Reynolds's *Cupid and Psyche* looks like it's been glazed with tar. And as for the Poussin—'

'There's more to it than cleaning,' interrupts Bill with a pained grin. 'It's a delicate business, bringing those beauties back to their prime.'

'I'm sure Professor Lamb can hear about these matters in good time,' says Maud.

'Of course, Maud, of course.' Bill buries his hands in his trouser pockets and turns back to his ledger.

She leads Don into the corridor. 'I'm sorry, Professor. Bill is passionate about the museum's collections, but he lacks – how shall I say it? – some of the social graces that others of us take for granted. I probably shouldn't say this' – she lowers her voice and halts her step – 'but he carries a hip flask.'

Don hears a volley of high, clipped bleats – before realising that it's him, laughing in his politest manner.

'A hip flask? Whatever next?'

'Yes,' she sighs, walking ahead. 'I suppose it's a generational thing. I've decided not to make an issue of it – for now. Let me take you to the Palladian Library. That's the name of the director's study – *your* study.' She seems to divine the question that's forming in his mind. 'It contains a bust of Palladio, eighteenth century, unattributed.'

'How very fitting. You may be aware that I published a book on Palladio's villas in 1979.'

Maud nods uncertainly and then stops by the final door on the corridor – the only door that isn't open. She turns the handle and stands back to allow him through.

The Palladian Library is an elegant room – square, dimly lit and lined on every wall with leather-bound books. The carpet is thick and soft and silencing.

'It's just as Maurice left it. And it looked the same when *he* became Director in 1942.'

'A room untouched by change.'

'*Quite.* Although I should warn you – we've ordered a computer for you. A concession to modernity, but it'll allow all kinds of things.'

Don wanders across the room. The director's desk faces away from a tall window with its own view of the garden. Oxblood leather armchairs are scattered about the floor like slouching bodies. A recess in one of the bookcases houses

Palladio's head and shoulders in pink-veined marble – genius repressed beneath eyes as smooth as melting ice cream. It is, he suspects, a nineteenth-century knock-off, the type of thing that populated half the libraries of Belgravia once upon a time.

He sits at the desk after Maud has left and rotates on his swivel chair. Outside, a lawn bordered by rose beds extends like a lake towards a cluster of trees. From a certain angle, with the road out of sight, the scene gives the impression of an idyllic country park.

*

In the first days after his arrival in Dulwich, he feels as if he is living in a dream. Every person he meets is new. Every place, every item of information, carries the shimmer of a fresh discovery. The smell of the museum hits him every time he walks inside, that mingled scent of varnish and other precious veneers.

Intermittently – as he studies exhibition schedules with Maud Berenson, or hears accounts of funding shortfalls, or consults with Bill Hoare on the fine points of cleaning Boucher's nymphs – he is filled with doubt. He asks himself what he is doing in this place, so far away from everything he knows. Then the image of *SICK BED* returns to him. The mangled metal and flashing light are like spasms of residual pain.

In the evenings, he sits in his bedroom – Val's room – and works on his book until late. Sometimes Ina Stables brings him dinner on a tray. On other nights, she seems as non-existent as her mother – their annex lies in deep silence – and he eats cold leftovers from the fridge.

Towards the end of his first week, he walks out and dines at a little Italian restaurant in Dulwich Village – veal *alla Milanese* and a bottle of Trebbiano. He feels extravagant afterwards, vaguely guilty. When he returns to the house, he telephones Val.

'It's so quiet here. So – different. Now I understand why you used to come away so often.'

'You're fortunate to be there, Don. Think of it as an endless sabbatical. You got out of Peterhouse at the right time. Things are terrible here. Erica Jay has just made a formal complaint against Bruce Day. Jay versus Day – but I shouldn't joke. She alleges racial discrimination. It's nonsense, of course – a misunderstanding, silly remarks at High Table blown out of all proportion. You know what a blunderer Bruce is. But she has the Master's support. He's insisting on a disciplinary tribunal.'

A college scandal. It seems small and faraway. What a relief, Don thinks, to be free of High Table and the Master and Bruce Day – free of every major or minor happening of Cambridge life. Still, a tribunal will serve the old fool right.

'I blame the Master's wife,' Val continues. 'Briony Davis. She's the power in that power couple.'

Holding the telephone to his ear, Don walks to the window, teasing out the curls of the electric flex. He looks out at the road. The streetlamps are amber against the night sky.

'By the way, Val, when is that Tiepolo oil sketch coming to the Brockwell? *The Martyrdom of Saint Sebastian*?'

'Soon, Don, very soon. We're finalising the terms of the bequest – the practicalities of transport. The estate of the Prince of Löwenstein will send you a letter confirming the donation.'

When he's off the phone, Don runs a hot bath and pours a glass of red wine. He has noticed that the bottles in the wine rack are always diligently replaced.

*

On Saturday, the weather is prematurely warm – almost like spring.

He wakes at five o'clock and wrestles for hours with his new chapter on the Venetian theatre. His brain brims with subtleties of costume and scenography, the ingenious device of the proscenium arch, the multicoloured morals of stock characters. By eleven, his concentration is waning. He peers between the drawn curtains. The buds on the horse chestnut tree are shivering in the breeze. The day beckons to him.

Enough of Tiepolo, then, for an hour. He will walk. Val told him to explore the green spaces of Dulwich and its environs – all except for Brockwell Park. He inspects a map of the local area that he has found in the kitchen, then heads towards Dulwich Park, strolling along peaceful residential roads and crossing a sports ground. And yet, when he reaches the park gates with their bulbous stone posts, a flash of perversity impels him to change course.

He asks a couple of strangers for directions as he goes, although his feet seem to know the way.

Brockwell Park lies behind iron railings running the length of Norwood Road, a busy thoroughfare separating Dulwich from neighbouring districts. From the pavement, the park is half hidden by oak trees planted along its perimeter. Beyond, the ground rises in broad swathes towards a house. Don walks alongside the railings, allowing vistas of the green interior to flicker out, until he reaches the entrance. The iron portals open onto three broad paths. He takes the middle course.

The park is serene and almost deserted. In the distance, rising above the far side of the hill, are two tower blocks – identical concrete stacks.

He feels bizarrely alive – exhilarated, optimistic. It is a baseless happiness, all the more captivating for having no object. He passes in and out of the bluish shadows of plane trees. On the path ahead is a little concrete pavilion. As he passes, he sees that it is a shelter for a bench, open on one side, and that the enclosure is swarming with rubbish and graffiti – words have been sprayed, scratched or marked in scalpel-sharp pen. He tries to untangle them. *CRYTZ, FAME, KROS, TERA, ZEPHYR.* Letters emerge before transmuting into arrows, crosses, a love heart, a scattering of senseless marks.

At the path's summit, he stops to admire the house, an early nineteenth-century pile in sandy bricks.

He penetrates deeper into the park. On a grassy slope, lying beneath an oak tree, is a group of five girls – young women, similar in age to his undergraduate students. With a glimmer of surprise, he notices that they are all asleep. They are absolutely still, arrested in tumbling attitudes. Perhaps they are sleeping off a drinking bout – sure enough, an empty bottle lies on the grass a few metres away from them. One girl is slumped forwards on a red bag marked *PUMA*. Her cheeks are flushed. Another lies on the ground in front of her, turned away, in a shiny black jacket with bulbous sleeves and tight cuffs; the letters *NAFF* are embroidered in different colours on the back. The soles of her trainers are filthy.

Something urges him to walk over and reach out to touch the shoulder of the nearest girl. He comes a step closer and hears low, erratic snoring. He stalls – seized by the thought that someone might see him and assume he is a party to their misdemeanours, or worse, a lecherous spy.

He draws back and walks on through the park, bemused by what he has seen, unable to believe that the stillness and languor of the scene were entirely real. Something about the place is working on his senses. The sweeping escarpments of grass, the trees, the balmy air . . .

He turns onto a narrower path and sees a miniature steam train with a string of buggy-sized carriages, gliding towards him on rails. It stops at a tiny platform marked by picket fences, and a mother and child clamber into one of the carriages. The train starts again and disappears into a cluster of bushes.

Close by, he finds model houses nestled in the shrubbery. They're like Dulwich residences shrunk to the size of dolls' houses, complete with pitched roofs and herringbone brickwork and mock Tudor beams. Behind, through the bushes, he catches sight of an empty bowling green that looks like a pool coated in algae.

He has walked in a giant loop and is close to the gate he entered by. A large sign displays a map of the park. There is a neat blue rectangle denoting a swimming pool. He didn't encounter this on his walk. He thinks of the outdoor pools that are said to exist in Cambridge, and guesses that the lido of Brockwell Park must be similar – real and yet unseen, and therefore not quite real after all.

He checks his watch and hurries back through the gates.

He dedicates Sunday to Tiepolo – reviewing, revising, rewriting. He keeps the curtains drawn.

The next morning, he takes a meandering route to the museum. Dulwich is growing familiar, little by little. He recognises the Village with its pretty vistas, the old tollgate with its white-boarded pavilion, the Venetian clocktower of Dulwich College.

When he arrives, he strolls through the different galleries and casts his eyes around the walls. He is getting to know the places of things – that view of Tivoli at sunset, that portrait of Gainsborough's daughters, wan with alarm. The Brockwell Collection is like a fly in amber. Its contents have barely changed since the 1770s, when the sugar baron Montague Brockwell founded it as a home for his art treasures. The people of the museum are part of the antiquated clutter: the stewards who stand in the corners like mute sentinels, and the visitors – there are only a few this morning – who wander on tentative paths.

There are numerous small studies by Tiepolo dotted around the place. But the new oil sketch, when it comes, will require a special position. After long deliberation, he identifies a site for the picture. A small Rubens painting of the god Bacchus currently hangs there – it will have to be moved.

6

Ten days after Don's arrival at the Brockwell Collection, there is an early-morning delivery. Walking up the path to the entrance, he sees a truck parked outside. Two men are removing a plywood crate from the back of the vehicle.

He watches, breathing clouds of vapour into the air. From the dimensions of the crate, he knows what it contains. He asks the men to take it straight to the Summer Refectory and place it on the mantelpiece, with the lid removed, for everyone to see.

Seated at his desk, he makes a last-minute addition to the agenda for the staff meeting. As he scribbles down the words, he thinks of the Tiepolo oil sketch being placed – this very moment – on the mantelpiece in the meeting room. He can almost see the picture being revealed as they lift away the plywood lid: the naked martyr tied to a tree, a reed-like arrow through his arm, and an impressionistic sky – boldly modern in finish. He fights the temptation to go and look. It will be a collective epiphany.

He waits until one minute before ten o'clock, when he knows all the staff will be assembled. Then he smooths his lapels and makes his way to the other end of the corridor.

One of the lamps in the passageway has blown. Passing through the dimmed section, he registers a painting on the wall. It has always been there, but the temporary absence of light makes it somehow more noticeable. The scene is a jungle fantasy by Henri Rousseau – a twilight vision of a tiger attacking two natives in a bed of rushes: a horse rears up in panic and one of the men tilts a spear at the predator's face. The tiger is monstrous

94

and beautiful, a picture of terrified rage. The entire scene is as delicate and unearthly as a piece of embroidery.

Don sighs. The picture was a coup of Maurice Forster's – a long-term loan from the Barnes Foundation for which no suitable place could be found in the galleries. It will have to go.

He sweeps into the Summer Refectory and assumes his place at the centre of the table, purposeful, determined – keeping his eyes studiously averted from the painting that he knows is at the end of the room. He senses, as he pours himself a glass of water, a certain mood around the table – a tremor of expectation. But let them wait. He will draw out the suspense.

Putting on his glasses, he begins to read the morning's agenda out loud.

Maud Berenson – who is seated opposite – clears her throat. Don stops reading.

'Professor Lamb – Don – if I may?'

'Yes?' He smiles indulgently.

It is only now, as he leans back in his chair, that he turns to look at the painting. As he does so, he raises one hand in a reflex motion, pursing and relaxing his fingers. The shock is bewildering.

It is not the Tiepolo oil sketch.

Instead, he is confronted by Caravaggio's *Boy Bitten by a Lizard*. The canvas is propped inside its plywood crate, cushioned around the edges by chunks of turquoise foam. Every detail is grimly familiar – the boy's naked shoulder and curling black hair, his scowl of pain as he springs back from the biting lizard. The image radiates pretence. The simulation of suffering, the showy play of light and shade, the rose that stands in a pitcher of water – too incidental.

He breathes in sharply and shifts his eyes to the table in front of him – the glass orb of the water jug and the vase of wilting violets behind. For an absurd moment, it seems as if reality is coalescing with the picture. The light in the room mellows as the sun passes behind a cloud.

Maud has risen to her feet and her hands are placed together in a gesture of prayer.

'The Counter-Reformation has arrived in Dulwich.' Polite laughter reverberates around the table. Maud's lips retract to display her teeth. 'This is the first painting to arrive for "Caravaggio's Muses". It will take pride of place in the Octagon.' The lenses of her glasses flash as sunlight streams back into the room.

Don's heart plummets and irritation races through him. The Caravaggio exhibition. Of course. Maurice Forster's final flourish.

'Thank you, Maud,' he says, keeping his eyes fixed on the table. He is on the point of returning to the agenda when there is another interruption.

'Sublime,' declares Bill Hoare. 'Magnifico!'

Don slides the agenda to one side and cloaks his face in a smile.

'A pampered boy bitten on the finger by a lizard – *sublime*? I hardly think so. Just look at his preposterous gesture – such affectation! – and that simpering face. To think, he had to hold that attitude for hours at a time. I'm afraid I defer to the judgement of Poussin on this artist. Caravaggio was born to destroy the art of painting. Such vulgar pictures can only be the work of a vulgar man.'

Bill licks his upper lip.

Maud's grin has set like plaster. 'Don – Professor. This painting is allegorical, *classical* – its source is the *Apollo Sauroktonos*, the god slaying a lizard. The violent act has been comically reversed – a Christian subtext resides—'

'My own sentiments align with those of John Ruskin.' Don places both palms on the table and closes his eyes. 'Caravaggio's pictures are *signs of evil mind, feeding upon horror and ugliness*.'

Poussin and Ruskin have spoken. He listens for noises of grudging assent, maybe a flicker of laughter. But the only sound is the far-off whirr of an aircraft. He opens his eyes and sees a chain of expressionless faces.

'This exhibition will be the culmination of many years' work, Don.' Maud's tone has become entreating. 'Maurice did so much to revive the reputation of Caravaggio.'

'Regrettably, yes. And I suppose the exhibition will be a success, if we measure success by the size of the crowds we attract. The artist is popular in that way.' He regards Maud with a smile that is no longer reciprocated. 'I hope that my tenure as Director will be marked not only by popular successes but by daring experiments. I must tell you – another time perhaps – about my idea for a Tiepolo display.'

'Another time, of course,' she says with polite acerbity.

He is about to say more, but then simply nods and returns to the agenda. The satisfaction of a few seconds ago has died. His mind sinks into regret. *A Tiepolo display* – it sounded like nothing. It was a mistake to mention it. If only the picture had been what he thought it was. He could have aired his plan in the presence of the wonderful gift, and it would all have made perfect – exquisite – sense.

The subject of 'Caravaggio's Muses' resurfaces only once, when Maud speaks – in a more subdued voice – about the shade of red that the Octagon will be painted.

'I'm thinking of Tuscan claret,' she says, to a fluttering of nods.

No longer listening, Don looks back at the painting. Sunlight is slanting through the skylight. All he sees now is a shining waxen surface – the tiny streaks and ridges of the paint beneath the layers of varnish. The boy's surprised face is nothing more than a sliver of jawline.

That evening, he edges through rush-hour traffic in the back of a taxi, headed for Leighton House Museum. The occasion is an exhibition of paintings by Lawrence Alma-Tadema, the great Victorian visualiser of the ancient world – and Don's first outing as Director of the Brockwell Collection.

Val's words repeat in his head. 'It's a coming-together of the art world. The great and the good will be there. Why do you think I'm coming?'

It is a rainy night. Through the windows of the taxi, the lamps of the Albert Bridge stream by like strings of blazing pearls. *The great and the good*. He braces himself against the nerves of a new situation, new expectations.

Just before seven o'clock, the taxi pulls up on a leafy residential road in Holland Park, not unlike those of Dulwich. Leighton House is a redbrick villa, square and serious on one side but veering on the other towards Moorish extravagance, with a beehive dome surging out of the brickwork. He sits for a moment in the taxi, prolonging the act of paying the driver.

As he steps from the car, he tries to imagine Frederic Leighton, the house's creator, emerging from the front porch – the patriarch of Victorian art. But it's too dark and wet for reverie. He runs through the rain to the door.

Inside, his feelings change like a song shifting into an unexpected key. Moving through a huddle of guests – other early arrivals – he finds himself in the turquoise-tiled core of the house. Abruptly, his senses dilate. He is drawn further in as if by some psychic lure.

He stands before a small pool set into the floor. A fountain dances and splashes. Moorish carpets and Roman-style mosaics surround the square of water. Decoration scales the walls like foliage – bands of green and gold, choked with manic pattern, ascending to a gold-painted dome. A thorny chandelier plunges from the apex.

The effect is showy to the point of grotesquery. Don tells himself that he hates it – that he ought to hate it – and yet he's overcome by a wild feeling. Sensations, hundreds of them, bleed out of the walls and congregate in his body. The surfaces and patterns work on him like a drug. Startled by his own susceptibility, he looks down at the wobbling water and tries to hold himself steady.

Shaking himself out of his trance, he walks back into the small antechamber close to the front door. It is filling up with guests. The air is heavy with their murmuring.

'Where are the Alma Tads?' says a man in a rasping voice, as if his life depends on knowing.

Don turns, uncertain if the question was addressed to him. Concurrent conversations race around his head.

'Oh, in a poky room upstairs.'

'Where's the champagne?'

'I've never seen *that* before.'

'I thought you weren't drinking—'

'Such dazzling brushwork – an avalanche of colour!'

The voices and their bearers are swirling around a bronze statuette on a plinth. Don examines the sleek figure. It is a nude Narcissus, cast from a Roman original, polished to glassy smoothness. Or perhaps Bacchus. He prefers the second possibility. How impervious the little god seems, and yet how vulnerable.

He walks upstairs, past a stuffed peacock. On the upper landing, a green-walled space not unlike the landing at Val's house, he discovers a recess. It is a closed balcony overhanging the ground floor. Through latticework he can see down to the fountain. People are milling around the water.

He feels safely alone, cocooned in the elevated niche.

'You were early too?' says a familiar voice.

Val has crept to his side undetected.

'I noticed you admiring the Arab Hall. I've been watching.'

'I would hardly say admiring,' Don replies. 'It's hideous. It confirms me in my view of the late nineteenth century, and Frederic Leighton in particular. What a thing to have built.'

Almost at once, Don regrets what he has said. He knows that his words were directed not only at Leighton House, but also

– in an oblique, semi-conscious way – at the house in Dulwich. An insubordinate part of him wants to ridicule Val's gift.

Val peers through the screens for a while. 'In my youth,' he says at last, 'I knew a man – he was very old by then – who modelled for Leighton in the 1890s. His name was Billy Raymond. A failed artist and a desperate alcoholic. The greyest, sickest wretch I ever saw. But he'd been so beautiful as a young man – so very beautiful – when Leighton painted him. Billy told me that he had been the model for *Flaming June*. And you know – even in his ravaged old face I could see the likeness.'

'But Val – *Flaming June* is a painting of a woman.'

Val turns and smiles. His eyes have a watery shine. 'So very beautiful.'

Changing the subject, Don mentions the arrival that morning of *Boy Bitten by a Lizard*.

'Caravaggio!' he hisses, as if the word itself were noxious. 'The antithesis of everything I've spent my career celebrating. Garish, superficial—'

'Ah yes. Maurice Forster's swansong – "Caravaggio's Muses". He had the idea for that show, oh, fifteen years ago at least.'

'I want nothing to do with it, Val. You should have heard Maud Berenson and Bill Hoare worshipping that picture of a hustler.'

Val laughs. 'Caravaggio's *bardassa*.'

'Hoare was in raptures,' Don mutters. 'But what if people think this exhibition is *my* idea, my debut? They'll say I've taken leave of my senses.'

'People? What people?'

'The people that matter. Cambridge people.'

'Oh, them.' Val lowers his voice. 'Remember, Don, that you never need to worry about what I think.' He runs his fingers over the latticework. 'But consider this: the Brockwell is not Cambridge. You'll find the people, the pace of things, different. Don't fight it, or you'll set yourself at odds with the world.'

'I suppose I spoke out of turn, telling them the truth about Caravaggio?'

Val leans towards him. 'Telling them *your* truth. *Your* truth. There are other truths, you know.'

'Oh Val, not you as well.' Don takes a step back. He feels the same as he did – for a moment – on the morning when they drove down from Cambridge. An embarrassment of intimacy. 'Shall we go and look at the exhibition?'

Val gives a frowning smile. 'Don, you need to realise, private views are not for looking at art. You should be downstairs in the Arab Hall, moving through the crowd!'

Val leads him downstairs and introduces him to the great and the good. Their names fly through his head, heard and forgotten in an instant. After ten minutes, Val catches sight of a pair of friends – two men in suits who have been ogling the Bacchus statue – and strides over to greet them.

Don veers sideways and pretends to examine the plumage of the peacock, waiting for Val and his friends to drift away.

After a few moments, another man joins him in mock admiration of the bird.

'Alma-Tadema's great revival, no?' demands the man, staring at the peacock and then at Don. Val has already pointed him out as the Head of Exhibitions at the Tate Gallery. He wears a cravat of crushed blue velvet.

'Unquestionably,' says Don, conscious that he hasn't seen the exhibition.

'Unquestionably,' repeats the man, with affectation. 'And you're the new boy at the Brockwell, eh?'

Don nods, uncertain whether the man is mocking him or trying to endear. They wander together into the crowd. The man watches Don from the corner of his eye.

'A very heterosexual painter, Alma-Tadema, wouldn't you agree?'

Don nods seriously.

'But camp as well – a camp heterosexualist, eh?' He grasps

two glasses of champagne and hands one to Don. 'Come on, I'll show you to the campest heterosexualist of them all.'

Don is introduced to the President of the Royal Academy, a wiry, unsmiling character who tells him (as if they're picking up an old conversation) that representational painting is dead, a relic, and that conceptualism is the future.

The coloured glass of *SICK BED* flickers like a light show in his memory.

'Don't you think,' says Don in a rush of confidence, 'that classical subjects lay claim to their own kind of modernity? Take the Tiepolo study that's just been discovered in Germany, *The Martyrdom of Saint Sebastian* – you must have heard.'

'Oh yes, the lost oil sketch,' says the Royal Academy President drily. 'It was reported in the *Art Chronicle*.'

Don finishes his champagne and nods. 'It hasn't been seen for two hundred years – longer. It hasn't *existed*, you might say, since almost Tiepolo's lifetime. It's a work of contemporary art – as new as anything that's just been made. It will go on public display the moment it arrives at the Brockwell.'

'Public display? At the Brockwell?' The man from the Tate is staring at Don from across the glinting blue band of his cravat. He seems angry and amused all at once. 'You must know something the rest of us don't. Hasn't it just been promised to the Frick?'

'Yes, that was my understanding,' says the Royal Academy President, whose concentration has already shifted to the far side of the room. He nods distractedly at Don and begins to extract himself from the group.

'The terms are still being agreed – practicalities,' Don insists, sounding overeager, hardly aware of what he is saying. 'It's a large estate – multiple bequests . . .'

No one is listening. New people have appeared and other conversations have overleapt his own. The man from the Tate has turned his bullish amiability towards a young woman. He fires out questions, interrupting her as she tries to reply.

Don looks around the room for Val, perplexed. Surely it can't be true that the rediscovered Tiepolo is going to New York. There must be – there will be – an explanation. Val will know. But he seems to have left already – he must have had to catch the train back to Cambridge. Don can't see him or the pinstriped men he was chatting with.

At nine o'clock, Don retreats. Outside in the cool, wet night, a taxi waits on the roadside, its engine turning over, ready to steal him away. He is exhausted, but not only from the effort of socialising. It is a deeper, engulfing tiredness. He sleeps as he is ferried back to the House Beautiful.

*

Don is standing by his bedroom window the next morning, still in his pyjamas, watching a rag-and-bone man passing on the road outside – an ancient Londoner, ringing a brass bell, pulled on an open cart. The horse looks close to death.

The phone on the desk rings. Val's voice is quiet – different from usual.

'I thought you would want to know that Bruce Day suffered a stroke last night. A massive one, the doctors say.'

'God – I'm so sorry.'

'It happened just as I was arriving back from London. He fell in Old Court, right in front of *SICK BED*. Dropped to his knees – flopped onto his back. It was dreadful to witness. That foul light was flashing all over him. A great man brought low.'

After the momentary shock, Don pictures Bruce lying on the cobbled path, his eyes open to the night sky. He feels curiously unmoved, but judges that this isn't the right moment to ask about *The Martyrdom of Saint Sebastian*.

'How is he now?'

'He's lucid, I think.'

'Lucid?'

'His eyes are the same. That stare. But he's terribly lethargic. He sleeps most of the time. They're keeping him in at Addenbrooke's.'

Don tries to imagine whether, even in death, the grey islands of Bruce's eyes would look different.

'It was the stress of his impending tribunal,' Val says. 'This is the Master's doing. *He* decided to inflict that show trial on Bruce – and for what? He'll have to go. The senior fellows are adamant.'

An old Cambridge sentiment rises inside Don – furtive ambition mixed with burning prurience.

'And who will replace the Master?'

'Oh goodness, Don, it's far too soon to say. You of all people know how long these things take. What a question to ask!'

Afterwards, Don takes a three-minute bath and dresses quickly. As he approaches the front door, he glances at himself in the Queen Anne mirror. He looks dapper in his black corduroy suit. Stern, lean, no younger than his forty-three years. Hairline fissures run across his forehead. The shadows beneath his eyes are heavy. And yet despite the signs of strain, despite mortality's inerasable incursions, he is elegant and trim. There is a brittle resilience about the figure he cuts. He will still do.

He is pleased to see, when he walks into the Palladian Library, that the sign he ordered for his desk has arrived. Someone has seen fit to put it there. A walnut triangle stained to a rich shade of brown and engraved with his name:

Professor Donald Lamb, Director

The engraved letters – picked out in gold – glint at him from the empty desk.

*

In the weeks that follow, *SICK BED* is no longer the ugly bruise it was for Don when he left Cambridge, just a fading impression.

But a new worry is rising to take its place – the Tiepolo oil sketch. Val assured him that the paperwork was almost complete, the shipment imminent. But Don is troubled, still, by the conversation he had at Leighton House – that suggestion of a diversion to New York. A misunderstanding, no doubt. But the men's surprised faces and sceptical words repeat in his mind with unpleasant clarity.

At noon on a Wednesday, he decides to call Val, who is sure to be in his study at Peterhouse, teaching or marking. Don knows the extension by heart.

The phone rings twice. There is a hissing pause.

'Hello,' says Val, sounding formal and remote.

'Val, it's Don. Listen, I'm sorry to trouble you, but—'

'I'm not here to take your call,' declares Val's voice. 'But if you'd like to leave a message and a number, I'll contact you *tout de suite*.'

Don hears a long, rasping beep.

'Val – it's Don. Perhaps you'd give me a call back. It's – well, as you might expect, we're all *very* eager to know when the Tiepolo will come. I'm having a Rubens moved into storage to make way for it.'

He tries to think of something else to say. The silence of the line, absorbing and trapping his voice, suddenly feels like an affront. He has the vague, unconfirmable suspicion that Val is listening as he records the message – there in his study, just not answering.

He hangs up.

Of course, he hasn't revealed anything to the staff of the museum. He wants the acquisition to be a big event, grandly announced. His first directorial flourish.

Val will answer him *tout de suite*, except that he doesn't. Days go by, and Don wonders whether to call again. He tries to deflect his attention to other matters. Val will telephone in the end; he always does. Don manages to dampen his present agitation with thoughts of future glory.

He has become a man of two parts. By day he is the Director of the Brockwell Collection. By night he is the author of *The Skies of Tiepolo*. He sleeps little. The remaining nocturnal hours are spent at the giant desk in his bedroom, examining the colour reproductions that spread in an orderly chaos around his typewriter. He adds new lines, using a ruler and a needle-sharp pencil, as he perceives new subtleties of design – new intimations of depth – within the pictures. He makes notes and types up his prose in feverish bouts.

But many hours are spent simply looking . . .

Tiepolo's ceiling frescoes, illusionistic visions of open skies, seem like whirlpools in reverse. Their energy increases as the eye moves away from the centre. Hazy sky spirals out to encompass airborne bodies, horses and chariots, columns and other fragments of buildings, entire flotillas of activity – all supported on cushion-like clouds that rise in fluffy tiers towards the apex of heaven. Around the edge of the scene there is usually a ledge, a fragment of cornice. It is a hard reminder of the realm beyond the world of the picture.

He has begun to take a walk each day, just after lunch. One afternoon, the air is mild and the sky is a luminous blue – spring is arriving. He strolls into the Village, passing the Crown and Greyhound pub, and then turns onto a road he hasn't walked along before, a sedate avenue composed of long rows of semi-detached houses. The rhyming pairs multiply in a gently winding course. For around a mile, he is carried along as if by a smooth current. Some of the trees dotted along the pavements are breaking into blossom.

He turns onto another road – busier with traffic – and realises that he is close to Brockwell Park. There will be time to circle the hill, and perhaps he will find the swimming pool.

He enters by the same gate as before, but soon becomes happily lost. He wanders along different paths, deep into the green heart of the place, and absorbs the slanting vistas. An archway in a brick wall reveals an enclosed garden: crisp, sculptural topiary and roses (some of them already beginning to bloom) are massed in dense arrangements between diverging paths.

As he climbs a shallow ascent, thinking again of the little bronze Bacchus of Leighton House, he experiences a leaden sensation in his bowels. Not far away, on a raised bank of ground, is a small building that looks like a classical temple, a pavilion-sized Pantheon.

Don goes in. The men's lavatory is a dank unheated chamber, as horrible as the park outside is lovely in the March sunshine. The air is thick with the smell of unflushable toilets and erupting urinals, mingled with an oversweet chemical scent that seeps out of small pink disks piled like macaroons in the porcelain bowls. Cracked tiles cover the walls; the terracotta floor is dark with grime. A tiled frieze runs around the room at eye level – blue garlands on white – but the white has yellowed and the blue is the blue of an old man's veins.

Don straightens his tie. In the corner are two plastic-walled cubicles – one with its door wide open. He goes into the open stall, unfastens his belt and lets his trousers and underpants drop to the floor. Sitting on the cold plastic seat, he holds the door shut with an outstretched hand (there is no lock) and allows the queasy sensation at the pit of his gut to overtake him, rippling like a slow spasm through his stomach and thighs, until his whole body seems to dilate and then contract around the hard mass at its centre, quivering with the effort of expulsion. He hears a sequence of gunshot splashes as he releases the gross load – cold water flies up and strikes him – and he emits a sigh that turns into a low moan as relief passes through him.

His fingers tremble against the door. With his free hand he fumbles for paper, but in place of a toilet roll he finds a hole in the wall between the cubicles. It looks like a small porthole, roughly cut into the Formica, exposing a jagged rim of chip-board. The space beyond is dark and impregnable.

He tenses. Something has moved – something in the next cubicle, through the hole. A body, or merely a shadow. Wasn't the room empty when he came in? He listens intently, but all is silence again. Forgetting the lack of paper, he reaches up and tugs the chain: the toilet judders, water belches from the cistern above, then nothing. When he pulls the chain a second time, it thuds and water spits feebly.

'Damn it,' Don mutters, perhaps for the hearing of the silent presence – the imaginary presence – through the hole. Hastily he pulls up his trousers.

As he opens the door of the cubicle, he is aware of a figure standing across the room, by the urinals. First he sees a pair of boots – obelisks of black leather in a pool of water – and then, rising above them, muscular legs clad in denim, a taut torso and a shaved head. There is a gurgling sound of urine draining into the urinal. Something about the man's motionless stance makes Don pause. It's as if a statue or an automaton is standing there, pissing mechanically.

He knows that he is staring, that his scrutiny has been overt and overlong. But any movement will give him away – reveal that he has been watching and waiting.

The man knows, perhaps, that he is being watched, yet he stays rooted to the spot. The gurgling ceases and at last he shifts. Planting both hands on the wall, he levers himself back from the urinal with a long sigh. His upper arms slide from beneath the cropped sleeves of his T-shirt – columns of white flesh. One of them has a tattoo – a band of spidery marks running around the bicep. It looks like calligraphy or ancient Greek. A couplet from Homer? Don squints to see.

The man slowly turns. He must have seen Don by now in his peripheral vision, and yet he seems not to have closed his fly . . . Don looks away too late – there it is, in a flash, hanging like a large white grub, sheathed and limp, another man's cock.

He is being coaxed into an assignation – he makes the deduction with peculiar calmness. He has read of such things. He knows the story of Simeon Solomon, arrested in a public convenience in Marylebone in 1873, then again in Paris a year later . . . career-ending indignities.

With morose eyes the man looks towards the cubicles, back towards the door from which Don has recently emerged; and yet he doesn't signal or blink. His face is hard-edged – fierce, even – but not, Don thinks, unattractive.

Suddenly he speaks.

'Are you ready, baby?'

His voice is low, gravelly and jarringly tender. It is too much. Alarm takes hold at last: Don stammers an apology and makes for the exit, flushed with fear and shame.

Again the man calls out, louder this time: 'Are you ready?'

Don escapes into the safety and light of the park, his heart pummelling. But something makes him stop and turn – another voice, different from the man's, shrill and infantile. A small child, no more than a toddler, is skipping out of the cubicle that was closed. The man scoops her up in his arms and holds her over his head, high in the air. His face is different now and he is full of gleeful baby talk. His trousers, Don observes, are zipped up. The child squeals with happiness – a piercing, unrestrained cry. He quakes at the sound. Through the doorway the man catches his eye, and his grin evaporates.

Don breaks into a run – down the grassy incline, through a cluster of trees. Plunging between bushes, he almost trips over the miniature railway line and narrowly misses the train as it rolls along. He only stops at the park gates, groaning in breathless agony, clasping his knees, feeling like a madman, or worse – a fool.

7

Once a month, Don takes a train to central London to meet Dirk Coltman.

Dirk is the Director of the National Gallery. He was a few years ahead of Don at Cambridge, and they have maintained contact over the years – contact of a polite, professional variety that has never quite blossomed into friendship. Since Don's move to Dulwich, their meetings have become a periodic ritual. For an hour, they indulge in subtle condescension and backhanded praise, harking back to earlier versions of themselves.

Don descends the steps of the National Gallery after one of these sessions, replaying in his mind something that Dirk said.

'You've got a Caravaggio show coming up, I hear – with the *Narcissus*. Very louche! Not the Don Lamb I know.'

'It isn't my show,' Don replied. 'Not my doing. It was Maurice Forster's idea – his last hurrah.'

'It'll be popular, though. Good old Forster.'

In a few casual remarks, Dirk managed to malign Don, ridicule the show, and then – by an insidious backflip – praise the show and Maurice Forster. But then their discussion turned to the attribution of an Italian altarpiece, and Don gained the upper hand.

Crossing Trafalgar Square, Don decides to catch the bus back to Dulwich. It will take longer than the train, but he is in no hurry. He will have time to reflect on the points he made, and the points he scored.

He flags down the 12. The Routemaster comes to a rattling halt. The grimy bus carries adverts on its front panels for *Les*

Misérables – a sad-eyed child engraved in tremoring lines – and *The Phantom of the Opera*. A conductor stands on the open platform at the back.

'All aboard!' he sings, although no one else is embarking. He has russet sideburns, and a cumbersome ticket machine hangs over his stomach. 'To Dulwich!' he exclaims in mimicry of Don's request, and busily winds his lever.

Don climbs to the upper deck, where peace can usually be found. It is almost empty. Two women sit together in the front row; one of them has a clear plastic bonnet on her head, spotted with raindrops. Behind them are two men, slumped on opposite sides of the bus, holding a conversation across the aisle. Don takes a seat at the back, near the top of the stairs, permitting a view of the entire deck.

The bus stops and starts around the southern rim of Trafalgar Square. It is clouding over – Nelson stands in isolation against the grey. Don takes out his copy of Grote's *History of Greece*. In the artificial gleam of the bus, the pages – already yellow with age – have a sicklier tint. His mind wanders into the safe space of Greek antiquity, as evoked by the graceful prose of the nineteenth-century historian.

At Horse Guards Parade, a group tumbles on board. He hears shouts and laughter below, followed by clattering up the stairs behind him. Nervously he strokes the pages of his book.

Six or seven young people thud past. They are all boys – so far as he can see – and not much older than teenagers. A boy with longish hair and a glinting lip ring glares at him as he passes. The bus moves off and they collapse into the seats with raucous laughter.

Raising his eyes every so often, Don observes the group. Two of them have begun to sing a low, rhythmic tune. The words are indistinct, but the cadences are hypnotic. The others are throwing a large white hat around the bus. The floppy object flies from side to side, accompanied by cheers and whoops.

The scene is like many he has witnessed, nothing unusual. But as he surveys them in covert glances, something gives him a shock. Among the young people is a man dressed differently from the others, not in casual clothes but a cream suit with a curious sheen. Don guesses that the white hat belongs to him. As it spins through the air, caught and hurled, the suited man chases it with flailing arms, staggering up and down the aisle between the seats. Like a lunatic he jabs the air, missing his target, his mouth gaping with hilarity.

Don sees with a twinge of horror that the man is not young – not young at all, despite attempts to rejuvenate his appearance. He is young-old, a pastiche of youth: the pink in his cheeks is granular powder, his smeared-back chestnut hair is dyed, and his eyes withdraw at the corners into deep ridges. Yet the young-sters have accepted him as one of their own – their taunting is good-humoured.

The young-old man shrieks with merriment. When he comes close, Don notices that his pearly suit is scuffed and stained. Its shine could be a coating of dried drool. With a desperate lunge he finally snatches back his hat. The gang erupts in cheers, and the singing subsides.

The other passengers – the close-knit women and the spread-out men – seem unperturbed. But Don is fascinated – appalled. He tries to resume his reading of Grote, but his attention keeps returning to the scene further down the bus.

From their excitable banter he gleans that the group have been out all night. And yet they are overflowing with energy. Sex permeates their conversation – remarks about men, about each other. All their talk is flirtation and obscenity. In the boys this is pardonable, but the voice that rises above the others – insistent and grating – is that of their older friend. His accent is Italian, and his speech hard to decipher, but when Don does pick out individual words, they are lewd and odious – a bleating stream of arses, cocks and fucks. Don is amazed that the young ones tolerate this creature, even enjoy his company. Don't they see how decrepit he is, how ridiculous?

The bus rolls past the Elephant and Castle shopping centre, a long slab of pink concrete soaking up the rain.

The two singing boys take up their refrain. The young-old man stands at the centre of the bus, his gnarled hands locked around the aluminium rails on the backs of the seats, and he casts his eyes across the top deck. Every aspect of him seems to gleam – his cream suit, his pink face, the whites of his eyes. For a moment he resembles the conductor of an orchestra, scanning the players with relish before he strikes the first beat.

Don tries to bury himself in Grote, but it is too late. The man saunters down the aisle towards him, singing along to his friends' duet, fixing his eyes on Don. His voice is high and cooing. At moments he breaks into operatic flourishes and snatches of other tunes – a line from *Mary Poppins* (or so Don believes), a bluesy lament, and then a string of wordless vocalising – scat made up of falsetto trills and guttural interjections.

Don lowers his eyes, but the man's horrible stare is like a siren song, forcing him to look back.

The bus jolts and the man loses his balance, but manages to redeem his fall into a cavorting dance. All the while he holds Don's gaze, singing with exaggerated movements of the lips. With one hand, he reaches up and plucks the cord that runs along the ceiling. The bell rings sharply. He strums the cord over and over, producing a frantic peal as he sings at the top of his voice. The driver shouts angrily from the deck below.

Don looks around in panic. The man's friends are watching with lazy amusement. The other passengers haven't turned around.

The man is almost on top of him – leering in mock fascination at the copy of Grote. He stops singing and murmurs, in soft, sibilant words, that he is glad, so very glad and *onorato*, to make the acquaintance of one so *eminente*. Don shrinks in his seat.

A quivering finger hovers above his book.

'And what is the good professor reading today?'

The good professor – how could he know? Don feels himself redden. He grips the book tighter. It must be pure chance, an idiotic turn of phrase . . .

'*Mi dispiace*,' the man croons. 'We both are bibliophiles.' A cloying smell wafts off him – perfume crossed with stale alcohol. He spins behind Don and peers down at the pages, before transposing a fragment of Grote into a lilting ditty:

'*Codrus is numbered as the last king of Athens –*
Codrus is numbered, oh Codrus, oh Codrus!
Yes, Codrus is numbered as the last king of Athens!'

The pages are spotting with flecks of spit. Don snaps the book closed. His disordered thoughts contract into a hard mass of anger.

'You shall move away from me, sir,' he says in a commanding voice.

Baby talk spills from the man's lips, then gives way to a smattering of kissing sounds. He clasps his fingertips together and holds them to his puckered mouth, as if he were drawing out the chirrups on a string. His young friends are now actively relishing the spectacle – egging him on with their laughter.

'Get away from me,' Don hears himself say. The man's smile falters and then returns stronger than before. He leans in, inspecting Don like a connoisseur appraising an artefact, and winks.

'This is harassment!' Don's face is burning. Finally the other passengers are taking notice – people are turning, pointing, murmuring.

He glances outside. Underhill Road – close enough to his stop. He will walk. He stands and pulls the cord.

He stuffs Grote into his pocket and elbows the vile apparition out of his way. As he retreats down the stairs, the man clambers after him with a peal of laughter.

Don reaches the lower deck and grips the bar. The bus creaks to a halt and the man falls down the stairs behind him like a ragdoll, howling with pain and mirth.

With a nod to the unreactive conductor, Don steps off the bus and secures his overcoat. He finds that he is shaking all over. He watches the bus heave itself from the kerb. The grotesque scrambles to his feet and stands on the open platform, leaning out like a rapt lover in a musical.

'Give him my love,' he cries out. 'Beloved boy. Crown him with flowers!' He presses his fingers to his lips and then throws them out in a parting flourish.

It is quiet and cool in the street. Don shivers as he lights a cigarette. Whether by accident or by an unconscious instinct – a subtle sense of precaution – he takes a wrong turn, down Lordship Lane, and ends up walking a circuitous route towards the museum. By degrees, he manages to shift his thoughts to work matters. A final painting is to be borrowed for the Caravaggio exhibition; it is a complex loan requiring tact and negotiation. A picture of dreamy, drunken musicians. For a split second his brain is poised to make a connection – but doesn't. Insurance, shipping dates, the probability (no, the certainty) that Maud will dispute the cost – these are the points Don's mind is joining as a fine, barely detectable drizzle starts to fall.

He walks along Dulwich Common, past the railings of Dulwich College, and slows his pace. He feels calm again – and unable to believe what happened on the bus. He stops and holds on to the iron spike of a railing, soothed by the spray that sifts through the air. He looks across the mown lagoon of the playing field towards the school buildings, and experiences a twinge of something like excitement or nostalgia. A nostalgia for what, he couldn't say – perhaps something that hasn't even happened. In a moment, the feeling passes. Recovering his breath, he begins to smile as he thinks of the raving attentions of the madman.

The bell tower of the school emits a single chime. A movement at the edge of Don's vision causes his smile to vanish. The stranger, the young-old man, has appeared from behind the trunk of a horse chestnut on the opposite side of the road. There he is again, as if by some conjuring trick. He must have got off the bus and followed Don all the way down from Lordship Lane. His eyes are exultant – his face a shining moon of joy. He raises a finger scoldingly, and as he sways across the road he lets out a victorious screech.

Panicking, Don walks as fast as he can towards the Brockwell Collection. For ten minutes he refuses to turn around, and yet he is conscious – at regular intervals – of the man's wheezing, tittering presence somewhere behind him. There's no hope, he realises, of shaking him off. He reaches the gateposts and paces up the path, still not daring to look back, praying that the man will be deterred by the aura of the institution.

With an effort, he slows to a normal pace and stifles his breaths as he walks past the girl at reception. He even manages to utter an inane pleasantry about the rain. The girl looks surprised. He hurries on – close now to the haven of the Palladian Library. He will lock the door and all will be well.

But in the Octagon, he is brought to a halt by Maud.

'Professor Lamb – I'm delighted you're here!' Her words are rich with insincerity. Sure enough, she is with a visitor – a man in a suit, thin and punctilious-looking. He has pale eyes and grey skin and his hair is greying.

Don gives an agitated smile and tries to pass.

'This is Sir Ronald Braun,' Maud says.

Don stares at her blankly.

'Founder of Pascal Electronics.' Her eyes narrow. 'Our chief sponsor for "Caravaggio's Muses".'

Ronald Braun gives Don a steely look. The skin around his mouth is dry and pinched, in a way that seems to prohibit smiling. His hand is cold and bony to the touch. Don has barely clutched it when a high, crowing noise breaks into the room, emanating from the lobby.

'Oh, the professorial rites!'

The words soar through the gallery like a hymn. The three of them turn around, two in stunned surprise, one in sham surprise and nauseous panic. Don holds the visitor's hand in his grip. He can't let go of it – as if paralysed by an electric shock.

'Learned friends!' the new arrival cries. He totters into the Octagon – a shambolic figure in face paint and raffish costume, all the more garish against the Brockwell's stately veneers. Maud, containing her astonishment, smiles wanly at the interruption.

'Sealed with a handshake – the sacred observances!'

The pale-suited creature comes nearer. His lips tremble with excitement and he extends his arms. He is preceded by the same rank fusion of wine and musk.

'Secret lovers!' he hisses in a stage whisper to Maud, before turning his shining eyes on Don and Ronald Braun, who stands silent and morose, waiting – with all patience and dignity – for matters to be explained.

The young-old man gives a cackle that devolves into heaving coughs. He points to a spot on Don's jacket where toothpaste has dried in a crust.

'A flood of sacred fluid,' he purrs, and rubs his fingers together.

'This man is mad,' Don says – or tries to say. His voice is constricted and the words emerge as stammered fragments. 'He followed me off the bus.'

The drunkard lies down on the marble tiles and kicks the air frantically. He looks like a child being tickled. Maud takes a step towards him and plants her feet apart.

'May we help you?'

The stranger ignores her. He has lapsed into a high-pitched repartee. It is similar to his singing on the bus, shifting between music-hall shrillery and sonorous Italian. Is it opera, Don wonders, or folk music? The words are too fast and fluid to discern – and anyhow, his senses are failing. The melange of competing registers dissolves into another bout of laughter. With hideous daintiness the man kneels forwards on the floor and holds his silk-draped buttocks towards the skylight, then lowers his trousers and underwear before rolling – in a single deft manoeuvre – onto his side, into a foetal curl. He peers up at Don with a childlike smile; his teeth are small and white and neat.

Before looking away, Don notices how perfectly smooth the man's backside is, and how white – like alabaster or the surface of a peeled hardboiled egg. Boucher's odalisque with her huge white arse, Caravaggio's slumberous baby, the *Sleeping Hermaphrodite* – images collide and condense in a horrible instant. Art history provides multiple commentaries but no answers, and in the end, Don is left with one image only – a lunatic on the floor.

'I'll call the police,' he hears Maud say, as if from a distance. She marches off towards the lobby, her heels striking the floor with staccato clacks. The man seems to spasm in time with the noise. A crowd of onlookers has assembled timidly at the sides of the room, around the doorways to the other galleries. They watch and whisper as the intruder lies there, rolling backwards and forwards, singing in a quieter voice.

Within minutes, two police officers have arrived. They pick the man off the floor – gesturing and gibbering as he rises to his feet – and help him back into his trousers. Maud apologises – in long, assiduous appeals – to Ronald Braun, who leaves without a word to Don.

Impotent against the tide of events, Don stands and watches. The police officers are guiding the stranger – now in handcuffs – towards the exit. With furtive agitation, turning from one officer to the other, he pleads with them to unshackle him, protesting that it's *degradante*. One of the officers relents. As the manacles are unlocked, the arraigned man starts to weep uncontrollably. He accosts Don with a stream of burbling reproaches.

'Sicilian dialect,' says Don in a brittle voice, turning to address the crowd. 'Incomprehensible!'

But everybody's attention has shifted to the doorway. The young-old man has shaken loose from his escorts. He walks ahead of them and flings out both arms to resemble, for a second, the figure of Christ the Redeemer, towering over Rio de Janeiro, a dazzling white guardian. As he reaches the entrance, he swivels his wrists and smacks the two Venus statuettes that stand either side of the threshold. A precise movement, perfectly judged. The ancient objects topple and plunge to the floor like synchronised divers, exploding into pieces.

A fine mist of marble dust rises from the rubble. There is absolute silence.

*

Don decides against any further trips into London for a while. The spring is turning into one of the balmiest he can remember, too warm to spend in that large, quiet house. And so he begins to stop off at the pub in the early evening.

The first visit happens by accident. As he walks by the Crown and Greyhound on his way home, an impulse directs him to go inside. Without further thought, he steps into a dim, reddish confusion of flock patterning and backlit bottles. Writing on a blackboard announces that Beaujolais is on special offer. He orders a glass and sits outside. The wine is full-flavoured, on the verge of sweet – not the fine vintage that Val keeps. Then self-control returns and he leaves, mindful of his book.

But the guilt of that first occasion fails to recur. On his next visit, he sits in the same place – at the table outside where the sun seems to linger longest – and enjoys a bottle of claret. He plans the next chapter of *The Skies of Tiepolo* in his head.

Soon it has become a daily event. From evenings spent in silent reflection outside the Crown and Greyhound, he acquires a faint suntan for the first time in years.

'You're looking so well, Professor,' Maud Berenson remarks. 'What's your secret?'

It amuses him to see himself enter this unforeseen routine. It is a routine that his Cambridge self would have frowned at, deplored. Sometimes he takes out a book – a history of La Fenice opera house or *The Stones of Venice* by Ruskin. But increasingly, he prefers to listen to the conversations around him or to follow his thoughts wherever they lead. That was the problem in Cambridge – incessant activity without fresh thought, the type of thought that can float freely and assume new shape . . .

As he sits on the terrace of the pub in the early evening, looking at the varied scenery of Dulwich, he perceives – with the force of an epiphany – that this is life after Cambridge. All of *this*. A serene kind of non-existence which is now his only existence. His new reality. He traps wine in his mouth and feels it seep into his tongue, engorging it, turning it into a soaked leech. His mind feels enlarged. Was there a life before Cambridge? Why has he excised it from his history? He reaches back, groping for the obscure chapter.

When he tries to recapture his parents, he sees the elderly, respectable people in his graduation photograph. His father, a local government official, was a diffident man who kept his emotions in check. In his youth, Antony had been a bellboy at the Connaught Hotel in Bournemouth, and all his life he remained conscious – in a cautious, wincing way – of the step up he had taken.

Don's mother was withdrawn, too, but with an artistic streak. Sylvia Plath and Gertrude Stein were her favourite writers. *Arbitrary blackness gallops in. Look at Me Now and Here I Am.* The poems of Paula Lamb were filled with variations on these formulas.

His memory has degraded with the years. He remembers them more as stock characters – outlines – than people in the round, and yet certain remarks stand out in high relief.

'Your mother couldn't have any more children after you,' his father told him as they walked Iris through a pine forest. 'Just as well for all of us, really.' Not unkindly spoken, the statement concealed far more than it disclosed. He still wonders.

Around the same time, at home one evening, his mother folded the *Sunday Mirror* and murmured, 'That Lord Boothby's been nancying around with Ronnie Kray – queer stuff.'

Don was thirteen and harbouring an awareness of his own queer stuff. For a while there was horror and denial. Could he really be one of *them*, he wondered, as he triangulated his life with those of Lord Boothby and Oscar Wilde and Kenneth Williams from *Carry On*. But gradually, desire became artistic – something he could feel and explain through paintings and sculptures, the strange familiar bodies of other ages.

His adolescent years were friendless – even then his shyness passed for high conceit. Art became his refuge, a place of exquisite stillness and stability, where even violence and agony were beautiful. He remembers discovering Giorgione's *Tempest* in the school library, the only colour picture in a survey of the Italian Renaissance: lightning breaking over a strange hinterland on the border of town and country, a girl cradling and feeding her baby, and looking on, a man in a red mantle – a soldier, the book claimed, except that he didn't look like one. More a young poet, aloof and circumspect. Don noticed how the man's thigh and calf glowed in the warm stormy sunlight, while the other leg remained hidden by shadow.

Giorgione became an obsession for a while. The paintings offered visions of a reality far removed from Don's grammar-school existence in Poole. They also hinted – and maybe this was the real attraction – at the possibility of a story without a resolution.

When he was seventeen, his mother found his diary under

his bed. The pages were filled with reflections on Renaissance art, the names of great art historians, and expressions of desire for boys at his school – some of them disguised in mythological references, others sensual and unmistakeable.

'I'll never get over this,' she said to him when he came home that afternoon. 'I'm going to stick my head in the oven.'

He recalls how she looked – sitting on the end of his bed with reddened eyes, the offending notebook on her knee, just below the hem of her knitted skirt. He felt like telling her that it wouldn't work: their oven was electric, not gas. Paula Lamb was no Sylvia Plath.

He smiles faintly at the memory and fills up his glass. That was only a few weeks before he left for Peterhouse, and only a few months before Anders Andersson sent his books flying down the stairs . . . *I'll never get over this*. Perhaps he never did. His life has been one of sexual abdication. Cambridge was an end as well as a beginning, and not just for him. Once he left home, his parents seemed to age by decades in a few years. They died not long after he received his PhD – first his mother, then his father, within six months of each another. The doctor said it was old age. And yet they weren't so very old – hardly older than Val is now. They just *seemed* so much older.

Dulwich is charming in the evening light – the striped awnings that flap lazily above the shops, the close-trimmed verges – and yet it is lonely. Never before has he minded the absence of love, the absence of someone to love or be loved by. Now he feels acutely all the things he lacks. What friendship can he claim other than his friendship with Val – and what, after all, is that?

The bottle of wine in front of him is three quarters empty. The ashtray is clogged with cigarette ends. A child's buggy trundles past the table, pushed by a young mother. A poodle prances behind – Don leans forward to fondle its bobbly crown. The dog licks him on the fingers.

He drains his glass and pours another. The sinking sun flashes in his eyes and warms his brow. He tries to think about Tiepolo's ingenuity as a designer of space, but can only see the peculiar blue of the painter's skies – that pale, creamy turquoise. It is all around him.

*

A week after the episode in the Octagon, virtually nothing has been said. The broken statues have been sent – quietly, in balled tissue paper – to Inigo Price of Lewisham, the best restorer in the area. A cracked tile in the Octagon has been filled with invisible resin. The conspiracy of silence among the staff is almost as strange as the occurrence itself. Don wants to break it but can't think how, and so he too stays quiet, becoming complicit.

As they walk down the corridor on their way to the Wednesday morning meeting, Maud leans towards him with a confidential look.

'The police won't be pressing charges against that poor man.'

'Poor man?'

She considers her words carefully. 'The one who followed you in the other morning. He'd suffered some kind of mental breakdown.'

'I'll say.'

'They've closed the investigation. Better for everyone, wouldn't you agree?'

Before he can answer, they have entered the Summer Refectory and the eyes of all the staff are upon them. Don takes his seat and commences in his usual style – a genial address to the people of the museum. But Maud's words have left a corrosive trace.

Alone in his office after the meeting, he dials Val's number – stabbing the digits.

'Hello.'

Don sighs.

'I'm not here to take your call. But if you'd like to leave a message and a number, I'll contact you *tout de suite*.'

'Call me, please, Val,' he murmurs. 'It's important.'

Slowly, as if considering the action very carefully, he replaces the receiver. This silence isn't like Val. He thinks back to their last conversation, at Leighton House; but what he remembers more than anything they said is the static image of Val beside him in the dark recess, looking through the gaps in the lattice-work, tracing the carved wood with his fingertips.

Later, he catches sight of Maud through the door of the Communal Office. She is with Bill Hoare, standing behind his desk and looking over his shoulder.

Something makes him linger – he's been meaning to ask Maud a question but can't (at the moment of seeing her) remember what it was. He stands unnoticed in the doorway.

'But you told me these would be ready by today,' Maud says.

Bill stares down at a pile of papers. His face turns red and he begins to stammer a reply.

'I don't want excuses.' Maud's voice cuts through the air.

'I've been so busy with the restoration plans for the Poussin,' Bill manages to say.

'It's not good enough, Bill. Not good enough at all.' Maud's fingers descend in an elegant swoop to his desk and her rings crack against the wood. 'I've never seen such shoddy work. And don't think I haven't noticed' – she places one hand on her hip – 'that flask in your jacket. I find it hard to imagine that our trustees would be convinced of its medicinal purposes.'

Bill pats the pockets of his tweed jacket, like a man searching wildly for lost keys.

'We need these condition reports finished and signed by Professor Lamb *today*.'

This final word is a *coup de grâce*. Bill's head descends under the blow, burning with shame.

'Of course, Maud. Today it shall be.'

Still unobserved, Don marvels to hear his name brandished like a weapon.

Maud looks up and smiles. 'Professor Lamb! We were just discussing the loan paperwork for "Caravaggio's Muses". Bill will have everything ready for you to sign by lunchtime.'

'My pen is at the ready,' Don says. He continues along the corridor.

Alone in his study, he looks out of the window. The grass is about to be cut, but for now – on this April afternoon – it looks like a meadow sprinkled with wildflowers.

The incident stays with him. Is it disapproval or fascination that he feels, or both? His empathy rushes to Bill, the helpless victim, then transfers (under the dictates of logic) to Maud – fearless, diligent, exacting. He knows that workplace relationships are a performance. A sustained mode of insincerity. They run on a delicate interplay of charm and coercion, and no one is more practised than him.

But he is left feeling dissatisfied – by what he saw, by his own reaction to it. He can't rationalise it, but it has the effect of making him care very little about the condition reports when they land on his desk at four o'clock, delivered by Bill with lengthy apologies for lateness. Don looks at him and perceives – more strongly than before – Bill's complete defence-lessness, the absence of a social façade. Once Bill has left, he turns again to the window and catches sight of his reflection, and he wonders if he – Don Lamb – is all façade. Perhaps façade is all he has.

Things have been different since the vandalism of the Venuses. He feels aloof and out of place in the museum, and senses that others here feel differently about him. His thoughts shift – retreat – to Tiepolo's gigantic allegory of the continents of the world, and he contemplates whether he needs to take some new approach. Is he right in everything he claims? Can the heavens really be measured like the portico of a building?

The following morning, Val telephones. He sounds breathless with excitement. He skips the usual preliminaries.

'We're proposing a vote of no confidence in the Master. Frank knows nothing about it. College council are meeting in a few minutes. An ambush is always best.'

'Val – I've been trying to reach you.' Don is unable to disguise his bewilderment. 'I left messages on your answering machine.'

'Answering machine? Oh goodness, I never listen to that. Besides, we're in turmoil here.'

'What's been going on?'

'Ructions like I've never seen. A struggle between two cultures, two temperaments, almost two eras – and only one can win.' Val takes a breath. 'College politics! You're well out of it, Don.'

'Not if I've fallen into something worse.'

'Worse than a civil war at Peterhouse?'

Don decides to be blunt. 'I'm not happy here. I wish you'd told me what it would be like. I regret . . .' He pauses, then resolves to say it. 'I regret leaving Peterhouse. You flattered me into a rash plan.'

'But Don, just remember, Peterhouse had become unbearable to you. Think of *SICK BED*. That's not going anywhere, I'm afraid.'

'Peterhouse was familiar, it was *me*. It was a bearable unbearable. Everything here is done by committee. There's no such thing as an individual decision. God, if I have to sit through another meeting on the cleaning of Poussin's *Triumph of David*—'

'Be patient, Don. You're an individualist, a great art historian.

These people aren't used to a man of your stature. You bridle at their little ways, their procedures, of course you do. That's just how Forster ran the place, I'm afraid. He was weak, hopelessly passive – such a *democrat*. You'll have the opportunity to impose your will.'

'All I want to do is write my book.'

'And you will. Why do you think I gave you the sanctuary of the house?'

Don's hand tightens around the phone.

'Val, listen. I've been meaning to ask you—'

'Next time Don, next time – I'll be late for college council. The ambush!' He gives a rasping chuckle. 'You'll acclimatise to Dulwich. The way to perfection is through a series of disgusts.'

8

He is awake at four o'clock in the morning. Another wasted evening: he curses himself for staying so long at the Crown and Greyhound.

He forces himself out of bed, crosses to the typewriter on his desk and begins to type, but the sentences are slow to come. He grinds the words out until sunlight signals to him from behind the curtains. Time to get dressed – another day.

Looking through the wardrobe, he comes across a blue velvet jacket. It must be a cast-off of Val's. He tries it on and studies the effect in the long mirror of the wardrobe door. It fits him perfectly. He slips his copy of Grote into one of the pockets.

The velvet shines like cobalt as he walks to the museum. As it is still early, he decides to take a detour through the grounds of Belair House, a neoclassical villa close to Montcalm Road – now a ballet school. He passes a large pond and treads up a sloping lawn in the direction of the white façade. Low balustrades extend from either side of the central door – rows of swelling white chess pieces. He stops here, rests one hand on the ledge and lights a cigarette.

All is silent and still apart from a pair of sprinklers that rotate with robotic jerks, spitting jets of water: phut, phut, phut . . . Perhaps it is an after-effect of hours of concentration, but he feels giddy. The grass has become greener – too green to be true – and the bushes scattered over the turf are like floaters streaking across his eyeballs.

He finishes his cigarette and walks in the direction of a sharp, high thudding – the wavering rhythm of a tennis game. The courts come into view from behind the curtain of a weeping willow. He walks around the tall enclosure of green mesh; the courts are empty apart from one, where two men are engaged in a vigorous rally.

Don allows his eye to roam discreetly over the court. It alights on one of the players – the man nearer him – a bronzed, athletic character in his early thirties with curling blond hair and a proud Roman physiognomy. The man thwacks the ball across the court, over and over, with brute thrusts of the racket. The muscles of his thighs and calves are developed and mobile beneath his skin. As he runs, the fine blond hairs on his legs catch the light. Finally the ball evades his reach: it bounces, curves erratically in flight, and crashes into the mesh – close to where Don is walking.

'Damn,' the man exclaims. His face breaks into a grin and he massages his curling hair. He stands at ease, swinging his racket and surveying the court. 'Good shot!' he calls out to the other player.

On the road leading away from the park, hedges form a dense screen along the pavement. Occasional gaps reveal the open plane of a playing field beyond. As Don raises his arm to push his hair off his forehead, he glimpses the green space over the glinting ridge of his own sleeve – and in that moment he recognises the jacket. It is the same velvet jacket that Val was wearing on the day they met. *I lecture on neoclassical sculpture*, Val said to him, *the tranquil exterior, the baroque inner life*.

The colour, that lenticular blue, gives it away. With wonderment, Don observes that the jacket still seems new, almost untouched, nearly three decades on.

Walking through the galleries, Don sees that Poussin's *Triumph of David* has been taken off the wall and placed on the floor. Bill Hoare is standing in front of the deposed painting, his fingertips wedged in the silk-envelope pockets of his waistcoat.

A young man in a T-shirt wheels an empty crate across the parquet. The painting is leaving today, Bill explains, for the workshop of Inigo Price.

Don looks at the oblong of green patterned wallpaper where the picture has blocked the sunlight for decades – centuries. He has noticed before how Inigo Price's name seems to be hallowed among the staff of the Brockwell.

'I have occasionally,' he says, 'I admit, struggled with what I might term the *austerity* of Poussin's figural constructions. One finds dignity of bearing, yes, and rigorous design—'

'It's the varnish, Professor Lamb. That's the problem. Hundreds of layers of the stuff – century after century. Inigo Price will see to it.'

'And yet, how shall I couch it?' Don goes on, buttoning the velvet jacket and raising his eyes to the ceiling. 'A certain *stolidness* of mood, yes, befalls his scriptural scenes. The question, of course, is whether that mood confers more than it detracts—'

'It'll look very different after it's been cleaned, Professor.'

Bill launches into a description of the process, and Don wonders what he and Bill must look like from a few feet behind – from the perspective, say, of the young man who is now unscrewing the crate, ready to entomb the painting. A slender figure, head erect, clothed in shimmering blue, beside a short, broad man in green tweed.

'It'll be a different picture in six months,' Bill says.

Don looks down at the canvas in its gilt frame. The skin of the painting catches the light, exposing hundreds of ripples and cracks. The colours have turned to pools of grimy ochre and black. Here and there are scuff marks – breaks in the varnished surface where light is swallowed up.

'*Six months?* To restore it to its original condition?'

'Six months is quick, comparatively,' Bill replies. 'As for its original condition – we'll never get it back to that. Not even Inigo Price can work a miracle.' He licks his upper lip.

Don takes a few steps around the painting. Somewhere within the gloom is a picture. His instincts lead him there – to the victorious David processing through the street with Goliath's head on a stake, to the joyous crowd beneath the portico. He turns to Bill in exasperation.

'The picture is there beneath the dirt. It's *there*. All it needs is vigorous cleaning.'

'Ah yes, Professor Lamb, vigorous. But it mustn't be over-cleaned. The whole painting would dissolve.'

Bill's hands are concealed in his trouser pockets. The tweed material, rucked up around his crotch, bobs and twitches. Germs of chaos swarm into Don's brain. He feels helpless – furious. What would Poussin have made of this? He finds himself bombarded by shards of memory – the metallic clatter of Gene Caskill's urine, the parted lips of Caravaggio's *bardassa*, the magic lantern of *SICK BED* and the word *caressible* in the urbane voice of Robin Hands. His brain screams.

'You will see that this picture is *cleaned*,' he says. Bill makes no reply. 'Back to its original condition, nothing less. And I want it back here in three months. Tell Mr Price that we don't require conjuring tricks – just an honest performance of his duty.'

Particles of sweat have formed across Bill's face. Don is quietly appalled by his own fierceness. But it's no matter. He pulls himself straight and feels the fine, even pressure of his velvet sleeves. As he marches away, he remembers that the Rubens *Bacchus* still needs to be moved to make way for the new Tiepolo – wherever the new Tiepolo is – and he feels a fresh rush of impatience.

In the grip of impetuous feelings, he has entered a side gallery filled with small paintings. His eyes pass over a multitude of details. The room is empty and warm. Before he has conducted a half-circuit, he feels tired. He sits down on the plush bench which appears to float on the floor upon a bed of tassels, and he feels its squishy back – studded with buttons – envelop him.

His gaze drifts across the grid of pictures. Amid the group

is a tiny study by Tiepolo – the twin gods Apollo and Diana, along with a retinue of nymphs, borne into the sky on rafts of cloud. He creeps around the outer edges of the picture, circles in to inspect the gods in their floating train, then tumbles into a clear blue space where the clouds have parted. The blue is that milky blue of Tiepolo's, saturated by light, the colour of the sea on a clear morning.

Someone has stepped into the luminous space of his meditation. His eyes refocus and he sees a young man in his early twenties, crossing in front of the Tiepolo painting. The way he moves is striking – a poised, purposeful motion, and yet leisurely, as if he has all the time in the world. Don is reminded of Egon Schiele in his self-portraits: slenderly built, dark hair rising in a stack.

The youth turns and looks at him. Don recognises him as the young man who moved Poussin's *Triumph of David* only minutes earlier. The eyes confronting him are dark and energetic.

A delicate feeling, something like embarrassment, makes Don look away. He searches with one hand for the copy of Grote in his jacket pocket, and opens the book at a random page.

When he looks up again, the gallery is empty.

The next morning, when he comes downstairs to the kitchen, he notices a newspaper on the table. It is the *Guardian* – Ina must have been reading it. He makes a pot of coffee, sits down and surveys the paper's contents in frowning silence.

He has almost reached the end of the news section when something makes him stop and turn back a page. A picture. It is black and white – dull and grubby on the thin paper – but he recognises the composition at once. With a squeezing sensation in his chest, he sees that it is the oil sketch for Tiepolo's *Martyrdom of Saint Sebastian*.

He brings his finger to the image and runs it across the tortured body of Sebastian. As he reads the headline, his finger stalls.

Lost Tiepolo heads to New York

He skims the details of the article . . . An oil painting that was thought lost for 250 years has been donated to the Frick Collection in New York. The picture, a preparatory study for Giambattista Tiepolo's celebrated *Martyrdom of Saint Sebastian*, came to light in a medieval castle on the Danube, where it had been used as an ornamental fire screen. It is one of numerous undocumented masterpieces from the collection of Klaus von Löwenstein, a reclusive German prince who died last summer.

So the rumour he heard at Leighton House was true. He sits back and stares into space. Val claimed – beyond all doubt – that he had secured the picture for the Brockwell; he said that he had persuaded the prince's estate. There must be an explanation. Perhaps, just perhaps, there were two oil sketches for the same work, both found in the castle of Prince Klaus.

For some reason, Don feels nervous, as if he is guilty himself of some gross mistake. He thinks unhappily of his appearance on *Shifting Perspectives* – Erica, Angela, his failure to realise . . .

His eyes switch between the white squares and the red lines of the tablecloth. Only now does he register that Ina's voice has been audible for several minutes through the frosted glass door to the annex. Its intermittence suggests that she is on the phone. Or maybe she is talking to her mother, whose own responses are so quiet – uttered in a frail, failing voice – as to be inaudible.

The door opens a little, not wide enough to reveal the space beyond it, and Ina comes in. She is holding a cordless phone.

'It's Val,' she says, looking solemn and curious. 'He wants to speak to you.' She speaks into the phone. 'He's right here – I'll pass you over.'

The phone has a telescopic aerial that makes Don think of a fencing foil as she holds it towards him. He takes it and brings it to his ear.

'Don – are you there?' Val sounds faraway. 'I've just been reading today's *Guardian*. You won't have seen it—'

'I'm looking at it now.'

Val's silence induces a new wave of foreboding. Ina, who has been pulling dusters out of a cupboard, glances at Don and then disappears into the hallway.

'What's going on, Val?'

'Oh Don—'

Val breaks off. His voice has become tight and peculiar. Don thinks for a moment that his friend is on the verge of laughter, before realising that he is fighting back tears.

'It turns out that Klaus promised that picture to the Frick twenty years ago. He knew what it was all along, knew it was an original Tiepolo, and he kept it hidden from me – *for years*. And now the Director of the Frick has produced a letter Klaus wrote back in the 1970s. A guarantee of the picture upon his death. Bona fide. Unarguable.'

'When did you find out?' Don is thinking again of that night at Leighton House. 'How long have you known?'

'Oh, there have been rumours for a week or two, but I thought nothing of them. The art world is full of empty gossip.' Val's tone is ragged and strangulated again. 'I assumed I knew the truth.'

The text of the newspaper shifts this way and that like print seen in a dream. Next to the reproduction of the painting is a photograph of Klaus von Löwenstein. A man with a corona of brilliant white hair – he looks a bit like the chaplain of Peterhouse, but more patrician, filled out and pacified by wealth. The traces of a handsome younger face are discernible.

'I'm so sorry, Don – for you, I mean. I know how much this picture meant to you. Your exhibition—'

'It isn't your fault.'

'But I should have known.' Anger and regret have ignited in Val's voice. 'I've been so caught up in Peterhouse politics. All that business with Bruce Day, and now this vote of no confidence in the Master. I should have investigated the rumours about the Frick as soon as I heard them.' He lets out a long, stuttering sigh.

With bitter irony, Don remembers Val's words to him after the disaster of *Shifting Perspectives*. *You should have known.* He has never heard his friend like this; Val, who knows everything, so helpless and humiliated. Even in his own misery and black confusion, he feels Val's grief, feels the radiant heat of Val's outrage. Looking back at the photograph, he wonders about Val's relationship with the dead Klaus – what was it, exactly?

For a long while, neither of them speaks.

'What happened with the Master?' Don asks in the end, wanting to dilute the mood. 'The vote of no confidence?'

Val tuts dismissively. 'The motion was passed. Effortless. The Master's not fighting it – he'll go quietly. Personal problems, apparently. He wants out of Cambridge. So we'll have a new Master before Michaelmas . . . Which *reminds* me.'

In an instant, Val's words are filled with life. He pauses for several seconds, rendered dumb by his own sensational recollection. Don waits.

'A new person is coming to the Brockwell.'

'A new person?'

'Oh Don, it's a perfect match – just the man for you.' Val is soaring from despair into sublime elation. 'And there's a poetic justice about it – I've only just realised. Wait till I've explained. I've found a deputy for you at the Brockwell. A man of intellect and drive!'

'But Val—'

'Don't worry, I've settled it with the trustees.'

'Why wasn't I consulted?' Don has begun to tear the *Guardian* in a long diagonal rip that severs Sebastian lengthways.

Val laughs. 'I know you so well, Don. I know what you require before you know it yourself. Just think, a capable deputy to shield you from the tedium of museum administration. Maud is already so busy with the Caravaggio show – it makes marvellous sense.'

'But who is he?'

'Well, that's the beauty of it. Right now, he's the Senior Curator at the Frick. He's thirty-two, younger than Jesus, a future great. But he wants to come back to London – he's British, you see – and I think I've convinced him. They'll be devastated to lose him. Don't you see, it's the most perfect revenge – a retaliation for their seizure of the Tiepolo!'

Don completes the separation of the newspaper page and screws the detached section into a little ball. 'Does he have a name?'

'His name,' Val says momentously, 'is Michael Ross. I got to know him when he organised that glorious Batoni exhibition a few years back. We've become very close. He's quite brilliant – *stunningly* knowledgeable. The BBC have just commissioned him to make a documentary about the Grand Tour. Englishmen on the roam in Rome!'

'I'm not sure about this, Val. I need time to think.'

'No, Don, you don't. You've admitted that you're finding the Brockwell a strain. Michael Ross is your solution. For what it's worth, I think you'll like him very much.'

Don succumbs to a heavy, creeping, suffocating panic. He knows that Val loves to be the puller of strings, the great fixer and impresario; for years, Don has allowed his friend to perform this role. But it no longer feels like an eccentricity to be humoured. He is aware of an urgent desire to pull back the other way and break loose.

Then he thinks of his unfinished book, the stack of typewritten sheets on the desk upstairs, and he rolls the little paper ball over the tablecloth beneath the palm of his hand. He isn't blind to the advantages of a deputy. If only he'd had the idea himself.

'I insist on meeting him before anything is decided.'

'Naturally. He's moving to London next week with his wife, Anna – she's a cellist in the New York Philharmonic. They're *very* eager to meet you. They'll be at the private view of your Caravaggio show. After that you'll interview him – the proper formalities.'

'It isn't my show, as you well know.'

'Oh Don, can't you see what a wonderful thing this is? It's one in the eye for the Frick. Let them have that miserable little Tiepolo daubing. A fire screen, that's all it was. You can still have your exhibition – Michael will help you!'

With the phone clamped between his chin and collarbone, Don reaches for his cigarettes, unsettled by the way Val has described this young friend – and even more unsettled by the violent revolution in Val's mood. He experiences a convulsion in his gut.

'Val, I must go, I'm sorry – I have a meeting. Maud Berenson – wall texts. We're swimming in it. You understand?'

'*A demain*, Don. And soon you'll have an eager young assistant to swim alongside you.'

The line crackles and dies.

Ina is in the hallway outside the kitchen door, polishing the gilded bronze statuette of Hercules wrestling with the bull. She looks up as he comes out. He wonders if she has been listening. Other questions follow in fast succession. Who is Ina Stables? A supporting character in the playlet that Val has written for him, a random detail? And why has he never seen or even heard her mother, that absent presence beyond the frosted glass door of the annex?

Ina watches him with muted curiosity, as if she has multiple questions of her own. Then she resumes her rubbing of the bull's rippling flank.

*

It is just after seven o'clock. Steadily, the terrace of the Crown and Greyhound is filling up with drinkers. People have been tempted out like zesty insects by the first intimations of summer.

'D'you mind if I sit here?'

He doesn't mind at all. A person shuffles up beside him on the wooden bench. Someone else sits down opposite. Soon he is surrounded by a whole party of strangers, young men and women. They are a loud, boisterous lot – amusing to listen to. He scans their faces. From time to time, they look back at him with passing bemusement. Snug on the end of the bench, he finds himself caught up in their breeziness, their love of life.

'Hey, mate, can I have a cigarette?'

The question has come from a girl sitting beside him. She looks boyish and scruffy in a ragged jumper. Blackened finger-nails. He holds out his pack of Lambert & Butler.

'Can I try some of your wine?'

'Well . . .' he begins.

She grabs the bottle and tips its contents – everything that remains – into her empty pint glass, virtually filling it.

He watches the red liquid frothing in the glass. Bizarrely, he doesn't mind. The girl's complicit grin has stalled his ability to react.

From snatches of their conversation, he learns that they are art students – artists. They are chatting away about a teacher called Malcolm. Some of them throw out slurs – 'He doesn't know a fucking thing' – and others come to Malcolm's defence.

'He's pushed conceptualism back into the realm of the real,' says one man, a smiling character in sunglasses.

'He's a one-trick Charlie,' chips in another male voice at the end of the table.

'You mean one-trick pony, dickhead,' says a girl.

'Malco doesn't know a fucking thing!' shrieks the boyish girl beside Don, and she gives him a hard prod, as if he were a stand-in for their absent teacher. Surprised by her own violence, she erupts in laughter. Before Don can object, she has pulled him into an apologetic hug and is raising her pint of wine – his wine – to the sky. He finds that he is laughing too, saying that it's quite all right and quite true – he doesn't know a thing!

The young man in sunglasses is watching him. He takes the sunglasses off. It's the boy from the Brockwell, Egon Schiele. Don comes to his senses and blushes deeply. The sunglasses were a mask. The young man looks back at him, seeming to apprehend the fact that Don has only just recognised him. He is pale and serious; his hair rises off his brow, except for a loose strand that falls above one eye. After a moment, he puts his sunglasses back on and turns once more to his friends.

'Alastair's a homo!' the girl beside Don suddenly declares. 'Alastair's a homo!'

'You can't say that,' says one of the others. 'You have to say *gay*.'

'*He's a big fucking homo*.' She cackles with delight.

'When did he come out?'

'He never needed to – just look at him!'

They carry on laughing and arguing, including Egon Schiele, and including – Don realises – the Alastair who is the subject of the conversation. He is a tall, long-limbed man with a pointed nose and an air of swanlike imperturbability.

Listening to their talk of coming out, Don wonders what it's for – all this truth-telling. He thinks of the Cambridge of his youth. There were swimming parties – sometimes in the nude, like Cézanne's bathers (not that he attended) – hidden kisses and embraces, romances of the passing moment. Like his romance with Anders Andersson, whatever that was. He told the truth when he wrote to Anders, and the romance withered in an instant.

He goes to the toilet and buys another bottle of wine from the bar. He is glad, when he returns to the table, to see that the group hasn't moved. His space is waiting for him. Gradually, however, the party thins out. One by one, people leave. They speak of getting back to the studio or say they're off to the Golden Heart.

But Egon Schiele is in no hurry. He stays at the table with two others, the girl who stole Don's wine and another man who wears an expression of permanent bafflement. The sunlight mellows. Their conversation slows. They seem content to sit there in each other's company, descending occasionally into affectionate teasing and in-jokes that Don can't hope to understand.

Half an hour later, the young woman and the baffled man get up and say goodbye, drunkenly and cheerfully. Walking away, she caresses Don's shoulder. It makes him feel excited and melancholy.

He is left alone with the young man from the Brockwell.

'Funny, seeing you out here.'

Don nods tranquilly – quiescent from the wine.

'In the world, I mean. Outside the museum.' He has an ordinary accent – estuary, Don would call it – and yet it sets him apart from most of the young people Don has known. 'I'm Ben.'

Don takes his hand. It feels smooth and cool. The fingers, busy with rings, close around his with stealthy force.

'Don Lamb.'

Ben laughs. 'Yes, I know.'

'You can call me Don.'

'Thanks, that's kind of you.' There is humour in Ben's voice. Only months earlier, if a student had spoken to him in this way, Don would have been aghast. As it is, on this warm evening in Dulwich, with spring melting into summer, he feels different – indifferent.

'I work at the Brockwell,' says Ben. 'Part-time. I'm at art college.'

'Do you paint or sculpt?'

Ben smiles at the question. 'Neither, really. I make stuff out of . . .' He shrugs, as if the right word doesn't exist. 'Out of nothing, sometimes.'

'That sounds like a riddle.'

'Yes, it is, sort of.' Ben pulls a crushed Marlboro packet from his denim jacket and flings it on the table. Don reads the inscription beneath the gold insignia. *Veni – Vidi – Vici.*

'And what about you?' Ben asks. 'What do you do?'

The question is a joke, surely. 'This you know. I am the Director of the Brockwell Collection.'

'Yes. I knew *that*.' Ben taps a cigarette from the buckled pack.

'And before that, I taught art history—' Don stops. Ben hasn't said anything, but the noise of the afternoon – a babble of voices carried on the breeze, broken up by laughter and the tinnitus ring of glasses – halts his thoughts, roaring in his ears like rushing blood. Ben is a riddler, like the teasing rogue of the *commedia dell'arte* whom Tiepolo's son sketched many times. A jester and a beguiler. 'How did you come to be working at the Brockwell?'

'I was doing shifts for a shipping company. Driving a van. We dropped off a painting a few weeks ago – a Caravaggio.'

'Yes, I remember. That was you?' He pictures Ben on the back of the truck and recalls his own mad excitement – his conviction that the Tiepolo had arrived.

'Well I was sick of being a van driver, so I asked Maud if there was any work going at the Brockwell. And she suggested I help with the Caravaggio install. So here I am. Got a few mates to help me.' Ben indicates the empty table, strewn with abandoned glasses.

There is silence, during which they each light a cigarette. A fine gust of wind glides around Don's neck, almost extinguishing his match. They look at each other and then glance away, as if through mutual embarrassment – each unwilling to concede that the other man is familiar – more familiar – than he is letting on.

'Have some wine,' Don says. He tips an inch of Beaujolais into a used pint glass.

Ben makes a thumbs-up sign and winks. Yes, a jester and a beguiler . . .

'Funny place, Dulwich Village,' he says finally.

'Is it?' Don looks at the shops and cottages across the road, the red latticework of the telephone box. He tries to see it through the other man's eyes, but all he sees is himself in the lenses of Ben's sunglasses, two miniaturised versions of Don Lamb, serious and proper in his blue velvet jacket.

'It's funny to me, yeah. Doesn't feel like London. Feels like somewhere from the past. It's not very *real*.'

'Dulwich is different from Cambridge, I know that much,' says Don.

'Is that why you left Cambridge? Change of scene?'

Staying silent, Don recollects his walk in Coe Fen on the afternoon of the radio broadcast, that sad ramble through the mist, ending with his shoe entrenched in a heap of dung.

Ben looks up the road in the direction of the Brockwell Collection. 'Why this place?'

Trained replies are on the tip of Don's tongue, but something stills him at the point of answering, like the calming hand of a deity. For several seconds, speaking feels as impossible as changing shape, becoming another creature entirely, a tigress or a bear.

'I don't know,' he says at last, released from his paralysis. 'I mean – Cambridge became deathly, in its way. And the things that had been beautiful – the trees, meadows, ancient buildings, all the things I used to love – became stifling.'

His words have run away from him. He is talking to a man he hardly knows, pouring out his private feelings, sentiments he didn't know he possessed. His rational mind warns him that Ben is a stranger and – more to the point – an employee, but the reminder comes from far away, like a voice heard underwater. Rationality is sinking beneath a deep blue sea of happy delirium.

'Cambridge sounds a lot like Dulwich to me,' says Ben. 'Small differences.'

'Oh no, they're not the same.' Don drains his glass. 'Nature is different here. It has a different . . . I don't know . . . a new *agency*, perhaps that's the word. The parks – they draw you in like honeytraps, haven't you found? And yet they don't imprison you, they're freeing – traps that liberate. They're – I don't know how to explain it.'

Ben stubs out his cigarette. 'Maybe it's you that's changed, Don Lamb.' There's an insolence about this use of his name, but the insolence seems to cloak another mood, something closer to tenderness.

'It's been a massive change for me – someone at my time of life.'

Ben laughs – a loud laugh, without restraint. His head falls back, and he is no longer Egon Schiele, sombre and intense, but a mischievous boy.

'Your time of life! You talk like you're a hundred years old.'

Don refills their glasses. 'How old are you?'

'How old do you think?'

'Twenty-two?'

Ben nods in a slow, noncommittal way that leaves the guess hanging. 'How old are you?'

'Forty.' Don shaves three years away.

'You look older.'

'I always have.'

'Or maybe you just *act* older. It's the way . . .' Ben considers for a moment. 'Your status. The way everyone calls you "Professor".'

Don wants to point out that he *is* a professor. And yet – he can't help admitting it – there's a growing pretence about the title and everyone's insistence on using it. Professor Lamb. The idea amuses him – the entire idea of *him*.

Ben appears to perceive the direction of his thoughts. 'Your clothes, too,' he says, and he reaches out to clasp Don's forearm. Don tenses with surprise. 'They're part of your *professoriality*.' He draws the word out, making it even more ridiculous as he stretches the vowels.

Professorial. The grotesque who followed Don into the museum used the same word: something about professorial rites. They sit for a while without talking. Don feels fuzzy and warm. The edges of things have softened, everything is vibrating. He laughs, surprising himself with the outflux of emotion.

'You know,' he hears himself say, 'you remind me of Egon Schiele. An artist whose work I hate, mind you.'

Ben smiles quizzically. He tells Don that he is heading to the Golden Heart in Spitalfields. Don should come too, if he wants to. They could take the bus right now.

'The Golden Heart,' Don murmurs. 'Where your friends went already? You should have gone too. Why did you wait?'

Ben flips his sunglasses onto his head and studies Don with his green-brown eyes, as if he's figuring out a puzzle. 'Come with me now. It'll be a laugh.'

Don shakes his head. 'You're very kind. But I must return to my work.' The vibrations in his head make thought slow. 'But I'll see you again – at the Brockwell?'

Ben doesn't reply. He just grips Don's hand – it is stronger than a handshake, and rougher – and then leaves.

Don sits there for some time, drifting in a flood of feeling, as the evening dwindles around him.

9

A breeze from the open window stirs against his naked shoulder. His maroon pyjamas are still neatly folded at the end of the bed. He forgot to put them on. His tongue is heavy with the aftertaste of wine.

He flings away the covers, gets up and pulls on a dressing gown. It is a silk kimono of Val's, black and embroidered with gold, that hangs on the back of the bedroom door, more for decoration than use. The slippery fabric strokes his bare hips and buttocks as he ties the cord.

On his way back from the bathroom, he wanders into an unused room on the opposite side of the landing. It is a bedroom without a bed, smaller than his own room, containing a harpsichord and architectural etchings by Piranesi. He peers out of the window, over the top of a vase of freesias. He can see down to the zinc roof of the annex and the jungle of the garden. *Il giardino povero*, Val called it. Some recent effort has been made to trim the overgrowth around the door on the side of Ina's quarters.

Before leaving the room, he scans the multiple framed photographs that have been arranged over the harpsichord. He doesn't recognise most of the people, although some are unmistakeable: Val and Pablo Picasso surprised by the camera from lunch al fresco, Val and Somerset Maugham beside a swimming pool – the novelist a grimacing geriatric by then. Further back in the array is a photo of Val as a young man – still in his twenties – at what looks like a university gathering. He is surrounded by art historians, some of the stellar figures of the twentieth century. Don recognises Ernst Gombrich, Erwin Panofsky and another renowned German scholar – Hubert something or other (the name escapes him), beaming charismatically at the camera.

As he descends the stairs, Ina is coming out of the kitchen. Over the banister, he sees a tray in her hands, spread with a Qianlong tea set. Steam rises from the pot and the petal-like cups. The set is a museum piece – he is amazed to see it in everyday use. The china vessels are as thin as eggshells and their white surfaces are speckled with flowers and scrolling figures. The patterns are doubled in the mirror of the silver tray.

'Don! I was just bringing you some coffee.'

He places his hands gingerly on the newel post. 'Thank you, Ina, but I really must be off.' He tries to flash her a gracious smile but isn't sure, from her reaction, that he's pulled it off. 'Well – a quick one before I leave.'

He sits at the foot of the stairs and presses his hands between his knees. Setting the tray on the step beside him, Ina pours two cups of coffee, black as ink, and hands him one.

The taste is overpowering. It hits his tongue like a stringent chemical. His first impulse is to spit it out. Then it's as if he has bitten into tarry liquorice; the liquid is warm and dry at the back of his mouth. He swallows. The aftertaste is bittersweet, more sweet than bitter.

'Do you like it?'

'It's extraordinary.'

'We've just been sent a sack of the stuff from a friend in Syria.' She lifts one foot – in a workman's boot – onto the bottom step and watches him with interest. 'I'll bring you a cup each morning if you like.'

'Oh, there's no need, really.' He takes another mouthful.

'It's no trouble.' She picks up her own cup from the tray. 'I'll be making it anyway for Mamma and me.'

He runs the fingers of his free hand down the side of the Minoan amphora that sits on the bottom step. He is surprised to find the coldness of metal where he expected the dull warmth of clay.

'What is this thing? It's made of metal.'

'Of course it is.'

'I thought it was an amphora. A Minoan fermentation vessel?'

'It's an old gas cylinder.'

Don leans over the object and examines its russet surface. With a kind of horror, he sees that the colour is nothing more than industrial paint, weathered and dusty, and that the circular neck of the vessel conceals within its rim a small brass tap. The moulded bands that run around the outside are standard-issue; and – most humiliating of all – what he had taken for a trace of geometric patterning is, he now sees, a half-erased serial number.

'Minoan – is that what Val told you?' There is a scintilla of amusement now in her eyes – he is beginning to be able to detect her buried reactions.

'No, he didn't. I just – I just saw it in a certain way.'

'I brought it in from the garden last year.' She drains her cup. 'I guess you see everything through an art historian's eyes, even the most random stuff.'

'I do try to discriminate,' he says quietly.

'It's possible to be too discriminating.' Her words are brisk, matter of fact. 'You stop seeing the thing for what it is.'

Don looks up and is struck by the sight of her – grey T-shirt, jeans, heavy boots – holding the antique cup.

'Val never told me who you are – what you do.'

'And you never asked,' she says in a lighter tone. 'I am – was – an athlete. Won an Olympic silver medal for hurdling. LA, 1984.' She takes the empty cup from his hand and reclaims the tray. 'And then I retired. Now it's nursing and conservation of antiques – much the same thing, in the end.'

'An Olympian,' Don murmurs. 'How marvellous. I was in

Los Angeles myself that summer, receiving the Getty Sword of Excellence.'

'You mean that little sword in your room? I thought it was a toy of some sort.'

He smiles at the idea. 'A toy for art historians. It was a prize for my research into the Rococo period.' He leans back, enlivened by the coffee. 'The real prize was the trip to California. I'll never forget the view from the Getty Museum across the city towards the Pacific – the simple conjunction of sea, sky and hills . . .'

His imagination is running loose and unchecked, but Ina is nodding, beginning to smile back.

'Ancient Greece on the west coast of America. That's what I've always loved about it, that thing of . . .' She starts to carry the tray back to the kitchen, then calls back: 'That thing of timelessness.'

When he arrives at the Brockwell, there are vans and trucks blocking the crescent of gravel around the entrance. Before he has made it through the lobby, he sees men in T-shirts and jeans moving through a maze of plywood crates in the Octagon. Hammers clatter against the mosquito whine of drills. Through a mist of sawdust, he sees that the emerald wallpaper has been stripped. In its place, a wine-dark shade is edging slowly upwards through the action of brushes and rollers.

He almost trips over a toolbox as he enters the gallery. A man with dark hair is standing on a ladder, peeling a sheet of transparent plastic film away from the wall with scrupulous care to reveal a band of text, ivory white on the new maroon.

CARAVAGGIO'S MUSES

Don can't see the man's face: he is turned away, intent on his work. Is it Ben? At the centre of the Octagon, Maud is holding a clipboard and reviewing the work with rapid eye movements.

'What's going on?' he asks, realising as he speaks that his palate is still thick with the savour of wine. He places his fingertips across his lips.

'We're hanging the Caravaggios. Did you forget?'

Even as Maud replies, he sees one of the pictures being carried across the room – Narcissus crouching in the shade, confronting his own reflection in a black pool.

'The exhibition opens next week,' Maud says. Her eyes settle on him.

Narcissus flips as two men rotate the picture. The bleary reflection stares down at the hard, clear form of the boy on the water's edge.

Don nods and looks back at the man on the ladder – still turned towards the wall, still peeling back the clear film. All his senses converge on the mystery figure, while the strange course of his conversation with Ina echoes somewhere in his deeper consciousness.

His daydream bursts as the noise of a drill rebounds off the eight walls of the gallery. He strides off in the direction of the Palladian Library, sensing Maud's eyes on him.

It is past eight o'clock as he sets out for home. The light is fading and the air is cool from a shower. He feels better at last after the stagnation of the day.

Walking under dripping horse chestnuts, he becomes aware of someone running behind him on the pavement. He turns.

'You're not stopping at the pub tonight?' Ben asks, recovering his breath.

'No. Not tonight.' Don starts to walk on. 'Don't let me delay you. You must have somewhere to be.'

Ben walks alongside him. 'Not really.'

'What are you doing now?'

'Wandering. Checking out the parks. I remember what you said yesterday – how they draw you in like honeytraps.'

Repeated back to him, Don's words sound farcical. What could he have meant? He winces to think.

'Don't they close soon, the parks?' he asks.

'I guess.' Ben sticks his hands in the pockets of his jeans. 'But I don't care if I get shut in. I mean, I'm not living anywhere right now.'

Don stares at him. 'You're homeless?'

'Oh, it's nothing major. I was staying with a mate at Dawson's Heights. Got kicked out – same old story. I often knock about like this. Sometimes I sleep at Goldsmiths, in the studios. No one seems to mind.'

They walk on, shaded by the regularly spaced trees. Don glances occasionally at Ben, whose gaze has drifted to the properties of Montcalm Road – stately villas receding into the gloom. Ben looks different up close. Paler, less assured than when they were at the pub. His hair appears darker, and it no longer sweeps back in a wild tide but hangs half across his forehead. His denim jacket is open. The neck of his white T-shirt is loose – stretched – to expose one shoulder.

For a second, their eyes meet. With his mouth open a fraction, thought restraining speech, Ben looks melancholic, less like Egon Schiele – that hard, saturnine handsomeness has softened tonight – and closer to one of the nameless subjects of Giorgione, perpetually young and never to be identified.

They are almost at the house. Don's conscience tells him that he has fallen behind on his book. But another desire, some feeling that has been growing in him since he saw Ben walk across the gallery the day before last, wells up.

'Come and stay at mine for the night. It's just up the road here. There's a spare room.'

Val, Ina, Ina's elderly mother, his book – objections crowd into his head like furious protestors. But they're too late. He has already said it. Ben's eyes stray lazily along the treetops, then back to Don, and he assents with a smile – and a grip of the professor's arm. His smile is easy and broad, but a trace of that cinquecento solemnity remains, like a note still reverberating.

Giving nothing away, Don is filled with mad delight. Long broad vistas open in his mind, like that sports field he glimpsed through the hedge of a Dulwich lane.

He gives Ben a lengthy tour of the house as soon as they arrive. He feels as if he too is entering the place for the first time, even though he knows every detail. He guides Ben from room to room, prompted by an unexpected pride in the treasures of the House Beautiful, undeterred by Ben's muted responses.

'This is where I work,' he says, opening the door to his room. 'And sleep.'

Ben walks straight to the bay window. He looks at the typed sheets and reproductions on the desk and floor.

'What's all this?'

Don follows him.

'Materials for a book I'm writing. Ceiling frescoes by Giovanni Battista Tiepolo, also called Giambattista. The last of the Old Masters, or the first of the moderns – it's a question I'm debating.'

He explains how each scene is a pageant in the air – and how every figure has a place within the larger scheme. Nothing is accidental, not the most casual of gestures.

Ben regards the masterworks with an expression that lacks, to Don's mind, the appropriate deference.

'Ceiling paintings,' he says, resting his hands on the desk. 'So you're looking *down* when you should be looking *up*.'

'I always work from reproductions. But I've seen all these paintings in their actual locations. Some more recently than others . . .'

Ben's eyes follow the meticulous pencil lines that crisscross the pictures. 'Looks like you've added some touches of your own.' He picks up Don's wooden ruler and balances it between his fingers.

'Perspective lines, yes. My intention is to map the skies of Tiepolo. I believe that the clouds, the figures, the air itself – all of it conceals a precise and beautiful geometry.'

'So you're a measurer.'

Don laughs politely. 'It's a little more complex than that. My book will challenge the entire way that Tiepolo has been defined. My colleagues in Cambridge call him a magician, a conjuror of fantasy. Wrong. Meaningless!' He begins to stroll around the room, warming to his theme. 'I will show that Tiepolo was, in truth, a *classical* painter. It's there in the construction of his skies.'

'Classical,' Ben repeats, as if only half understanding – or half agreeing.

They go downstairs to the sitting room. It seems bigger than ever, a majestic space coated with damask wallpaper of apricot and blue. The twin colours vie for pre-eminence in the lamplight. In the centre of the room is a sofa covered in pink velvet, a Napoleon III piece resembling a huge flower.

They stand facing one another.

'Got anything to drink?' Ben asks.

Don fingers his lapel, nods and retreats to the kitchen. He slides a bottle from the wine rack (replenished as usual) and opens it. The pop of the cork releases a sweet, musty aroma. Not a sound comes from Ina's annex.

Ina – he breaks into a sweat. He hasn't thought of her once since they arrived. Has she gone to the cinema, gone to bed early? He stands close to the frosted glass door and listens – nothing. His heart relaxes. He begins to invent a plausible story.

In the kitchen fridge, he finds a piece of French cheese on a dinnerplate. When he returns to the sitting room, wine and cheese in either hand, Ben has settled on the pink sofa, drawing one leg underneath himself so that his boot squashes into the velvet. He starts asking questions as soon as Don walks in. He wants to know more about Tiepolo.

Don takes two glasses – Val's best crystal – from the walnut credenza. As he pours a large measure in each and hands one to Ben, he delineates the context of Venice in the eighteenth century – the intricacies of trade, war and patronage. He has found some matches on the credenza, and moves about the room, lighting various candles.

'But what about the sky?' Ben interrupts finally, picking up the piece of cheese – ignoring the crackers and knife that Don has arranged on the plate – and taking a large bite. 'Why was he so obsessed with painting the sky?'

Don talks about the shade of blue that Venice produces – a blue that occurs when the sky is thinly veiled by mist rising off the water. Tiepolo saw this colour. He transferred it into his pictures. Don calls it Tiepolo Blue.

'Look between the bodies,' he says, 'at the blue spaces – those are sometimes the most beautiful parts of the painting.'

'Tiepolo Blue,' Ben echoes. 'I could use that.' Then he tells Don about a show called '*Aperto*' that happened two summers ago in Venice. Some of his friends were included in it.

'I'd like to have seen it,' says Don, thinking that he would love to see Venice again – the metallic lagoon with its stale aquatic perfume, the campanile rising beside the pale pink glory-box of the ducal palace. He hasn't visited in years. Not since his radio programme.

'We'll go,' says Ben. He lights a Marlboro and inhales deeply.

Don lights a cigarette too, and releases smoke from his nostrils in fine jets. A minute elapses without a word between them, and he begins to wonder what Ben is thinking – whether his silence signifies something. He realises that his body is tensed, as if he's about to deliver a keynote lecture. Excitement – that new illicit force – is running up and down his nervous system like trapped energy.

'When I was your age,' he suddenly says.

Ben looks amused.

'When I was your age, I read *The Stones of Venice* – Ruskin, you know? Perhaps you don't. Anyhow, such *feverish* erudition . . .' He loses his train of thought, then regains it. 'Venice grew in my mind. I had so many fantasies about the place – the Gothic city state ringed by water, famed for its painters of colour, a place of colour and sensation rather than hard form, literally floating . . . I suppose it sounds ridiculous.'

'Not really,' says Ben. 'I mean, we're all ridiculous, aren't we, in our own way? What would we be – any of us – without that?'

Don feels a spur of encouragement. 'Venice, the Venice of my imagination, was so different from Poole, where I lived. My childhood was very ordinary, believe it or not. But when I finally went to Venice – I must have been twenty-one – it was shrouded in fog.'

'We'll go,' says Ben again.

Ben turns slightly and his head shifts into profile. Don traces the definite, delicate edge of his brow and nose. Cigarette smoke drifts through the yellowish light of the room, and he reflects on the concept of exhalation as the expression of the soul – the momentary release of the spirit into the world.

'Next year. Why not?' Ben is watching him with an expectant expression.

Why not? Why not . . . Don checks the clock on the mantelpiece. All that racing energy has found an escape route. He feels exhausted.

'I'm afraid that before any thoughts of visiting Venice, I must go to bed,' he says with brittle jollity. 'Would you like to see your room?'

As he leads Ben upstairs, he has the bizarre sensation of falling and floating simultaneously. He grips the banister hard.

He shows Ben into the spare room on the floor above his own. It is a narrow space with a single bed and a suite of framed prints by John Flaxman; Val calls it the servant's room. Standing in the doorway, Ben looks at him with drowsy eyes – he seems to be waiting for something. Don feels a faint rush of fear. In his mind, he crafts apologies, excuses, a late change of heart. But all he says is, 'Goodnight, Ben.'

With nimble steps, he goes back down to his room and finds a sheet of blank paper. He writes a note to Ina. A former student has come to stay for the night. *Possibly longer*, he adds in a postscript. He thinks of writing more, but can't think what else to write, and so he leaves the remainder of the page blank and takes it down to the kitchen. He places it on the table, angled towards the door to the annex.

He lies awake for a long time. His room feels different. The whole house appears, by an invisible but palpable change – a shift in the texture of the air – to have acknowledged its new inhabitant. Through the grey-brown darkness, the walls and curtains crackle with life.

He wants to go upstairs and check that Ben is really there. But he stays still, lying on his back, afraid to move in case the creaking of his bed should send reverberations through the walls, into Ben's consciousness.

He listens to his own breaths and counts them. Sleep creeps over him. It is a light sleep, thought-filled and vigilant.

He wakes to the realisation – a dim realisation, slow to cohere – that he hasn't actually woken. Not fully. The thinnest membrane of a dream still encases him. And yet something is pressing close. A body. He feels the nearness of a man's face – breathing, animate, almost touching his own. Warmth radiates into him. He waits for the seam of air between their two bodies to close; his limbs tense and his neck strains to raise his head. But his mind recoils and his body snaps awake.

The room is dark – it is still night. His heart is racing. He lies still, listening to the silence, and rolls his eyes around the room. All he sees is the bluish outline of the window behind the curtains. But he has the prickling awareness, an aftersensation breaching the membrane of his dream, of Ben's presence – right beside him, only seconds ago. The sound of a footstep, perceived in his sleep, loiters in his inner ear.

He climbs out of bed. The door is ajar.

Out on the landing, the green wallpaper emits a weak glow. Treading carefully, withholding his weight from each step, he climbs the stairs. Before he reaches the second-floor landing, he sees that the door to the servant's room is slightly open. Wasn't it closed when he left Ben? He stops and listens and hears nothing. But as he climbs a few more steps, the sound of slow, somnolent breathing comes from the doorway. He tiptoes to the threshold and looks through.

Ben is lying on the bed. He has pulled off his T-shirt and is lying on his side, with the sheets furled busily around his bent legs – the material has slid down just far enough to uncover the crest of his hip. Moonlight spills through the window. In the celluloid glow, Ben looks like one of the plaster casts from Pompeii, a victim suspended between sleep and death. His features are still – affectless. His body is slim, but with the suggestion of strength in the smooth masses of his upper arms. Don focuses on a portion of his shoulder. With every intake of breath, it makes a fractional movement.

Is Ben only pretending to be asleep? Did he not creep downstairs, moments earlier, and watch Don in the same way, coming close enough for them to touch? Don tries to imagine what Ben would have seen: the sleeping professor in his maroon pyjamas, hands one atop the other like a saint on top of a sarcophagus. He grits his teeth and decides that it is impossible. Ben is deeply asleep.

He returns to his own room, fearful that he won't sleep again for hours – and yet, when he lies down, he is unconscious almost at once.

In the early morning, he washes and dresses at speed. It will be better, he thinks, if he doesn't see Ben until they're at the museum – formality will resume. He glances up the stairs towards the servant's room before going down to the kitchen. The note he wrote to Ina has gone.

Before leaving, he decides to check the sitting room and clear away any remaining evidence of last night's dialogue by candlelight.

He stops dead in the doorway.

Ben is lying asleep on the velvet sofa, fully clothed except for his denim jacket, which lies slumped on the floor with one sleeve reaching up. Or pretending to be asleep: almost at once, he opens his eyes.

Don grips the door handle, lost for words. The intimacy and ease of last night are like a half-remembered dream, inaccessible now. He feels himself changing colour.

'Did you sleep down here?'

'I came down in the night. I couldn't sleep.'

'Have you seen Ina? The housekeeper, I mean.'

'Housekeeper . . .' Ben grins and buries his head in the sofa, then looks back at Don. 'No, I haven't seen anyone.'

He sits up and stretches. Don notices the fine dark hairs on his forearms, and the taut upper arms – extending out of the T-shirt – with their concealed strength. He feels less certain, after all, that Ben didn't spy on him last night.

Ben adds – almost as an afterthought: 'Would you mind if I stay here for a bit? Just a few days?'

Don has noticed a full glass of wine on the arm of the sofa. He thinks of the various ways he could say no.

'Perhaps for a few days – I think there's a spare key I could lend you. Let me have a look.'

*

Fifteen paintings now hang around the Octagon. Alone in the gallery, Don tiptoes in a tight circle as he looks at each picture – noticing, as he always has, how Caravaggio's faces and limbs loom with garish clarity out of fetid shade. Most are smirking, drowsy, effeminate boys. Street dwellers: their mythological guises are a sham. They hold lutes or armfuls of flowers or fruit. The fruit is bright, blooming and ready to rot.

John the Baptist is hugging the neck of a ram, breaking into a laugh. Don comes to a halt. The picture holds his attention longer than the others – induces a new reflection. The play of light and shade (the quality of chiaroscuro he has always found so overblown) is precisely that – a game. As studied and stylised as a hard-edged spotlight. This is theatre, the artist is saying, this is *cinema*, and here are the mechanics – here are the actors. The way the body shines out, puncturing the biblical subject, is all part of it. Not some accident of the artist's grosser nature, but the essence of the thing.

*

It has been three days since Ben arrived at the house, and Ina hasn't commented on the note Don left for her. She seems to have accepted Ben's presence in the same tacit way she accepted his own. She can't *not* have noticed, he thinks. But it's as if the real inhabitants of the House Beautiful are the paintings, statues and artefacts she spends her time polishing and preserving. The human dwellers are mere passers-by.

Ben works irregular hours at the museum. In the evenings, when Don returns to the house, he finds Ben in the sitting room, on the velvet sofa, drawing in a sketchpad or inspecting camera lenses or rifling through shining streams of negatives.

'Will your friend be staying for long, Don?' Ina finally asks as she prepares coffee in the kitchen. The question is casual – conversational.

Don doesn't know. He doesn't want to predict. He feels a frisson of satisfaction to have introduced a character of his own to the House Beautiful – a person not vetted or approved by Val.

Later that morning, he is sitting in the Palladian Library, poring over the list of guests for the evening's private view of 'Caravaggio's Muses', when Val telephones.

'I'll stop by at the house this afternoon, before the reception. Let's meet there. We can enter the fray together!'

Don makes a nonchalant reply, distracted by thoughts of the fray. But afterwards, off the phone, Val's echoing words fill him with dread. Too late, he guesses that Val will stay at the house tonight – in the servant's room.

He fills a tumbler with wine from a bottle he keeps in a chest close to his desk. Ben will be busy all afternoon with last-minute adjustments to the exhibition. But after that . . . Don sips from his glass. He will have to find a way of explaining the situation to Val, or making Ben disappear.

At four o'clock, as soon as his schedule is clear, he leaves the museum – ignoring the activity in the Octagon – and rushes back to the house. With panting relief, he sees that Val's car is not in the drive. He runs up two flights of stairs and gathers Ben's things – clothes, books, sketchpads and Walkman – and carries them in a tumbling pile down the stairs. His own room is too obvious a hiding place, and the cupboard under the stairs is crammed with his belongings from Peterhouse. He looks around for another option. Finally, he tries the doors of the lacquered cabinet on the staircase landing. The interior is a black void. He spills Ben's things inside and shuts the doors.

All that remains is to tell Ben – warn him off, keep him away.

Val arrives at five o'clock sharp, his Mercedes swishing into the drive.

'How lovely to see you,' he says as he sweeps into the hall, preceded by his familiar scent of cologne and tobacco. 'You look wonderful, Don, very dapper. Isn't that my jacket? I can see you're quite at home already.'

Don follows him down the hall. He wonders whether Val knows already about Ben. Has Ina informed him? But Val is overflowing with news from Peterhouse. He leads Don straight into the sitting room and busies himself at the credenza, explaining how the prospect of a new Master has triggered furious discord.

One of Ben's books, *The Brutality of Fact: Interviews with Francis Bacon* by David Sylvester, is lying on the velvet sofa. Don reaches over and slides it beneath a cushion.

'It'll be in the newspapers,' Val says, pouring two glasses of brandy. 'You mark my words. I've never seen such murderous anger.' He passes Don a full glass and holds up his own. 'I've been looking forward to this evening. Your first private view.'

Don lights a cigarette with unsteady fingers. 'I wish I could say the same. This exhibition, Maurice Forster's swansong, whatever you want to call it, is nothing short of an embarrassment.'

Val studies him for a moment, then recovers his smile. 'Drink that quickly, we need to leave. *They're all waiting for you.*'

IO

Hollyhocks crowd around the gateposts of the Brockwell Collection, their heavy buds like satellite dishes clustered on masts. A churn of voices and clinking glass has escaped into the night air.

Don and Val walk up the path and into the lobby. With dismay, Don realises that Ben won't be here. The crowd is affluent, middle-aged, and – he decides from a quick survey – middlebrow. Conversations are playing in a knowing and humorous key. It's the kind of polished society that Val loves. Trays decked with flutes of champagne float past, emanating pale fire. Don manages to scoop a glass.

Val's eyes light up and his lips separate – the tokens of recognition. 'Don, let me introduce you . . .'

His introductions are like assaults, precisely timed and relentless. Just as Don is beginning a conversation, Val propels him on.

'And this is . . .'

'You *must* meet . . .'

'And surely you know . . .'

Val's ammunition is inexhaustible: the Octagon and the outlying galleries throng with important people. Don is carried along on waves of smiling repartee. People joke and he finds himself missing the point or understanding too late. Every so often, he catches sight of Maud. She slips with ease between the groups, her silver jewellery flashing in time with the lenses of her glasses, her intonation rising or falling as the moment demands.

Val whirls Don towards a young couple. They embrace Val fondly while Don holds back. The woman has dark brown eyes and her hair, also dark, falls in loose undulations. Her dress is a plunging column of silvery blue that leaves her slender arms exposed. She catches Don's eye and holds it unerringly until he looks away.

The man is regaling Val with some hilarious tale. He looks familiar – tall, athletic, with a broad smile and dark blond hair flowing back in waves. There is an air of easy virtue about him – the semblance of somebody unbruised by life, free of cynicism or calculation.

'Don, this is Michael Ross,' says Val.

'Delighted,' says Michael. His teeth are almost flawless. He wears a navy-blue blazer. His trousers are daringly white. Don looks into his eyes and feels that he is encountering a spectre of decency and strength.

'And Anna Ross,' says Val with a wave of the fingers.

Don takes their hands in turn and is delighted and honoured and looks forward, of course, to knowing them better.

This, then, is Michael Ross – soon to be his capable deputy. Don has a face to put to the name. But the face itself is more than a little familiar. It has a sturdy, Apollonian handsomeness.

'Have we met before, perhaps in Cambridge?'

'Unlikely,' says Michael with good humour. 'I studied in California, at Berkeley, and went straight from there to the Frick.'

This accounts for the American twang in his British accent – an educated accent, like Don's, but less fussy, less fastidious.

'Yes, indeed', Don says, fastidiously.

'But I've met you many times, so to speak, on the page. Your work on Palladio—'

'Oh, you're very kind,' Don interrupts, not waiting for Michael to elaborate.

Still the wife's eyes rest on him. Without looking back, Don senses her attention.

'And *Anna* is a cellist!' interjects Val, as if this is the real point of interest – the fundamental truth that their circumlocutions have been leading to.

'Well – yes. I'm just doing occasional performances for now,' she says with a hesitant smile.

'I understand you were in the New York Philharmonic?' Don says.

'That's right.' Her eyes widen. 'I was.'

'You'll find other things,' says Michael. The remark seems a little quick, a touch overconfident. The uncertainty returns to Anna's eyes.

'Do you come to the Brockwell often, Mrs Ross?' Don asks.

Anna laughs, casting off her reserve. 'I can't say I do. We've only been in London three weeks. Why, do you?'

Don marvels at the strangeness of her question. He is sure he is being mocked, and yet there is something beguiling about her failure to be serious.

'We'd love to have you for dinner, Professor Lamb,' says Michael. 'Perhaps after my interview for the job.'

'A mere formality!' Val sings.

'Call me Don. I would be delighted. Where are you living?'

'We've just moved to Craxton Road,' says Anna.

'Then we are neighbours.'

His mind is whirring. Clearly the Rosses have moved to London on the promise of Michael receiving the position. Anna has had to sacrifice hers. And they have been here three weeks already. He perceives Val's guiding hand. But before he can ponder the matter further, quiet spreads through the galleries.

He hears a rhythmic thudding and creaking. Through a break in the crowd, he catches sight of the ancient figure of Maurice Forster, on leave from his nursing home, driving a walking frame with feeble determination across the marble tiles of the Octagon. Forster appears to have shrunk to the size of a child: his felt suit hangs from him like a costume out of a dressing-up box.

On either side, Maud and a woman in a nurse's tunic guide him – by creaks and thuds – to the centre of the room. An insane grin has spread across Maud's face.

It has been decided that the old man – too forgetful to make a speech – will read his favourite passage from Shakespeare by way of a welcoming address. Forster pulls a ragged piece of paper from his jacket. He commences, in a frail voice, to recite.

Easing his way to the front of the crowd, Don manages to pick out the words.

The king doth keep his revels here tonight.
Take heed the queen come not within his sight;
For Oberon is passing fell and wrath
Because that she, as her attendant hath
A lovely boy stolen from an Indian king:
She never had so sweet a changeling.

Forster reads with painful, faltering effort. As line follows line, Don experiences a creeping – profound – attack of déjà vu. It isn't simply that he recognises the extract. The words are hyper-charged. They sink into him like a portent.

And jealous Oberon would have the child
Knight of his train, to trace the forests wild.
But she perforce withholds the lovèd boy,
Crowns him with flowers, and makes him all her joy.

His mind rushes back to the sight of the horrible creature in the white suit, accosting him on the bus and pursuing him into the museum.

He is barely listening by the time Maud steps in front of the trembling Forster and delivers words of thanks and praise. She concludes with an expression of heartfelt gratitude to the exhibition's chief donor, Sir Ronald Braun, sadly indisposed and unable to be present. There is an outbreak of applause and Maurice Forster is escorted from the room.

The crowd spreads out again and voices multiply into a spirited babble. Hardly anyone is looking at the exhibition – too much conversation is to be had. Don finds himself away from Val's guiding hand, alone finally, in front of *Boy Bitten by a Lizard*. By leaning in to examine the tips of the boy's flexing fingers, he makes an oasis for himself – a protective bubble where he won't be disturbed, at least for a minute.

But almost at once there's a voice in his ear, not much more than a whisper.

'He looks like a right tart.'

He springs back from the painting.

'A right tart,' Ben repeats, louder.

Don frowns but knows that a smile is breaking through. 'Please lower your voice – this is a private view. There are people . . . I didn't think you'd be here.'

'Doesn't seem very private to me.' Ben turns back to the painting. 'I think he was more than just a muse. Look at his eyes. The way his shirt falls off his shoulder. You can tell.' He looks at Don with gleeful eyes. 'Can't you?'

Don draws close. 'I suppose so. But listen, I need to tell you something. It's about you staying at the house tonight—'

Ben's attention has switched sideways. His humorous glint has vanished. Don turns and sees, with a surge of panic, that Val has appeared.

'Have we met?' Val asks with an icy smile.

Don feels his own smile hardening into a grimace. Did Val hear the tail end of what he was saying? He wonders if he should reveal, right here, this second, that Ben has come to stay. A strangled laugh breaks out of him.

Val's question – *have we met?* – lingers in his eyes as he glances at Don and then back at Ben. He assesses the situation – speculating, surmising, disapproving, all in the space of a second. Even in his paralysis, Don is struck by the sight of them together: generations apart, mutually hostile and yet uncannily alike. It's as if the older man is looking askance at his spry younger self.

Ben looks away from Val without answering. 'You should have called the show "Caravaggio's Bumboys",' he says to Don. 'That's what they were, after all.' He shrugs and wanders back into the crowd.

Val watches Ben as he goes. 'Whoever that was, I suspect there are guests here worthier of your attention.' He peers at Don. 'What is it? Are you all right?'

'He shouldn't be here,' Don mutters. 'He's one of the art handlers.'

'Jesus Christ. Get a grip, Don.' Val squints into the middle distance. 'Ah, Letizia!' He sails forward, his hands extended like battering rams capped with jewels.

Don follows, embarrassment having turned to anger – but whether the anger is with Ben or Val or himself, he can't decide. Turning his head, he sees that Ben has begun to talk with Michael Ross. They're laughing. His heart shrinks by an infinitesimal degree. Anna Ross is with them, but as she listens (or pretends to listen) she scans the room and her eyes meet his. She is, he guesses, in her mid-thirties. Possibly older. The blue of her dress gives a bluish tint to her dark hair.

Val beckons him into a circle of beaming guests. The way that they call him *Professor* is grating. Tonight, he feels the obverse of his old self. There is a lull in the conversation. Don looks around the circle of faces. It dawns on him that everyone expects him to speak. He stands there in tense embarrassment.

'I'm speaking on the radio tomorrow morning,' Val finally remarks, addressing the group.

'Indeed?' says Don.

'Yes, for *Shifting Perspectives* with Robin Hands. Haven't you been on it yourself? We're discussing post-war British architecture. The concrete revolution, to be exact. The Festival Hall, the Hayward Gallery, the Barbican Centre. When did Modernism become a period style? Fascinating stuff!'

'Oh, how marvellous,' somebody drawls.

'Carbuncles,' says a man in a three-piece suit.

'I assume you're appearing as the voice of scepticism,' Don says.

'Why scepticism, Don?' Val allows his eyes to dance around their small audience.

'Only because you're one of the great defenders of the classical tradition.' Don attempts a laugh.

'You think that because I admire Palladio, I must automatically disdain concrete?' Val's expression is one of perfect innocence.

Don clears his throat. He blushes. Val has attacked those very buildings in the past, he is sure of it.

Val stretches out a finger and pats Don's lapel. 'So much classical beauty is to be found in the places we least expect – in the buildings we might instinctively recoil from. The Barbican Centre, for me, is an ancient Greek citadel – a Mycenaean palace stripped down to a Brutalist shell. Walk across its courtyards and you're in the home of Agamemnon – megaron, propylon and all.'

There is a murmur of laughter and approval.

'Absolute carbuncles,' says the man in the suit.

Don moves away, perplexed and furious. Valentine Black, the arch neoclassicist, defending concrete monstrosities: it makes no sense. Val is lying. Either that or reality is wearing a new face. He finishes his champagne in a gulp.

As the crowd begins to thin, he steps into the circular chamber – accessed through a narrow doorway – that is the burial place of Montague Brockwell. Ben is alone beside the marble sarcophagus.

'Listen, Ben. Val is coming back to the house tonight – his house. You won't be able to stay.'

Ben looks up, roused from his reverie. He appears thin and ghostlike in the dark tomb.

'Val . . . Your friend? I don't think he likes me.'

'Well, it's hardly a surprise. What on earth made you say that?'

'Say what?'

'What you said in front of Professor Black! About Caravaggio's boys.'

'Oh, *that*. Just to see how you'd react, I guess.' Ben's seriousness is dissipating. He leans back against the sarcophagus, spreading his fingers over the marble lid. 'Come on, Don. Don't pretend to be outraged. So it's his house, is it? Are those red pyjamas his, too?'

Don takes a step forwards. So Ben did spy on him that first night.

Ben stands up straight. Don can smell wine on his breath. For a second, they are almost close enough for their faces to touch. Then Ben sways back a little and smiles.

'Don't pretend you care,' he whispers.

Don steps back, his head swimming.

'I'll sleep on the sofa downstairs,' Ben says.

'No, I don't think—'

But Ben has spun around and exited the tomb, leaving Don alone with the remains of Montague Brockwell. Gloomily, he returns to the brighter light of the adjoining gallery. There are farewells to say. And then . . .

The crowd is thinning. Val is standing at the entrance, bestowing parting words to the guests.

'I know, Mrs Penrose, wasn't it *moving*? And can you believe Maurice will be ninety next spring?'

Don comes and stands beside him.

'I take it you'll be staying at the house tonight?'

'Oh no,' Val replies as he waves at the exiting stream. 'I always stay at Albany before a radio appearance – John Richardson's flat. So much more convenient.' He bends forward to kiss a patroness. 'Listen, Don' – he drops his volume, placing an arm behind Don's back – 'I wasn't going to mention it this evening, but it's been playing on my mind. I understand there was a disturbance here the other week. That the *police* were called.'

'Yes – a vagrant wandered in and made a scene. The Venus statuettes suffered some damage, but they've gone to Mr Price for restoration. Very unfortunate, but – well, nothing to worry about.'

'Not quite nothing. Sir Ronald Braun was furious. I had to intervene to persuade him not to withdraw his bequest.'

'You know Braun?'

'He's an old friend.' Val hesitates – he seems to have more to say. He sighs and lowers his voice further. 'People seem to think the . . . *intruder* was somehow connected with you.'

'But that's nonsense. I'd never seen him in my life. He started harassing me on the bus and followed me here.'

'Of course, Don. I don't doubt it.' Val glances around the room. 'But you are responsible for this place now. Its reputation rests on your shoulders.'

'For heaven's sake, Val, I told you—'

But just at that moment, Don is forced to break off to say goodbye to a pair of guests, and Val slips away like a character whose part has been played.

Don's dreams are garbled and grotesque. They resound with the words *megaron* and *propylon*. He wakes very late, his head blazing with pain and his heart beating fast. At once he hears Val's voice on the radio, which he left on overnight. *Shifting Perspectives* is airing.

'The Hayward, after all, is a beautiful piece of rosewood joinery. Pure Arts and Crafts!'

'I'm surprised to hear you say that, Professor Black,' says Robin Hands chummily. 'I'd always thought of you as a champion of traditional architecture.'

Don pictures the host – the architecture of his hair, the ochre tan, the glinting lenses of his spectacles. He turns into his pillow and closes his eyes.

'And you thought correctly,' Val replies. 'But I am – if you will – a true ancient Greek rather than a narrow neoclassicist. I worship beauty in all its forms.'

Nausea sweeps into Don's throat.

*

When he is shown into the Summer Refectory, Michael Ross looks just as he did at the private view. Everything about him exudes a glow, from his bronzed hair and face down to his sparkling teeth.

Michael takes a seat on the opposite side of the table from Don, who is flanked by Maud and Bill. He sits away from the French-polished surface, at an angle, casually.

'Have you been on holiday?' is the first question Don can think to ask.

'No,' Michael replies, and then – sensing Don's meaning – 'this is only a tennis tan. What weather we've had. I've never known a spring like it!'

His demeanour is bright and candid – it stops just short of being cocksure.

'Perhaps I might ask about your experience of restoration,' begins Bill.

Michael spreads his hands on the table. 'One of my keenest interests!'

Don is lost in recollection. Tennis – that's where he first saw Michael, in Belair Park. He remembers now the sight of Michael charging across the court as the ball swerved from reach. It makes sense, of course. The Rosses have recently moved to Dulwich. But the realisation brings no relief.

'And if I may ask you about your time at the Frick,' Maud

is saying, 'could you describe a situation in which you deployed the resources of a team to' – she looks down at her notes – 'manage and resolve a problem?'

Michael flashes and glimmers like a brass statue in the midday sun. His reply is polished and robust. The interview proceeds, with Don's concentration flitting between the Summer Refectory and the tennis court in the park. Swipes, lunges, passionate dashes . . .

When the time comes for Don to pose his questions, he snaps into life and demands that Michael expound on the progression of the Renaissance into the Baroque. Just when and how did the shift occur? Is *evolution* or *revolution* the appropriate term?

Smoothing his hair, Michael declares that he prefers to think of it in terms of *involution*. There follows a long exchange about Poussin and the merits of a poststructuralist analysis. Michael is fluent and unflappable. With dismay, Don sees that he is weathering the interrogation with ease, relishing the back-and-forth as if it were another game of tennis. But then the appointment was a foregone conclusion, just as Val said.

It is past nine o'clock as he enters the house. Closing the front door, he thinks he can hear singing – different voices in rhythmic interplay.

As he walks along the hall, he perceives low conspiratorial murmuring coming from the kitchen. Ina laughs – an unfamiliar sound. He walks into the kitchen and finds her and Ben together at the table. They look up and stop talking. Between them are tumblers of wine: they have opened a bottle from the rack.

He stays in the doorway and watches them, unable to quell the jealousy that has kindled in him.

'Don!' Ben cries out. The excitement in his voice is irresistible.

Don smiles. 'Don't let me interrupt.'

'Ina's been telling me about the Olympics.'

'Ah yes,' Don says. 'The summer of '84.'

'And she knows all about Goldsmiths College. The new art scene.'

'Come and have a drink, Don,' says Ina. 'I've ordered a take-away. Jambalaya.'

To his mild surprise, she begins to prepare a cigarette on the gingham tablecloth, pulling shredded tobacco out of a cloth bag and sprinkling it along an oblong tab of paper. She startles him by pushing a spare seat towards him with her leg.

'I have a book to finish,' he says with a wracked smile. 'It won't write itself.'

'They'll give you another sword at this rate,' Ina says with a delicate twinkle in her blue eyes. 'We can all go back to California.'

'I'll come!' Ben pours more wine into the glasses and looks from Ina to Don with a smile that's somewhere between innocent and mischievous. 'We can get a house in the hills. It'll be like living in another dimension. Hockney's *Bigger Splash* . . .'

Don walks out of the kitchen with Ben's absurd fantasy bouncing through his mind. He feels impatient – annoyed. And yet the short conversation has sparked some deeper emotion. What has he created here? Ina must have told Val about Ben by now, he thinks, as he passes the stern Regency faces in the hall. But Val has said nothing: he is like a gambler deciding when to enter the game, hedging his bets.

He notices again the gas canister at the bottom of the stairs. Is it possible, he wonders, that Ina hasn't said a word after all?

Around ten o'clock, as he works at his desk, he hears the front door closing below. Ben is on his way out: Don sees him crossing the driveway and turning right in the direction of the bus stop. With the Caravaggio exhibition open, Ben is no longer needed at the Brockwell Collection. He seems relieved to be free of the museum. He has more time for his art, for life beyond Dulwich.

Don works into the night, hammering the typewriter in a two-fingered frenzy. He forces himself to the end of each sentence like a man blundering down a dark passageway. Hours later, he sits back and exhales. The house and the night outside are silent. With slow movements he stands and pulls off his shoes, then slithers into bed. His heart throbs with a dull pain, but his brain is empty: thought is dead.

Before long, morning intrudes on the room. He wakes and checks his watch – six o'clock. He crawls out of bed and stumbles over to the desk. Without sitting down, he reads the pages he wrote in the night. His hands grip the back of the chair and his knuckles turn white. The writing is terrible. Hectoring, repetitive, pompous . . . he trembles at the idea that it will ever see the light of day. He tries to tear the pile in half, but the paper is too thick. It buckles in his hands.

He treads out of his room onto the landing. He has an intuition that Ben is still gone. He tiptoes upstairs to the servant's room and finds, sure enough, that the door is open and the bed untouched. Ben's things have reappeared in various places – a pile of clothes, sketchpads and pencils, *Interviews with Francis Bacon*, a splayed toothbrush – assurances that he will be back. Don brings his face close to the undented pillow and tries to pick up a trace.

He goes back down to his room and surveys his own scattered attributes, so different from Ben's – the colour reproductions, neat jottings, books pinned open at critical pages and stacks of typewritten sheets, all spreading across the floor from the nodal point of the desk.

The phone on his bedside table suddenly drills through the silence.

'I'm sorry to call so early, Don. I suppose I've woken you.'

'Goodness no,' says Don, pulling the phone cord back to the desk and feeling the quick tightening in his chest that a call from Val always now prompts. 'I've been busy working on my book.'

Does Val know yet? Has Ina told him? Hastily, Don begins to change the ribbon on his typewriter with one hand as he holds the phone to his ear.

'Well I hear that Michael Ross performed *magnificently* in his interview.'

'I don't know who told you that.'

'Michael did, of course.'

'I see. Could Michael be suffering from an inflated opinion of himself?'

'All he suffers from,' Val professes benignly, 'is the confidence of a young man at the height of his powers.'

'He's of the new generation, I'll say that much. He twisted a discussion about Poussin's *Triumph of David* round to modern French philosophy. Apparently the painting is about temporality – no, *temporalities*. Nothing to do with the victory of the shepherd boy over Goliath. Who knew?'

'Ha!' exclaims Val with mock disgust. 'I remember when Cambridge awarded an honorary doctorate to that dreadful man Jacques Derrida. I added my name to the letter of protest. Still, you must remember, Michael is barely past thirty. All the brilliant young minds in the world are caught up in this continental sophistry. Believe me, he's a man after your heart. He did a *stunning* show at the Frick on the hidden radicalism of the classical male nude. Heartbreaking!'

'A man after *your* heart, then.'

'A man after our mutual heart.'

Our mutual heart – Don turns the phrase over like a marble.

'I had a funny thought, the other day,' he says. 'I imagined this house as my own home.'

'Don,' Val says, softly and firmly. 'It is your home now.'

'I know, but it was more than that. I imagined a family was living here, like my own family, from the past. A father and a mother and a child – a boy. And I was the father, and then at other times I was the son, growing up in the place. I was all of them, the woman too. It was like – I don't know – an alternative life. Multiple alternative lives.'

Over the phone line, Don hears an intake of breath and a long sigh.

'Really,' Val says at last. 'I thought that you were safe from that kind of thing.'

Don begins to laugh. 'I am. It wasn't real. In my dream, the house was like a stage.' Or, he supposes privately, like Ben's vision of Los Angeles – a testing ground for other realities.

'The house is real,' Val says with sudden seriousness. 'And your place in it. What could be more real than that?'

*

It is early in the evening. Ben is on the velvet sofa – half sitting, half lying – and drawing in a sketchpad. Don has brought his typescript downstairs. It lies heavily in his lap.

The book is still staking its claim, if only just. He makes periodic efforts to annotate the pages – a footnote here, a subclause there, a careful sharpening of expression – just one word substituted and the meaning breaks through like a shaft of light. But he feels unable to write new passages. Mostly he listens to the scratching and scribbling of Ben's pencil.

Ben smokes rollups one after the other. Their smell makes Don nostalgic, as if their present tense – here, together in this room – is already the past.

'Where did you go the other night?' he asks.

'Soho. With the Goldsmiths crowd. You should join us some time.'

Don thinks back to the scene he witnessed at the Crown and Greyhound, and tries to imagine Ben among that exuberant group again. For a second, he feels like a guest on the threshold of Ben's life, detained by his own reserve.

'Thank you, Don,' Ben says, continuing to draw.

'What for?'

'For letting me stay here.'

Don says nothing. A hidden reservoir of feeling has opened up, and he suddenly wants to change the subject.

'What have you been working on?'

Ben flips the sketchbook closed and smiles.

'I've been stealing things,' he says. 'Stealing pieces of other works.'

'What pieces?'

'Anything, really. I've started making collages out of other people's paintings. I take photographs. Sometimes I turn objects from paintings into pieces of sculpture. Like Francis Bacon's warped mattress – you know, the one with a woman dissolving on top of it?'

'I'm trying to remember it,' says Don.

'Or that amazing structure in Antonello da Messina's painting of Saint Jerome, the desk and bookcase. I turn them into real objects, plaster casts, plywood models. Sculptural fictions, I call them.'

Don listens, ingesting these mysterious details. Bacon, Antonello, sculptural fictions.

'I've been looking at this house for ideas,' continues Ben. 'It's a strange place.'

'Strange?'

'It wasn't made for living in. Everything's been so – *carefully* placed. It's a museum.'

Don casts his eyes over the furniture, the wallpaper, the closely packed spines of the books – bands of tan leather and gold tooling, a complete set of the *Journal of the Warburg and Courtauld Institutes* – and he marvels again at the fact that Val could have amassed all this. The paintings are good enough to be in a museum. The drawings, too – including that exquisite study of a dead cat by Chardin.

'Val has some very fine pieces, if that's what you mean.'

'What I mean is, it seems like a set-up. The whole thing's unreal. The only *real* part's the garden – Christ, have you been out there?'

Don stands up, afflicted by contradictory emotions.

'If this house is a ruse, then it's a very elaborate one. But I suppose you're unused to the tastes of Valentine Black. This place embodies his view of art – his sensibility. Decorous yet decorative, tempered by an inner restraint.'

He rests his hand on top of a small bronze by Auguste Rodin which stands at the centre of the room, on top of a Pompeiian tripod.

Ben is watching him from the sofa. Don keeps his hand on the bronze – beginning to hold his pose unnaturally, like a television performer who knows the cameras are rolling. Ben stands and touches the ends of Don's fingers with his own. He lifts them – playfully prises them – off the Rodin. Don tenses. What would Ben do, he wonders, if he reached out and touched him back – stroked his neck . . .

Ben breaks the livewire between their fingers and looks out of the window. The view is photographically still – the shaded driveway, the road beyond. Then a car purrs past. Its headlights send elongated beams rippling across the stucco leaves of the cornicing.

Ben laughs suddenly. 'Tempered by an inner restraint. That's *you*, Don. Tempered and trapped in this house. Come on, why don't we go out?'

'Out where?'

'The Crown and Greyhound.' Ben sits down on the sofa, bouncing gently as he lands, and stretches back to grab his leather jacket from the floor. 'Why not?'

The teasing question – *Why not?* – announces its own solution. His book has stalled – he might as well admit it. His mental powers are at a low ebb. They will return, of course, but why force it?

In a single elegant movement, Ben stretches out his feet and wraps them around Don's leg. He is wearing red socks.

'Let's go.'

Feeling the grip of Ben's feet, Don waits for the call of Tiepolo – that familiar call to order – but he hears nothing except for a faint crackling in his ears, like distant fire.

They walk through the Village and sit outside the pub at the table where they first spoke to each other. Don buys a bottle of Beaujolais. The last trace of daylight is fading from the sky.

'Tell me about your pictures again,' Ben says. 'Tell me about that colour – Tiepolo Blue.'

Don lights a cigarette and outlines the master plan of his book once more. It is so much easier in the darkening warmth, outside the pub.

'The way you look at those pictures on your desk,' Ben says, 'measuring the sky . . . You're always looking away from the *people*. The actors, the story, the *life*. You're looking into the background, at the stuff that's not supposed to matter. Clouds and air. It's like looking at the Kennedy assassination film and thinking how blue the sky is, or how green the grass is next to the pavements – the sidewalks, I mean – while the president's being shot in the head.'

Don is beginning to enjoy Ben's random points of reference. The day of Kennedy's death rises through his memory. He sees himself as a boy, sitting in the front room in Poole with his parents, around the radio, while a ferry drifted across the harbour beyond the window. His mother was seated in the corner, stifling sobs.

'But what would the assassination *be* – in our minds, in our memories – without that video?' he demands. 'And what would that *video* be without the blue of the American sky, that mid-twentieth-century blue, or without the pink of Mrs Kennedy's dress? Or, for that matter, the peculiar perspective of the film – elevated and oblique, a dress-circle view of the motorcade? These are not minor details!'

He reaches for his glass. He has landed on his metier, colour and depth of space. He is about to launch on a fresh excursus – he is raising his hands as he prepares to speak – when something about Ben's expression silences him.

'Have you ever been in love?' Ben asks, watching him with solemn intrigue.

Don drinks a long draught of wine, then another, as he considers Ben's enquiry. He knows, and yet doesn't know, what to say. The question is offhand, off-topic. Ben watches him, perhaps not requiring a reply.

'I have never had a lover.'

'That isn't the same thing.'

Don shrugs and drinks. Ben is still watching him, tracking his thoughts. Don wants to throw the question back. Has Ben ever been in love, and who would Ben fall in love with – a man, or a woman, or both? With Don?

Ben's thoughts have moved on. He plunges into another stream of conversation, saying something about stealing as an art form. As if to make his point, he reaches out and takes Don's glass – steals it straight from his hand – and downs the contents.

They smoke and drink until they're the last people outside the pub. The street is dark and deserted. The trees and pointed rooftops are featureless masses against the clear night sky.

At closing time, they wander back through a silent Dulwich Village, arguing happily about the role of beauty in art. Ben has taken their half-empty bottle of wine from the table. They pass it back and forth as they make their way along Montcalm Road.

Ben has stopped on the pavement, in the middle of a statement. He holds out both arms, the bottle swinging from one hand, and breaks into a grin.

'Art doesn't need to be beautiful!' he cries out. 'Art should be deranged!' He looks at Don with imploring excitement. His face is animated by an interior, pulsing light. His eyes refuse to move. They are locked on Don, waiting.

Don meets the gaze of his new friend. Art, beauty – the time for scholarly correctives has passed. This is his reality now – life after Cambridge. *This*. He takes a step towards Ben, brings his face close, his lips . . .

Ben pulls away, by just a couple of inches, and bursts out laughing. It is a ghastly sound. His eyes are wide, still, but with amused surprise.

'What are you doing, Don?' Ben's voice is quiet, but deafeningly lucid in the motionless night. 'Come on. It's late.'

Ben walks on ahead, with the wine bottle swaying from his fingertips. Don watches him recede by five, six, seven steps. Cold devastation steals over him, all across his body, like the hemlock that Socrates drank to kill himself – a slow, incremental death. He laughs artificially to break up the horror. He walks on behind Ben, sensing the dark depthless shapes of the houses and trees closing in on him, not wanting to catch up.

PART II

11

In the early summer, Dulwich feels different. It is no longer the sedate suburb it was when he arrived – more an idyllic garden in which the houses and shops are scenic follies. He notices the detail and variety of things: the horse chestnuts bulging with leaves, the picket fences that border the pavements (white as cricket screens), the strips of manicured turf at the roadsides, and the mock-Elizabethan houses with their pastel-pale pebbledash.

His pictures and notes remain laid out on the desk in the bay window. Tiepolo's skies cover the surrounding floor in the same complex formation. But his attitude towards his book has changed. The old obsessive enthusiasm has disappeared.

'Inevitable, Don, absolutely inevitable,' Val insists, when Don admits on the phone that progress has slowed. 'You find yourself in new climes. So what if the book waits a while longer? It may be the better for it.'

Perfectly wise, Don thinks. So what, indeed. Yet something about the pronouncement unnerves him. New climes . . .

The House Beautiful is preying on his mind. In the sum of its parts, it is just that, beautiful. *Exquisite.* Everything about the place – the furniture, pictures and objects – is so right, so unimpeachable. A model of decorum. Yet there is a lurking germ: a discordant note, almost imperceptible, nothing quite as blatant as that gas cylinder on the stairs. The shimmering lacquered cabinet, the champagne tint of the oval mirror, the plaster bust of Antinous with its rosary necklace (like black beetles in single file) – there is something wayward in these charming details. He tries to define it whenever he catches glimpses.

On every ascent or descent of the stairs, he looks at the black cabinet on the half-landing. In the gleaming surface, his reflection dissolves into dabs and flecks, scattered like petals on the surface of a pond.

He begins to wonder if Ben was right about the house. He has the growing sense that the place has somehow been contrived – made up like a stage set to disarm him. Val has kept it for decades as a kind of shrine. *How little you knew*, the older man seems to be saying, through the silent media of French polish and finely cracked paint. *How little you knew about any of this.*

'You know, Val, the longer I spend on this book, the less grasp I have of it,' he says. 'The end point is like a mirage that keeps jumping away from me.'

'Fatigue Don, fatigue,' Val surmises from the other end of the line. 'And who can blame you? New burdens, new—'

'Climes?'

'Exactly.'

But is it just that? Tiepolo's towering, populated skies are beautiful still – perhaps all the more beautiful when he looks at them casually, without his accustomed acuity, passing through the bedroom with other things on his mind – or nothing on his mind at all. He prefers the overall effect of the outspread pictures – prefers this to the nagging pedantry of a paragraph, an argument, a chapter. Does the artist's trip to Milan in 1730 matter, really matter, as much as he thought?

Tiepolo's colours are more of a lure to him now than his own thesis. Sometimes he thinks that he sees the painted skies in real life. As he looks above the gabled rooftops of Dulwich, the blue air is fresco-faint.

*

It is Michael Ross's first day. There is a buzz of excitement at the Brockwell Collection – the mood seeps through the galleries and offices. Not even Don is immune. He brushes his velvet jacket – Val's jacket – with both hands and walks from the Palladian Library to the Summer Refectory, knowing that Michael will be present for the weekly meeting.

He enters to see Michael standing with a group of staff and looking more lustrous than ever. The staff are laughing at something he has said. Michael's eyes penetrate the dim room like search beams, finding their way to Don.

'Professor!' He bounces forward with an outstretched hand. He isn't wearing a jacket. His sleeves are rolled up to reveal forearms as sturdy and browned as fresh-baked loaves.

'*Don*, please,' Don appeals, conscious of the attentions of the others. 'Call me Don.' He waves everyone to their seats.

Don watches Michael intermittently during the meeting, intrigued. He observes the way in which Michael listens to Maud Berenson, with his chin in his hand and an expression of ardent concentration on his face, as she reads a report on visitor numbers. When she has finished, Michael sits back and plants his hands on the table.

'These numbers foretell a magnificent summer,' he says.

Maud's lips retract and her eyes light up. 'Indeed!' she replies, almost breathless with pleasure.

'Very well, very well,' says Don, more genial than usual – Michael's presence is casting its golden light upon them all. 'Bill, let's hear your conservation report, please.'

Bill delivers an update on the restoration of the Poussin, currently at the workshop of Inigo Price – the plan of action is more vigorous than first proposed. But the real transformation is in Bill's manner. Gone are the trembling and cowering. He works his way through the plan with doe-eyed humility, like an old artisan explaining the fine points of his trade to a royal visitor. He kneads his hands while he speaks and looks up, every so often, for approbation. He looks to Michael Ross.

At the end of the meeting, Don rises to his feet and – as usual

– notes his own reflection in the surface of the table. He is about to leave when Michael comes over.

'Don,' he says – *Professor* has already been dropped. 'Anna and I would love to have you over for dinner. When would be good?'

Don feels Michael's warm glow radiating into him. He is powerless against it. But too much familiarity won't do.

'I shall check my diary, Michael,' he says. 'How very kind.'

*

'Ladies and gentlemen, may I have your attention please? Before you lies a pageant of art – a *cornucopia* of paintings and drawings, bronze bodies and marble busts (I must request that you don't touch) – Giordanos and Guercinos, Lelys and Zoffanys, Roubiliacs, Riberas, Tiepolos. Welcome, ladies and gentlemen, to the Brockwell Collection!'

It is Friday morning. Ten or so visitors have assembled in the Montague Room, having noticed a sign in the lobby when they entered the museum:

For the Director's Tour – a personal view of the Brockwell Collection by Professor D. Lamb – please gather in the Montague Room at eleven o'clock.

They follow the Director through the museum. He strides ahead, pointing and professing. Only in the Octagon – the setting of the Caravaggio exhibition – does he fall inexplicably silent, passing through without a word.

For fifteen minutes, Don expounds on periods and styles, on the curious place of British art within the grand European picture, on the deceptive charms of provincialism, on the rise of the mercantile classes . . .

'Montague Brockwell, who amassed this collection, was the epitome of the new middle class of the eighteenth century. A merchant who built his fortune on the sugar trade. And what riches that fortune bequeathed!' Don gestures at the walls. 'These smaller works by Tiepolo are the museum's special claim to fame. And this bust of Alexander Pope by Roubiliac, sculpted when the poet was suffering from consumption – *well*, it possesses such a haunting likeness that my predecessor (the great Maurice Forster) was moved to speak to it. That's right. He truly believed he was communing with the author of *The Rape of the Lock*.'

Don leads them on, past a picture of two small boys on a country road. One of the boys chews a lump of bread; the other is lying on the ground and smiling at his companion.

'Urchins,' he sings with a wave of the hand. 'John Ruskin described them as *ragged and vicious vagrants*. And who could disagree? Please, this way.'

He maintains a relentless pace.

'I wish to end this morning's survey,' he declares, turning on his heel, 'with *this* picture.'

He has stopped in front of a painting by J. M. W. Turner, depicting a ship caught in a storm.

'The principal interest of this picture is the *sea*.' Don rises on tiptoes as he enunciates. 'It is the noblest sea that Turner ever painted. The artist imagines the aftermath of a tempest. The waves are still restive – see how they rise in vast and mighty ridges! The storm clouds are receding in a slanting bank upon the horizon, dyed incarnadine by the setting sun.'

He is impressed, even startled, by his own lambent eloquence. As he speaks, he notices that Michael has wandered into the gallery and is standing at the back of the group, fractionally apart. He seems poised to interrupt – he is raising a finger – but Don silences him with a mild frown.

'This is the painting,' he says solemnly, 'upon which Turner's immortality rests. Ideal, pure and truthful.'

Don smiles and closes his eyes to signify the conclusion of the talk. He opens them to a chorus of non-reaction. He is about to take his leave, but one member of the audience is coming forward with intent.

'Don – forgive me, Professor Lamb.'

'Yes, Michael?'

'The subject of the painting – surely – is the massacre of African slaves.'

Don turns to look at the picture. It is the first time he has looked properly, beyond rapid glances. He feels his heart contract. It is a picture by Turner, just as he said, and shows a stormy sea . . . but it is not the picture he thought. A vessel lurches in the mid-distance, and in the foreground, hands and feet rise above the waves. Scattered bodies are embroiled in a shoal of monstrous fish. He is looking at *The Slave Ship*, Turner's exposure of the slave trade – dead and sickened men have been fed to the sea.

'Ah yes, Michael, that is the case . . .'

The gallery must have been rehung without his knowledge – the pictures swapped around. He is about to confess his mistake. But as he opens his lips, Michael is already walking through the group, taking command.

'It's an indictment of human trafficking,' Michael asserts, looking eagerly at each of the visitors as he speaks. 'That's the true point of interest.'

'An indictment, yes,' Don interrupts, turning back to the picture. 'A tragic episode subsumed within the larger scene.'

'You speak as if it were a minor detail,' Michael says.

'No detail in Turner's art is insignificant,' Don retaliates, wondering if anyone can detect the strangled quality of his voice. 'No one can deny the barbarity of the scene, the inhumanity – I knew that our visitors would see for themselves the gruesome truth! But the point of this picture' – he grasps for some slender thread of meaning – 'the point is that *Nature* is indifferent to the slaves' predicament. Nature doesn't care. Nature's indifference heightens the human tragedy!'

Satisfied with his new interpretation, he wills Michael to allow him the final word.

'Nature doesn't care, but how about the artist?' Michael persists. 'Surely *he* cared deeply?'

Don is aware that he is blushing furiously. He is desperate to snatch back control of the hijacked lecture but feels that Michael has taken his authority away, confiscated it like a bag of sweets to be redistributed – with smiling magnanimity – among their visitors. He gives his cufflink a pincer-like squeeze.

'The implications of this picture extend to the museum itself,' Michael continues. He is now standing on the opposite side of the painting from Don, addressing the group. 'Montague Brockwell became rich off the back of slave labour. It's a dark truth that we have to face as custodians of the collection.' He smooths back his leonine hair. 'Anyhow, excuse me – I've rather butted in. Please, Don, carry on.'

'Not at all, Michael. We should all be thanking you. You've brought the tour to a resounding conclusion.'

Twenty minutes after Don has returned to his study, his heart is still beating fiercely.

*

Ben is still living at the house, still coming and going. He and Ina have grown closer. Don finds them together in the kitchen in the early evenings, chatting away and smoking rollups. Contemporary art seems to be a shared enthusiasm, and the films of Pasolini.

It has been more than a fortnight since Don and Ben went to the Crown and Greyhound, and neither of them has mentioned what happened. Don hasn't been able to expel the memory. The image of Ben's face and the sound of his laughter – breaking through the silence of the night – are like ghosts that refuse to be exorcised.

He senses – hopes – that Ben has forgiven him. They have settled back into something close to their old familiarity, and yet Don senses the presence of a barrier – a subtle reciprocal reticence – where there wasn't one before.

It is Sunday morning, and Don is watching Ben from over the top of a book. Sunlight streams through the window of the sitting room.

'Where do you go in the daytime, when I'm at the museum?'

'I go to Goldsmiths,' says Ben, without looking up from his drawing. 'To the studio.'

'But when you're not at the studio?'

'I've been exploring – walking from place to place. Brixton, Herne Hill, Crystal Palace.' Ben looks up – past Don – out of the window. 'Brockwell Park.'

'Brockwell Park?'

'Yeah. I've been swimming. Haven't you been to the lido?'

Don's thoughts splinter. 'The lido . . . in Venice? It's pronounced *lee-do*.'

'In Brockwell Park. There's a pool.'

'Ah yes.' He remembers the small blue oblong on the park map. 'Lidos were all the rage once – a product of the health and sanitation craze of the interwar years. I believe there's one on Jesus Green in Cambridge, not that I ever went.'

'I'll take you to this one. We'll go.'

'I'd like that.'

'Well, let's go. I have spare trunks – unless you want to go nude.'

Outside, the sun is casting fragments of light across the driveway. Don stands up, possessed by contrary desires to go out – now, with Ben – and to retreat upstairs. He thinks with envy of how easy everything is for Ben – how easy he finds it to translate ideas into actions, how easily he forgives.

Narrowing his eyes against the light, Don thinks again of their walk back from the Crown and Greyhound, along the dark road.

'I can't,' he says, feeling desperate. 'Another time.'

* * *

He sits at his desk and immerses himself in Tiepolo's frescoes. More and more it is the space between the figures that preoccupies him, to the exclusion of anything else. He worries about how this fascination with thin air will advance his thesis.

At the sound of the door closing below, he raises his eyes and sees Ben crossing the driveway, a rucksack slung on his back.

For the first time in many days, he tries to type a new paragraph. Before he has completed a sentence, his thoughts have returned to Ben.

In a rush of anguish, he brings his fists down on the typewriter keys. Letters and cyphers stutter onto the page. Striding over to the wardrobe, he rummages through piles of clothes he hasn't touched since arriving in Dulwich. He finds an old pair of red swimming trunks – a flimsy vestige of his undergraduate years (and even then they lay unused). He grabs a towel from the bathroom and rushes out of the house.

He has made his way to the far side of the park. He follows an unknown path bordered by bushes, and then steps out onto a broad, open plane of grass that sweeps down towards the outbuildings around the lido. The long, low structure reminds him of barracks.

Midway across the slope is a fat-trunked oak. He stops and rests his hand on the bark. The urgency of his desire to follow has burned off in the heat of the day. He feels calmer but less certain.

The position offers a panoramic view of the lido complex and surrounding park. In the distance are two tower blocks, the spike of a church steeple, and miles away in the City, the grey stripe of the NatWest Tower – blanched by aerial perspective.

He sits at the base of the tree. The grass is thin here. He makes a cushion with his towel. Thirty metres away, the outbuildings of the lido block the pool itself from view. Visitors come and go, passing through an oblong archway guarded by turnstiles.

He is no longer sure whether he wants to see Ben – or be seen – but he stays and watches in a patient lull, letting the minutes float by. The tree provides a smattering of broken shade, but the heat is soporific.

Perhaps Ben didn't come after all, he thinks, just as cramp breaks out in one foot. He stands and rolls his heel on the grass. At the same moment, a group of people file out of the archway. Ben is one of them.

Don catches sight of his hair first, wet from the pool, and his sunglasses. The familiar denim jacket is hanging open to reveal his bare chest. Other people cross in front and Don loses him for a second. Then he retrieves Ben's smile. It is the same smile he observed on the evening when they first met – a broad, assured smile, made slightly enigmatic by his sunglasses.

Ben turns to one of the others and appears to say something. He catches hold of the person's shoulder – Don can't tell who it is – and pulls the friend towards him in a jostling movement, bringing their two faces close.

Wishing he had binoculars, Don tries to work out if any of the people are those same characters from the Crown and Greyhound – the Goldsmiths gang. But the group is scattering and the sun is playing games. It falls in blinding splashes.

Ben steps away from the others – starts to walk backwards across the grass in Don's direction. Still facing the lido, he raises both hands to the sky and spreads his fingers wide. His jacket lifts away from his waist to reveal a narrow strip of back. The sunlight glints in his wet hair, strikes the rings on his fingers, flickers all over him like an animate being.

Don is distracted by a pair of girls who have begun fighting at the entrance to the lido. Their hands and legs slice through the air in a yelling, spitting frenzy. One of their bodies buckles. He hears a piercing scream.

Ben is closer now – walking straight towards his tree. Like a skulking voyeur, Don skirts around the trunk, keeping on the far side as Ben passes.

Once Ben has disappeared between the bushes up ahead, Don runs the other way, past the lido, out of an unknown gate. Pacing back to Dulwich, he looks this way and that, afraid to be spotted by the object of his obsessive thoughts. Underneath his fear is a heavy, foolish melancholy. He is ashamed and darkly amused by his strength of feeling. Is this jealousy, even now?

This idea, working in subtle alliance with the unworn swimming trunks bundled under his arm, takes him back to the moment when he stood on Magdalene Bridge and watched Anders Andersson. He wonders if for Ben, too, beauty and charm are ever-replenishing gifts, to be given away freely.

It is getting dark when Ben returns to the house. He sits downstairs listening to Kiss FM. The noise of the radio draws Don away from his work.

He walks into the sitting room to find Ben spread across the sofa in jeans and a white T-shirt. He looks comical, flung out on Val's Napoleon III centrepiece, and the sofa looks comical beneath him.

Don can smell chlorine coming off his hair, as well as a fainter scent of rollups.

'Back from the lido!' He states the obvious with strained jollity.

Ben turns a languid eye on him. 'Lover, you should have come.'

Don shivers. He feels reproached, mocked, strangely elated.

Ben sits there and says nothing. He seems to fluctuate – under Don's scrutiny – between tenderness and indifference.

*

A few days later, Don is walking up the path to the museum when he encounters the gardener again. Paul is standing close to the path, in the same spot where Don first saw him – a man in his thirties, with a slim build and refined features. He is holding a pair of secateurs.

'Hi,' he says in an offhand way.

Don stops, at a loss for words, and then nods towards the gate. 'I think,' he says, then hesitates. 'I think the hollyhocks . . .'

Paul watches him with sharp, kind eyes.

'So extravagant . . .' Don is floundering.

'Too extravagant?' says Paul, with humour. He brushes his apron and places one hand on his hip – the hand is large, browned by the sun – and looks down the garden, towards the gate, with the wry scepticism of a man playing along with another person's illusion.

Don tries to rally himself against the dreamy torpor that the encounter has instilled.

'Yes, perhaps – I mean, yes, *definitely*, far too extravagant. Something ought to be done. Some cutting back.'

Paul holds up his secateurs and snaps them open and closed like castanets. He seems to wink, although it may be a nervous tic.

Don cuts across the grass, taking a shortcut to the door. He feels odd, different from himself, as if some chemical – adrenaline compounded with subtler forces – has been injected into his bloodstream.

Later, as he sits in his study, Val telephones.

'You'll never believe the rumour that's going around Peterhouse.'

He waits to hear what he'll never believe.

'Briony Davis – you know, the former Master's wife – is having a, a, an *affair* with the poetess. The artist in residence, you remember. Erica Jay. A *liaison*.'

Don pictures Briony Davis, wife of the deposed Master, naked and pale against the darker body of Erica Jay, each perspiring and heavy-limbed, neither of them youthful, and yet alive, unashamed, in love.

'Sapphic love, Don! The Master's wife!'

The news would once have held him spellbound. Today he feels detached. It's as if he's hearing about an intrigue from long ago, or a tawdry piece of fiction.

'Well of course, no one dares speak of it,' Val continues, interpreting Don's silence as a desire for detail. 'But everyone knows, *everyone*, even the undergraduates. The rumour is flying on the winds of Cambridge. It'll be in the papers, and *Private Eye*, mark my words. Such a scandal. By the way, have you considered what you'll wear for the Benefactors' Dinner?'

'It's a black-tie dinner,' Don replies, inspecting an infrared photograph of Poussin's *Triumph of David* that happens to be lying on his desk. 'That, I would have thought, eliminates the need to consider.' He cradles the heavy Bakelite phone in the tips of his fingers and swivels in his chair to look out at the garden. The roses are coming into bloom.

'Black tie is for run-of-the-mill guests, Don, but you are in an elevated position: the new director.'

Val's thoughts are whirring – as they often do during telephone silences. Don can sense their machinations in the hum and fuzz of the line.

'In previous years,' Val finally says, 'I have worn a beautiful suit – pure white satin. It's hanging in the wardrobe there in Dulwich. It would fit you perfectly.'

'A satin suit?' Don chuckles. 'I don't think so.'

'I insist, Don. It's imperative that you stand out from the sober crowd.'

'Yes, but not as a carnival performer.'

'Think about it, at least.'

Don looks out of the window as the conversation floods onwards. Paul is crossing the grass. He crouches in a swift movement to inspect something, then strolls on, beyond the window's field of view.

12

Michael and Anna Ross live fifteen minutes' walk away, on a parade of semi-detached redbrick houses leading in a gradual descent to Brockwell Park. Without realising it, he has passed their house often.

He sets out early and walks slowly, extending those fifteen minutes into half an hour. In one hand he carries a bottle, taken from the rack in the kitchen. He pauses often to sample the balmy air or to study the effect of the evening sun on the asphalt pavements, or to glance over fences at gardens that are flowery or paved or obscured by dark leylandii.

It is eight o'clock as he unfastens the small iron gate of number 190 and walks up the front path. He presses the doorbell.

Within seconds, Anna answers and kisses him on each cheek. Her perfume has a sharp, bright edge, and she wears a floral print dress. He senses in her the same quality that he noticed at the private view, a sort of penetrating detachment. Is there a latent sadness, he wonders, in her eager smiles? She leads him into a dim hallway paved with hexagons and quatrefoils.

He follows her into a small sitting room where Michael is sitting on a leather sofa, a book in one hand.

'*Willkommen*, Professor!' he cries. 'Not a second late. Here to free me from Heidegger.' He is wearing spectacles that confer a premature middle age on him.

Misinterpreting Don's outstretched hand, Michael passes the book.

Don receives Heidegger's *Being and Time*, observing that the copy is new. 'There's a saying – isn't there – that all western philosophy is, in the end, a series of footnotes to Plato?'

Michael beams at him without a word.

Anna comes forward with bottles of wine. 'Would you like a drink, Don? Red or white?'

'Thank you – red would be marvellous.'

The room is lined with art books. He glimpses the names of Paul Gauguin, Jacob Epstein and Mariam Schwarz. Through French doors, he sees a patio strewn with white blossom. The petals have gathered around large, dark boulders.

'What a lovely house.'

'Oh, it isn't ours.' Anna hands him a glass. 'It's owned by Dulwich College. A schoolteacher lived here, but he's just retired to Sicily.'

'Taormina,' Michael says, folding his arms and looking every inch the hero of the cricket field.

'A friend of Mike's organised the house for us,' Anna explains.

Don sits on a small armchair in the corner and holds his glass of wine steady on his knee. 'Valentine Black, I presume?'

'Yes, that's right.'

'And you're staying at Val's place, aren't you?' says Michael. 'The villa of the mysteries!'

Don nods and wonders what Michael means. There is an insinuation that they are all in Val's debt – but it's more than that. *The villa of the mysteries*. He grips the stem of his glass.

There is a silence before Anna speaks.

'Did you live in Cambridge a long time, Don?'

'All of my life.' He looks through the French doors as if regarding the long span of years. 'Of course, my work has taken me to Italy many times – Venice especially.'

A timer goes off in another room. Anna apologises and retreats. Michael glows in the lamplight.

'Have I mentioned,' Michael says, 'that I'm going to Italy in the summer to make a TV programme?'

'Val said something about it. Rome and the Grand Tour?'

'Not just Rome. The producers want me to hike over the Alps and down through Italy – Turin, Florence, across to Pisa—'

'And Venice, surely?'

'Oh, I don't think we'll bother. Just the important stop-offs. They want some countryside footage as well. I'm going to swim down the Arno, all the way through Florence.'

Anna returns from the kitchen. Michael draws her onto the arm of the sofa and plants a kiss on her cheek.

'I'll be demystifying the Old Masters! Making art accessible.'

Don sits very still. 'You may not know that I made a BBC programme myself, in the early eighties. A radio series. It was called *A Venetian Odyssey* – a little survey of paintings and palaces, not a bit like the *Boy's Own* adventure you seem to have planned.'

He speaks with casualness, but he notices that his hand is trembling.

'Goodness,' says Michael. 'Another era! I had no idea, Lamb.'

This use of his surname, he thinks, must be a hangover of public-school camaraderie.

'I'd love to hear it,' says Anna. 'You must lend us the tape.'

'Oh, I don't have anything like that,' Don replies. 'It was a brief excursion from academic life. When I returned to Cambridge, I had twenty PhD theses waiting to be read. That was my reward for a summer of media stardom. I do hope' – he switches his gaze back to Michael – 'that you'll be able to fit these travels around your duties at the museum.'

'I began a PhD,' says Michael with a rueful grin, ignoring this last remark. 'But then, you know, *life* started. All of a sudden, I was Associate Curator at the Frick. Far too busy to finish the thesis. I turned it into an exhibition instead. I couldn't have done it without Val – he was a massive support.'

Don surveys him blankly, unable to keep pace with his own racing suppositions.

'Mike's thesis was a study of horses' backsides in fifteenth-century battle paintings,' says Anna, still in the compass of her husband's strong arm. She starts to laugh.

Michael's expression is different from before. A humourless smile – unspontaneous. He gently disentangles himself from Anna.

'That's a bit of a flippant way of describing it. It was from a poststructuralist angle. *Posteriority* and the early modern gaze.'

Anna remains perched on the arm of the sofa, watching Michael. Don wonders if he can detect muted pity in her face – or disdain. He crosses his legs and withdraws a cigarette from his packet.

'May I smoke?'

The Rosses exchange glances. Michael stands and gives him a clap on the shoulder. 'It's good to have you here, Lamb.'

'Why don't you come into the garden, Don?' says Anna.

She thrusts open the French doors and leads him onto the patio. The three of them walk among the boulders, which he now sees are clods of bronze – squat, globular forms resembling hardened lava, glazed in a tarry patina. Flecks of blossom blow across their blackened surfaces, clinging momentarily before wafting off.

'The teacher who lived here was an artist as well,' Anna says. 'He called this series *The Emperors of Rome*.'

Without forethought, Don kneels and puts down his glass. Tucking his cigarette between his third and fourth fingers, he feels one of the bronzes with both hands as if he is remoulding its surface.

'My departure from Peterhouse was hastened by the arrival of – I suppose you would call it an outdoor sculpture.' He has begun to pick the blossom off piece by piece. The Rosses watch him with polite curiosity. 'Although I would refrain from affording

James Cahill

that eyesore the status of sculpture. I said as much on the radio. It was the mischievous doing of a self-styled artist called' – he pauses, wondering what to call her – 'Angela Cannon.'

'Ah yes, Cannon,' says Michael. 'I know the name. And – well – who could forget your comments on the radio?'

Don is still crouching down with his hands on the bronze. He looks up to see that Michael is grinning broadly.

'Tell me,' Michael carries on, 'didn't Val have something to do with the commissioning of that sculpture at Peterhouse? Some kind of festival of contemporary art and poetry, wasn't it?'

Standing back up, Don bursts out laughing. 'Valentine Black? I think not! He was as appalled as the rest of us.' He draws a stream of wine into his throat, down to his gut. 'I couldn't be part of an institution that was prepared to traduce the name of art.'

'I'll mix some Pimm's,' says Michael brightly. 'The first of the summer!' He disappears indoors.

Once they are alone together, Anna's face seems to alter. A tension has dissipated. Only now, in the relaxation of her features, does he perceive the strain that was there before.

They stand and look across the garden. The patio is bordered by a low balustrade, beyond which the lawn recedes in a serpentine course between bushes and trees. The foliage is gaining depth in the dimming light. At the point where the grass disappears into a cluster of elms, a stone Cupid holds up a bird bath. From somewhere beyond comes the muffled roar of a train.

'This has been a big change for us,' Anna says. Her eyes follow Don's to the end of the garden. 'The move back to England. Mike's new job.'

'Do you miss New York?'

'I miss everything about it.'

With a casual question, he has touched on an unexpected depth of feeling.

'I never thought we would come back,' she says. 'I mean, I'm from London originally, but there's nothing to keep me here.

Mum and Dad died a long time ago. I was their only child and they were late parents.'

He nods in surprised recognition, figuring that Anna is older than she looks.

'I'm sorry.'

'Oh, don't be. What I'm saying is – I miss having a purpose. It's impossible not to feel busy in New York. The life of the place, the pace, all that energy. Dulwich feels incredibly . . . I don't know . . . *static*.'

'Like a picture?'

'I'm sure it's just me. But then' – she laughs bitterly – 'I'm really *not* busy any more. I gave up everything to come here. I'm starting all over again. It happens to lots of people – I shouldn't complain. You're starting again too, in a way, at the Brockwell Collection.'

'I suppose. But I have a position. That makes it easier. You have to create a position for yourself, in a place you don't know.'

The sun is low in the sky. It fires a valedictory ray through the trees, and the edges of Anna's hair catch the light. Absentmindedly she uncreases her skirt.

'I do feel free, though, in a weird sense,' she says. 'I wonder if you have to lose something – lose something that really matters, or that you *think* matters – in order to be free. Not that I've lost everything, by any stretch. I mean, look at this place. We were in a studio apartment before, in Brooklyn.' She drinks and continues to gaze out at the garden, pursuing its end point. 'But to lose the thing that matters to you can be liberating as well as tragic. Like a loss of self. Like being drunk. Am I making sense? Maybe I *am* drunk.' She turns to him and smiles through her seriousness.

'I think I understand. It's different for me. I haven't been flung out into the void. Even so' – Don rests both hands on the balustrade – 'I do sometimes wonder what I'm doing here.'

He has said more than he intended. Anna is nodding. Her

brown eyes seem to rise out of a deep well of thought, fastening on him, drawing the words out. She laughs.

'I haven't quite fallen into the void. I'm playing with a local strings group, the Orpheus Sinfonia. Your curator at the Brockwell – Miss Berenson, isn't it? – has asked us to play at the Benefactors' Dinner.'

'Ah yes, the high point of the Brockwell's social calendar.'

'Pimm's for anyone?' Michael bounds onto the patio, clasping a jug clogged with amber fluid and wobbling lumps of fruit.

As they sit down for dinner, Anna puts on a record from one of her orchestral concerts: Brahms, Liszt, Stravinsky.

Michael sets down three cocktail glasses stuffed with a lumpen, glistening substance the colour of pink opal. Taking a spoonful, Don sucks away the creamy gloop to detect the hard carcass of a prawn on his tongue.

As the music pounds and swells and then plunges into phrases of exquisite lethargy, they talk about the political landscape – endemic sleaze in the Tory party, a resurgent Labour (surely they'll win at the next election) – and then topics closer to home, including the Benefactors' Dinner.

Deftly, like an actress in a dramatic scene, Anna clears the cocktail glasses – Don's is still smeared with prawns – and sets down a main course of pork tenderloin and potato gratin. Michael gives an exhaustive account of the Ribera exhibition he organised at the Frick in 1989, and Don is compelled to feign appropriate responses – nods, hums, polite chuckles, murmurs of disapproval – to the twists and turns of the interminable story. What a bore Michael can be.

He is conscious, as dinner progresses, that he has not broached any of his own prepared subjects. He has been a passive listener, polite and retiring. Anna, too, is quiet again in Michael's presence.

Just as Michael appears poised to embark on a fresh tale, Don leaps in.

'I presume you saw Julius Fould's essay in this month's *Burlington Magazine*? About the Assisi frescoes?'

'Oh – yes. I had a skim. Feather-ruffling stuff!'

'My feathers were ruffled, if that's the metaphor you prefer, by the woeful lack of attention to liturgical context. A singular lack of nuance—'

'Oh, I don't know about that, Lamb. Isn't Fould's point that liturgical subtleties were as good as irrelevant, so far as the painters of the frescoes were concerned? They were craftsmen, not theologians.'

Heat passes through Don's neck. 'I should read a little around the subject of the Basilica di San Francesco, if I were you,' he says with a brittle laugh. 'But of course, I forget – you have Heidegger to keep you busy.'

He seems nearly to have finished his wine again. Anna stands and takes another bottle from the sideboard – Don's gift of Beaujolais.

Pudding arrives, and sweet Sauternes. At last there is silence around the table. Don's teeth sink through a mush of raspberries and break into meringue.

'You're not married, are you?' Anna says.

Almost at once, Michael tuts and smiles at her and says, 'Darling!'

With his mouth full of sugary rocks, Don watches. Anna's question was casual, without a subtext; she probably meant to confirm what she already knew. But the way Michael looked at her – with a smile steeped in scorn – has worked its way into Don's heart like a hypodermic syringe. At the same moment, the record player unleashes a rogue wave of percussion and strings. He crunches and swallows.

'I have been, yes,' he says. 'Married, I mean. With a wife and a son. Some years ago.'

Michael lets out a fragmentary laugh, then stops – as if his throat has snapped shut. There is an annihilating silence.

'Where are they now?' Anna asks.

'Dead.'

Don stares at the pepper shaker. He is as shocked as the Rosses. Something like diabolical possession has taken hold of him. Panic and exhilaration rise through his chest. Stravinsky beats in his ears like rushing blood and he feels the fixedness of Anna's eyes. He looks up at her.

'Oh, Don.' Her voice is barely audible.

He looks at Michael, and what he perceives – alarm inlaid with bright hostility – is a delicious goad. 'From Asiatic cholera,' he says.

'Cholera?' Anna gasps. 'But that was eradicated years ago.'

'Not quite, I'm afraid.' His voice quavers with emotion that has flooded into him from some unknown place. 'I keep a framed photograph of each of them in my bedroom. Wherever I travel, the pictures travel too. They are always with me. It sounds absurd, but I kiss them every night before I sleep.'

No one speaks. Anna places her hand on Don's.

'I'd rather not talk about it any more, if you don't mind,' he whispers.

'I don't mind at all,' says Michael. His tone is drained of its usual charm.

Dinner finishes quickly. Michael barely speaks again except to tell Anna not to open another bottle. Don feels as if he is swimming on a tide of unreality.

When he leaves, Anna stands at the front door and kisses him again on the cheek, and for a moment he feels sane. Michael has retreated into the house, declining to say goodbye.

'I'm sorry,' Don says. 'What I said before . . .' But the grasped-for explanation flies out of reach.

Anna's eyes are dimly luminescent, like parallel moons. She reminds him of a picture from Picasso's Blue Period – a beautiful woman cast in chilly nocturnal light.

'It's okay, Don. Everything's okay.'

'Goodnight, Anna.'

She closes the door.

He walks in the direction of Dulwich Village. But his pace slows. The night is inviting him to linger. The urge intensifies into a decision to turn around and go back in the direction he has come. His manic head has returned – he is swimming again, thrashing against tides of orchestral music. Only the dark void of the park will restore peace.

When he passes the Rosses' house, it is dark apart from a narrow bar of light separating the curtains in an upstairs window.

He reaches Norwood Road and skirts the park. The main gates are locked, but by a stroke of luck, the small side gate is ajar.

The park is dark and the air is still – so still that it's like being indoors. He hears a dog barking somewhere ahead. He isn't the only night-time wanderer. Otherwise the place is silent. At the crest of the hill, Brockwell Hall looks like a toy, flattened by darkness, stripped of detail.

Wading into the gloom, he considers the ridiculous lie he told – Asiatic cholera, a wife and son. So improbable, so fanciful . . . Michael knew at once, and Anna must have seen through him after a second's reflection. Perhaps that was what he wanted, to be seen through all the way.

He has reached the top of the hill. He glances over the iron-work balcony of Brockwell Hall and the semi-circular bulge of the drawing-room window, then slowly circles the building, listening to the soft thud of his feet on the gravel bordering the house.

On the far side of Brockwell Hall, the park is a landscape of shadows. Trees and bushes loom as black masses against the greyer darkness of the grass. A short distance away, in front of a thicket of shrubs, is a paler shape – a compact white object. He strains to make it out. As he does so, it moves slightly. He treads carefully towards it and realises that it's a dog, with the conical face and shrunken eyes of a bull terrier.

Don comes closer. The creature is watching him, standing guard with its head raised and its front legs planted apart. It is tethered by a lead to an iron water pump that must have served the house once. Suddenly, the dog lets out a single vicious bark. The noise is explosive. Startled and intrigued, wondering if the animal has been abandoned, Don walks diagonally past it, around the settlement of bushes beyond the pump. He peers further into the gloom of the park.

A rustling within the bushes stalls him. He peers through a gap in the wall of leaves. Beyond is a secret clearing, ringed all around by thick shrubbery, where the grass is uncut like the grass of a meadow. In the middle, two men are lying on the ground, writhing and rolling around one another. They are naked. Their bodies are hard to tell apart in the darkness – both are large-limbed, with solid backs and buttocks and calves. They form a single restless outline as they wrestle and tussle in silence, half buried in the swaying grass.

The moon slides out from behind a cloud. Don glances behind him and sees the facets of the house picked out in dim, steely light.

He turns back. The clearing within the bushes is more visible now through the gap: the grass appears as thousands of slanting lines, some of them yellowed, many of them top-heavy and swaying with seed heads. At the centre, the two men have changed position. One is on his knees, turned slightly away to present a view of his ghostly-pale rear. Don catches sight of his erection, nodding gigantically – the man holds it with both hands, as if to tame it. The other is still lying on his back in the grass. The kneeling man pulls the horizontal one towards him with a swift, muscular effort, like sliding open a drawer. The man underneath raises his legs – knees bent – off the ground; he lets out a high, sharp gasp. Their two bodies join and unjoin mechanically, slowly at first, then with faster and firmer movements.

Don watches, transfixed by an intense, prurient curiosity. He is struck by the soundlessness of their actions. All he can hear is quickening, overlapping breathing. The face of the lying figure is obscured by the hatching of the grass. The other man is turned away still, bowing his head as his body shunts back and forth like a piston.

The shunting becomes faster. Suddenly, the man underneath lifts his head into full view. He releases a terrifying groan and the whites of his eyes shine moistly. The dog lets out a volley of barks from the other side of the bushes.

Don turns away and steps creepingly back towards Brockwell Hall, past the dog, which lunges at him as he goes by, catching itself on its lead with a clanging thud.

He winds his way round to the front of the house. At the bottom of the hill, Norwood Road runs as an amber thread along the edge of the park. Sifting two fingers through the gaps in his shirt, he feels his heart beating. His fingers are clammy. He withdraws them and undoes a couple of buttons. He wonders about opening his shirt to allow the air to spread across his chest – or taking off all his clothes and standing there, naked before the world.

From behind him comes a muffled howl. A fresh explosion of barks tears through the night.

*

There is a quiet knock on the door of the Palladian Library. So quiet that at first Don mistakes the sound for the rustle of rose vines around his window. But it comes again, slightly harder.

'Come in!'

Bill Hoare's face appears in the doorway.

'Professor Lamb' – he is out of breath – 'we'll be gathering at twelve in the Cosway Room. You remember, to inspect the restored Venus statuettes?'

'Ah yes.' Don remembers. The demented intruder, a bizarre scene in the Octagon and himself somehow to blame . . . He pictures the marble dust rising from the rubble.

'Will you be able to join us?'

He removes his reading glasses. 'Us?'

'Well, I shall be there, as Head of Conservation. Mr Hamilton's coming – he paid for the restoration. And Inigo Price, of course. You'll remember how they were when he started – broken in hundreds of pieces—'

'Yes, yes, I remember.'

'And Michael Ross said that he would attend.'

It has been almost a week since he went to dinner at the Rosses'. He and Michael have barely spoken, beyond curt exchanges on museum business. The strange thing is, Don doesn't care. Not deeply. Beneath the wincing embarrassment, the sporadic fear he could have expected, is a different mood – sprightlier, darker. It amuses him to think of Michael going to Val and relating the tale. *But no, he can't have meant it. Cholera? You must have misconstrued* . . .

'Fine, I'll come. Give me ten minutes.'

Bill shakes his jowls gratefully and shrinks from view.

The Cosway Room is an out-of-the-way chamber, rarely frequented by visitors, containing the museum's Greek and Roman antiquities. These amount to a pair of marble busts – supposedly of Roman emperors, but damaged beyond recognition – a tray of oxidised coins, and a marble altar that Don has privately identified as an eighteenth-century fake. The two Venuses have been placed on top of the altar, newly repaired and considered too vulnerable to return to their former pedestals in the Octagon. ('Not after what happened,' Maud advised. 'We couldn't risk that again.')

The others are already assembled when Don arrives. Inigo Price is fussing learnedly over the statuettes, pointing out their invisible joins and chromatic integrity. He is a tall, skinny man with pointy features and thin mousy hair. His brown suit is of an outmoded cut – fat lapels, flaring shins. His moustache runs along his upper lip like eyeliner.

'Please, carry on,' says Don, although Inigo shows no sign of halting.

Don stands at a polite remove. Bill is installed in a gilt-edged chair, obliterating the pinecone that was placed there as a deterrent. To one side, Michael listens with fierce attention.

'Such fine pieces of Roman statuary,' the restorer professes. 'In the eighteenth century, they were owned by none other than Bartolomeo Cavaceppi, who re-carved the breasts of the goddesses to their current refined proportions.'

Don looks at the statues, each arrested in a stance between standing and crouching. One is positioned frontwards to display the goddess's breasts; the other is turned to reveal her buttocks and twisting back. But something is different – not right.

'You will observe the chaste simplicity of the figure,' Inigo declares, tracing Venus's midriff with his finger. With his other hand, he produces a metal torch from his jacket – it looks like a tiny truncheon – which he flips acrobatically between his long fingers to turn on the lamp.

Don feels sure that changes – additions – have been made. Following Cavaceppi's lead, Inigo appears to have modified the curvature of each figure, accenting and amplifying her shape by every trick of the restorer's repertoire. The Venuses have become overly buxom, salacious – coy in the wrong way.

Michael strokes his chin and nods. Hamilton, the diamond dealer who funded the reparation, has lost interest and is turning to examine one of the Roman emperors.

Inigo guides his torch across the statues' surfaces, every dimple and cleft, and relates the complexities of his craft. But Don is distracted by a growing awareness of Bill on that antique chair. He seems more massive than usual – a huge, self-engulfing form, inert as a totality yet appearing to palpitate and squirm within his own vast contours.

Bill isn't listening to a word of the restorer's speech, and yet he is looking intently at the Venuses. Out of his tweed folds he has extracted a miniature telescope. He holds it to his eye and ogles the goddesses with slackened lips. His other hand remains submerged in his trouser pocket, disappearing into his crotch.

'Each Venus was bathed for many days,' Inigo says, 'in a bath of purifying fluid.'

A fine glitter of sweat has broken across Bill's face. The noise of his breathing – an accelerating airborne tide – breaks through Don's consciousness.

'It's the very finest piece of restoration work I've seen,' bursts out Michael. 'The setting of the pelvis and the groin – such precision!'

'You flatter me, sir,' says Inigo, bringing his fingertips to his moustache. 'I will confess, the reconstruction of the pubic mound on this figure required unusual patience.'

Bill lets out a rattling sigh.

*

Ben goes regularly to Soho, Shoreditch and other, remoter parts of London, often for the whole night. Sometimes, close to dawn, Don hears movement in the hall below, and from the footsteps he knows that it's Ben, back from a night-time excursion.

His other, larger life is reclaiming him, Don supposes. The idea rouses a buried fear.

On other nights, Ben stays in. He sits in his accustomed place on the pink sofa, and they drink Beaujolais until late. Facing each other across the lacquered coffee table – its surface glowing like a lake at sunset – they smoke and drink and chat for hours. They talk about art and life. Ben's perspectives are bizarre, maddening, captivating . . .

These evenings remind Don, with dual pleasure and sharp pain, of their earlier evenings together, and their outing to the Crown and Greyhound.

*

He has been making final arrangements for the Benefactors' Dinner – his head is awash with names, titles, roles. The house is silent when he returns. He guesses that Ina is in the annex with her mother. Ben is out – no matter, he will be back. His clothes are slumped around the sitting room like proxy versions of him. His leather jacket, smelling of cigarettes, hangs around the back of a walnut chair. He has left other oddments around the room – a sketchpad, scalpels, pencils, a plastic bottle of glue. Don picks them up, one by one, and turns them over in his hands.

He pours a glass of wine and goes upstairs to his room.

When he opens the door, a slice of paper flutters across the carpet. He looks around. His Tiepolo pictures have been disturbed. Decimated. His first thought is that a wild animal, a bird or rat, has invaded the room. But the window is closed.

He steps over the threshold. Tiny irregular scraps of paper, thousands of them, are scattered across the floor. They look like leaves or sweet wrappers – ragged, perforated shapes. His entire archive has been pulled out of the wardrobe, and the cardboard boxes lie across the room, their contents spilled and cut into pieces.

He treads over the carpet. Some of the pieces of paper are partly intact; he is able to make out details. He kneels and sees that the pictures have been cut with painstaking care – hollowed out with a scalpel – so that the sections of blue sky are gone. All that remains are the human figures and animals, the chunks of architecture and puffs of grey cloud, detached from the skies they once inhabited – left behind like corpses.

He stays on his knees for several minutes, succumbing to a rising grief, and tries to think back to the previous evening. Ben arrived home around eleven. They drank for hours in the sitting room, well into the night. That much he remembers. Did they go upstairs? Did Don pull out the boxes of pictures and show them off, giving vent to a late-night stream of consciousness, talking volubly of Venetian masques and ballets and the parapets that divide earth from the heavens? Perhaps – but the details are lost from memory.

All he knows for sure is that Ben came back here during the day. He must have crept in while Don was at the museum and desecrated the collection piece by piece with his scalpel. An act of vandalism – hateful – and yet done so lovingly, with such perverse care. It must have taken many hours.

Unable to think, barely able to move, he lies down on his bed and sleeps.

Once the shock of the discovery wears off, Don feels strangely unperturbed. It's as if the surgical removal of the blue expanses has brought a kind of peace.

Even so, he intends to confront Ben. The mutilation of his property is a crime that cannot pass unpunished. He will inform the police – or threaten to. He will expel Ben from the House Beautiful.

And yet, like a guilty child, Ben evades him. He returns to the house in the daytime – Don knows he's been there from the staggered movements of his possessions. But like a ghost afraid to be sighted, Ben waits until Don is asleep or at work before appearing. For almost a week, he skulks in Don's shadow.

Then, on Friday night, Don comes home to find him lying in the sitting room, face down on the sofa. Glancing across the unlit room, he assumes that Ben is sleeping. But as he stands by the door and watches, summoning up the nerve to wake him, he hears an odd noise – long, juddering sighs, sobs that are almost without sound, buried deep in the padded velvet.

Don backs out of the room. The sight has induced in him an anguish of embarrassment. More than ever, he senses the vastness of his ignorance – of people, of Ben especially. He thinks dimly of Ben's wider life, those characters around the table at the Crown and Greyhound. He knows next to nothing about that life. But this too is a kind of bleak epiphany. Wasn't it Socrates who came to realise that he knew nothing? And Socrates had Alcibiades, that young tearaway whom he loved and forgave – forgave everything – because Alcibiades loved him back, in his loveless way.

He no longer feels able to extract retribution. When he next sees Ben, a couple of days later on the stairs, they look at each other before speaking. Each of them sees that the other is reluctant – or unable – to broach the matter of the pictures. When they do speak, it is about nothing in particular. Ben is getting ready for an exhibition in Oval the following month, maybe Don would like to come. Don can't promise – there's the Benefactors' Dinner to worry about first.

Having failed to mention it, they seem by a silent agreement to have made the subject unmentionable. Life carries on, but Don leaves the tattered pieces of paper where they are on his bedroom floor, like the rubble of an archaeological site, the sacred dross of a Roman ruin.

13

'I really can't apologise enough,' Val says.

'But the dinner's this evening. You're chairman of the trustees. How can you not be there?'

'You know how things are at Peterhouse, Don. One crisis succeeds another. Perhaps you've forgotten that we are in search of a new Master – the college is a headless body, *acephalous*. I've never known a situation like it. Move Michael Ross up to my place. He'll be able to help you with that bore Herb Thackeray.'

Afterwards, Don finds Val's white satin tuxedo and matching trousers concealed inside a nondescript bag in the wardrobe. He lays the outfit on his bed and regards it pensively. He strokes the slippery material with one finger. Val has advised him to fix a carnation to the lapel; he can pick one up from Portia's Florists in the Village.

No matter that Val will miss the dinner. Don is the Director, and he will be resplendent.

He arranges other items on the bed – shirt, silk tie, underwear and a pair of patent leather shoes, shiny as molten tar, that he picked up from a charity shop on Norwood Road.

'Just be yourself,' Maud said to him a few days ago, when she came into the Palladian Library to find him studying the table plan. But nobody – he reflects now as he stands before his bed – behaves entirely like himself or herself. Not at events like the Benefactors' Dinner.

* * *

The day passes routinely enough, although a flurry of preparation has spread throughout the galleries as caterers and flower arrangers set the stage. While he gets dressed at home in the late afternoon, Don drinks a bottle of Beaujolais. He is on to his second by the time he leaves for the museum.

His splendour turns heads the moment he walks into the pre-dinner drinks reception. He is fashionably late by an hour. Maud, busy with a group in one corner, stares at his suit.

'Where have you been?' she asks under her breath, having broken away from her group. 'You look . . . extraordinary.'

'Thank you, Maud. Thank you indeed.' Don picks up a flute of champagne from a nearby formation.

Passing into the next gallery, he notices Michael talking earnestly with another group of guests, and begins to circle in.

'I think it's so important,' Michael is saying, 'that we ask ourselves who our audience is. Who is the exhibition for? Have we made it *accessible*? We have a duty—'

Don swerves in a different direction and drinks a long forgetful draught.

Not far off, he finds Anna Ross alone in front of a painting. Her dress is black and fitted, and her arms are pale beneath high-cropped sleeves. Her hair is untied – casual but carefully arranged. She turns to him as he comes near.

'Hi, Don.'

'Anna . . . How are you?'

'Not bad. I always get nervous before a performance.'

'Of course, you're playing. The string quartet!'

She looks at him with curiosity. 'I guess it's also the nerves of any event like *this*. The formality of it all. Do you feel the same?'

Before he can reply, she carries on.

'It's the chatter and circling – there's a sparkling randomness that I never seem able to grasp.' She sighs. 'Michael seems to have it cracked.'

Just at that moment, as if to corroborate her point, Michael's hearty laughter resounds through the room.

Michael knows the part he has to play, thinks Don. A second later, he wonders if he said the words aloud. Either way, Anna seems to have read his meaning. She nods, surveying him with her brown eyes.

'We're the same,' he says suddenly. 'I mean, I feel the same as you. These events, these situations, they demand a sort of artifice – a performance of self.'

'Well, you seem to have your social armour on tonight.' She indicates his jacket with an uncertain smile.

'This? Oh, it's nothing. A gift from an old friend.'

They are both poised to say more, but then Anna begins to step away.

'I mustn't hang around – I'm playing in a moment.'

She brushes past him, so lightly that it might have been an accident.

The rising hum of voices smothers his thoughts and adrenaline drives him into the Rubens Room. A table the length of a train carriage has been draped in white cloth and blazoned with silver, crystal and china. Gilt-embossed cards mark the places like tiny headstones, and ivory-white candles rise like triumphal columns along the crowded route. Lilies explode in clusters of white and green.

The gallery is filling up with friends and patrons of the museum – an urbane crowd, regally dressed. As he wanders apart, Don finds himself looking at them as if from a great height. He feels as though he is soaring in the clear air of Tiepolo's frescoes. The milling guests are flotsam, a band of cherubs and demigods playing their minor parts.

He catches sight of Agnes Penrose, a grand lady of Dulwich who has bequeathed various small masterpieces to the museum, and he is moved – on an impulse – to take her hand and draw it to his lips.

'Charmed,' he says. '*Delighted*.'

Without returning his smile, she starts to speak. But Don is sweeping ahead.

Anna and the other members of her quartet are tuning up in the corner of the room, hovering around a single note with a tightrope-walker's precision. They are seated beneath Peter Lely's *Nymphs by a Fountain*. Fenced in by music stands, they form a demure counterpoint to the painted scene – naked nymphs lolling in the open air. Don is musing on the contrast when their four bows move in tandem. The tune is Purcell's 'Chacony'; the strident opening chords awaken a distant memory. Anna seems to attack the cello, plunging her bow and clamping down the strings with manic energy.

Between pieces, the gong sounds. Don circles the table and the guests follow him like a train of acolytes in their tuxedos and shining gowns. The evening sun slants through the skylight and dances across the cutlery and glass, mingling with the flames of the candles. He is reminded of the altar of a Rococo chapel he visited once in Andalucía – a static riot of creamy plaster, worked metal and pearlescent flame. Everything in the gallery has reached a heightened state of brightness and colour. The red carnation in the lapel of his jacket, which he had worried might appear excessive, chimes (as if by perfect pitch) with the splendour of the scene. Venusberg, he tells himself, must have looked as lovely as this.

The guests take their places. Their actions seem more stylised, their motions more decorous, against the music. At the head of the table, Don is flanked by the museum's biggest donors, an elderly American couple called the Thackerays. On his right is Herb – a retired oil magnate, already busy explaining why he moved from Texas to London. On Don's left is Betty. She is a tiny, wizened woman with feathers on her head, mink around her shoulders, and an enamel brooch printed with a reproduction of *The Blue Boy* by Gainsborough pinned to her velvet lapel.

'My,' says Betty, touching his arm with her jewelled fingers. 'This really is some jacket, Professor Lamb.'

Michael, three places down the table to Don's right, is talking to the Director of the Whitechapel Gallery. He is close enough to be impossible to ignore, yet hard to hear over the general hum. Their eyes meet occasionally as they pursue parallel conversations.

The brilliance of the room gradually dims until the pictures on the walls are imageless portals. The white wine accompanying the soup is replaced by Anjou rouge. Guinea fowl, glazed to the complexion of burnt caramel and laid on a pyre of risotto, is delivered by white-sleeved attendants.

In defiance of gravity, the red wine rises through Don's body, from his stomach into his chest and up to his brain. The candle flames multiply like fireflies in the glass and silverware. The outlines of people blur. The flavours of the food become indistinct and yet more potent, a slow deluge of texture and sensation. Sweet sauce congeals on his palate and around his gums. Conversations blend into a rapid stream out of which he sifts Betty Thackeray's appeals for a Joshua Reynolds exhibition. Her frail hand strums the table and occasionally touches Don's own, the lightest of touches, like the stroke of a bird's wing.

But against the softening of forms, Don is aware – increasingly – of the profile of Michael, three places away. While other bodies mingle into glowing plasma, Michael becomes, by some chance effect of the candlelight, more distinct and robust. His Roman countenance stands out like an imperial portrait on a coin.

'When, Professor?' demands Betty with growing passion. 'When can Sir Joshua be rescued from obscurity?'

'I would hardly say he's fallen into obscurity,' Don replies languidly. 'But if anyone is going to restore Reynolds to favour, then Donato Esposito is the man.'

'Esposito,' Betty repeats, Americanising the vowels and poring over the word as if it were a marvellous relic.

The word 'demystification' causes Don's ears to prick.

Michael is preaching the new philosophy – his usual mantra. Don distinctly hears him mention Jacques Derrida. He wishes that Val could be here to interrupt – to halt Michael in his tracks and send that voguish French idol toppling to the ground. Worst of all, the guests around Michael are listening intently, hanging on his words. Herb Thackeray leans in and cups his ear while he trowels risotto with his other hand, absorbing the tenets of poststructuralism with beady eyes.

Under the pretence of listening to Betty, who is now bemoaning the state of funding at the Guildhall, Don tries to eavesdrop. As the dishes are cleared and pudding is served, fragments of Michael's speech reach him.

'The classical revival in this country was half baked . . . A synthesis of invented histories . . . *syncretic*, I would say, and *agglomerative* . . . a formulaic shorthand for beauty . . . but ultimately, in my view, deeply conservative.'

Michael's tone, whatever he is talking about, is assured and throwaway. The Director of the Whitechapel Gallery nods furiously. Don's blood warms.

'A thoroughly old-fashioned art historian . . . a slave to the old iconographic method.'

Who can he be talking about? Is this a public attack on Valentine Black, or – he swallows a glug of wine – on him?

Betty turns her attentions at last to the guest on her other side, but in the same moment, Herb claps Don's right arm.

'C'mon, Lamb,' he says, helping himself to wine. 'I know you wise guys, you intellectuals. You like to vanish up your own asses. I know about art, same as you, I know a Rubens from a Velázquez. Hell, I know the moderns too, like I know my own kids. Picasso, Pollock, you name it.'

'He went off the boil, intellectually,' Michael is saying. 'Lost the respect of his peers.'

Again, their eyes meet. Don is convinced now that Michael is speaking about him.

'You okay, Professor?' asks Herb. 'More wine?'

Michael's words continue to flit across in snatches, until suddenly his voice is loud and clear.

'It's the fate of so many brilliant minds. Imagination starves itself to death, and what are you left with? Crushing prejudice – and childish lies.'

Don stares down at his untouched peach melba. He knows he shouldn't care. If anyone else were saying these things, he could perhaps withstand the assault with a cool smile. But something about Michael's expression, that glow of virtue, makes the words unbearable.

He picks up his knife and strikes the rim of his glass. The tremulous ring subdues the room. Standing up, he slides a piece of paper out of his jacket pocket. The table extends like a runway before him, lined with expectant faces. He clears his throat.

'I came to the Brockwell, as many of you know, from Peterhouse, Cambridge. My career there was long.' He takes a mouthful of Anjou. 'Some have ventured to call it illustrious.'

Herb chuckles.

'From the oldest of Cambridge's colleges, I have crossed, if you will, a professional Rubicon to arrive at this small but perfectly assembled compendium of western art – the Brockwell Collection!'

A smattering of applause.

Don goes on to enumerate the achievements and aspirations of the museum – just the kind of speech that his guests expect. He stumbles and loses his place at times, but his thoughts are rushing ahead.

'I have been called a lover of classical forms,' he declares, shifting abruptly from minor fundraising triumphs to his final cadenza. 'I make no apology for my belief in the beauty – and, yes, the moral and aesthetic superiority – of the Greco-Roman tradition, as it has permeated our greatest art and architecture. Beauty, virtue . . .'

He tails off for a moment and picks up his glass, waving it in a panoramic arc.

'There are those in the museum world who would decry these values,' he says gravely. 'Those who, for all their education, claim that beauty and virtue are stifling notions – elitist principles, *mystifying*!' He articulates the word with theatrical stress, prompting Herb to sneeze into his napkin. 'I dedicate my directorship to the preservation of truth and beauty!'

Another polite round of applause, and yet the sound harbours within it a rumble of suppressed talk and uneasy laughter. Don commands silence by extending both arms. His satin sleeves spread like wings. The glass in his hand is a crimson lantern.

'I will finish by saying a little, if I may, about the rising generation of museum men and women, for they are the future of this institution and others like it.'

'Hear, hear,' comes a voice from the end of the table.

'They tell us that we must champion openness, that we must ensure *accessibility*. Fine ideas! But while they preach such high ideals – and forgive a pedantic scholar for rebuking hypocrisy – these young democrats speak in a language that *no one* understands.'

His strength of emphasis causes Don to totter slightly, leaning into the table. He recovers his balance.

'A pseudo-philosophy full of puns and flippancy, a creed riddled with evasions and enigmas, taught by charlatans. An insult to those of us – and there remain a few – for whom art history is a serious matter. *They* are the true agents of mystification.'

'Quite right,' Betty murmurs. 'Amen to plain speaking.'

The audience is noiseless. Only the chink and gurgle of a bottle emptying into a glass, somewhere along the table, breaks the silence. He has been artful and subtle in his insinuations. He casts an eye around his audience, dimly perceptible in the candlelight. Michael has a serene, abstracted look – reactionless as a statue.

Yes, he has been too subtle by half. He decides to add a coda. The cutlery bounces as he lands his hand on the table.

'Take my new deputy director.' He fires the words into the flickering silence. 'Mr Michael Ross, as celebrated a curator as you could hope to meet, a gift to the Brockwell, newly arrived from Manhattan. We welcome him here tonight. The Frick's loss is our gain!'

There is an eruption of clapping – a violent release of energy; the guests have elected that this should be the end. Michael fixes his masklike smile on Don. He is waiting – he knows there will be more.

'You will hear the mantra of accessibility upon his lips,' Don cries in a singsong tone over the dying applause. 'Fine words! And such fine lips, too! And yet – and yet' – he fortifies himself with wine (*such fine lips* – what does he mean? But there's no time to reflect) – 'this man reduces the glories of art to trendy axioms. Axioms!' He sweeps his glass through the air. Betty Thackeray touches his arm in a gesture of support.

'A lover of continental *cant*.' This alliterative missile produces a loud titter. Don strokes the carnation on his lapel, turning his eyes on Michael, who meets his gaze with inscrutable calm. 'I fear I shall have my work cut out in making a serious classicist out of this young wordsmith,' he adds with a silvery laugh. 'But he is, to be sure, a celebrated curator. The Frick's loss is our gain!'

He sets his glass down – empty now – and bows to signal the end of his oration. Leftover lumps of peach melba flash at him, orange and scarlet, from out of the ranks of glass and silver.

No one speaks. Then, gradually, as if applause has been passed over or forgotten, conversations break out furtively along the table. Everyone seated close to Don – Michael included – turns away and falls into evasive chatter.

As he stares at them, Don feels an overpowering need. He strides from the room.

Entering the gents, he surveys himself in the mirror and is dismayed to find that his satin jacket is streaked – from collar to waist – with red wine. It gives the impression of his carnation having exploded and leaked its lovely dye. The flower looks limp. He wonders if the dim light of the gallery concealed the spillage, and then ponders whether Michael somehow conspired to spill it there. Never mind. The speech (*the speech* – so long in the planning, so swift in the execution!) will have diverted attention from this trivial flaw.

He floods the toilet with piss. It sprays in wayward fashion, dancing off the floor and walls, flying in glittering arabesques.

He returns to the table. There is a noticeable lull as he takes his seat. Michael looks at him, with a look that gives nothing away – serious but disquietingly serene.

'What rhetoric,' Betty Thackeray says, with what he perceives to be an unnecessary shot of irony. 'I love a man who can thump the tub.'

Don smiles obsequiously.

She lowers her voice and leans towards him. 'We knew you weren't a wimp, me and Herb. I guess you could say we're cut from the same political cloth. Herb hates them smooth-talkin' liberals.'

'I'm afraid you've quite misunderstood me,' Don says. 'As far as politics are concerned, I have no interest. Truth and beauty will do for me. Would you please pass the wine?'

It should have been a moment of triumph. But as he says goodbye to the guests in the lobby, he feels desolate. He is uncomfortably aware of his blemished jacket, but there is more to it. A needling worry. Did his points hit home, and what – come to think of it – *were* those brilliant arrow-tipped points?

The guests file past, saying little, and he is horrified to observe the faces of people he recognises from other times and places.

Robin Hands, the radio host, sweeps past – pretending not to recognise him – and then the grey and impassive figure of Sir Ronald Braun, who declines to shake his hand. They are followed by Frank Davis, one-time Master of Peterhouse. He is not accompanied by his wife.

Frank nods at him – a hard, sceptical nod – and simply says, 'I'm sorry, Don,' as if he is offering condolences.

Don has the unpleasant suspicion that Michael managed to slither from his grasp at the very moment he tried to strangle him. Truth and beauty have run away to hide like mischievous children. Perhaps they have taken Michael with them: he is nowhere to be seen as the guests file out, a modulating stream of colours, into the cloudless, starry night.

Walking home, he is surprised by a voice. It calls his name – a soft but definite sound. He looks around at the trees, fences and rubbish sacks – disembowelled and spewing over the pavement. Not a person in sight.

Finally – at the mercy of his sluggish senses – he sees that a car has drawn up parallel to him. It is a beige Ford Escort. Its engine turns over.

'Don!'

He steps towards the open passenger window. Even after he has seen her face, it takes him several seconds to comprehend who it is. He rests his hands on the edge of the window.

'What are you doing out here?' Anna asks.

'I'm going home.'

'But this is nowhere near your place.'

'Isn't it?'

'Get in, I'll drop you back.'

He tries to stand up and knocks his head on the frame of the window. Surely she can smell the clouds of wine rolling off him.

'Get in,' she says again with a gentle laugh.

Without a word, he opens the door and climbs in. The rounded end of her cello case protrudes between the front seats like a third head. Quiet acoustic music plays on the radio. They sit for a while with the engine humming. Anna seems in no hurry to move on.

'I suppose you heard,' he says, then falls silent. The speech he made at dinner has mutated, in the short time since he walked out of the museum, from a ringing victory to a disaster. The cool night has rearranged his feelings, eroded his assurance. 'Why haven't you gone home?'

'Insomnia.' Anna keeps her eyes on the deserted road. 'I drive around most nights. All over the place. It's my substitute for sleep – roaming around London in the car.'

She taps the gear-stick and the car edges forwards. Don watches the street slide past and feels a tide of air through the window. She extends her bare arms straight, over the top of the wheel, and he studies the arrangement of her hair and earrings and dress. There are tiny lines around her eyes. She must know that he is staring, but she seems unconcerned.

He is frightened of what she'll say – about tonight, about the dinner party at her house, about Michael. He waits to be confronted by damning facts. But she just steers the car as if hypnotised. His heart grows heavy. He can feel it filling up with regret.

'Tonight was terrible,' he whispers. 'I lost control.'

The words sober him as he utters them, making him realise how drunk he was. Anna accelerates along an arterial route. Semi-consciously, he reads the signs: Clapham Junction, Herne Hill, Tulse Hill.

'No, I'm wrong,' he murmurs. 'Not a loss of control. More a case of *that man*' – he pinches his wine-spattered jacket – 'wrapping himself around me.' They stop at an open crossroads, and the indicator ticks loudly. 'Did you hear what I said? At the dinner, I mean – all those things I said?'

'I was sitting in the next gallery with the quartet. We had our own table, servants' quarters – never mind that I'm married to Michael.' She glances at him – a fast, humorous look that fades in a second. 'But yes, I heard.'

No judgement, no reproach. Nothing that she's going to verbalise, at any rate. He feels the heavy clump of the carnation on his chest and unfixes it, tugging off the petals before dropping it from the window. It hits the car door with a damp tap.

Anna's gaze is level and unreadable. 'Tell me,' she says.

He stares out of the window for a while before speaking. 'I've always hated big events, just like you were saying earlier. But tonight, some insane power took hold. It felt incredible. Breadth and depth, that's what I was feeling. Powerfully unlike myself. It was as if I was flying . . .' He tails off, then starts again. 'And then those words came out, and I thought they were marvellous. I'd never felt more real. Oh God.'

'Have you read *Doctor Faustus*?' she asks, changing down gears for a red light. 'Marlowe.'

'I haven't read the play. I know the legend.'

'A gap in your reading.' She laughs and turns to him. 'Well, Faustus was the greatest scholar of his age, a man of *immense* status. He made a pact with the Devil, and won fantastic power, the power to do anything he wanted. He could even conjure Helen of Troy like *that*' – she snaps her fingers above the steering wheel – 'out of nowhere.'

'I remember the Helen scene. I must have seen a production once. She comes to him like a beautiful ghost.'

'*Sweet Helen, make me immortal with a kiss.*' Anna watches him as she quotes.

'A tale of hubris.'

'But it's not the hubris that's interesting. It's that Faustus couldn't transcend his human brain, his desires. His character still controlled him – the proud scholar, the petulant man.' She laughs loudly, as if at a preposterous joke. 'Helen of Troy appeared, and he was still *that man*.'

'And Faustus was so unlikeable,' he says. 'I remember that too. So unsympathetic.'

'A total bastard?'

'Yes, exactly.'

'Well' – she lifts both hands momentarily from the wheel in a kind of shrug – 'who isn't disagreeable at some level? I reckon we're all as bad, or as good, as each other when it comes down to it. We're all hypocritical, self-regarding, whatever you want to call it.'

'Oh, Anna. I wish I could . . . feel more. I wish I always felt like *this*.'

They speed along for some time, over a flyover, before she answers. Her face is a disc of light against the reeling South Circular.

'Don, don't you ever ask yourself what it is that you want?'

The image of his destroyed pictures, hundreds of fragments strewn across the carpet, floats through his head, and he tries to imagine what Ben is doing now, this very moment. Does she expect an answer? Is she even asking him, or is it a question posed, via him, to herself?

He tries to plunge into the undisturbed waters of his mind, but it's as if he is meeting his own reflection, knocking the image into shivering distortions as he attempts to touch and hold and invade his own body. His eyes refocus and he catches sight of himself in the wing mirror. He looks terrible.

'I wish I didn't have to go back to being that person.'

'Maybe it's enough just to desire something more,' Anna says. 'To want to become larger than yourself. That Helen encounter was a failed attempt, but what a failure.'

Before long, by a kind of magic, the car has re-entered Dulwich. He recognises the gateposts of the Brockwell Collection and the drinking fountain that looks like a lopped obelisk. In another minute, Anna is pulling up alongside Val's house.

'I don't want to go back.' Don utters the words to himself, barely audibly. The wine inside him is beginning to turn to poison – the catalyst of a hangover.

'Nor do I,' says Anna. 'Try being Michael's wife. It's true, though, what you said.' She giggles. 'He does have remarkable lips. Like a Van Dyck. He's very conscious of them, believe it or not.'

They stop talking, and sit with the engine running, just as it was when she picked him up. Don's heavy heart seems to pin him to the seat, next to her, with the radio pulsing in the near distance and with Anna's face – eyes, earrings, hair – appearing to close in on him. A sudden impulse makes him want to grab hold of her, kiss her . . .

'You know, Don,' she says, arresting his fantasy, 'you're not as bad as you think you are. Or as good.'

His heart wobbles and he feels tears rushing to his eyes. Then in an instant he is laughing, and so is she.

*

He doesn't make it into the Brockwell until twelve. He has missed the weekly staff meeting, slept through it completely. What would have been unthinkable only a week ago is now a matter of small relief.

He shuts himself in the Palladian Library and locks his door from the inside, praying that no one will knock on it. Soon, however, he becomes nervous that no one has. The silence is maddening. Hours pass in the form of a slow, cumulative dose of guilt and regret.

He is too weak and discomposed to work. So he sits facing the window and watches the serene, unchanging garden. Occasionally, Paul appears, going about his work. For a while, he is close to the window, pruning the roses – apparently unaware of Don's silent, morose presence behind the glass.

At some point, Don falls asleep in his chair. When he wakes – perhaps only minutes later – he turns to see that a piece of paper has appeared on the floor from under his door. Feebly, he rises and crosses the room to collect it.

It is a typewritten note from Maud, requesting a meeting with him at nine o'clock the following morning.

*

At five minutes to nine, he ambles across the front lobby, past a crowd of schoolboys loitering around the books and card carousels. A few of them are laughing at the contents of a book. He attempts to see what it is – Kenneth Clark's *The Nude*, perhaps. He can't be sure.

A few minutes later, Maud stands facing him across his desk.

'It has come to our attention that you may be suffering from exhaustion,' she says. 'Nervous exhaustion.'

Don smiles. '*Our* attention? I don't believe anyone else is under that misapprehension.' He opens a small walnut box that sits on his desk, a recent purchase from Dulwich Village Antiques, and removes a Turkish cigarette. 'In fact, I've never been less exhausted in my life.' He brandishes the unlit cigarette as if it were the key to his vigour.

'Your behaviour at the Benefactors' Dinner was bizarre. Embarrassing. Unacceptable.'

He has been wondering about offering a defence, some kind of explanation. A joke gone wrong, academic badinage that wasn't delivered in quite the way he intended . . . But even in his head, his reasons seem preposterous. And so he says nothing and concentrates on maintaining a face of calm, slightly wistful dignity.

'We – and I have the backing of the trustees – recommend a fortnight's rest—'

His mask slips. 'This is Michael Ross's doing.'

'—pending a review.'

'A review?'

'Your position as Director is probationary for the first six months.'

Don sits back and turns slightly in his chair. The schoolboys are wandering in the garden.

'You can tell Michael Ross—' he says, then breaks off. He strikes a match and holds it, forgetting to light the cigarette, until it burns his fingers. He shakes it violently to death.

'I will notify the staff that you are taking a leave of absence.' Maud's pearl necklace gleams in the dusk of the unlit room. 'Two weeks. Health related. Try to see it not as a suspension and more as a . . . temporary relaxation of your duties.' She smiles and then frowns, as if remembering too late that this is a serious matter. Her face is a cross-wiring of emotions.

'Val Black won't tolerate this.'

'Val knows all about it.' There is quiet triumph in her voice. 'I called him in New York yesterday.'

'New York? What are you talking about? Val is in Cambridge. I spoke to him on the morning of the dinner.'

She looks doubtful. 'Perhaps he hadn't left at that point. But he's there now. He went for the unveiling of the new Tiepolo at the Frick Collection.'

'Why on earth would he do that?' Don hears his voice hoarsening.

'Well, he's a trustee. And the guest of honour, I should imagine.'

Beneath his desk, Don pulls the cigarette to shreds.

The first day of his suspension is long and empty. The house is lifeless. Ben is at Goldsmiths. The annex is its own sealed world. He traipses up and down the stairs, spending long actionless periods at the kitchen table and at his desk.

All day he waits. Finally, in the evening, Val telephones. The line is scratchy.

'I hope you know, Don, that I wanted this whole sorry matter dismissed *out of hand*. But it was out of my power. All of the other trustees were there at the Benefactors' Dinner. They witnessed your – your *tirade*, shall we say, first-hand. Perhaps if I'd been there . . .'

Don inhales deeply. 'How is New York, Val?'

The line goes silent. For a moment, it seems as if Val has hung up. Then comes a shuffling, airy sound. Val is moving, or whispering – possibly – to another person in the room. 'Sweltering,' he says at last. 'New Yorkers hate the city in the summer. I rather love the broiling heat. It's a brief visit – very brief.'

'Too brief to bother mentioning?'

The pause is shorter than before. 'I thought you had enough to worry about. Was I wrong?'

'Tell me what happened at the Frick. You're a trustee there? And *The Martyrdom*—'

'You'll find out soon enough,' Val interrupts, with a smoothness that can't entirely disguise his annoyance. 'Not everything is as you might imagine, Don. Things are more complicated. *Life* is more complicated.' He sighs. 'There was a setback. American scholars—' he checks himself. 'Nothing to concern you, though. You have your own crisis to navigate.'

'It'll blow over.'

'Not just like that. A report will have to be sent to the trustees. Fortunately for you, I will be the author.'

Over the crackling line, Val gives an improvised recitation of the report he intends to write. Professor Lamb was exhausted and overworked. Struggling under the burden of authoring a major book and running a museum, he suffered a lapse of judgement. A period of leave will restore him to health. He will carry the Brockwell Collection to new heights.

'You'll be in the clear after a fortnight, Don.' Val's voice has softened. 'Remember Milton. *What though the field be lost? What is else not to be overcome?*'

Val will step in and save him. Perhaps the facts are just as he has them. The Frick Collection received the Tiepolo painting on a long-forgotten promise – and Val really was detained at Peterhouse on the day of the Benefactors' Dinner, before flying out to New York the following morning. Perhaps . . . But Don perceives that he is skirting the boundary of an enshrouded truth.

The next morning, he is sitting in the kitchen when Ben rushes in. His hair is wet and he clutches his rucksack in one hand. He tips coffee granules into a mug, saying that he needs to catch an early bus to Goldsmiths.

Ben is amused, and not remotely scandalised, when Don tells him what has happened.

'You're better off out of there for a while,' he says. 'I can't see how it matters.'

Don studies him for a while. 'Well,' he says with strained nonchalance, 'if you take a nihilistic view of life, then I suppose nothing matters. If you believe that a life's work is no more than an art-school game – if destruction is all your joy . . .' He falls silent, seized by a surprise emotion.

Ben watches him with intrigue. Don strains to detect some hint of an admission in the young man's eyes, the slightest signal of contrition for the sliced-up pictures. But all he sees is serene good humour.

'You're free,' Ben says with a shrug. 'Unfixed – for a while. What are you going to do?'

Don sits and listens to the sounds of Ben opening and closing cupboards, running a tap, clicking his rucksack closed. He feels strange – plaintive and excited. What does the rucksack contain, he wonders? Should he demand to inspect it? In his mind's eye, he sees himself grabbing the bag, and Ben wrestling him for it – a furious, hysterical fight in the kitchen.

'I'll go out,' he murmurs, as Ben leaves the room. 'To the park.'

As the day passes, Don feels a burden lifting. His phase of relaxation has coincided with the start of July and even warmer weather. In the early afternoon, he walks down to Brockwell Park.

He climbs the hill to Brockwell Hall and looks for the spot where he saw the two men in the night. Walking around the house and across the broad plateau of grass beyond, he seeks out the iron water pump where the dog was tied. He can't see it. Did he imagine it? He walks a while further, and suddenly the pump has appeared – having risen up, seemingly, from the ground. He strayed further that night than he realised.

Beyond the pump is the large crop of bushes where he stood before, a miniature forest of glossy laurels. He finds a point where the bushes divide inconspicuously, and pushes his way through the partition, closing his eyes against the scratching, rustling leaves. He opens them to see a bright oval of long grass, completely enclosed by shoulder-high shrubbery. The space is larger than it looked at night, perhaps ten metres across. The sun spills across the grass, some of which has turned a blanched, brownish hue.

He walks to the middle of the plot and lies down. The sky is an uninterrupted blue block. In his ears is the lethargic buzzing of bees and other insects. A white butterfly flutters across the peaks of the seed heads, close to his hand. He imagines that he has been transported to his own small piece of Arcadia. The intermittent noise of the London park – barks and laughter and children's voices – is just an illusion, a memory of his urban existence, and *this* is his true habitat, a parcel of prehistoric Greece.

He thinks of how the two men lay here and seemed to merge, at first, into a swivelling, urgent, muscular whole.

The grassy enclosure is shadeless. He has grown hot. And so he removes his jacket. A little while after, he unbuttons his shirt and eases off his shoes and socks.

Who will find him here – who can even see? With new boldness, he removes his shirt and vest and kicks off his trousers. He makes a pillow for himself with his rolled-up shirt. Only his underpants remain as he lies back in the dry, bouncy grass, feeling it tickle his neck and shoulders. Solar warmth radiates through his body.

Thoughtlessly, as he looks up at the sky, he runs a finger beneath the waistband of his underpants, this way and that.

He goes to Brockwell Park every day for the next fortnight. The luminous summer is loveliest at the beginning of the day, before the heat has built. He stands each morning next to Brockwell Hall and watches the sunlight roll across the rooftops of south London. Sometimes he stays in the park until well into the afternoon, dozing in his secret enclosure.

*

'Oh, you'll love this. SICK BED has been incinerated. Burnt to cinders.'

Don checks his watch – it isn't quite seven o'clock in the morning. He clutches the phone to his ear and reaches for the glass that he left beside his bed the night before. He drinks a long, slow mouthful of stale wine, while Val says something about life being stranger than art.

'Well, Don? Say something! Did you hear what I said? There's nothing left of SICK BED but a charred husk.'

'Good.'

'Yes, perhaps. But the thing is, it was *deliberate*. Erica – Angela Cannon, I mean – came and did it herself. She called it a performance. Everyone was there, the whole college, standing around the court like we do for Remembrance Sunday. She set fire to the thing and it burned for hours, *violently*. Soaring flames! It was like Dido immolating herself on the pyre. Some of the bottles had been filled with gasoline. Horrific explosions, glass everywhere. You should have seen it, Don, just horrific. But rather wonderful too. An autodestructive end, she called it.'

Don drinks again and looks around the room, over the lip of his duvet cover. Sunlight prises its way through the gap between the curtains. He feels the rays on his hand. He knows that a reaction is demanded of him. But it is his final day of freedom before he returns to the museum, and every impulse is coaxing him towards the park. He wonders how to end the call.

Val hums quietly – as if intrigued by some private thought – before he speaks again.

'It really did gain something, you know, in the act of performance – just like her poetry. The remains of *SICK BED* will stay on the lawn in perpetuity. An autodestructive end – just fancy that.'

14

Everyone is pleased to see him back. Suspiciously pleased. Michael gives him a sportsmanlike clap on the arm and says something about cobwebs being blown away. The words pass over Don in a wave of good cheer. He meditates afterwards on what exactly Michael said, and what he meant.

He is interrupted by a knock on the door of the Palladian Library. Maud strides into the room, her face alive with pleasure. She is followed by a tall man with long black hair who holds a plastic cube. For an insane moment, Don imagines that he is witnessing an arcane ritual – Maud as a high priestess, ecstatic with ceremonial fervour . . . The man sets the cube down heavily on his desk.

'Your new computer, Professor Lamb,' she says.

Don stares at her, then at the black box and keyboard.

'You'll find it immensely useful,' she says, as the man kneels and fiddles with wires and plugs beneath the desk, his hair dropping around his face like a veil. 'Thank you, Hashem.'

Inwardly, Don vows never to use it.

'We'll have you connected to the web in no time.'

'The web?'

She gives an august smile. 'The World Wide Web. Haven't you heard? The Brockwell is going to be *connected* – joined to the electronic cosmos. It's the future!'

*

They are in the sitting room, late on a midweek evening, drinking wine. Back in their happy routine.

'Tell me about who you were before,' Ben says.

'Before what?'

'Before you became Professor Don.'

Don lights a cigarette. 'There's really nothing to tell. I became who I am – who I *really* am – when I went to Cambridge. Cambridge made me, I'm sure of it.'

'I'm not.'

They both laugh.

'I mean it,' Ben says. 'Cambridge wasn't your mother. You didn't slip out from between the stone thighs of King's chapel.'

'King's *College* Chapel.' Don can't resist the temptation to correct. 'And I'd say they're more like hoofs than thighs. Ruskin, in fact, compared the chapel to a table turned upside down with its four legs in the air.' He takes a long drag of his cigarette and squashes it into an ashtray. 'I grew up in an ordinary home. Very ordinary. People assume, because of how I sound, that I come from a world of money and connections and iron-gated privilege – like Val. But I don't.'

'Then why do you sound the way you do?'

'I don't know. I suppose I cultivated it.'

'It sounds to me as if Cambridge *unmade* you. Took away whatever had been there before.'

Don pauses and lights another cigarette. 'But I'm not sure what that was. My father was a local government official in Poole. My mother painted watercolours and wrote poems. An artist manqué, you might say. They died a long time ago. They were already old when I was a boy. What does that tell you?'

He is struck, as he says this, by the memory of what Anna Ross told him. She is also an only child, without parents, in exile from her former life.

'Cambridge made me an outsider, a strange kind of renegade.'

'You – a renegade?' Ben looks at him archly.

Don casts his eyes over the ceiling. 'Back when I was a student, there was a socialist uprising in Cambridge. The Garden House riot. The hotel next door to Peterhouse was hosting a delegation of Greek officials, and a group of students stormed the place. It was a protest against the Greek regime. The ringleader was an undergraduate in my year, one of those public-school types who had converted to Marxism. I forget his name, but he came banging on my door in the middle of the night, telling me to join the battle. They had broken into the hotel and were smashing the place up. Just another kind of tyranny. I kept silent – pretended to be asleep. I was thinking of the hotel staff, the men and women who would have to clean up the next day – I suppose it was to do with the fact that my father had once worked in a hotel. I felt closer to *them* than to the revolutionaries. Respectability had never seemed so entrancing – so right.'

'Jesus, Don.'

'I'm just telling you how I felt.' He sits forward and looks hard at Ben. 'Maybe I was always an outsider. I was an odd child. I lived in books – in here.' He taps his head with one finger.

'Yeah, I can just see it.'

Don meets Ben's humour with sad seriousness. 'The drive to achieve was always there. That's what makes your mode of life so odd to me.'

'*My* mode of life?' Ben is trying not to laugh. He leans over to the coffee table and fills their glasses.

'Your wandering existence, your pleasure in doing nothing. The long hours of drinking. It would be torture for a man like me. I never took a day's rest at your age.'

'But look at you now. You're more drunk than I am.'

Don is about to object when the stick of ash that has grown out of the end of his cigarette crumbles onto his sleeve.

'I don't believe you, anyway. About never taking a day's rest.' Ben stands and walks to the mantelpiece. From a dense cluster of pictures – Val's dead relatives, classical statues, Dresden cathedral bombed into ruins – he plucks a small photograph in a silver frame. 'Haven't you seen this?' He holds it under Don's eyes.

The picture is black and white and hard to make out – an angular mosaic of light and shade. Then he sees it: a group of men in blazers, on the cusp of adulthood. They are on board a punt. At the back of the boat, apart from the others, sits an older man, perhaps in his late thirties. He is lean and handsome; his black hair sweeps back in a mass from his forehead. The sidelong glance and wan smile are unmistakeable.

'It's Val,' Don murmurs.

'Yes. And who else?'

Don's finger lands on the glazed surface. Among the four figures at the front of the boat is a young version of him, Don Lamb – a delicate, dark-eyed boy, looking down at the water in sombre abstraction . . . It produces a tremor of shock to see himself – and to know that he looked like that, once. The picture must have been taken from another boat or from the bank of the river – but when? The other figures are turned away or cloaked in shade. Only the expressions of Val and Don shine out – the older man watching the younger one, the younger one lost in thought.

'We look so young.' Don brings the picture close to his eyes.

'But it's you all right. Even I could see that. I noticed it the first night I stayed here.'

The picture has the effect – peculiar to black and white photographs taken on sunny days – of reality sharpened, of an unremarkable event bathed in the sheen of a film still. A play of light and shade . . . He wonders what he was looking at, over the side of the boat – his own reflection in the water? Or was he simply shunning the camera?

As he stares, he can sense Ben's amused disdain for everything the picture represents – blithe privilege, narrowness of experience, guiltless elitism.

'I don't know,' he says at last, looking up. 'It's hardly me at all. What parts are the same? The cells of my brain have replaced themselves, every one of them, since then. I have no memory of when it was.'

They look together at the picture. Then Ben says, 'I think he was in love with you. The way he looks at you—'

'Val? Impossible.' Don's laugh descends into a throaty cough. He reaches for his glass.

'Is it?'

Don attempts to cast his mind back to those years when Val was his doctoral supervisor, but the memory that comes to him – ambushes him – is recent. Val in the Fellows' Garden, only eight months ago, turning to him with that bizarre declaration: 'I love you.'

For the first time, like a drug beginning to take effect, the possibility races through his head – before doubts rush in to counteract it. He lays the photograph on the sofa.

'It is possible to read more into images than is really there. A compulsion to narrativise—'

'And sometimes it's impossible to miss their real meaning,' Ben interrupts. 'And sometimes that meaning has to do with who's been looking at the picture and what they've been feeling. I mean – what is this picture doing on Val Black's mantelpiece? Come to think of it, what are you doing in his house?'

'You know very well. This is my temporary home.'

'You're in his house, sleeping in his bed, doing a job he's given you.' Ben is suddenly exasperated. 'His stuff' – he glances around the room scathingly – 'is all around you. It's as if he's here now – as if this *house* is him.'

'You're being ridiculous. I see Val more rarely than I ever did in Cambridge.'

'But how often do you speak to him? How often does he phone?'

Don doesn't reply.

'I'd say,' Ben persists, 'he has you as close as he can get you.

It might be from a distance, but he's still sitting there, watching you. He may not love you the way he did, but he's still – I don't know – obsessed.'

Don stands and returns the picture to the mantelpiece. As he does so, another picture catches his eye. A man and woman – probably Val's parents – sitting on a sandy beach. Dark-haired, handsome, beautiful, on holiday. The buildings behind them are 1950s concrete blocks. It doesn't look like England.

'It's odd,' he says.

'What's odd?'

'No one has ever spoken to me about my life. Not in this way.'

'Does it bother you?'

'No, I don't think so.' Don's words float out like a chain of bubbles. 'It's odd, too, that I hadn't seen that photograph. Or maybe I had seen it, but without looking closely, without really seeing it.'

His whole body feels liquid and volatile. Could it simply be the vertigo of seeing the picture? He looks at Ben, who is looking back at him, and he reflects that Ben is the same age as he was then.

'I think,' he says slowly, 'that I may have drunk too much.'

The following morning, a newspaper cutting arrives in the post. It is a snipped-out paragraph from the *Cambridge Echo*, enclosed in an envelope without an accompanying note.

Last Saturday, Peterhouse College was the unlikely setting for a work of performance art. A sculptural installation in the college's quadrangle was deliberately set on fire, causing a sequence of minor explosions. Angela Cannon, the artist behind the spectacle, described it as 'a metamorphosis'.

Don carries the fragment of paper into the sitting room.

It is just what Val used to do at Peterhouse – leave little

cuttings from the newspapers in Don's pigeonhole. Items of humour or mild interest. But this is not a joke he wants to share in. He decides he will give the cutting back, hide it inside one of Val's books.

He skims the shelves in the sitting room, passing along the different categories – French and German literature, metaphysical poetry, aesthetics. Stopping at this last section, he notices a slim yellow volume. He tugs it out. *The Neoclassical Pose* – Val's first book. The spine cracks as he opens it. The pages have turned a rich ochre. The typography – sans serif, mid-century – is almost quaint in its simplicity. He reads a few pages, and is struck once again by the book's style. Lucid, assured, but also radically unadorned – purged of commas and adjectives. There is a stark, surreal bluntness about it, despite the sophistication of the arguments.

He returns Val's book to its place, still holding the newspaper cutting, and moves to the shelf containing classical literature. There is certain to be a copy of the *Metamorphoses* of Ovid.

Sure enough, he soon spots an edition of John Dryden's translation of the Latin text. It is marked with gold lettering on its red spine. The second it takes him to read the spine seems to expand infinitely. It is his book – his copy – the book that he thought was lost or thrown away. The one in which he concealed his letter to Anders Andersson, decades ago, after the letter came back to him as a silent symbol of rejection.

He slides the book off the shelf and opens it. His own name is pencilled in the inside front cover, in his own writing. How has it ended up on Val's shelf? Staring into his mind, he chases after all the streaming possibilities, tries to hold on to them. Only one thought remains in his grasp. It is that he gave or lent the book to Val – they often swapped books in those days.

He stands holding the volume, as still as a character in a painting. Would he have removed the letter beforehand? He had hidden it in the pages like a relic inside a casket, never to be extracted. Something tells him that if he had remembered about the letter, he would never have given away the book. The probability that he passed the book to Val without thinking – the letter still concealed within it – settles down deep inside him.

He flicks through to see if the letter is there, knowing that it won't be. He shakes the book by the spine.

And then – could Val have thought the letter was for him? With a spasm of unease, Don wonders whether he actually addressed it to Anders by name. It is just conceivable that the letter was an impersonal declaration, made out to no one in particular, in the manner of a classical apostrophe. A mad boy's love song.

He snaps the book closed, slides it into his pocket and circles the room. No, impossible: Val was too clever, too cynical, to believe it was for him. He always understood the truth of things. Don can see him now – the young Professor Black, already an academic star in the late 1960s, raising his eyebrows at his student's handwritten confession and then folding it away.

*

He is reading the Saturday edition of *The Times*. Gossip about the unravelled marriage of Charles and Diana has pushed all real news to the margins.

'It's the opening of that show tonight.'

'What show?'

Ben has woken, having slept for half the afternoon on the velvet sofa.

'That exhibition I told you about. Want to come?'

Pitching himself onto one elbow, Ben explains that the exhibition is at an old betting shop near the Oval cricket ground. He and some friends are displaying their work. He suggests that they walk over there.

Don folds his newspaper. It is a sultry afternoon. He is wearing a linen jacket over a tieless shirt, his typical summer attire, but he feels hot and constrained. He fingers the buttons of his shirt and unfastens another one. With his knuckles he skims the haze of stubble at the top of his neck. The idea of a pilgrimage through south London strikes him with the force of a grand plan.

They set out at four o'clock and walk down to Herne Hill, passing the Rosses' house on Craxton Road, then treading the border of Brockwell Park, on towards Denmark Hill. In the heat, people fill the streets. On a mound of grass at the foot of a tower block, two girls in crop-tops are bending over with laughter. They are in their early teens. One of them sits down on the grass and rolls onto her side. Her hair falls in a curl across one eye. The other eye meets Don's as he and Ben pass.

They come to King's College Hospital – a montage of buildings from different eras, Modernist accretions around a Victorian nucleus. On the pavement outside, the doors of a wailing ambulance fly open. A body is strapped to a stretcher beneath blankets, ending in a bald pink head like the tip of a frankfurter. Paramedics rush the bundle onto a waiting trolley.

The road widens into a junction. A young woman walks across their path, pushing a buggy. The plastic handles are bubble-gum pink.

'It's a relief to have left my work behind,' Don says, after many minutes of silence.

'But you never really leave it behind, do you?' replies Ben. 'It's in your head wherever you are.'

Don's eyes rifle through the mess of the road junction, a chaotic interface of billboards, traffic lights, railings and signs.

'That may be true. When I look up this scruffy road, I see the idealised structures of Piero della Francesca's pristine city. Does that seem ridiculous?'

'Yes, a bit.'

Don is undeterred. 'Look ahead – the converging pavements,

the cylindrical building at the junction. You could build a frame around the scene and it would resemble a painting of the Italian Renaissance, structurally at least: the world receding to distant points. You could draw lines over the surface of the image, mapping the recession of space.' He tilts his head back and squints. 'Then – just imagine that system of lines applied upwards.'

'That's what you're doing with Tiepolo's paintings?'

'Precisely. Their infinite blue space can be dissected, triangulated. Infinity is only an illusion.'

'But what's the point?'

'It's not a simple case to explain. The book has reached a very difficult stage.'

Ben turns and grins ironically. Perhaps he knows that the book hasn't advanced in weeks. 'When you stopped just now and looked at the sky, you weren't measuring it. You weren't thinking about classical proportion. You were *feeling* something.'

They pass Camberwell Green. Ben says he knows a pub close to Burgess Park; he identifies it from its green-tiled façade. They stop for a half of lager. The dark interior – even darker on this sunny afternoon – is filled with smoke and silence.

Afterwards, they come to a straggling parade of shops. Teenagers hang around the entrances. Plastic boxes stacked outside a greengrocer's release the sweet-acrid scent of fruit and veg. The next shopfront consists of a glass sarcophagus arrayed with raw meat – cross-sectioned, minced, cubed, patterned with creamy fat and skewered with star-shaped pieces of green card that announce prices and weights in scribbled pen. The colours of objects, their small details, enter Don's vision like new phenomena – things he's never seen.

'To be honest with you,' Don says as they turn onto John Ruskin Street, 'I have spent little time in London over the years. When I did come it was usually to Bloomsbury, the academic precincts. Cambridge was my world.'

'You never thought of leaving?'

'Not until last year. Before that . . .' He thinks for a moment. 'I couldn't think why one would want to live anywhere else.'

Ben looks straight ahead. 'You couldn't see beyond Cambridge. But I reckon it was more than that. There are whole parts of your life that you seem to have forgotten. Things about yourself. Academia should have been called amnesia, in your case.'

Don nods, thinking of life at Peterhouse and how each year resembled the last, and how people never left or changed – how life was a rolling present tense. But that is in the past, now.

'Perhaps a dimension of time has entered my life at last,' he says.

'Let's hope so.' Ben starts to laugh. 'Only time will tell.'

Don's eyes trip along the shopfronts – Ladbrokes, Timber Sales, Off Licence, We Buy Gold – and he falls into a kind of trance. Everything is visual noise and vivid sensation. An unused shop is plastered with posters repeating the name of Jah Shaka. Ahead are two policemen. The metal crowns of their helmets flash erratically. A lorry has stopped in the road, arousing angry shouts and volleys of car horns. Its back end is shuttered – a blank panel, ridged horizontally. They come to a second-hand furniture shop where half of the stock seems to have been turned out on the pavement. Padded armchairs and battered tables, clapped-out sofas, electric fires and a Formica chest rise in ramshackle piles, the flotsam of two decades ago. A young woman is sitting in one of the armchairs, watching life go by. She is gaunt, lank-haired, and wears a black leather jacket, jeans and leather boots. Don wonders why she has stopped here and where she will go afterwards. As he comes near, she closes her eyes against the sun.

He isn't aware, at first, that they have arrived. They are among a mass of people on a stretch of pavement beneath the skeleton of a gas cylinder. The crowd is unlike anything he has seen. Men and women in rough, inelegant clothes or few clothes at all (he sees bare arms and legs clothed in tattoos), characters who seem sexless or both sexes at once, faces of different colours . . . He smiles to think of the Caravaggio opening at the Brockwell, and then the Benefactors' Dinner. He feels intrepid and bohemian.

Ben nods and grins at person after person. Don follows, mesmerised – conscious of glances in his direction. These people who are so utterly alien to him are, of course, entirely familiar to each other. He is the alien – the trespasser.

'A guest not worthy to be here,' he murmurs aloud, muddling and misquoting George Herbert.

'You what?' says a woman standing nearby. She smiles to reveal a gap between her front teeth.

The crowd's feverish mood is emanating from a small door, buoyed along on jet streams of cigarette smoke and a general odour of lager. Above the doorway, the words *CITY RACING* are painted in blockish script – white letters on racecourse green, the spur of the 'G' ducking into a horizontal underscore.

An old woman approaches Don. She is tiny and world-worn, with a pinched, impish face.

'Used to be a bookies,' she says with a wink.

Her accent is pure cockney, almost a parody of cockney. Her breath smells of booze. Ben comes over and hugs her and calls her 'Sandra love'.

'This is my friend Don,' he says.

Sandra turns back to Don. 'Ah yes, we've heard all about you.'

My friend Don. He deposits the words in his memory as the crowd tugs him further in.

Standing close to the shopfront are two men who seem out of place – solemn and upstanding, into their fifties and dressed in matching woollen suits of tawny brown. Their silk ties, too, are matching – baby blue. They stand slightly apart, observing the throng like sentinels.

Sensing kindred spirits, Don approaches the men and extends his hand.

'Professor Don Lamb,' he says, with the aplomb he is used to summoning at social events, but sensing at the same time the absurdity of the appellation among these people, in this place.

The taller of the two men takes his hand. His eyes are large and inquisitive behind thick glasses. His hair is thinning but neat. He looks like a schoolteacher.

Immediately Ben is there, stepping in. 'George, this is Don.'

'Delighted to meet you,' says George in a genteel voice. 'Where are you a professor?'

'I am – was – at Peterhouse Cambridge.'

George smiles wisely. 'The land of punts and cunts, we always call it.'

The other man, his stooge or shorter double, chuckles with amused disdain. Don's aplomb falls into pieces on the cutting-room floor of his brain. He smiles like a fool.

'This way, Don.' Ben guides him over the threshold.

The gallery, as Ben calls it, is emptier than the pavement. It consists of two echoey rooms. The walls are whitewashed, and the ridged concrete floor is coated with a slick of grey paint. The air smells of paint and cigarette smoke. Someone has left an upturned bike on the floor.

Open bottles of beer stand on a table. Don picks one up and drinks.

'Where's the exhibition? Where's the art?'

'Just look around,' Ben says, under his breath.

He and Ben walk in separate directions. He notices now that the upside-down bike has a plank of wood balanced along its top edge (really its bottom edge – the tips of its tyres), and that photographic prints have been arranged in a row along the wooden ledge: photos of a man's naked crotch, providing a repeating view of pale, outspread thighs and a modest belly. The man's genitals have been blocked by objects – apples, a banana, a bunch of red flowers.

Across the room, on a small television, he sees a video of a figure in a gorilla suit, jumping up and down until the suit falls away to expose the spindly, naked man inside.

As he watches, Don fastens his jacket button with one hand and unfastens it again. Ben comes up behind him and puts an arm around him – a loose, careless gesture, precisely calculated – and leads him away.

They walk into the next room. The space is smaller, and empty apart from a single picture in the corner. It is a large work in a frame. It appears to be entirely blue: a panel of light azure, possibly an abstract painting. But as Don comes close, he sees that it is a mosaic – thousands of fragments of paper, all fractionally different in tone, stuck together into a vast composite. Some of them contain wisps of other colours – pink, grey or pale yellow. In places, thin graphite lines flit across the blue.

With a shock he sees, in the meticulously cut sections of paper, the silhouettes of bodies he knows. His eyes trace the profile of the flying horse Pegasus, and the contours of Venus sitting plumply on a cloud. The figures remain as outlines – ghosts – in the sea of blue pieces.

Only the skies – those missing skies from Don's desk and bedroom floor – have been admitted to the picture.

He stares in amazement. 'What have you done? My Tiepolo skies . . .'

'I appropriated them,' Ben says.

Don feels as if he is disappearing into the composition – so meticulous, perverse and purposeless. He tries to summon an appropriate reaction, a feeling of outrage.

'I was going to call it *Annihilating all that's made in a blue heat haze*,' Ben says. 'But that seemed too long – too clever.'

All Don feels is a strange buoyancy. The room around him – its noises and the people who come and go – recede into nothingness. Ben disappears.

There is no perspective – no point of unity. Just granular space extending in every direction. His eyes swim across the variegated colour and his whole body feels giddy. His mind tries to instil borders, but it's as if the picture has streamed beyond its edges – as if those edges were only ever an illusion, there to assuage his intellect. Judgement, discrimination, the rulers and callipers of fine analysis, have all fallen away, just like the scalpelled details of the paintings, leaving – what? He holds his breath and then lets it go in a rush. A raw, untameable sensation.

'What do you reckon he's looking for?' someone says behind him, prompting muffled laughter. 'Maybe he's lost his coat in there.'

The sounds are close yet removed, like voices heard from the interior of a dream.

Breaking away at last from the picture, he retraces his steps to the front door.

Outside, above the iron frame of the gas cylinder, the sky is cooling. It looks like Ben's collage, a million fractured facets. Ben is a few feet away with a group of friends. He comes forward and thrusts another beer into Don's hand. The bottle is cold and slimy, and the label slides around on the glass. His friends turn and watch Don with expressions of benign intrigue.

'So what did you call it, the picture?' Don asks, raising his voice above the noise.

Ben leans close – Don can feel his breath on his ear. 'What *you* called it. *Tiepolo Blue.*'

Don nods and drinks the bitter contents of the bottle. The riotous pitch of the party fills his head. Then, with a beckoning touch of the arm, Ben is letting him know that it's time to move on.

'Let's go,' he says. 'Let's go to Soho.'

They walk around the wall of the cricket ground. A bank of floodlights looms overhead, angled towards the invisible field. They pass blocks of flats, drab friezes of brown brick – only the strings of laundry on the balconies betray the life within.

Then they come to a narrower, darker road lined by office buildings with plate-glass façades.

The road opens onto the embankment. Traffic shoots past. Beyond is the Thames, a metallic strip beneath the pink sky.

They cross the road and stop at the parapet. The tide is high; water laps beneath them. Don is halted by a surge of feeling. Ben stands next to him – their arms touch – and they stare out across the river at the blunt oblong of Millbank Tower and the needle points of the Palace of Westminster. Cranes are scattered across the city, mechanical flamingos asleep on their spindly legs, liquorice-black against the sunset.

He has felt it before when he is alone with Ben, but never so strongly – a clash of exhilaration and anguish, and a sense of infinite time that disappears – always – before he can catch hold of it.

They cross Vauxhall Bridge, where Ben points to a new building on the riverfront. It is a giant Babylonian stack of cream stone and green glass. Don calls it Thatcherite Egyptomania. Ben laughs at this and lights two cigarettes at once. He puts one in Don's mouth. Their eyes meet and Don shivers, although the air is still warm. Then he inhales and feels his body flood with evening calm.

They trek through Westminster and Whitehall and Trafalgar Square. Pigeons squabble and scatter while a busker strums. The National Gallery lurks at the edge of the square. Don thinks of Dirk Coltman, his old acquaintance at the gallery, and realises that he can't remember the man's face.

At last they come to Soho. Ben knows the place with a sleepwalker's intuition. They slide into a pub called the French House, an intimate, shabby hole that feels like an underground cell, a centre of resistance. A ginger-haired woman is singing 'Smoke Gets in Your Eyes', accompanied by a blind man at the piano. Her ageing face is blazing red and her leather skirt ends well above the knees. She smokes while she sings – *When a lovely flame dies . . .* – and opens her mouth to reveal a black throat. Her voice is like pulverised terrazzo.

They wander afterwards through the narrow streets of Soho, past women posing in doorways and past little shops, neon-bright inside open doors, that brim with masks, thongs, whips and dildoes in different shades and shapes, all standing to attention in neat ranks. Don is reminded of the grotto emporia of Venice. Out of the side alleys blows a reek of rubbish and cigarette smoke. Sex is in the air – it permeates the place.

Ben leads him on a zigzagging course through passages dark with grime, beneath a bridge of sighs. Over a solitary doorway, between rubbish bins, Don sees a flashing neon sign: *CALYPSO.*

'That's the Roman spa,' says Ben. 'Homos go there to fuck.'

'*Greek* would be more appropriate.'

They laugh together, and Don wonders – as he often has before – whether Ben counts himself as one of *them*, those men, the homos. Ben probably wouldn't tell him even if he asked. Ben is like a blithe spirit, a sylph who refuses to be caught.

They settle outside another pub and watch as people pour out of the Prince Edward Theatre. A new musical version of *Antigone* is playing.

Ben tells him things, as they stand outside the pub, that he is too drunk to understand. Things about love and revenge, and – odd as it seems – Valentine Black.

Ben is touching Don's wrist and talking in a secretive, urgent voice. The night has taken on the chromium glow of a dream. Are Ben's words, Don wonders as he lounges against the wall, a warning? Is there a warning glow in the lights of Soho, the amber tints of the drinks?

'He wants me away from the house, away from you,' Ben says as he lights one cigarette off the butt of another.

Life seeps past in a warm, unclean flow – a noisy tide of shouting and laughter and car horns and distant music. It overlaps with Ben's voice, like one current of water twining around another.

Don reaches and takes Ben's arm – the cigarette falls from Ben's mouth – and he tries to say what Ben said to him, weeks earlier – that casual, heart-stopping rebuke: 'Lover, you should have come.'

But the words won't issue – they tumble and spill.

At a certain point, memory itself bleeds out into the night, into the fetid drains of Old Compton Street.

*

He wakes early. Light is spilling into the room. Opening his eyes, he realises that there is a man next to him. A blatant, naked presence in his bed, turned away from him – uncovered, legs crossed, arms tucked under the pillow.

For a second or two, before he can make sense of things, he looks at the untensed muscles of Ben's back. The skin is almost reflective. Its gentle topography and minute pores are all that's logical – all that's real.

Then it makes sense. They must have returned late – a taxi from Soho to Dulwich, Don paying – and staggered upstairs. Ben came into the wrong room, accidentally or not accidentally, and flopped into the wrong bed. Don glances down at his buttocks and thighs, four rounded forms (one of them marked by a mole) divided by tight crevices in the shape of a skewed cross. Even as he allows his eyes to linger, he is filled with alarm.

He, at least, is still wearing underwear. Surely, therefore . . . but he can't remember. Everything after that pub in Soho is a beige blank.

As he scans Ben's shoulder blades and the shallow depression running down the centre of his back, he reflects on how close tenderness comes to brutality. His desire to gaze is also a desire to feel, hold and possess.

He edges closer. He brings his lips towards the sleeping body until they're about to touch Ben's skin. When his mouth makes contact, he is surprised by the heat that radiates into him. The scent of Ben's body is a subtle, subcutaneous lure. Don detaches his mouth and slides down the bed. He touches the different sections of the line that runs from the centre of Ben's neck to the top of his backside – with such lightness that only that pulse of warmth in his lips lets him know he's made contact.

Close to his buttocks, where two small dimples appear, Ben's skin acquires a coating of ultra-fine hairs, almost invisible except at close range. Don holds still and feels them tingling against him.

He slides backwards. Gradually he eases himself up on one arm. He leans – slowly and carefully – in order to peer over the horizon of Ben's hip.

Ben snores explosively. Out of his body comes an odour of stale alcohol. Don draws back.

Moving in slow motion, willing the mattress not to creak, Don slides from the bed and, gathering his clothes in his arms, tiptoes from the room.

He doesn't feel hungover that morning. His senses are electrified. Just before the staff meeting, as he walks along the corridor past Henri Rousseau's painting of a tiger hunt, the lost final section of his night in London comes back to him in a bright, lucid jolt.

It was late in the night. They had left the pub in Soho and gone to a subterranean place, a noisy labyrinth of staircases and chambers. They met a man on the stairs, an actor who Ben knew, and they sat with him in a vaulted cave and drank Red Stripe beer. The man must have been in his fifties, but he had a boyish, excitable face – he seemed far younger. Don recalls their meandering talk – how they chatted about Saint Sebastian, Jerusalem, delphiniums, the war in the Balkans.

The actor was sitting between him and Ben for hours. As they chatted, the man plucked a stack of photographs from his pocket, saying they were stills from a film he'd appeared in – a film made by an artist who'd died a year ago. The pictures showed marvellous reconstructions of Caravaggio's paintings using actors and theatrical lighting. Close to the originals, but ingeniously different. Unmistakeably fake. With a grin, the actor pointed to an image of himself in the role of the flagellated Christ.

In the Summer Refectory, the meeting has already begun. Michael Ross appears to be chairing it: he sits back from the table with a leg crossed and the agenda draped over his knee, rotating a pen in his fingers. Don circles the table and takes his seat.

'I want to display the work of an artist who died not long ago,' he declares, interrupting Maud Berenson as she describes a new initiative for school groups. 'A filmmaker called Derek Jarman.'

The room is silent. All eyes are on him.

'Is this on the agenda?' asks Michael.

'He once made a film based on the life of Caravaggio,' Don tells them animatedly. 'A fictional version of the painter's life. An experimental film. It would be a sensational addition to our Caravaggio show.'

Maud, who has been studying her notebook intently, raises her eyes. 'Thank you, Professor Lamb, for that imaginative proposal. But this is a picture gallery, not a cinema. Where could a film possibly go?'

'I've already thought of that. We will black out the Octagon – cover the dome, curtain the doorways, and project the film across an entire wall, over the tops of the paintings. A cinematic mirage on top of the painted scenes.'

Silence. Bill Hoare masticates and swallows.

'It would need to go to the board of trustees,' Michael says.

'Quite,' says Maud. 'And besides, we must consider our regular visitors. We have a loyal following. Who would this be for?'

Don stares at them, remembering his amazement as he saw the pictures in the darkness of the cave. If only he could make them understand. But Michael has already moved to the next item on the agenda.

He attends to usual matters that morning, but by the afternoon he is overcome with inertia. It is a dull, heavy feeling that makes him want to escape. His mind beams out the vision of Ben beside him in bed – a trespasser, but as guiltless and still as the marble *Sleeping Hermaphrodite* of imperial Rome, that beautiful aberration of nature unearthed near the Baths of Diocletian, carved by unknown hands.

He goes outside and sits in the garden on a bench next to the rose beds. The weather is lovely – a dazzling sun, a spotless sky. The garden glitters with colour. Egg-yolk cowslips pierce the lawns.

It is then, by the sudden clearing of a neural pathway, that he remembers another perfect summer afternoon decades ago. He and Val and a few others had gone punting on the Cam – a rare event. Don was feeling drunk, probably for the first time. He remembers lying down in the boat so that his head came close to the water. The calm surface threw back a facsimile of the sky.

Afterwards, off the boat, he and Val were alone – walking back to Peterhouse through Coe Fen. The meadows were spinning. Grazing cattle stood around. Val put an arm around him as they walked – swayed, staggered – over the hillocky grass, and told Don how much he loved him. Then Val tried to kiss him – the memory causes his heart to pound. Don remembers pulling away with a stream of stuttering refusals, and leaving Val there in the meadow, amid the cows.

They never spoke about it afterwards. He feels certain of this. And yet everything around the recollection is a dark blur. How could he have forgotten? He thinks back to the love letter he hid inside Ovid's *Metamorphoses* – the book he gave to Val – and he tries to enter the heart of his friend.

It is true what Ben said. The photograph on Val's mantelpiece – which must have been taken that day – tells a story. The love of an older man, still young himself, for a younger man who didn't know how to return it. Perhaps the raw memory of Anders Andersson was already a defensive reflex, foreclosing other possibilities. Perhaps that book, with its abortive letter, had already reached Val's hands before the fateful day on the river.

The sun's rays sustain their gentle assault. He feels sweat breaking on his forehead.

Over the years, he and Val have settled into comfortable familiarity, the easy repartee of friends who work together, dine together, complain and plot and reminisce together. Rarely have they touched on what they really feel.

Has an element of Val's early passion survived? He gazes over the circle of lawn; the trees are like volcanic clouds of richest green. At some level, he has always known, but he has evaded the knowledge – repressed it – content to believe that their intimacy is an intellectual affair and nothing more (just as Ben said, his academic's life has been one of amnesia). For one of them, though, it has always been an affair of the heart.

The house is empty when he returns from work. Too empty. There are no discarded clothes, no art materials. The whole place is suspiciously tidy.

For an hour or more, he waits in the sitting room. Then, leaping up, he hurries upstairs – both flights – and bursts into the servant's room. The bed is made and empty. The floor is clear. Every sign of Ben has been erased.

Don descends again slowly. He wanders around the house, looking for any stray token, until the atmosphere is stifling and he has to leave. Outside, the sun is still shining. Walking into the Village, he finds himself opposite the Crown and Greyhound. He decides to sit outside and let some time elapse. Perched at the edge of the table, he burns up the vacant hours with wine and cigarettes.

The inkling that Ben has gone – and won't return – is hardening into certainty. Was it embarrassment at the accident last night, ending up in Don's bed? No, not that. He can't believe Ben would care.

Back at the house, he stumbles upstairs and collapses on his bed. He lies fully dressed on one side of the mattress, across from where he saw Ben that morning. He looks for signs – indentations – in the sheet, but the patch of linen keeps gliding off the edge of his vision. He pulls off his shirt, shoes, trousers, underwear – flinging each item on the floor until he's naked.

When he wakes, he is still alone. It isn't yet morning but most of the night has passed. He is lying at a strange angle across the rippling wilderness of the bed. The duvet has fallen to the floor. Electrical signals pour through his mind, mingling images of Ben with the fuzzy reality of the room.

He draws his knees up to his chest and tries to quell his churning thoughts by watching the lightshow on the ceiling of his closed eyes. After a while, he is conscious of a ravenous hunger. He summons all his remaining strength and goes downstairs, not caring that he is naked, gripping the banisters with both hands. In the kitchen fridge there is a packet of cheddar cheese. He tears the wrapper open and sinks his teeth into the cold, hard block. As he does so, he wonders if he can detect a flicker of light behind the frosted glass door into Ina's annex

– a dim, pale light that reminds him of the dog he saw in Brockwell Park, before he knew it was a dog.

Passing back through the hall, he sits at the bottom of the stairs and looks at the gas cylinder that he once mistook for a Minoan pot, and he winces to think how he recoiled from Val that day in Coe Fen. He wishes he could remember what happened afterwards. But he sees only the instant of rejection and the look of horror on Val's face, a mirror image – probably – of his own.

He runs his hand across the dusty surface of the gas cylinder and rocks it gently on the carpeted step.

Even now, a quarter of a century later, it seems absurd. Valentine Black with his life in London, his galaxy of connections . . . why would he care about Don in that way? Don returns to what Ben said when they looked at the photograph, about Val watching from afar, cajoling and controlling, even to the point of sending Don away from Peterhouse, but telephoning him still, guiding him always. The thought comes to him that they have been held apart, all these years, by what seemed to hold them together – the ritualised performance of a friendship.

When he next speaks to Val, some days later, the performance resumes. They talk about the election of a Master at Peterhouse. Don tries to rationalise away his deductions. Whatever happened was long ago. They're different people from the men in the photograph. As he said to Ben, the very cells of his brain have changed. What is memory anyway but a hologram – an illusion?

15

For days, he expects to see Ben. But every evening the house is deserted, and the only person he finds is Ina, going about her rounds.

He stands facing the pink velvet sofa. Lost in thought, he doesn't notice that Ina has walked into the room. She is standing next to him, holding out a cup of black coffee.

He looks into her blue eyes and takes the cup.

'So he's left, then, for good?' she says.

'I don't know.'

She crosses to the mantelpiece and starts to dust the ormolu clock.

'You know, Don, maybe it's for the best. He has his life to lead.'

'Of course he does. He always did.'

She looks back. 'And not only that. You have your life too. Sometimes these things run as long as they're supposed to, and after that . . .' She puts down her cloth and wanders over to where one of Val's pictures is protected from the sunlight by little damask curtains; she fondles the golden cord. 'After that you set each other free.'

Don watches her in silence. He doesn't know what to say. Not for the first time, he wonders who Ina is – and he knows with fresh regret that Ben could have told him. Has he misconceived – underestimated – her role? He pictures the three of them singing together in the kitchen, or watching Pasolini films.

'Besides,' Ina says, letting go of the cord. 'Val doesn't like guests to stay too long. Except for you, that is.'

Don nods with grim resignation. 'So you told him? Val knew all along about Ben?'

Her eyes hover on him. 'No, I didn't tell him. Didn't you? Are you saying he didn't know?'

Before he can answer, she smiles – it's the first time he's seen her really smile – and closes her eyes for a second. She shrugs and trudges from the room.

*

A week passes, then another.

He knows that Ben won't return. He can feel it. Again and again, he reminds himself that Ben never intended to stay. It was a passing visit, a temporary fix.

But Ben's disappearance is like a death. Don can't rationalise his physical absence. He walks into the sitting room every day, hoping madly, with a sprinting heart, to find Ben there. All he sees is the empty pink sofa.

He searches for distractions, but the grinding routines at the Brockwell leave his mind free to wander. His book now seems like the work of another person, alien from him. And he can't bring himself to look at the little cut-out figures that litter his bedroom carpet.

Everywhere he goes, he thinks of Ben – laughs in his head at Ben's comments, rehearses Ben's insults with sad glee, and curses himself for every professorial remark, every fastidious quip, every prim denial. 'Lover, you should have come,' Ben said. So why didn't he? Couldn't he have done things differently?

In the evenings, he walks from the museum back to the house, then leaves the house again almost at once, stepping into the lengthening shadows. He walks from Dulwich to the Oval, along the route that he took with Ben only weeks earlier. He walks the same route several times. Sometimes he becomes hopelessly lost. He goes back to the bar in Soho with the piano, and listens as a young man in a blond wig sings 'I Cain't Say No'. The man casts his thick-lidded eyes around the room, meeting Don's gaze.

In the spare morning hours before work, he takes buses all over London, looking for Ben from the top deck. On Charing Cross Road, he sees a man in a leather trench coat and a turtle-neck sweater – his hair is dyed, his fingers are flecked with paint – sauntering along with a stare like a hawk's. Another time, he sees two men fighting near Camberwell Green, and nearby, an old woman with a limp and a dog.

But he never sees Ben. From his vantage point at the front of the bus, he searches in vain.

One afternoon when his schedule is empty, he leaves the museum at lunchtime and catches the bus to New Cross. He asks a stranger the way to Goldsmiths College. He ascends the front steps, adopting a professional air and gait that now feel artificial. The Victorian building has a dilapidated grandeur, at odds with its reputation as a crucible for new art.

He walks into an echoing lobby and wanders along the first corridor he comes to, checking the faces of people he passes. He drifts up and down a chilly staircase. There is a vague indus-trial smell, like the residue of fumes. A door opens and students spill out in a laughing, shouting scrum. A girl bumps into him, and he looks down to see that her tangled hair is thick with plaster dust; her hands too are encrusted with plaster. It looks like ghostly make-up. In a few seconds, the stream of bodies has raced ahead, splitting into other rooms and corridors.

He turns onto a broad corridor lined with giant canvases turned back to front against the walls. A gap in the canvases reveals a door. He leans against it; voices are audible beyond. He opens the door a couple of centimetres and listens.

'I want you to think of painting as something more than pigment on a surface. What do we mean when we talk about painting? Painting is a process, but it's also a discourse.'

Don opens the door further and peers inside the room to see

students sitting on orange plastic chairs in a large circle. Light streams through two massive windows, hitting the room in misshapen oblongs. With them in the circle is an older man. It is this character – grey-haired, lugubriously handsome – who is speaking in a ponderous American accent.

'Painting is not just a physical object. It's the forces that gave rise to that object – the creative act, if you like – and then the responses the object provokes, its *reception* in the world beyond the studio, beyond the intentions of the artist. It's the words people speak, the judgements they make. What I'm saying to you now, today, is part of the sum total of *what painting is.*'

Unseen, Don looks around the circle of students. Their faces are so different from those he lectured in Cambridge. Some are black, one is bearded like a young Rasputin, and some are made up with bone-white foundation and eyeliner.

'Painting's dead!' shouts out a girl with bright red hair. 'It died with the Madonnas and the angels.'

'What about Bacon?' demands a young man.

'He's dead,' she snaps back. 'Didn't you know?' She rolls her eyes and sticks a cigarette between her red-painted lips.

Their teacher watches them calmly. 'It's living in this very conversation. Don't you see? *This* is a form of – an extension of – painting. This conversation.'

A young woman raises her hand. 'Does talking about something automatically reinforce it, make it real? What if it's totally theoretical?'

'In art,' says the man, 'everything is theoretical. And everything is possible. Anything that's conceivable is real, in art.'

Without meaning to, Don has opened the door yet wider. They turn – all of them – to look at him.

'Can I help you?' says the older man.

Don scans the faces that are turned in unison towards him – making certain that Ben isn't among them. 'I'm an art historian,' he says. 'A professor.'

The man has risen from his chair and is walking around the circle towards him.

With a rush of excitement, Don recognises one of the students. It is the girl who drank his wine at the Crown and Greyhound. Her hair is different – short, chopped away. She looks exhausted. She is wearing torn jeans and a T-shirt riddled with holes. (Is it her nipple, he wonders, that shows through one of them?) She stares at him without a hint of recognition.

Don smiles and begins to wave, but the teacher blocks his view.

'Whoever you are, you are interrupting my class. Please go.'

The man places a hand on Don's arm and edges him back through the door.

'Get out of here, dickhead!' the girl shouts, and then, addressing the teacher: 'Deck him, Malco.' She laughs wickedly.

The door slams and Don is alone in the corridor. He bangs on the door with both hands.

'Do any of you know where Ben is?' he shouts.

He tries the door handle again, rattling the aluminium lever and pushing with all his weight, but it has been locked from inside. The teacher is calling out threats. Don rests his head on the door and repeats the question in his head: *Do any of you know?*

He wanders back through the arteries of Goldsmiths College. Passively he registers the notices that litter the walls. He tries another door and finds himself in an empty studio – a large room with the same towering windows. One of the windows must be open a fraction – he can feel a mild wind. A yellow mattress, soaked with stains that resemble continents, is slumped against a wall like a collapsed drunk. Nearby, a wooden table overflows with honeysuckle. The greenery seems to grow out of the table's centre, creeping around its legs. He catches a whiff of its sweet, elusive scent.

One consolation is that Ben, so long as he remains unfound, will stay the same in Don's imagination. His eyes, his hair, his smile – none of these will age or mutate. Beauty is a short-lived tyranny except in the mind, where it can reign forever. Don stands alone in the empty studio and stares at the strange things there.

On the journey back, he sleeps and has dreams about rampant honeysuckle and mythic characters – fluid, unrememberable beings.

He wakes as the bus is arriving in East Dulwich. Just as he steps off, a car swerves to overtake the stopped bus. He hears horns and screeching tyres – a near collision. Another car must have been coming the other way. Sure enough, a second later, a black Mercedes appears from behind the bus – moving fast in the opposite direction.

The road is clear again. Don is coldly aware, as he crosses, that the driver of the Mercedes looked like Val. He is certain, too, that there was a second man in the front, a passenger. But their clothing was what he saw first – matching black suits and black ties. Funeral clothes. He didn't have a chance to fasten on their faces.

The insane idea comes to him that Val and Michael Ross have kidnapped Ben – stowed him in the boot of the car. Then a more prosaic guess: Val is on his way to a funeral.

But his mind is filling with rational doubt. Surely it was just the car that he recognised – and Val's is not the only Mercedes of that model. He is sure, as well, that the driver (even from a snatched glimpse) was too taciturn – too rigid and lifeless in the face – to be Val, who always loves a good funeral.

The letters, labels and loan requests that cover his desk matter less than ever. Beside them, the new computer sits like an incubus, confronting him with an insensate stare.

He opens a drawer and takes out the red book with gold lettering – he keeps it close now. He flicks through the pages, as if willing to let chance dictate which story he will land on, but conscious of the one he wants to find.

The Cyclops, Polyphemus, fell in love with Galatea. He was driven mad by longing. He searched out his beloved, only to find her in the arms of the handsome Acis. In horror and agony, he threw a stone at Acis and killed him. Reading the myth again, Don thinks of an ink sketch in which Polyphemus gazes through a chink in the rocks – a murderous eavesdropper – just as Acis lifts the naked girl into bed. He wonders if Ben is lying somewhere now, dozing beside a new lover.

He closes the book and strokes the cover.

There is a knock, and Maud's head appears from behind the door.

'Professor Lamb, would you come, please? We have an emergency.'

He follows her down the corridor and through the galleries to the Nicolaides Room. People are clustered like mourners around a large painting. Bill is among them, as well as Inigo Price, the expert restorer, with his brown suit and millipede-thin moustache. Don recognises the picture as Poussin's *Triumph of David* – returned to the Brockwell after its spell of cleaning, and yet bizarrely changed. The details of the scene – the creases of the clothes, the fluting of the columns, the expressions of the women who crouch to watch the heroic boy as he parades through Jerusalem – have been burned clean away. The shady recesses have flattened into sandy wastes.

'I asked Mr Price to clean it vigorously,' Bill warbles, his eyes wide with fear. 'I said that vigour was essential.'

Mr Price bows his head. 'The acids in my cleaning fluid may have been too stringent. I can't apologise enough.'

'It'll take years to restore,' Maud bursts out furiously. There are tears in her eyes.

She and the rest of the crowd are looking at Don, waiting for his verdict.

He gazes at the remains of the painting. He is struck, most of all, by the shimmering loveliness of the scene in its dissolved state. It's as if a fine gauze has descended over the picture. The figures in their flowing robes have turned to soft-edged impressions. Hard forms have become crops of weightless, powdery colour. And yet the colours themselves have survived – strengthened, even. The whole thing pulses with blue, orange and umber. Goliath's head is an ochre silhouette, as featureless as a face seen against a light-filled window.

'It reminds me of the work of that later French artist, Pierre Puvis de Chavannes,' Don murmurs. 'Or then again, Seurat.'

Maud glares at him. 'Is that all you have to say?'

He regards her solemnly. What ought he to say? He knows that the blame is his: that posturing, bullying insistence on a vigorous solution. He turns to Bill and is on the point of telling the abject man that it's all *his* fault, that he has destroyed a masterpiece. But the old automatic words of censure have drained away.

'Go back to work, Bill,' he says softly. 'And everyone else. We won't change the situation by staring.'

'But what are we to do?' demands Maud, nearly hysterical. 'If only Michael were here.'

'If only,' Don repeats pensively, before his faculties sharpen. 'Where is he?'

'Didn't you know?' For a moment her distress abates; there is a gleam of sarcasm in her eyes. 'He's in Rome this week, filming the first part of his documentary.'

Don looks back at the Poussin that is no longer a Poussin. 'Well, I daresay Mr Price can rectify the matter.'

Maud is incandescent again. 'What, after ruining the picture in the first place? How can we let *that man* anywhere near it?'

'Ah, it'll take no time to put right,' says Inigo, raising his fists jubilantly. 'A month – no, less! I have just the pigments.'

*

267

His schedule seems emptier these days. The staff trouble him less with their demands. Every Friday at eleven o'clock, he gives the director's tour, although attendance has been decreasing by the week.

One morning in early August, his audience consists of three people – a pair of elderly women and a decrepit man for whom a stool has to be found. Don tries to maintain his usual alacrity, but his aged visitors force him into a ponderous pace.

The culmination of the tour is Peter Lely's *Young Man as a Shepherd* – a painting of a long-haired youth gazing into space, a musical pipe in one hand.

'Historically, this painting was called *Boy as a Shepherd*,' Don tells them. 'Of course, the boy Lely painted wasn't really a shepherd.' He points at the daydreamer in the picture, feminine and aristocratic in twilit parkland. 'Nor was he a boy, for that matter. Lely portrayed him between stages – boy and man.'

He waits and looks at the three aged faces. Only one of them appears to be digesting his words, a woman whose sharp eyes confront him through the twin portholes of her glasses – and doubts appear to be playing on her mind.

'Where does the pastoral disguise end and the real life of the model begin?' Don demands. 'Look at the way his finger touches the staff – strokes it. He's not using it, he's just feeling it. Look at the way he holds the pipe. He's only playing at being a shepherd. And consider his face! What was he really thinking about as he stood in Lely's studio in that costume? Perhaps the Latin epigrams he was supposed to have learned for his tutor. Art, you see, hasn't concealed *life*.'

'I really don't know what you mean,' the woman says. Her eyes are steely, adversarial.

'And why do you say he's not a boy?' chimes her friend, a small lady with snow-white hair. Having appeared deaf up until now, she speaks with surprising acidity. 'Butter wouldn't melt!'

Don breathes deeply. 'The youth is playing a part, whoever he is. His hands are too delicate to be those of a shepherd. What do we really know about him?'

'Butter wouldn't melt, I know that,' repeats the lady with white hair. 'Is it because he's got lovely long hair – is that why you say he's not a boy?'

Don turns back to the boy in the painting – more urbane than a shepherd and more knowing than a boy. He sighs.

'Yes, partly it's the hair. He's more than *one* thing – a model, a character, the two together. A boy and a man, both and neither. Can't you understand?' He has begun to stammer, tripping over his words in the pursuit of meaning.

'I don't see what that has to do with art concealing life,' says the first woman. 'So what if his hands are delicate?' Her expression has taken on an ironic glint. 'So are yours.'

Don feels a dreadful urge to grab her by the wrists and shake her out of her obtuseness. He imagines the shock breaking over her face and the attendants running to restrain him. She stares, waiting for an answer. Does she have a psychic intuition, he wonders, of what he is meditating? He dives into the abysses of her tiny pupils.

Abruptly, the old man on his stool, who has been silent throughout, emits a wheezy chortle.

Don looks down at the frail figure. For a horrifying, delirious moment he believes that he is looking at Maurice Forster. But in an instant, the resemblance has vanished. The man is shrivelled beyond recognition – time has withered him into anonymity. His eyes are closed and a gnarled stick lies between his stick-thin legs, steadied by an unsteady hand. He could be anyone.

Don tries to smile. He knows that he has failed dismally.

'Thank you for attending this morning's tour.' His voice is faint and tremulous.

The old man opens his eyes like a creature waking from hibernation and regards Don with a gap-toothed sneer – as much of a sneer as his ancient face will permit.

Later that day, when the galleries are quiet, he returns to Lely's picture. He repeats in his head the words that fell on deaf ears. He thinks of the artifice of his own role, here, in this place, and asks who – or what – will shake him free. Involuntarily, he stretches out his hand and touches the tip of each of the boy's fingers. The veneer of the painting wobbles at his touch. It feels smooth, dry and unexpectedly warm.

*

On Saturday night, he traipses around the house. The quiet is oppressive. Ina and her mother have gone to Brighton. She has left a vegetable casserole in the fridge.

He wanders into the kitchen and looks in a listless way at the turquoise cabinets and the tablecloth with its overlaid grids of red on white. He tries to open the door to Ina's annex. It is locked. He leans his head on the frosted glass, but the choppy surface discloses nothing.

In a kitchen drawer, he finds a key with a tag marked 'Back door'. This defunct route to the garden is behind the sofa in the television room adjacent to the kitchen. He goes through and heaves the leather chesterfield out of the way. The upper half of the door is glazed, but the view outside is blocked by a bush. He unlocks the door – the key turns surprisingly smoothly – and shoves it into the wall of leaves. It opens barely an inch, with a sound of crumbling mud. He shoves again, and again – forcing the door into the thicket. The bush snaps and sags and finally admits a narrow path into the garden.

It isn't quite dark outside. As he kicks his way through the brambles, he realises that the ground underneath is hard – paved. The stones are only visible where they run along the side of Ina's annex – the shrubbery has been cut back here to create a narrow path. The rest of the garden is covered in a deep, undulating tangle of green that rises into a tall barrier at the end of the annex. As Don wades through the thicket, waist-high in weeds, his leg comes up against something hard. He pulls away fistfuls of creeper to reveal a rusting metal grill and a beige panel – an old fridge or oven.

Ripping at the foliage, he sees that the creepers conceal other objects – old tins, scaffolding poles, tyres stacked in a cylinder, glass bottles caked in grime. Woodlice scurry as he dislodges an empty litre bottle of Courvoisier. He continues to tear at the greenery. Buried in a mound of ivy is what looks like a car engine, a compression of blackened tubes and valves, and next to it, a heap of old clothes – leather jackets, jeans and a fur coat piled up like geological seams. The fabrics have been reduced almost to compost but are still identifiable – just – as what they once were.

Don looks, aghast, at the rubbish that the garden of the House Beautiful conceals. It's as if the rag-and-bone man has emptied his cart, day after day, into this place. How could Val have allowed it?

Something further up the garden catches his eye. Where the foliage closes in around the annex and obscures the depths of the plot, a figure is partially visible within a mass of honeysuckle. He makes out a hand with flexing fingers, and the outline of an arm and shoulder. The leaves have been trimmed neatly – precisely – to uncover the edge of the statue.

Wading across to the annex, he tries Ina's garden door. It is locked. He peers in at the windows. All the curtains are drawn. In one window, however, a narrow gap reveals a portion of a darkened room. He makes out the rim of a disc or plate, inscribed with grooves and spattered with hardened clay.

16

There is a place in Herne Hill called The Sphinx, a pub on a street corner. He has passed it numerous times on his walks, and observed the blacked-out windows and lovingly tended hanging baskets. A flag in rainbow stripes hangs above the door. In the early evening, a queue of men always fills the pavement outside.

Don finds himself passing The Sphinx more often. From the opposite side of the road, he scans the waiting men, noting their matching shaved heads and the gleam of their leather jackets in the last of the sunlight. One evening, when his thoughts are drifting, he crosses over. He shuffles along the queue, allowing his velvet sleeve to brush the leather elbows.

The following night, he returns to the same spot and asks someone for the time.

'Are you in a hurry, mate?' says the man with a wink.

Don wanders on a few steps, and then sidles into the queue. He stands there for ten minutes or more, listening to the banter around him – obscene, good-natured, malicious. The cutting humour – much of it too quick to comprehend – reminds him of Ben. He must look strange here, out of place. He inhales the cigarette smoke that drifts through the queue. His heart is beating hard as he goes inside.

'Fiver!' shouts a woman seated in a booth inside the doorway. She has black lipstick and short black hair gummed into spikes. 'Know what kind of pub this is, mate?'

Don nods and hands her a clean banknote.

Inside, the place is crowded, dark and bewilderingly loud. He stands at the bar and places one hand on the slippery ledge.

Rows of bottles flash their contents at him. Noise sweeps across him in an unbreaking wave, carrying splinters of conversation.

'Vauxhall isn't what it used to be, but then it never *was* what it *was*.'

'She scores every night, that one.'

'I'm not one of those made-up poofs. Keep your make-up to yourself, you old cow.'

'Felipe's a cunt.'

He turns and tries to locate the sources of the remarks. Heads and bodies, jostling to reach the bar, block his view. Men look at him with indifference or suspicion or something else – a sort of smirking irony.

He turns back to the bar. 'Do you serve Beaujolais?' he asks above the pounding noise. 'Beaujolais supérieur, 1989.'

The barman shrugs, not hearing or not knowing.

'Have a vodka and pomegranate juice, babe.'

The suggestion comes from a voice behind him. He spins around and sees a slim black man of around twenty, regarding him with amusement. His features are refined, pretty; he wears a close-clinging T-shirt of pastel blue that leaves his arms bare almost to the shoulders.

'Thank you,' says Don, and turns to the barman again. 'A vodka and pomegranate!'

'I'm Herman,' the young man says, pushing closer.

'Melville?' says Don with a smile.

Herman returns the smile, tinged – almost imperceptibly – with contempt. 'Just call me Herman, man. And this is Sid.'

He indicates a man to his side. Sid grins to reveal jagged teeth. He is Herman's antithesis – short, squat and pale. He wears a red T-shirt that barely contains his belly and hairy arms. The stubble that surrounds his mouth and covers his head is greying, like an old dog's. They are with a third man named Darryl who listens and says little. He has a dark moustache and bloodshot eyes.

Don pays for his drink and stands at the bar, sipping the sweet mixture. He finds that the three strangers are observing him, reeling him in by smiles and glances. Sid and Darryl are like dissolute versions of Bill Hoare and Inigo Price, he thinks. Herman is describing a string of hook-ups with lorry drivers. In a fast, fluid voice, he tells of liaisons in lay-bys, under motorway bridges, in a field beneath the stars. The whiteness and physical bulk of the drivers is a recurring detail – presumably because of the contrast to Herman himself – dark, slender, pliant as a ballet dancer. But one trucker wore red fishnet tights beneath his jeans.

At each lurid turn of the story, Sid dissolves into laughter. His eyes fill with tears and he reaches to touch Don's arm. Darryl looks on, impassive, and breathes through his nose, occasionally muttering an insult in response to Herman's revelations.

'I stayed all night with that one,' Herman says. 'She dropped me off in Wolverhampton.'

'Slag,' Darryl intones.

Don's curiosity is growing. He likes the way they substitute the female pronoun for the male. When Herman pauses to light a cigarette, he tries to tell them about the *castrati* of eighteenth-century Umbria.

'She's got a brain on 'er,' says Darryl to the others.

Sid crumples with laughter. Don laughs too. These men, about whom he knows nothing, are captivating as well as nightmarish. The place they inhabit is a kind of marvellous hell. Soon he is filled with excitement. He laughs without restraint. He begins to tell them of the sexual peccadilloes of the emperor Heliogabalus, and Sid leans forward and gives him a bristling kiss on the cheek.

'When you gonna tell us who you are?' Herman asks.

He tells them that his name is Don (no *Professor*, no surname) and that he found The Sphinx by accident.

'No one finds this place by accident,' says Herman. He takes Don in with his solemn eyes, scanning the knitted tie and the velvet sleeves before circling in on Don's face (lips, teeth, hair – greyer now than in earlier days), landing finally on his eyes. His gaze is penetrating. It's as if he knows all about Don's nocturnal rambling and the reason for it.

Sid proudly declares that he has been coming to the pub since 1971. 'It was a battle for sexual liberation back then,' he shouts over the music, with an unfocused gaze. 'Always a battle. But there was solidarity.' His round face looms close.

Don's thoughts scatter and reform like starlings. 'Sexual liberation,' he says deliberately, 'began for me in Brockwell Park.'

Sid touches Don's arm and his lips fall open. 'You're daffy, you are.' Turning to the barman, he calls out: 'Reg, get this daffy one another jar.'

Herman has been silent during this last exchange. He leans forward and whispers in Don's ear.

'Don't talk to me about liberation. I've seen guys dropping dead all over, not so long ago. Half the men I once knew in this pub.'

Ben told him about this modern-day plague. It was in the cavernous place where they drank Red Stripe with the actor, in that final phase of their night together. Don looks at the bodies filling The Sphinx, glowing lilac and lemon-yellow in the disco lights that pivot overhead. Two men in leather jackets are kissing. Bare heads – one scrawny, the other fleshy with ripples at the back. The force with which they bury themselves inside one another gives him a tingling shock.

'Listen to me, man,' Herman says. 'There is no liberation. You think you're free but it's just another prison. One prison, then another, then another.'

Don looks into Herman's dark, agitated eyes, then glances back at the men in their gnawing embrace.

'I'm listening,' he says.

At that moment, people start jostling around them. Don sees a plume of blond hair and a fur coat. Inside the fur is a boy, made up and willowy – he throws Don an unreadable glance through rings of mascara. His face is morose and beautiful. He is whisked along by a muscular man in a white singlet. People seem to fall away in the presence of the couple, allowing them a clear route through the pub.

Darryl has noted Don's curiosity.

'That was Princess Di,' he says drily.

Herman bursts out laughing. 'Di and Freddie!' he exclaims. 'That's what they're called. Princess Diana came to this place with Freddie Mercury, years back, dressed as a boy. We like to remember.'

Don joins the rest of the crowd in watching the couple, who have stepped onto a low platform and seem to be preparing to sing. He watches in silent wonderment until he feels Sid's hand again on his arm.

'Don,' he says tenderly, and he opens his other hand. A gold chain is curled inside his palm like a sleeping snake. Attached to it is a nugget of polished brass.

'My first boyfriend gave it to me. He was called Don too. I want you to have it.'

Sid's fingers reach into Don's collar and fix the pendant around his neck. Don tries to formulate words of gratitude, but he finds himself unable to speak.

*

The morning after his trip to The Sphinx, his hangover has seeped into the core of him.

Around mid-morning, as he reads a letter from Agnes Penrose (when, she asks, will the museum be renaming a gallery in her honour?), he suddenly needs to be sick. The vomit is rising in his throat as he hurries along the corridor. In the cool of the tiled lavatory, the nausea eases off, then returns in a surge. He swallows hard and fixes his eyes on the floor. The light grows dim and the room turns a strange shade of avocado.

Tiles press against his cheek and temple. His shoulder is aching where it hit the floor. Recovering consciousness, he sees the doors of the toilet cubicles as a curtain of blue plastic separated from the floor by a strip of empty space. Through the gap, he makes out two brown leather shoes planted on the floor. Trousers have fallen around them like a punctured balloon – mildew-green tweed.

He lies still and breathes in surreptitious spurts. Clearly Bill didn't hear him fall – the feet are motionless inside the cubicle.

His eyes are locked on the shallow heap of tweed. An elasticated waistband runs along the top edge of the trousers, plunging into an open fly. The ends of a leather belt trail onto the floor. There is something odd about the trousers beyond their volume. The empty pockets have flopped inside out, and their white lining has been trimmed to make an opening at the base of each. Hair-like wisps of nylon run along the cut edges, evidence of a clean scissor snip. Bottomless pockets. Escape tunnels for hands. In the same instant, he sees that Bill wears no underwear.

The feet shift. There is a sound of rummaging inside the cubicle, as the tweed is hoisted up. Don holds himself rigid. He calculates that he can get up and escape while the toilet flushes. Except that Bill has no intention of pulling the flush – he is already unfastening the lock. The door opens with a whine, and Don hears a gasp followed by a warble.

He closes his eyes. By a reflex of self-protection, he imagines that he is a corpse in a coffin. A lead-lined container on board a gondola hearse, bobbing across the Venetian lagoon in rain as fine as mist.

Bill is kneeling over him, shouting his name.

'Wake up, Professor Lamb, wake up – Don! Oh God, oh Christ, no, please no . . .'

Bill tries to check Don's pulse with a jabbing finger. He gives Don's face a panicked slap, but the blow does nothing to break the deathly languor. Bill's palm feels as soft as a soaked sponge.

'Oh Don, oh Jesus no.'

Don stays cadaver-still and pictures the waters lapping the edges of the old gondola. He thinks of Anna Ross, standing on the prow in a black raincoat and large sunglasses – and Ben, pale with grief, reedy and unwell but beautiful too in the dreary light of the lagoon.

He hears the taps gush. Water is raining on his face – thrown in desperate handfuls. It is warm, like piss. Bill is preparing to administer the kiss of life: Don hears the sound of lips opening and closing. He opens his eyes and forces a startled groan.

'Where am I? What happened?' He looks around madly, trying to mimic the terror of the Lazarus restored to life.

'Don, Don, oh Don.' Bill crouches over him, an enormous terrified presence, his face livid and glazed with sweat. 'Don't get up.' He tries to loosen Don's tie, stabbing uselessly at the knot and knocking the golden nugget that lies beneath his collar – Sid's gift.

With a pang of alarm, Don foresees Bill having a heart attack. He raises a hand and pushes back the huge, quivering figure.

'It's all right. I'm fine. A momentary loss of consciousness. Low blood pressure. It's happened to me since childhood.'

Bill breaks into sobs and buries his head in Don's chest. The sound is dreadful – smothered growls and shrieks deprived of air. Don feels tears soaking into his shirt, forming a giant pool of relief.

'It's all right,' he repeats. 'Get up.'

Bill's sobs sink deeper into his chest.

'Get up!' Don is losing patience.

Bill withdraws a little, and Don is able to slide out from under him and climb to his feet. He catches sight of himself in the mirror. A dark patch has spread across his shirtfront.

'Are you all right, Bill?' Don's own voice sounds far off. 'Can I do anything?'

He hasn't finished speaking when a new resolve takes hold. He places his hands inside Bill's armpits and heaves him up, straining against the incredible load. Shakily, reluctantly, Bill rises to his feet. Don guides him from the room.

As they shuffle along the corridor, Bill's giant arm slung around Don's shoulder, Maud and Michael emerge from the Communal Office in eager conversation. Their voices stop dead.

'What's happened?' Maud asks through taut lips. 'Is he ill?'

Michael looks coolly at the pair of them, at the pitiful figure of Bill and at Don's soaked shirt.

'Nothing to worry about,' Don says. 'Some fresh air – that's all he needs.'

He moves behind Bill and clasps each of his shoulders, then steers him between Maud and Michael like a tweed barge.

'Come outside Bill, into the garden.'

In the sunshine and flowing air, Bill brightens at once. He walks upright, although he keeps a hand draped around Don's neck in a redundant, oddly intimate way. They walk along one of the quieter paths at the garden's periphery, a gravel route that winds beneath yew trees and between beds of luscious rhododendrons broken up by little weathered rocks. To one side, set back from the path in a niche of dark laurels, is a bench made from scrolling iron, painted white. Facing back towards the museum, it offers a covert view – framed by the branches of an overhanging willow – of the lawn outside Don's study.

'I didn't know this spot existed,' Don says.

'It's like countryside – manmade countryside,' declares Bill, sitting down and beckoning Don to join him. '*While fish love*

*the floods, and bees suck thyme, or grasshoppers sip dew, still
shall endure thy honour.'*

The lines are unfamiliar. It is beguiling to hear them in Bill's
voice.

'Virgil, *Eclogues*. I remember it from school. There's a saying
that Virgil invented the summer, if you catch the drift.' Bill
chuckles and sniffs away a residue of tears. 'That was before he
became an imperial propagandist – an Augustan slime.'

Don nods, allowing Bill's words to sink through the depths of
his perception. They gaze together at the garden. Paul strolls into
view on the sunlit lawn. He is wearing wellington boots and a
green apron; his sleeves are rolled up to reveal bronzed arms. In
one hand he carries an uprooted plant, a fern of some kind, whose
muddy roots trail almost to the ground. Reaching the centre of the
lawn he stops, turns, and catches sight of them through the trees.

'Morning Don. Bill.' He waves, fluttering his fingers, and
smiles. His voice is dampened by the breeze. 'I didn't know you
were out here.' He nods towards their green enclosure. 'How
do you like my little piece of picturesque?'

Don raises one arm and smiles back, keeping his hand in the
air until Paul disappears behind the willow branches.

'He calls you Don,' Bill says with amused surprise.

'We're friends,' Don replies.

With searching, sympathetic eyes Bill studies Don's face. He
seems poised to say something, then settles back on the bench
and exhales.

Breeze, birdsong, the buzzing of insects and distant vehicles . . .

After an interval, Bill says: 'I feel like an idiot, overreacting
like that before. I should have been helping you.'

Don is staring at the spot where Paul was standing moments
earlier.

'I didn't faint.'

Bill turns on the bench with his entire body. 'No?'

'I mean, I did – but it wasn't low blood pressure. I passed

out because I'm hungover. Only for a second. I pretended I was still unconscious because' – Don grips the edge of the bench – 'I didn't know what else to do.'

Bill's lips part, his eyes enlarge, and then he breaks into a big, boyish laugh.

'I'm sorry, Bill.'

'Ah, it's quite all right.' Bill's laughter subsides.

'Not just about today. I mean – for all of it.'

Bill nods slowly and straightens his trousers. Don is about to speak but Bill halts him with a wave of the hand.

'You know,' he says, leaning back and finding his waistcoat pockets, 'it all reminds me of something that happened at Sussex back in the '60s.'

And he embarks on a long story involving a drunkard who played dead all the way to the mortuary. Don sits and listens and only occasionally does his concentration wander as he looks to see if Paul has reappeared.

'*Booze*,' Bill suddenly declares, straightening both legs so that his shoes lift off the ground, and prompting a blackbird to flutter into the trees. 'Sent to gladden our hearts. If only that was all it did. But who am I to talk? You should have seen me in those days. I used to drink like a fish. My God, it's a miracle I'm still here. Came off my motorbike several times. Here . . .'

From his jacket, he produces a pewter flask and holds it out. Don takes it and unscrews the cap to release a scent of cognac. He brings it to his nose and smells the harsh, sweet vapour, then replaces the cap and returns the flask to Bill.

'Thanks. I'd better not.'

Bill takes back the flask with a shrug and drops it into one of his tweed cavities. After a second, he sits up straight, delighted by a thought.

'Do you know what they used to call me? Bill the fish. Yes, that's right. *Bill the fish* – because I drank like a fish.' He laughs uproariously.

'Say those lines by Virgil to me again,' Don says. 'Wasn't there something about fish in the streams?'

Bill repeats the fragment and their two heads nod in time to the verses.

After Bill has left to inspect the varnish on a Canaletto, Don sits for a while in the niche, then wanders further down the path into an unknown extremity.

The path narrows and curves between walls of laurel. The gravel gives way to trimmed grass. There are weeds along the borders, daisies and dandelions, but they have been left there on purpose – interspersed with pebbles and trimmed into yellow flowering clusters that seem brighter as the route darkens. The path is a cul-de-sac. At the end, enfolded by hedges, is a small shed with a flat roof. Its horizontal timbers are stained black. The frame around the single window is yellow – newly painted.

Don peers through the glass. It is some kind of garden store. Paul's shed. The interior is orderly and spare, like an armoury. Pairs of black wellington boots – clean, gleaming – stand in a row, rising in height to thigh-high waders. One pair is slimmer and sleeker than the rest, more like jodhpurs. Bamboo canes, hooked at one end, lie sideways on a shelf. Against the back wall, sacks of peat are stacked in the shape of a couch and topped by a blanket. Above, hanging from hooks, are a coil of yellow hosepipe, a clawlike rake, and a complicated harness – all leather straps and shining buckles. His eyes wander over the small details. Paul is somewhere else, in another part of the garden, but these are Paul's identifying parts – like the attributes of a saint. The tokens of martyrdom.

*

On the Sunday morning after his trip to The Sphinx, he wakes to remember a dream more real than the curtained gloom of the room around him. He dreamed about Ben. They were teenagers, both of them – younger than Ben is now. They were in bed together, in a room different from this one. Ben had transformed – by one of those slippages that dreams permit – into a sculpted, immaculate body, unblemished as polished stone. Don leaned forward and kissed him, then took hold of the hard bulk of Ben's penis . . . Seconds later, he realised that it wasn't a real penis but a plaster cast, held together by strips of duct tape.

As the dream recedes, he still feels the phantom presence in his hand – real and then abruptly ridiculous. He turns over in bed and presses his own semi-hardness against the mattress and senses the residue of his desire.

There is one place he hasn't yet looked – the lido in Brockwell Park. Something has kept him from going, even though he knows that it was one of Ben's haunts. He looks out of his window and sees a spotless blue sky above the tips of the horse chestnuts and the tiled crest of the house opposite. It will be a hot day.

Perhaps it's because of the dream that he decides, at this moment, that he will go swimming – a desire to convert the insubstantial image of Ben back into a living being. He pulls out the pair of red trunks from among his clothes and puts them in a Sainsbury's carrier bag along with a bath towel.

When he walks onto the poolside, his towel slung over one shoulder, he sees a large rectangular island of water. The heads of early-morning swimmers bob above the turquoise surface. The pool is surrounded on three sides by single-storey outbuildings, strips of suburban Modernism that remind him of Ina's annex. Above is a sky made of vibrating blue corpuscles. The noises of the city – car horns, whirring traffic, the banging and grinding of building works – linger on the breeze, becoming abstract: a faint, trembling energy, like sounds refracted through a dream.

He leaves his towel on the concrete and walks to the edge of the water. He feels like the porcelain-pale boy of seventeen he was when he last swam outdoors. That was on a beach in Poole, the summer before he left for Cambridge. His parents were seated on the sand behind him; Iris was running in vast loops on the shoreline. Here he is now, nearly forty-four, wrapped in the same clinging trunks, lowering himself gingerly down the steps towards the water.

The cold is shocking. For a second it turns his brain rigid. Then he is in – drawing himself under the water, rising into the deep, forgetful of which way he is moving. His head breaks the surface and the sun shines in his eyes.

He lies on his towel afterwards, propped on one elbow. The lido has become busy. Swimmers travel up and down the lanes of the pool, or flail about happily. The pool sides are crowded with people. Two girls sprint past him and jump, one then the other, sending geysers leaping into the air. Through his half-closed eyes, air and water become the same substance – pure blue, the same blue as in Tiepolo's frescoes, only stronger, as if the skies of the paintings have concentrated into a brilliant essence.

He loses track of how long he lies there. At some point he realises that he has been sleeping, or virtually sleeping. He remembers that he came to look for Ben. Sitting up, he scans the figures around the sides of the pool, somehow knowing that he won't find him here.

Later, he reclines on the sofa that was Ben's favourite place, thinking. He lifts a glass from the floor and takes a mouthful of wine. It floods his windpipe. Fighting for breath, he returns the liquid in a red deluge onto his shirtfront.

He removes the wine-soaked shirt. Underneath is a vest of

the type he has worn since he was a boy – a white singlet. Sid's gold chain hangs over his chest. He feels cold. He puts on his velvet jacket and goes to inspect himself in the Queen Anne mirror in the hall. The combination of jacket and vest makes him look like one of his counterparts from Cambridge, a fashionable ideologue from the Faculty of English. But he looks younger, too – a modified version of himself.

It isn't yet midnight. He leaves the house and sets out on a walk. He stops at Starburger on Norwood Road for a Beef Zinger. The plastic table where he sits has been bolted to the floor; he studies its milky, translucent surface as he chews. A crowd of drunk men pile into the shop, singing 'Nessun Dorma'. Afterwards, Don walks to The Sphinx.

Herman and Sid and Darryl are there. They recognise him at once, absorb him into their group as before. He feels no reticence in their company. He listens to their talk, watches their reactions, waits for a sign.

Herman smiles at Don's vest, running an enquiring finger around its bottom edge. He slides the warm palm of his hand under the material. Don stands there and lets him do it. He touches Herman's fingers through the vest and holds on to Herman's hand – clasps it tight, guides it across his stomach.

*

On his next visit, he wears a vest again beneath his jacket. It is a hot, close night – and he prefers this look to the one he adopts at the museum. He finds it easy to loiter outside the pub now. He joins the queue and exchanges a remark or two with the skinheads who make up most of the clientele.

He finds Sid alone in the same spot, drinking ale and watching the dancers who strut and sway under the disco lights.

'Where are Herman and Darryl?' he asks, after Sid has given him a prickly kiss.

'Found another party. They've gone to where it's at.'

'And left you here?'

Sid plants his hands on the bar and stares into space. 'Oh, they pick me up and toss me aside. That's how it is. We're all the same. I don't stay put either. I drive a lorry, see. Always on the move.'

'Is that why Herman likes you?'

'That and the rest.' Sid pats the region of his fly and his eyes crease. 'But listen.' He turns to Don, suddenly serious. 'They come, they go. I don't waste time remembering. I'm here now, tonight – fuck the past – it's now that matters.'

Don thinks over these words. The old urge to dispute – to dismantle Sid's meaning – comes and goes. Part of him, a residual part that won't quite shift, thinks that Sid is a fool, without intellect or responsibility. What are his pleasures but drinking and random assignations? Don reflects on his own self-denial, those self-shaping years of study. That was his pleasure – his happiness – once.

He can't think of a riposte. *They come, they go.* What else is he doing on these long nights of wandering?

Touching Don's arm, Sid tells him the story of the other Don, the boyfriend who gave him the gold chain. A dismal tale – the man was run over and killed by his own car on a beach in Tangier.

'After that, I knew that anything could happen, at any time,' Sid says with a bleary smile. 'Life is like – I don't know, water running through your hands. You try to catch hold, but—' He sighs and slaps the bar. 'I go where the night takes me. It's all out there – fucking and freedom and, and – two more ales please, love.'

The barman levers out two frothing pints. Sid slides a glass towards Don. 'You try to catch hold', he says again, more solemnly this time.

They stand against the bar in silence and drink long draughts of beer, watching the dancers.

17

On the afternoon of his forty-fourth birthday, he retraces once more the route that he walked with Ben to City Racing. The gallery is closed, and the surrounding streets are heavy with a mood of summer deadness. There are few people around. On a back road in Kennington, a cat wanders across the pavement – a small striped cat, like a pygmy tiger – and jumps up to position its front paws on his knee, as if desirous of climbing his leg. He meets its liquid yellow gaze before it drops to the ground and plods away.

The drab throughway of Black Prince Road brings him to the Thames. The lights of the city cast a beige tint on the clouds. He remembers how it was with Ben – a pink sunset and a dizzying sense of promise. The feeling hasn't gone, but it is mixed now with a rawer pleasure – the harsh, concentrated taste of freedom.

He turns left and walks along the river. It occurs to him that Ben took him on a longer route than was necessary, past the ziggurat of green glass and glossy stone on the south side of the river. Halfway across Vauxhall Bridge, he looks down at the churning currents. A barge passes underneath, smothered with ropes and chains. Would it be quick, he wonders, to be swallowed up by the water? He thinks of Lethe, the river of forgetfulness, and tries to imagine the flavour of the Thames: a salty, oily, sour suspension. It is hard to believe that it would bring forgetfulness.

On the north bank, he stops at the Morpeth Arms and drinks a brown ale, then another, and then goes on – past the Tate Gallery – towards Westminster.

Underneath Millbank Tower, a grey-haired body is wrapped in a blanket. He pulls a bunch of coins from his pocket and scatters them around the insensate head. The man snorts as the coins slide off his bearded cheek and curls his fingers like a baby in sleep.

On the lawn outside the Palace of Westminster, a reporter is delivering a broadcast to a TV camera. Don walks behind her, across the triangle of grass. He recalls being in the same spot years earlier and seeing a sculpture by Henry Moore – two giant fragments of bone, magnified into bronze chunks. And yet – he stops in his tracks – the Moore sculpture has disappeared, been removed. In its place, on the same granite plinth, is a plaster replica of the Venus de Milo.

He stops and examines the statue, so familiar to him. Rapidly he perceives that it isn't a faithful recreation of the ancient figure, but an act of desecration. The plaster has been doused with a substance that resembles pigeon shit: rivulets of black, white and glistening green streak down the body from head to foot. Venus's midsection – that lovely point where she swivels within her drapery – has been cut out and replaced with an alien object. It slices through her anatomy like a magician's box. It is an oil drum, caked in rust and turned on its side to present a gaping cavity.

A shin-high stanchion has been erected around the freakish totem. Just inside the wire stands a brass-plated sign.

Mariam Schwarz (b. 1910)
Meretrix
1984
Originally commissioned for the
Games of the XXIII Olympiad, Los Angeles

He reads the information and his brain begins to whir, but then he thinks of what Sid said to him – it's *now* that matters. Fuck the past.

The light is fading by the time he reaches St James's Park. The warm weather has drawn people out – they stroll and lie around the green pockets of the park. He moves among them and watches the pelicans. Across the lake, framed by trees, is Buckingham Palace. He dreamed once of becoming Surveyor of the Queen's Pictures. But tonight, the palace and its art treasures signify nothing. A gigantic garden folly – that's how the building appears to him now.

The moon has risen. He counts two stars – pinpricks of cold radiance in the lilac sky – then three, four . . . A distant plane adds a fifth spot to the group. It drifts sideways like a star that has come off its moorings. Jangling emotions – rival forces of optimism and melancholy – compete to possess him.

In Soho, he goes to different bars, losing track of the hours. He meets people and drinks with them and has conversations that run off the surface of his memory. In the early hours, wandering through the back alleys, he comes to a place that is familiar. A burst-open mattress lies against the wall. There is a smell of drains and gutters clogged with rubbish, and yet the air is cool and bracing. Above a doorway, neon letters spell a single word. *CALYPSO*.

A man in a long anorak loiters near the door. They exchange a few muttered words, and Don gives him a cigarette. The man's breath is strong and beery as he leans forward for a light. His face is lined. For a minute or two, he and Don smoke in silence and look at one another. The man seems younger as he edges into the pink glow of the sign. Then, by a kind of telepathic cue, he is leading Don beneath the neon letters, through the door.

Beyond is a tiny room, bright as a laboratory. A young skinhead sits in a glass booth. His leather jacket is open to reveal a bare, bony chest.

'Two pounds,' he says, almost before they've made it through the entrance.

The stranger pays and moves on, as if passing through a toll. Don produces a shrivelled note from his pocket and hands it through a gap in the glass. The boy gives him a pair of folded towels with his change. Don rests his hands on their warm, bobbly surface.

'Where's Calypso?' he asks.

The boy throws him a sceptical glance. 'Are you fucked?'

Don surveys him through the glass. He is barely an adult but has the glower of bitter experience.

'That way,' the boy eventually says, and he tilts his head towards another door.

Don goes through and finds himself in a humid changing room lined with lockers. Everything – the floor, the walls, the locker doors – is maroon. There is a thick odour of sweat. The man who led him in is already undressing, proudly displaying his nakedness – a lanky body and a large, swaying cock. Don takes off his clothes calmly, as if disrobing for a ceremony, and stows them in a locker that refuses to lock. Realising that he has no swimming trunks, he keeps his underpants on.

His silent partner smiles and tugs at the waistband.

'You don't need those.' His voice is gravelly – expressionless. He holds out a towel. 'Just this.'

Don slides out of his underwear and draws the towel around his waist. Embarrassment has deserted him.

They pass into a dark corridor. Underfoot is a track of grooved plastic. Faint neon strips overhead light the way, but it's too dark to see to the end. The air is close with steam, chlorine and something else – a bodily base note. The man walks ahead with a casual slink. Then, in an instant, he has disappeared through a gap in the wall.

Don goes on alone. He turns onto another corridor, identical to the first one except that it branches off, on both sides, into darker byways. Around the mouths of these tributaries there are clusters of men – they stand in silence, all wearing towels around the waist, like initiates in a secretive cult.

No one speaks and yet the air seems to hum with a sound of breathing, murmuring, shuffling.

As he walks on in a near-trance, Don makes out the shape of a man walking ahead of him – a bare back and a broad pair of shoulders. Coming closer, he perceives that the man's hair is white and thinning: the strands give off an eerie glow. He sees also that the man is following someone else – a younger, slenderer character who walks ahead of them both, moving at an erratic speed, sometimes slowing to a near stop and at other times hastening away. Whenever the man with white hair comes close enough, he extends his hand to within touching distance of the younger man – but then the lure moves on, never admitting a moment's contact. The refusal seems almost conscious.

The slow game of cat and mouse continues for a minute or more, until suddenly the young man slips behind one of the blue plastic doors that line the corridor on both sides. The old man swings around as if losing his balance and leans heavily against the door. He lets out an agonising sigh.

Don passes around him and quickly loses his way in a maze of splitting passageways. From behind closed doors, he hears an undertone of voices and moving bodies. Condensation trickles down the walls in rivulets. The corridor – the entire maze – seems to be perspiring.

He turns a corner and sees light. At the end of the passageway is a bright open space. He comes to an octagonal room draped with ivy of iridescent green. In the centre is a raised jacuzzi, coated with a mosaic of turquoise tiles and backed by a tumbling rockery. Above the bubbling water, bunches of rubber grapes hang from a plastic vine.

The jacuzzi is empty. Don climbs the steps and lowers himself into the warm water. He basks in the purling liquid, breathing in clouds of steam, cogitating everything he has seen in this fantastical place.

After a while, a man climbs the steps to the jacuzzi. In his side vision – taking care not to look directly – Don sees that he is tall and light-haired, almost blond. With practised panache, he flips aside his towel and enters the water. His body is toned and trim. His cock is as neat as a statue's. In a swift, swooping movement, the man's body disappears beneath the foam and he settles on the other side of the jacuzzi.

Don knows that he is being watched – intently watched. He resists the temptation to look back. But curiosity works on him until he glances up.

He knows the man. But he can't think where from. He looks again. The man is gazing straight back at him across the bubbling water with a calm, amused, astute expression.

'How are those hollyhocks looking?' he says. 'Better?'

It's Paul. So unembarrassed, and so happy, apparently, to see him. Don tries to speak, attempts a reply, but the right words elude him. He scrambles through the water to the steps and heaves himself out. Snatching his towel from the floor, he rushes down a passageway, different from the one he entered by, shocked beyond anything he's felt in his life. It's as if he had descended to an underworld, a realm of drifting shades, only to encounter a real, vigorous person – impossibly real.

As he retreats, embarrassment gives way almost at once to regret. He slows his step and repents fleeing. And yet, as he treads onwards, he knows that Paul has followed. He can feel a presence close behind him, so close that his shoulders tingle. He refuses to look back, afraid that the presence will fade into absence if he dares to turn. He wills it to stay.

In slow motion, he passes along a sequence of closed doors, leaning on them as he goes, feeling each one rattle against its lock.

'Fuck off,' comes a voice from behind a door.

He moves on. Another closed door – his head rests on the

plastic and he sees the vapour of his breath on the blue laminate. But then the film of moisture is falling away and the door is succumbing to his weight. He falls inwards, stepping onto a hard blue mat. The door closes slowly behind him.

It is pitch black. The air is moist. He feels his way into a brick-walled cabin, stroking the walls and ceiling. He sinks to his knees and waits for his eyes to adjust.

He senses that he isn't alone. The man behind him crept in as the door swung closed. Don's hand is suddenly in contact with a warm section of arm or calf. There is no noise, no movement. The man's breaths are hot and regular. Their two bodies are charged with a power which builds as they remain completely still. The darkness relents and he makes out a wave of hair, and then he sees Paul's eyes – like moonlight breaking through cloud.

He tips his head back like a stargazer and senses their heads drawing together, and even though he has anticipated what comes next, the sensation of the kiss amazes him, shocks him out of consciousness. The desire to touch, hold, invade the other body (always before now a phantom in the waters of his mind's eye) has crossed into reality. *This was supposed to be impossible.* He brings his hands around Paul's head and draws it close. *Kiss me again.*

The liquid crackle of their mouths is compounded by other motions. Paul's hands are working their way up and down the massive form of his own erect penis. Don slides his hands beneath Paul's (an intuitive movement, quicker than thought) and runs them over the warm, slippery column. It feels strangely separate – autonomous – in the dark. He looks down and sees, through the thick gloom, that it is topped by a golden stud.

Their two bodies furl around one another. The distinction between his own limbs and Paul's, between their two heads, their two cocks, blurs in and out of existence. He feels himself being rolled onto his knees by Paul's large hands. His body goes light, less out of fear than a luxurious kind of enervation – a thrill of powerlessness. Out of the darkness, something splashes between his buttocks and across his lower back; it oozes like cooking oil down his thighs. The hands, full of calm intent, are closing around his hips – warm and softly abrasive. The golden stud touches him between the buttocks, a cold droplet that makes him shiver, and then noses its way into him. His head sinks. A spasm of sharp pain gives way to a slower, duller sensation of ingress that ripples all over him.

The movement quickens. As the thrusts become harder and faster, his whole body begins to be usurped. The golden stud is frisking deep inside him. Mingled pressure and fullness come in unrelenting waves. He reaches for his own cock, touches it, keeps it in a state of taut expectancy.

In another weightless motion, he is flipped onto his back. Paul's palms are pressing against the undersides of his thighs, gently easing them upwards until his knees are brushing his ears. Paul presses close – presses into him – and brings his open mouth almost to Don's. With a sound like a cry of pain, Paul shunts harder. Don tenses. A warm flow passes through his abdomen. The surge of energy intensifies – then dissipates – in his own abrupt release.

He tumbles to earth, emptied of himself, and lies on his side. For a long time, he stays motionless, feeling the other warm body just behind him – lying just as still.

When he wakes, he is stretched like a stranded sea creature on the mat, and alone.

After walking around the maze like a soul in limbo, Don finds his way back to the changing room. His clothes are still there, stuffed in an open locker. Men are arriving as he dresses – sullen characters in business suits. It is seven in the morning. The cycle never ends. He feels faint with disbelief as he pulls on his clothes.

His mood is an unstable element as he walks along the bleak, bright streets. The further he travels away from the otherworld of the previous night, the more his elation – that dazzled, questioning state – sinks beneath an encroaching hangover.

With the few dirty coins he has left, he buys a pack of cigarettes on Beak Street. He smokes one, then another, as he walks towards Oxford Circus. He descends the steps of the tube station and pushes his way into the fast-flowing crowd of commuters. On the concourse, between a photo booth and a row of telephones in hoods of smoked glass, he sees a vending machine: two clear plastic cylinders filled with coloured balls. The red and blue and yellow sweets remind him of a painting he saw at Goldsmiths that day when he wandered into the empty studio.

An escalator carries him deeper into the earth, and he feels himself borne along the tubular, tiled passageways, and then spat out onto the platform.

A train screeches into view and its doors slam open. It is packed – there are no free seats, just a blue pole to hold on to. The carriage lurches through the earth and the windows turn as dark as interstellar space. The odours of CALPYSO circle Don's head, persistent as the memory of the place, rising out of the gaps in his clothes.

A smarting sensation runs up and down his arms and legs. He prays that someone will get off and vacate a seat. But with each stop, more bodies flood into the carriage and press around him, carrying scents of respectability.

A woman's voice catches his attention.

'There's an article here about Francis Bacon, the painter.'

His stomach skips and shimmies. Ben loved Francis Bacon. He remade objects from Bacon's paintings and called them sculptural fictions.

'Did you know he died in Madrid?' She is sitting behind an outspread newspaper, speaking to a friend beside her.

'Oh yes. I think I knew. I was never sure about his paintings.'

Don closes his eyes and fights the urge to vomit. Unmetabolised alcohol rises through his brainstem, infecting the right and left hemispheres, spilling between conscious and unconscious thought like floodwater in a ship's hull.

'Listen to this: "A vehement atheist, Bacon died in the care of Sister Mercedes, a nun of the Order of the Servants of Mary. She became, in his final days, an angel of mercy."'

He grips the pole – harder, tighter. Not long. The train is burrowing under the Thames. A man opposite him yawns. Don can see his back teeth and their black fillings.

Retreating into the centre of his mind, he leaves his body behind – a wrecked shell clinging to the vertical metal bar – and listens with closed eyes for the stations, broadcast in a woman's computerised voice. Vauxhall, Stockwell, Brixton.

As the doors slide apart for the final time, he opens his eyes and registers the expressions of the faces that file past him – faces of bored indifference or muted disapproval. He follows them onto the platform. The train door closes on his foot and he wrenches it free.

He should go to bed and sleep – perhaps just die quietly beneath the duvet, with the curtains closed. But a powerful impulse urges him to reach the museum. Step by step, he fights his way from Brixton to Dulwich. Every sensory experience – the sunlight, the sound of traffic, the rushing movements of passers-by – is a knife through his brain. Christ on the road to Calvary must have felt something like this. A car hoots as he stumbles into the gutter.

Nearing the gates, he knows that something other than stoicism is driving him forward. It is the desire to see Paul again, and to ask: *Was it real? Did it happen?*

The girl at reception, Georgia, smiles sweetly as he hurries through the lobby.

For an hour he sits at his desk without moving. His mind and body are feverish. But through the swelling sickness come rushes of elation – a heady, defiant pride. He wants to go outside and find Paul, and tells himself that last night can't – mustn't – be the end. But then fear and creeping reticence take hold again: what would he say to Paul? How would he begin?

He fights to remember what happened in the pitch-black cubicle – strains to recapture every detail of every sensation. But as he thinks back, his brain begins to overlay the warm darkness with other images, and one in particular: Ben, on that final morning before he left, lying on the bed. Naked and unexpected. The image is like an apparition, temporarily vivid and then maddeningly hard to retrieve. He chases it until he can't be sure of the details. Tiny fragments survive – the edge of Ben's shoulder, the hairs on his lower back.

His mind craves stronger, clearer images. The new computer faces him from across the desk. Looking back at it, he has an idea of the kind that only a torrid hangover could inspire.

He switches on the machine and it lights up with a hum. Encoded text spurts across the screen. Then he sees a pane of bright blue, littered with emblems. He tries to remember the instructions he received about the World Wide Web. 'It's a thing of genius,' Maud said. 'A wonderful new resource. The telephone will be our hotline to the world.'

With agitated clicks of the mouse, he fumbles through the options – confirming, denying, retrying, opening, closing. *Okay.*

A crest appears in the centre of the screen. It consists of a miniature globe alongside a tiny pictographic computer and telephone. A whistling sound breaks out, followed by a series of bleeps cutting through a whoosh of radio noise. The pips and blasts continue and a chain of blue dots flashes up – one after another. Don stares as if hypnotised.

The screen reforms into a grid of panels that resemble tablets on a church wall. He moves the white arrow of the cursor to the panel labelled *Search*. A white box with a flashing cursor invites him to type. He remembers how the technician told him to insert plus signs between the words.

The + Sleeping + Hermaphrodite

The screen turns into a screed of blue text. It looks like nonsense, but as he casts his eyes across the garbled phrases, choice words spring out: *Villa Borghese, Louvre, Napoleon, Horace Walpole*. Pearls of possibility. With a trembling finger, he clicks the mouse. The page changes again and he sees a field of bleary grey and white.

He wonders if the computer has broken. The picture – if it *is* a picture – is mired in fog. But then a strip of harder, darker tone appears along the top. The strip gradually enlarges, like a Venetian blind descending slat by slat, to reveal a clear photograph. His heart contracts at the sight. Marble thighs, crossing legs, that petite swivelling back and Bernini's magnificent marble mattress, supplied in the 1620s but very similar – he now sees – to a cheap airbed with its cushioned convexities.

And yet the image isn't right. Too stylised, too like a statue. It doesn't align with what's in his head. He searches again.

Beautiful + male + body

Another barrage of blue text. He selects a promising line and finds himself transported, by a single click, to a webpage titled *The Beautiful Male Form*. The words blaze out in mauve and blue at the top of the screen. Beneath is a vertical parade of blurred pictures. In some, he can make out the outlines of bodies. After a few seconds, these too begin to crystallise. Suntanned young men stare back at him from a century's remove through a veil of sepia. They wear laurels in their hair, and fig leaves – a masquerade of modesty.

As he scrolls down, the images shift into colour. A near-naked youth pulls on the horns of a ram, aping St John the Baptist in the wilderness. A muscular hero tiptoes on the end of a diving board in a Californian utopia of palm trees and cerulean sky. Lime-green captions inform him that the pictures are covers from magazines called *Physique Pictorial* and *Epicene*.

Still his mind strives after a clearer image – something closer to how it was. He taps the search panel and types.

Beautiful + male + prostitute

This takes him to another webpage – florid script and a backdrop of flock patterning – and a detour through the demimonde of Victorian male brothels.

But there is too much text, too few images. Most of the pictures are mugshots of Oscar Wilde.

He tries again.

Beautiful + male + whore

Another mass of options in blue, another page of abstract capsules. As the computer whirrs, he discerns blue skies, treetops, smiling faces, glistening shoulders . . .

He hears his own intake of breath. These are colour images of modern men, unclothed and out of doors – naked bodies sprawling on sandy beaches, or reclining in the shallows of a river (the water slides like a pellucid blanket over bronzed limbs), or striding in the piebald light of a forest. Individual men and men in groups, white-skinned and black-skinned, like demigods in the sun, proud and taut in every part.

He strikes the mouse – the page jumps down. The scenes begin to change. The landscape settings are replaced by interiors – dimly lit, scantily furnished. He peers intently, waiting as the fragments assemble. One rippling character is hunched over another in a wrestling match: their two bodies strain and pulse with exertion. A glassy oblong resembling a storm by Turner recedes to disclose a man lying back on a concrete floor with his feet raised. His legs, dusted in black hair, are scissoring to reveal his innermost parts, the penetralia. It's obscene, but Don is unable to avert his gaze. His mouth has gone dry.

His finger guides him along the chain of images. He sees two oil-slicked lovers in an artificial grotto with a painted sunset behind them – Hadrian and Antinous, maybe, in their Egyptian hideaway – and then a rose-tinted room, inhabited by a smiling youth. His naked top half is sharpening into life. He has gaudy red roses in his hair. The fug dispels to show him holding out his engorged penis with an imbecilic smile. His eyes are dreamy and sly.

The pictures are all of the same model now. His poses change from picture to picture – kneeling, squatting, front view, back view, arms raised behind his head to show crops of black hair. In one picture, knee-high leather boots sleeve his lower legs; they make his thighs seem paler – more naked. In the next, he is wearing a tiny leather jacket, and beneath it a brassiere of pink lace and matching knickers that do little to conceal his sidelong erection – it bursts out to one side like fruit spilling from a string bag.

Don scrolls to the bottom of the page. In the final picture, the boy's hair is encircled by a wreath of flowers, his eyes are closed, and his lips – curling in an expression of rapt oblivion – are parted to reveal a sugary flash of teeth. An exploded pearl curves in the shape of a lasso.

Crowns him with flowers and makes him all her joy.

A noise returns Don to his senses. Behind him, he hears scuffling and a high-pitched laugh.

He spins around in his chair. At first, he sees only a cluster of stripy ties and purple blazers through the window. Then there are faces – multiple faces – flaring with excitement, eyes wide and mouths gaping. A group of schoolgirls – aged maybe twelve or thirteen – have gathered around the window. He bangs on the glass and waves them away angrily. They continue to point and shout. One girl has pressed her face up to the glass, squashing her nose flat.

Straightening his trousers, Don turns back to the computer. The picture on the screen is abject, farcical – a pantomime. He jabs at the keyboard to expel it. But the image refuses to vanish, provoking louder expressions of delight from the audience outside.

Panicking, he kneels and pulls the plug from the wall. The computer dies with a plummeting sigh.

More girls are rushing across the lawn to see. They come in twos and threes and larger groups, linking arms and swarming around the glass. One of them brandishes an uprooted hollyhock, taller than a man, with which she beats the pane.

Don shouts uselessly – incomprehensibly, then grabs the curtains and wrenches them shut. He stands still, the fabric clamped in his hands, listening with a thumping heart to the laughs that multiply in the garden. He stands there for many minutes. Eventually the noise dwindles and there is silence again. Unable to move, he studies the particles of light that puncture the unlined fabric.

When at last he relaxes his grip and looks out, the garden is empty. Sunlight falls in golden pools, the flowers are radiant, the leaves of the trees are vibrating with a scarcely detectable rustle. He wants to go out but doesn't dare.

He falls into his chair. Last night already seems like another life. He tries desperately to climb back into it. His memory is a stroboscope of blanks and vivid flashes.

Turning back towards the room, he notices something at the edge of his desk, on the opposite side from the computer screen, that must have been there all morning without his realising. A single hollyhock head, its pink flowers opening out of a stack of closed buds – cleanly snipped, standing in a glass of water.

*

'There's a parcel for you, Don.'

Ina is hunched over one of the Regency portraits in the hall, applying some kind of putty to a chip in the gilt frame. She doesn't look up as he comes through the front door.

A large object, wrapped in brown paper, is propped against the wall of the hallway. It is a flat oblong, almost as tall as him. Written on the paper is a single word in black capitals: *DON*.

He knows at once what it is.

'When did it come?' he asks, trying to sound casual. 'Who delivered it?'

'I don't know, I'm sorry. It was on the doorstep when I came back at five.' She smooths the filled section of frame with a metal spatula, stands back to inspect her work, then withdraws to the kitchen.

With a few swift movements he slices the paper open to reveal Ben's collage – hundreds of shards of painted sky under a sheet of glass. He balances the picture upright on the floor, kicking away the swathes of brown paper, and sees that a piece of paper has been sellotaped to the plywood on the back. A note:

I'm sorry I had to cut and run.
Returning to you your Tiepolo Blue.
With love,
B.

He rests his head against the top of the frame and closes his eyes, as if overcome by exhaustion.

He opens his eyes, still leaning against the picture, and traces the near-invisible joins between the parcels of sky. A thousand shades of blue. Whatever happens, he has this.

Ina has left a plate of eggs and ham on a tray outside his room. The yolks are like yellow eyes on the plate, monstrously dilated. Too consumed by memories to think about food, he allows his gaze to drift between Ben's picture – now propped against the wall of his bedroom – and the familiar view through the window. Finally he cuts out the yolks and eats them in abstracted silence.

He leaves his room to go to the toilet. On the way back, some vague inclination prompts him to cross the landing and go into the spare room where Val keeps his collection of architectural etchings and, ranged on top of the harpsichord, personal photographs. Ignoring the designs of Piranesi, and the glares of Picasso

and Somerset Maugham, Don crosses to the window that over-
looks the garden. It is getting dark outside.

He is startled to see a person below. An old woman with grey
hair is kneeling at the edge of the garden, just outside the door
to the annex. She wears a faded summer dress and holds a pair
of garden shears. She is clipping away at the honeysuckle around
the statue. Don watches as she erodes the foliage, leaf by leaf (or
so it seems), to reveal the hip and lower leg of the stone body.

It grows dark in this time, and yet a dilute light – presumably
coming from the kitchen window – shines on the old woman
and guides her work.

The statue, Don now sees, is a nude Venus carved from marble,
not unlike the ancient statuettes belonging to the Brockwell, but
larger and more modern – a smooth-surfaced creation of the
nineteenth century. One side of the statue remains buried in
dense honeysuckle, as if the body were rising sideways from
green water, but he can now see the goddess's solemn face, her
hair tied back in undulations, her demure breast and leg gently
bent. The marble has an apricot glow that makes him suspect
it was dyed once upon a time.

Even more intriguing than the goddess is the tiny woman
who works away with the shears – patiently, persistently. The
elusive mother. She really exists, and clearly isn't bedridden at
all. Don observes that her complexion is dark – southern
European or Middle Eastern. There are some streaks of black
still in her grey hair.

By that strange telepathy that alerts people to the fact that
they are being observed, the woman turns and looks up at the
window. Her face, although old, is handsome and shrewd
beneath dark eyebrows. Their eyes meet.

18

Don is reading the *Metamorphoses* when the phone rings.

It is Maud – at her most formal. 'Professor Lamb, may we come and see you?'

'We?'

'Michael Ross and I.'

'Come through – I'm short of time this morning.' The phone cracks like a whip as he slams it down. This doesn't bode well. He slides the book under a pile of papers.

Maud and Michael enter the Palladian Library in silence and stand side by side before his desk – a parody of a marriage portrait. It is Maud who finally speaks.

'Professor – Don. It is my duty to report that the museum has received a letter – an anonymous letter – concerning your behaviour.' She looks infinitely grave.

'Oh yes?' says Don, doing his best to seem breezy. 'Not a commendation, I take it?'

'I have asked Michael Ross to be a witness to this meeting.'

She unfolds a piece of paper and holds it out with a shaking hand. It is a typewritten letter, unsigned, addressed to the trustees of the Brockwell Collection. It requests that the goings-on of Donald Lamb be investigated as a matter of urgency. A drunken vandal brought into the Octagon. Blithe indifference to the affairs of the museum. And an incident of sickening indecency witnessed through the window of the Palladian Library.

They know.

Maud holds out the page just long enough for him to register the contents, then steps back and refolds it.

Don thinks of feigning a hearty laugh – of snatching the paper from her hand and tearing it into confetti: rip, rip, rip. He will dismiss the accusations as fiction. He will demand hard evidence. But his head has stalled. He is aware that he is staring inanely.

'We are obliged to take these accusations very, *very* seriously,' Michael says, fixing his eyes on Don. 'The trustees have asked us to speak to you today—'

'Guilty at the point of accusation? You decide to trash my name on the basis of an unsigned letter – a letter written, I might add, in the most ridiculous language, and unsigned, I assume, because it was composed by you.'

'Why would anyone make this up?' Michael demands. His eyes are fuller than ever with zeal.

There is a prolonged silence before Maud recaps the charges.

'Callous disregard for the museum, on multiple occasions, and a most *appalling* display of behaviour witnessed through the window of your study – by *children*!' She appears to steel herself for what she must say next. 'Masturbation.'

The word hangs like poison gas in the air.

'Children,' Michael echoes. It is the first time Don has seen scorn – pure, undisguised scorn – pass like a black shadow across his radiance. 'Playing in the rose garden on their first trip to the museum – their first encounter with works of art. And what do they see when they look through the window of the director's study . . .'

His voice has risen in volume and pitch until he can no longer articulate. He stands there, struck dumb by outrage.

Don listens, feeling as if he is in a dream. But his ego, what remains of it, is rallying.

'As for the allegation of – masturbation,' he begins, 'it's a lie.' (*If only*, an inner renegade voice breaks in. If he hadn't been interrupted when he was . . .) 'And as for them being uncorrupted innocents, they were in hysterics of laughter. How old do you think—'

'We have thought long and hard,' Maud breaks in, 'about whether to refer this matter to the police.'

Something snaps in Don, but his exterior remains placid. He crosses his legs and contemplates the pair of them.

'Then you'd better tell the police about the *Sleeping Hermaphrodite* in the Louvre. Gross indecency in carved marble.'

In his mind's eye he sees the boy on the computer screen, the garland of flowers and the flying line of sacred fluid.

'The executive committee have served us with instructions,' Michael says, seeming to revert to an agreed script.

'Their decision is that you leave the Brockwell Collection immediately,' says Maud with the same mechanical calm. 'Pending a full investigation. I must ask you, Professor Lamb, to be off the premises by midday.'

The midday sun is dazzling, but the mood in the corridors of the Brockwell is sombre. Silence hangs throughout the museum, broken only by whispers. The silence is heaviest in the Palladian Library: Don has already left.

He walked from the room as Michael and Maud stood at his desk, snatching up his nameplate and his copy of the *Metamorphoses*, leaving them to confront an empty chair. He walked straight into the garden, where the sun was high in the cloudless sky.

In his study, impeached by Michael and Maud, he felt horror and anger. He told himself that he would speak to Val, challenge the decision, see his dignity restored. But outside, as he wanders along the paths, it's as if the heat of the day is purging all outrage, leaving only a trace of contempt and – strange as it seems – a spreading euphoria.

With his nameplate sticking out of his jacket pocket, he takes a long and winding route towards the gate of the museum. He comes close to the window of the Palladian Library, the scene of his downfall. Roses surround the glass in a blaze of red and white. They are blooming all over the trellis that frames the window. In time, he imagines, they will encroach on the window-sill and feel their way into the building. They will engulf the place (every wall, picture and statue) with their thorns and flowers. Other plants too will wend their way inside; honeysuckle will grow around the director's chair and desk and that fatal computer, smothering them with fragrant creepers.

He looks around, suddenly forlorn, wondering if he will see Paul. He traverses every path, waits for a long while on the bench in the little niche where he sat with Bill, and then treads the secret winding tunnel to the garden shed. But the shed is locked and the garden is empty. Paul must be on a day off.

And yet, Don thinks, the place is full of Paul: he is there in every blade of grass, leaf, twig, and eruption of petals. Close to the niche, Paul's little piece of picturesque, Don plants his nameplate in the flower bed – driving it into the soft earth like a stake.

Wandering into the Village, he stops by the pink granite fountain that stands on an island of weathered paving at the centre of a small roundabout. He sits at the fountain's base between two stone boxes planted with poppies. The space is like a throne. He stretches out his legs.

From this vantage point, he observes the shops and cafes of Dulwich – so neat and decorous – and tells himself again that it is all over. There can be no doubt that Val knew already. As chairman of the trustees, Val allowed this to happen. And soon, everybody will be aware.

He knows that he won't go back. The Brockwell Collection, like Peterhouse before it, has cast him loose. Ben told him to set himself free, and now he has. He only wishes that Ben were here to share in the absurdity and elation of the moment.

A woman with mounds of red hair and a leather skirt saunters past and glances at him with surly inquisitiveness – a man slumped on the ground, wearing a velvet jacket that has become scuffed around the elbows. He would feel shame – terrible, consuming shame – if he weren't convinced that he is in the process of a mental re-wiring, a vital recalibration.

He stays for hours in his sunny throne. Late in the afternoon, he catches sight of Michael Ross crossing the road in the distance. Michael hasn't seen him. He is walking in the direction of home, striding with the air of a man who has done the right thing.

Don feels his hand sink into the stone box beside him, through the thicket of poppies, into the damp soil. He clenches a handful, then his hand relaxes.

Michael, he thinks, is like a proud young god – the golden-haired Apollo, striding down from Mount Parnassus. A figure at the centre of his own universe. What a relief to be out here on the edge, beneath the fountain. Once Michael is out of sight, Don thinks of Tiepolo's allegory of the four continents. With electrifying clarity, he sees the figures around the fresco's borders, the bustling sideshow that he usually skimmed over as he made his earnest calculations: men from all reaches of the world, and a carnival of animals – birds, horses, a draped camel and an antediluvian crocodile. He detects their bestial reek in his nostrils.

He looks up. The sky is a canopy of pale turquoise. Higher up, it dissolves into the blinding eye of the sun.

The sound of the telephone is like a rainstorm of tiny blades. 'I'm disgusted by what's happened, appalled. I spoke to every trustee, every single one. I begged them to reconsider. Such prudishness. Such rashness. And a man of your repute!'

Surfacing from deep sleep, Don cradles the receiver to his ear. It is nine o'clock in the evening – he must have fallen asleep when he lay down to rest. His forehead is tingling from sunburn.

Val is a smooth torrent of excuses and appeals.

'I'm sorry I couldn't warn you. I was legally prohibited, you see. I want you to know that you have my full support. I'll fight for your reinstatement. I'll speak to Michael. I'll speak to Maud. I'll make them understand, all of them.'

'I wouldn't bother.' Don's voice is arid, sluggish with sleep.

'I'll do whatever I can. You know that, don't you?'

'Do I?' Don turns over on the bed. There are long, doleful faces in the creases of the counterpane.

'Of course you know it, Don,' Val says with sorrowful impatience. 'I've been there for you since . . . since—'

'It doesn't matter,' Don interrupts. 'This was all Michael Ross's doing.'

'Ah, but Don, you mustn't be too hard on Michael.'

Sitting up, Don looks over to where Ben's collage leans against the wall. 'It doesn't matter,' he says again.

'Listen. You must understand. Michael is having marital problems. He's left Craxton Road. I'm telling you this in strictest confidence.'

'It's none of my business. Or yours.'

'His wife,' Val goes on, ignoring him, 'is a beautiful and gifted woman.' He measures out his words like fine thread. 'But you see, Don, she suffers from the *most* terrible bouts of depression.'

'Oh?'

'You wouldn't think it to look at her – or talk to her. Such radiance! But Michael has had a very great burden to bear. They were so young when they married. At least, Michael was. It all happened, I suppose, before he knew what he wanted.' Val gives an artificial chuckle. 'I fear you and I have too little experience in these matters.'

Don pictures Anna beside him in the car that night. Val hasn't once mentioned her by name. Bouts of depression, a great burden – what is the truth of it?

'I have to go, Val.'

'Remember, Don, I'll do everything I can. You'll be back at the Brockwell in no time!'

Not believing Val, he hangs up. He looks around for his address book and finds the Rosses' phone number. Michael is gone from the house, according to Val. But as for Anna . . . He dials the number and the phone rings: five, ten, twenty times. Where is she? At thirty rings he gives up. Perhaps she is out on a drive – her escape mechanism, her dream substitute.

*

He stands at the window of the harpsichord room, looking down at the garden – a new habit in the evening. The honeysuckle has been clipped to reveal the entire statue. Venus holds an apple in one hand. He recognises her now – a sculpture of the mid-nineteenth century by John Gibson. His derelict intellect hasn't lost all its points of reference.

After a while, the door to the annex swings open. The frail figure of Ina's mother hobbles into the garden with a bucket in one hand. She is wearing the same dress as before, and an apron. She produces a large paintbrush and with painstaking care begins to apply a clear fluid from the bucket to the statue, concentrating on the featureless crotch.

Mesmerised, Don watches as the old woman proceeds to gather honeysuckle clippings from a neat pile on the ground, and to apply them – with fastidious care – to the delta between the statue's legs. In time, she has adorned the region with a thick crop of green, as if she were restoring to the de-sexed goddess her biological dues – a triangle of lush, leafy hair.

Then, brushing stray honeysuckle from her hands, she pulls from the pocket of her apron two handfuls of what look like rose petals – dark red clumps. She clasps them to the statue's chest and begins to massage the marble breasts, making slow, circling motions with both hands.

After several minutes, seemingly exhausted from the effort, she drops the crushed petals to reveal nipples flushed with dye.

*

The long walk into London is no longer a search for Ben. The trip itself, with its endless small vistas, is a repeating discovery. He wakes early with a perverse feeling of optimism – and he pursues the mood through the roads of south London, up to the river, over to Soho.

On an overcast afternoon, he is walking past King's College Hospital, where a low brick wall runs beside the pavement. A line of smokers – patients and staff from the hospital – are stationed along it. Some are in wheelchairs. A wiry old man whose legs have been amputated is perched on the wall, a cigarette clamped between his lips. His thighs are tightly wound in bandages that have begun to turn nicotine yellow.

As Don strolls along the pavement, past the straggling line, he is distracted by the twin mounds of the bandages – and he collides hard with someone walking out of the hospital: a man in a flimsy gown, trailing a tall metal rod on wheels. The man tumbles to the ground, a flailing mass of gangly arms and a pale naked back, spotted with moles. The metal rod totters and crashes after him. A soft plastic pouch springs off the end of it and bounces over the pavement, trailing a clear tube, which – Don sees now – feeds straight into the man's arm.

People rush to help. The man yelps inarticulately, staring up in horror. His head is emaciated – a brute conjunction of irises, nostrils and mouth. Don stands back, murmuring useless apologies, apparently invisible to everyone.

Everyone except for a man seated further along the wall, next to a few other smokers who haven't shown concern. The man is staring at him. He looks very like Val, Don thinks, becoming conscious of a pain in his shoulder where it hit the man. In less than a second, he knows that it *is* Val – seated two metres away, with a charcoal-dark cigarette tucked between his fingers.

Val looks at Don without surprise or warmth. He is dressed oddly, in a long raincoat buttoned over a kind of collarless shirt, Indian in style. Don stares, the commotion of the fallen man rushing to the edges of his consciousness.

'Val.'

Val nods in recognition, and Don senses that his inertness is a mask, concealing deep unease.

'Hello, Don.' He shifts slightly along the wall to make space.

Don puts his hands in his jacket pockets and remains standing, remembering the dull anger he felt when they last spoke, and trying to align that feeling with what he now sees. Not a voice at the end of the phone line, but Val himself – uncannily physical. He is the same as ever and yet somehow changed. His face is smooth and tanned, but less shapely – fuller in the cheeks, spongier in the temples. Don notices with a frisson of shock that his neck, exposed by the shirt, is an old man's neck.

'What are you doing here?' Don says, glancing up at the hospital.

'Mamma is unwell.'

For a few bewildering seconds Don thinks that Val is talking about his own mother. But the way he says *Mamma* – the same as Ina – redirects Don's memory.

'What's happened?'

'She had a heart attack. But she'll recover – they think.'

He thinks of the old woman in the garden – the strain of her last performance.

'Where's Ina?'

'Inside. I'm waiting for her.' Val shifts again. 'And what about you? What are you doing wandering the streets when you – *we* – should be fighting for your reinstatement?' He looks along the pavement to where the patient is being helped up, then back at Don.

'It's too late for that. You know it is.'

Val lets the cigarette drop to the ground. With a fresh spasm of surprise, Don sees that he is wearing leather sandals over his naked feet – smooth, angular feet. The toenails are pared and neat and bizarrely shiny.

'Why are you pretending that you'll help me?' Don says. 'What's all this pretending for?'

Val's eyes widen slightly, betraying an inner alarm. 'I don't know what you want me to say, Don.'

'I want you to tell the truth.'

'All right. Fine. There have been times when I haven't told you things' – Val looks into the middle distance and raises both palms – 'but only because your good opinion means everything to me. More than you've ever realised. If I haven't told you things, I've only been trying to preserve – to protect—'

'To protect yourself?'

Val stares back. 'Something bigger. Your faith in me.'

There is raw sincerity in Val's face – and yet, Don tells himself, Val is more than just the man sitting on the wall. *This* is only one version. In the past year, his friend has become a disembodied force whose nature and intentions evade reasoning. Is it possible for a force like that to be kind, caustic, loyal, malevolent – all of these things at once?

The amputee is being lifted by a burly nurse into a wheelchair. The pavement is almost empty now – most of the other smokers have drifted back to the hospital. The sun has broken through. Val crosses his leg over his knee, cupping his hand around the tips of his toes. The stones in his rings catch the light as he releases a long, steady sigh. He seems to have more to say.

'I was going to telephone you, Don. We weren't supposed to meet like this, here – I didn't plan to tell you this way.'

'Tell me what?'

'I'm afraid I must ask you to leave my house.'

At the far end of the wall, a lone elderly woman is sitting in abstracted silence. Suddenly she smiles – as if to herself – to reveal a thick seam of gum.

'May I ask why?' The steel in Don's voice surprises him.

'I understand you brought a homeless man back to the house, to live there.'

'Homeless?' Don laughs, despite his rising bitterness. 'He was an artist. But that was weeks ago. Months ago.'

'What were you thinking?' Agitation breaks through Val's voice. 'That house is sacred. God knows what he's stolen.'

'Nothing. He hated the house, every trinket.' Don's voice quietens. 'Anyhow, he's gone – long gone.'

'And you must go too. I want you out by the end of this week.'

A car alarm has gone off in the distance. Val's eyes stay fixed on him.

Don wonders if Ina has finally informed on him. But an instinct tells him that Val knew about Ben from the start. Perhaps Val did, after all, hear them speaking at the Caravaggio private view; but he has waited until now – kept his cards in check.

'I have a new tenant arriving,' Val says.

'A tenant?'

'It's Michael Ross, if you must know. He has separated from his wife and I've invited him to stay at Montcalm Road until his situation is – resolved.'

Don wants to laugh again – to show Val that he doesn't care. But he is blocked by an anger that closes around his throat like clamping fingers.

'Michael Ross . . . I might have known. You drop him like a stone into my life, all that nonsense about a capable deputy, and now he's pushing me out of the house. What game are you playing, Val?'

Don lets the silence mount, knowing he won't receive an answer – not one that lays things bare.

Val's eyes have widened again, come alive with excitement or anger. 'You think it's time, do you, to probe beneath the surface? Down into the reality of things? Well' – a faint note of satire enters his voice – 'you always did want to measure the depths.' His eyes scan the pavement and the road beyond with sudden, gleeful despair. 'Haven't you considered the possibility, Don, that the surface is a better place to be – up on the level of forms, tones, words? A safer place? Feeling can exist there, too, you know.'

'And what about the baroque inner life? Weren't those your words, once?'

'I'm terribly upset, Don.' Val's voice is altered. 'I wanted my house to be your home. Our beautiful house . . . I wanted it so badly. You know that.' He has lifted one hand and is holding it – fingers stretched – towards Don. It hovers there, then drops.

Don knows it and has always known. With a shiver, he perceives that all the *what ifs* he has been toying with, those vague ideas of other lives lived inside the House Beautiful, have their mirror image in Val's own fantasies. The object – the epicentre – of those fantasies has been him. Living in Dulwich, he has been providing Val with an intimation of what might have been – an image of the life they might have led. He thinks back to the letter he wrote and hid in the pages of a book; perhaps Val still has it somewhere. For a moment, undiluted sorrow, carried on a tide of perplexity, wants to break from him.

Val looks away down the road, breathing steadily.

The pity of moments earlier has scattered into harsher reflections. The man seated on the wall is someone else now – someone different from the friend Don is trying to summon in his mind. It is far too late.

'I'll leave today,' he says. 'I'll find a room down by the park.'

Val's attention springs back, as if he has been presented with a piece of needling gossip. 'Which park? Not Brockwell Park? It's full of drunks. Very rough.'

'Yes, there.'

Don leaves Val on the brick wall. He doesn't look back. Further along the road, he sees Val's car parked. The alarm is shrieking but the car seems unharmed. Its bonnet is like blackened glass, imprinted with a dim version of the sky.

The typescript for *The Skies of Tiepolo* is as thick as a phone book. He tucks it under his arm and fills a carrier bag with clothes. Ina and her mother, he supposes, are still at the hospital. Perhaps it's for the best. He will disappear, just as Ben did, and the life of this beautiful, static place will continue as before.

He follows the familiar route to Herne Hill with the bag swinging from his fingertips. On Half Moon Lane he looks for a sign that he has seen before, on his nocturnal walks, pinned to a nondescript door between two shops. *ROOMS TO LET*.

He rings the bell. The door is opened by a woman with streaks of blue in her hair. Lines of despondence slope from the corners of her mouth.

'The room's a hundred quid,' she tells him on the narrow, dark stairs, without looking round. 'That's a hundred a month.'

She leads him into a dingy room on the third floor. Net curtains hang across the windows. The yellow plaster of the walls is falling away to reveal scabs of brickwork, and the cork tiles of the kitchenette are flaking and rotten. A lightbulb hangs from the ceiling, shaded by a husk of tin foil. On a table sits an ancient telephone, its wire tumbling and snaking across the carpet.

The bathroom is a filthy tiled cell shared by the whole house. It is no matter: he will shower every day at the lido.

He leaves his bag at the flat and walks back through Herne Hill, keeping his typescript under one arm. Building works are taking place inside one of the railway arches: traffic cones and temporary barriers are scattered inside, and a cement mixer turns over a bellyful of grey sludge. The next archway is darker: it seems to have excluded summer from its confines. Inside, he sees a group of tramps gathered around a wire brazier. Beards conceal their faces and long coats cover their bodies. Smoke drifts feebly from the smouldering mass of rubbish in the cage of the brazier.

Stopping on the pavement outside the archway, Don observes the men as they stand around the smoking mess, murmuring and passing a plastic bottle between them. Inspired by some exterior force, he steps forward and stands among them. Two of the men shuffle apart to admit him to their circle.

Don inhales the smoky air for a while and peers at the faces around him – pinched, pleasureless, without expression. Then he pulls a bundle of sheets from the typescript and chucks them into the brazier. Flames eat away at the edges of the paper, feeding on the dry fuel. Tears of excitement and desperation brim in his eyes, dissolving his vision. He chucks in another pile. The flames grow and enclose his work.

One of the men holds out his hands to warm them.

'What you doing, you mad git?' says another man to Don.

'An autodestructive end,' Don replies, looking into the flames.

'Ah well,' says the man, who has just taken a deep swig from the bottle. 'Same goes for any of us.' He looks back at Don with sad, inebriated sympathy. 'Here—' He takes the remaining pages from Don and throws them onto the fire in one go.

The man with his hands extended over the fire has begun to hum a tune.

Don returns to Dulwich and lets himself back into the house. One thing needs retrieving. With an effort, he carries Ben's collage downstairs, bumping it against the carpeted steps, and manoeuvres it through the front door. Like Atlas holding up the sky, he balances the picture on his head – using both hands to steady it – and bears it across the driveway and through the streets. The frame casts a dark rhombus on the pavement.

The walk is a trial of strength. Sweat pours from his face and pools beneath his clothes as he carries the collage to Herne Hill. Thrusting it up the stairs to the bedsit, he hits the frame against the ceiling and the glass splits. When he finally gets it into his new room and props it against the wall, he sees that it has turned into a double mosaic – blue tesserae overlaid by splintered glass. The cracks spread like the veins of a leaf.

This place will do, he thinks, as he lies on the bare mattress with its dense accumulation of smells. It is more than adequate. That man is free whose life is simple. He read it somewhere once, long ago. Finally he knows it to be true. He stares at Ben's picture and listens to the traffic outside.

*

The phone rings for nearly a minute, but this time Anna picks up.

'I thought you must be out.'

'I'm sorry, Don,' she says. 'I was at the bottom of the garden.'

She sounds out of breath, but just like herself – and pleased to hear from him. Perhaps that house on Craxton Road feels different now that she's alone.

'I heard that Michael's moved out.'

'Yes,' she says, and the pause that follows suggests that everything – or perhaps nothing – remains to be said. 'Can we meet, Don? Some time today?'

'Two o'clock in Brockwell Park? I'm living just over the road now.'

A few hours later, they meet at the park gates and set out together on the ascending path that he usually walks alone. It is another blazing summer day; the clouds are stretching in anamorphic designs across the sky. Anna's printed dress flutters in the breeze. Her arms are bright in the sunlight – untouched by the summer.

'I love it here,' Don says at last. 'I've grown to love it. I swim most days, now, at the lido. You see . . .' He clutches his hands behind his back, wondering how to say it. 'I've been put out to pasture.'

'I know what happened, Don. All of it. And I want you to know that if there's anything I can do . . .'

'Don't worry about me. I'm free.'

She looks sideways at him, gently sceptical.

'And what about you?' he asks. 'Are you all right?'

'This thing with Michael was inevitable,' she says in a single exhalation. 'I knew for a long time that it would end – it was just a matter of when.' They walk for a while in silence before she adds: 'I'll go back to New York in the autumn.'

'I'm sorry.'

He wonders whether he means, by this, the break-up or Anna's departure – or if some deeper feeling has escaped into words.

They pass Brockwell Hall and the water pump. He tells her about his chance meeting with Val outside the hospital.

'He looked so odd. So out of place. He was wearing a rain-coat and an Indian shirt, without a collar. I don't think I've ever seen Val without a tie.'

'Maybe he thought the same about you,' says Anna with a passing smile. She slows her pace as they climb another slope. 'Could it have been a hospital gown, underneath his coat?'

'I suppose so.' He tries to eject from his memory the image of the patient he knocked to the ground: half-naked, stick-thin, losing his hold on life. 'But – no, it can't have been. He said he was only visiting.'

They are at a high point of the park, a second peak beyond Brockwell Hall, on one side of a delving sweep of land that Don has privately named the valley.

'Val's going to be spending more time at Montcalm Road, I think,' Anna says. 'While he's being treated.'

'Treated?'

She looks out over the falling – rising – ground. 'Val has liver cancer.'

He follows her gaze, nodding slowly. 'I didn't know.'

Neither of them speaks for a while. He thinks back to how Val looked outside the hospital – that slight loss of definition. Suddenly older. He wonders if it's bad and supposes it must be.

'I didn't know,' he repeats.

'You mean, he didn't tell you.' She turns to him. 'This is why I wanted to see you, Don. How much do you know – really know – about Val?' Her eyes are limpid and searching. 'Did you know that Valentine isn't his real name?'

'What do you mean, Anna?' He feels a tautening inside him.

'He's called Eric James. He was born around here, in Brixton. He came from nothing. Started calling himself Valentine as a teenager. The house on Montcalm Road belonged to a German art historian. Schwarz, he was called – Hubert Schwarz – a Jewish refugee.'

Schwarz – Don has read the man's work, of course. A leading scholar of neoclassical sculpture: clever, fastidious, German. But he has been dead for decades.

'Val went to live with Schwarz and his wife in Dulwich when he was fifteen,' Anna tells him. 'He abandoned his own parents and became like an adoptive son to the Schwarzes.' She stares at him defiantly. 'Didn't you know any of this?'

Don stares back at her, processing the information with fascinated horror. Anna tells him how Hubert Schwarz and his wife lived a Bloomsbury-style existence in the 1940s, sharing and swapping lovers, opening their house in Dulwich to artists and writers, people like Auden and Britten, Peggy Guggenheim and Kenneth Clark – as well as a precocious teenager from Brixton. Val adored the couple: he emulated their manners, their taste, even their accent – that faint trace of German. Val's house – the art, the furniture – isn't Val's at all. And Schwarz, of course, means Black. An adoptive son. An invented life.

'Didn't you know this?' asks Anna again.

Don shakes his head. In all the years of their friendship, he has been content to believe that Val emerged from the dull chrysalis of youth in a fully formed state. For the first time, he sees fragments of that chrysalis lying about like clues. He thinks of Val's book, *The Neoclassical Pose*, published in 1960 – before Schwarz's death, presumably under the great man's supervision.

They walk on, through a cluster of trees, and arrive at the broad incline leading down to the lido. Don catches sight of the oak tree where he hid from Ben.

'I'm sorry, Don,' says Anna.

He touches her on the arm. 'Don't be.' He manages a grin. 'Remember, we've both broken loose. And we live on the same corner of the park. We should meet here again.'

They part at the oak tree. Anna turns and heads south – back in the direction of Dulwich. Don carries on towards the lido. He shouts goodbye to her as she goes, and she turns with a look that seems to signify many things: tenderness, regret, a bright melancholy.

A hand is on his shoulder, shaking him. Someone is speaking – an incoherent but gentle noise. He sees the lifeguard. Her face is known to him – she has woken him on other occasions. She looks concerned. He sits up and tries to placate her, but all that issues from his mouth is a crackling gasp.

'Mister,' the girl says. 'The pool is closing. You must go.'

Don sits up with an acidic gasp. The empty sides of the lido look mournful. The sun is going down.

He stands shakily and pulls his trousers on. The nugget of metal on the chain round his neck swings and hits his chest as he fumbles with his fly.

His vest, he realises, is missing. He pulls his velvet jacket directly over his bare torso and leaves it unbuttoned. The gold chain glints against his sunburnt chest.

As he walks away from the park, his mind begins to fill up

like a vacuum unsealed. Anna's revelations about Val are too many to contain in his head; they seem to describe several lives rather than one. Soon the shuffling facts are mixed up with a litany of names. Michael Ross, Maud Berenson, Michelangelo Merisi da Caravaggio, Angela Cannon, Erica Jay, Eric James, the crazed fop who invaded the Brockwell (did he have a name?): he feels them chasing him along the quiet roads.

He has wandered far off course, down to the South Circular Road. He floats along until he has come almost as far as Dulwich Village.

He thinks of going to the Brockwell Collection. He could go straight in and confront the spectres who have been haunting him. Then it occurs to him that the place will be closed: it is getting late. But perhaps he will go anyway. He will try all the doors – the front entrance, the fire exits – until one permits access, and he will roam through the corridors and galleries. He will sit in the Palladian Library and gaze upon the rose garden in the powdery twilight, and wait for Paul.

He is distracted by the sight of a boy of perhaps seventeen, walking parallel to him on the other side of the road. Staying level, he continues to look.

The boy is the same as the one he saw years earlier, reflected in a leaded window as he walked along a passageway of Peterhouse, just before he met Val for the first time in the Fellows' Garden. His own youthful image – dark-haired, eerily pale, a closed container of thought and desire. He remembers how Ben asked him what he was like when he was young. The answer has walked into view.

The boy is walking at an idle saunter. He wears a suit and school tie; a dark red rucksack swings from his back. He turns and glances across at Don – an indifferent, fleeting look.

The face is identical, Don thinks. Not just a close resemblance but a doubling. He looks back and sees himself, remote yet present, as if each side of the road were a discrete moment in time.

They have turned up Montcalm Road. Don follows from a slight remove, keeping on the opposite side. He watches as the boy comes closer to Val's house, and he is struck by the thought that *that* is where he is headed – that he will go up to the front door and enter. But as they draw level with number eleven, the boy walks on, past the house, with another momentary glance back.

Don waits in front of the house, clasping his knees. His body is weak. Having lost sight of the boy, he wanders through the Village and soon finds himself on roads whose names he doesn't recognise.

Outside a newsagent, the headline of the *Evening Standard* is printed on a sheet of tatty paper behind the grill of a news-stand.

WEST END FINAL
DAY OF CRISIS

The boy with the maroon rucksack walks straight out of the newsagent – and their glances meet once more.

Don follows him, turning from road to road. He doesn't bother to keep a distance any longer. Fate forces him on. He is lost and has only this strange young guide, a stranger he knows, to lead him on.

Suddenly the boy alters his pace. His slouching gait quickens into a stride. In an instant, he has turned into the front garden of one of the semi-detached houses that line the road on both sides, mirror images in brick and timber. The garden gate slams behind him. Up the path, key in door, open, closed, gone . . .

Don stands at the little wooden gate – still rattling in its frame – and stares at the front door with its lunette of glass panes. He feels cheated, as if he has lost, at the last moment, at some protracted game. The sun is sinking fast in the sky. Down the long vista of the residential street, the steel frame of Crystal Palace Tower rises – stark, steep and naked – against the fabulous architecture of the clouds, a pillar of phosphorescent cumulonimbus.

He has begun to wander away when the door of the house flies open. He turns. A man has appeared. He is huge and bald and angry. Letters that make no sense are branded across the front of his shirt. Don walks on, but the man has marched onto the pavement and is striding alongside him, unpleasantly close – standing in his way, blocking his path.

'What you following my son for, mate?'

Don regards him gloomily and attempts to pass.

'Come on, pal. What's it all about? He says you followed him for a mile.'

Mate, pal – terms of endearment that signal ill intent. Don feels light-headed. He holds on to the top of a garden fence and looks into the man's face. It is bullish, perplexed, a shade frightened. What business does Don have, after all, following an unknown teenager through the streets?

'I'm free to go where I like. Your son means nothing to me.'

'Then why are you following him, chum? Are you a perv, is that what it's about?'

Don starts to explain – a case of mistaken identity, a deceptive memory. He was walking the same way, he works in the area. He is, he should explain, the Director of the Brockwell Collection.

The man stares at him, trying to compute.

'I'm free,' Don begins, 'in my imagination—'

The man draws near. 'Get out of here,' he growls in a horrible baritone. 'If I ever see you again, I'll kill you.'

Axioms about liberty swirl in Don's head, refusing to be verbalised. With dignified calm, he walks away.

'Hey, mate, you got the time?'

Two men are walking towards him on the pavement; he tries to step around them.

'Oi, stay and talk to us.'

One of them seizes Don's arm – hard – and starts to pull him back.

'Five quid, come on mate, don't be like that.'

Don breaks free with a muscular wrench and runs. They are running after him, preceded by loud threats, but adrenaline speeds him on. As he sprints, their shouts begin to fade, and he knows that he has outrun them.

He has run back to familiar territory – a road leading into the heart of Dulwich. It is almost dark now; the night is spreading a sepia tint over the streets. Everything feels preternaturally calm. The houses are flat and colourless; their roofs are like triangles of folded paper.

He stops at the Crown and Greyhound, which is quieter than usual. He doesn't feel like Beaujolais tonight. Instead, he orders a bottle of sweet Alchermes liqueur.

Standing at the bar, he looks at the framed photographs that cover the walls. Many of them show people in this very pub at various times in the past. The interior is recognisable in the backgrounds of the pictures – the curving bar sculpted from mahogany, the panes of frosted yellow glass, the textured wallpaper coated in mustard yellow. For a long time, his eyes browse the unknown faces in the familiar setting.

Among the pictures is a black and white photograph in which two women sit at a table, convulsed with laughter. One of the women is young, in her twenties, and has platinum-blonde hair, white as lit magnesium and styled in a 1960s bob. She clutches – caresses – the arm of a much older woman – darker in complexion and dark-haired, beautiful despite her advancing years – who throws back her head and closes her eyes. The blonde woman is about to sink her head in her friend's chest.

Outside, he drinks a glass, then another – until the night air acquires a silken complexion. The near-miss with the two men on the pavement has unlocked a wild, nervous excitement that refuses to die down. Leaving the remainder of the bottle, he walks through the Village, without forethought or intent, until he's back outside the house – Val's house – on Montcalm Road. It looms dark and significant. Not a single window is lit.

He still has the key – a bundle of metal in the pit of his trouser pocket. He never gave it back; Val never asked. He turns it over in his hand.

With a burglar's stealth, he walks up to the door and opens it – automatically, unthinkingly. The key slides in and seems to turn itself. Don steps inside and detects the familiar smell of polish and pictures and books. He closes the door behind him.

The hall is dark. Through the gloom, the gilt statuette of Hercules wrestling with a bull glows murkily. He makes out the creature's massive buttocks, rearing into the air, and the bullet hole of its anus. Tiptoeing, he passes along the hall. He remembers about his remaining possessions, stuffed away in the cupboard under the stairs.

He tries the cupboard door but the brass handle is rigid – uncompliant.

The door to the kitchen is closed. Ina and her mother are asleep, if they're at home at all – if the mother is even alive. The house feels more than ever like a mausoleum: Val's beautiful things are its entombed corpses. The furniture, so decadent and overlarge, seems to block his way with conscious intent – the hulking mahogany chest, the semi-circular table with legs slender as those of a greyhound, the walnut console that thumps his shin as he goes past. He bites his lip to quell the pain.

He mounts the stairs with the grace of a ballerina, and yet the house mutters in protest. The lacquered cabinet on the half-landing glowers back at him with a thousand smudges of muted light.

He has reached the first floor and the entrance to his old room. Darkness hangs about the door like a cloud. When he strokes the brass knob, it gives a tinny, tittering rattle. He turns it and pushes. The darkness is absolute.

He switches on the light and squints in the sudden blaze.

The room is different. There is a decency and neatness about it that makes him certain that Michael Ross – although not here – is living at the house. A mean, stifling orderliness. The bed is made up like a bed in a hotel. It has been positioned against a different wall from before. The desk is clear apart from a hard-back notepad that lies closed.

His eyes pass over the vacant surfaces, all bathed in rosy light – the walls, carpet, curtains, the bed with its champagne-coloured bedspread. The room shimmers and the air grows pinker than before – it seems to have been ionised, every molecule charged.

Someone is coming.

Don hears steps. He stands still. The sound stops, then starts again – a rhythmic brushing noise – and he realises that it's the rush of blood in his ears.

His attention returns to that one article, the notepad. He walks over and opens it. Michael's writing covers the pages in graceful lines.

Just where do we locate meaning? In the work of art, or in the viewer, or between the two – in the world?

Don turns the pages – page after page of beautiful script. A large object slides from inside the pad. It is an envelope, yellow and black: a Kodak wrapper. He lifts the flap and removes a cache of photographs, secured with a rubber band.

At the top of the pile is a view of Rome on a grey day. The Palatine Hill, dotted with ruins and crowned by a row of stone pines. He pulls off the rubber band and feels the glossy prints sliding out of place. Another picture shows the ruins of the forum. In the distance is Michael, strolling amid the broken stones in a short-sleeved shirt and white trousers.

There are many more photographs. The Capitol, the Tiber, the Galleria Borghese, all with Michael roaming near or far – on the roam in Rome. The weather is always grey and oppressive. One picture, taken from a bridge over the Tiber, shows Michael's head and shoulders emerging from the river. His teeth are clenched with the strain of defying the currents. The sinews of his neck bulge like ropes.

Swiping through the pictures, Don comes to one that isn't of Michael in Rome. For a second, he feels nothing. Then it's as if his head and hands are being bombarded with static electricity.

19

The Sphinx is heaving. He finds Sid and Herman at the bar. Darryl isn't there.

'She's working nights,' Sid explains.

Don orders a vodka and pomegranate.

'You're late,' Sid tells him. 'It's past midnight.'

'Late for what?'

'Just late,' Herman chimes with a shrug and a melodramatic roll of the eyes.

The vodka and pomegranate straightens out his head. He leans against the bar and listens to a new story of Herman's – an erotic escapade, much like the old ones. He is distracted from the tale by two passing figures. They look identical. He gazes at the ponytails sprouting from their two bald heads.

'They're from St Martin's,' says Herman, following the drift of his gaze. It is a cryptic utterance, Don thinks. Sybilline.

The identical men turn towards the bar, and Don observes that their faces are not identical at all, even though they are both young. One is youthful and fleshy, but the other is sickly, his cheeks sunken and pitted.

'It's still happening,' Herman says. 'It could happen to anyone.'

Don stares back at Herman – dark, young and fierce. Is he an apparition?

'Are you . . .' He steps closer, chasing his own enquiry into words. 'Are you an oracle?'

Herman stares at him with sealed lips. 'Who the fuck are you, man?' he demands. 'What are you even doing here?' The words fly out of him, hard and bright.

'I wanted to see you,' Don says. 'This place – you and Sid.'

'Tell me,' Herman says. 'Are you just a racist professor or are you something more than that? Are you being *you*, or are you performing the same old shit?'

Don leans towards him. 'I've never felt more real. I wish I'd known all of you a long time ago.'

Herman's expression has softened, become humorous. 'You really are a dumb cunt.'

'That's Professor Dumbcunt to you!' says Sid, with a double dose of camp.

Herman laughs, then grips one of his teeth between his finger and thumb.

'Come here, then, lover,' he says, and he leans into Don's face. He pushes his strong tongue into Don's mouth, where it deposits a small hard object with a bitter taste.

Don has swallowed the pill before he can reject it.

Herman draws away and laughs joyously. His eyes are wide. Don laughs too as he looks from Herman to Sid.

'Dumb cunt yourself,' he shouts in a rush of excitement.

He detaches himself from his friends and levers his way through the crowd.

The toilets at The Sphinx are lit by a single fluorescent strip. It gives the room a bluish pallor, and turns his hands and bare chest into glowing shapes. The music from the bar is a distant thud.

He finds a cubicle with a lock and shuts himself inside. Then he pulls out the photographs and flicks through Michael's pictures from Rome. He comes to the picture that he glimpsed in the house. It is a photograph of Ben.

Ben naked from the waist up and grinning madly, pointing a camera into a mirror. Don feels something close to physical pain, seeing him again on that small oblong of photographic paper. He can tell that the picture was taken at Val's house –

Ben is framed by the bevelled edge of the Queen Anne mirror in the hall.

Just how did one of Ben's private snapshots become mixed up with Michael's travel pictures? Did Michael find the photograph and decide to keep it?

He sits back for a moment and feels a dizzying, preposterous sensation pour through his brain. It is like a shower of dayglo water. He bends forwards and spreads the photographs in a messy arc across the black tiles of the toilet floor.

There are other pictures. Ben in a different mirror, the flash of the camera obliterating everything apart from his face and naked shoulders. Ben's torso abstracted by shade and fractured light as he lies back on a sofa.

Someone bangs on the toilet door. 'Are you okay in there, love?'

Don ignores the voice. He continues to spread the pile out. The floor seems to be wet, like a pool of black water. The photographs float like colourful petals on its surface. As he slides the prints around, he has the sensation of running his fingers through liquid. Ben has captured himself standing or lying or crouching in the dusk of a curtained bedroom – the spare bedroom upstairs. Each time his face is averted or half obscured, and his undressed body is broken up by shadows. Don looks for allusions to statues and paintings, but the poses never quite conform.

The music from the bar seems louder. It drives its beats into Don's head. His eyelids droop from time to time, but the images remain crystalline.

The eerie hue of the pictures shifts as the sequence progresses. The colours change to twilight blues and lilacs. The shutter speed slows to produce floating, spectral images: Ben swigs from a glass bottle, vanishing into a boozy blur. He lights a cigarette and merges into the watery flame.

Suddenly, Don's brain moves like a muscle in spasm. Two legs have appeared in the bottom corners of a picture. They point inwards towards Ben, who kneels between the feet, looking back at the camera with a glower.

Don's tingling fingers sweep the photos across the tiles. Michael Ross goes from being a marginal presence (a stray limb, a fuzzy glow of naked flesh) to a participant: hazy and indistinct, but *there*, in the room. He lies alongside Ben on the mattress, turning away from the camera to conceal his face, or sits on the edge of the bed, seen from behind. His leonine hair is a halo of pale light. Then they're tangled around one another. Their faces are cloaked in shadow or swerving out of focus, but the gaps are easy to fill. Michael's teeth flash out – bared in pleasure or pain – from the shadowed mass of their conjoined heads.

'*In flagrante*,' Don murmurs, so quietly that it might just have been a thought.

The toilet floor has disappeared beneath a carpet of photographs – they are multiplying, swarming . . . He gathers up the dropped prints and returns to the bar, to Herman and Sid and the relief of their banter.

It is close to four o'clock when he leaves The Sphinx.

*

He lies in his bedsit, sprawled on the mattress. His insides, from his throat down to his lower gut, have been sliced, diced and minced into sickness. The perspiration collecting on his forehead seems to have been pressed out from deep within, through the sieve of his skull. But his mind is sparkling. The nausea breaks into phases of sparkling lucidity.

He revels for a moment in the knowledge that he has the power to destroy Michael – to ridicule and monsterise him. He feels the power of a murderer about to strike. But then he remembers Anna, and the power evaporates out of him. He lies face down, poisoning himself with the chemical smell that his body is releasing.

And what about Ben? He is there in each of the pictures – the leading character, the ingenious creator. To expose Michael would be to expose Ben. Don thinks back to the first time he saw Michael, playing tennis in Belair Park on a spring morning, and wonders if Ben was the other player – if they knew each other all along.

Maybe he can challenge Michael privately. Let him know that he has the photographs, reduce it to a hidden transaction. But what would he get? Ben, the Brockwell, Val's love and understanding – all these are like shed foliage now.

He forces himself from bed. He staggers to where he left the contents of his jacket when he got home, scattered across the table – coins, keys, the stolen photographs . . .

Except that most of the pile is missing. Only the snapshots of Michael in Rome are there. At the bottom of the stack, he finds that single portrait of Ben grinning at himself in the Queen Anne mirror. But the rest of the pictures – including all the shots of Ben and Michael together – have disappeared. He checks his pockets. Nothing. Could he have dropped them? Did he leave them in The Sphinx?

His stuttering hands rummage through the newspapers, bottles and plastic cups that cover the table, feeling their way through the rubbish like mice. Can he be sure, he wonders, that he saw what he thinks he saw? And yet the memory is so vivid: picture after picture of Ben and Michael in artful poses and erotic entanglements. He can still see the images floating on the surface of the dark floor, pinpricks of clarity amid the fug of the night.

He gives up the search and lies down. When he sleeps again, he has a vision of Ben and Michael against a backdrop of turquoise satin. They look like paper dolls, locked in exaggerated poses. The blue material is draped across the wall and spread across the bed to create a blue boudoir. Their bodies are bathed in light, absurdly naked, and the blue satin makes them appear airborne. One of them is a falling Icarus, the other a soaring Apollo. But their gestures are antic and ridiculous – they are running and somersaulting mid-air, their legs splaying, their penises rearing up like ornamental prows. Ben blows an invisible trumpet. Michael holds his thumb to his nose and fans out his fingers.

For a long time, he rifles through the strewn chaos of the bedsit, but at last he finds the number. It was in his pocket the whole time. A direct line to Professor Black's study in Peterhouse, scribbled on a torn-off corner of paper, tucked in the secret compartment of his wallet.

Val sounds surprised, prickly at being telephoned.

'Hold on a minute, Don,' he says. 'I'm in my study – with a student. Let me take the call next door.' The line blanks out, and Don counts the seconds. Val's voice reappears, brighter now: 'I *must* just tell you, the college is talking about nothing else—'

'Val, listen to me.'

'Wait, you must hear this – do you remember that young Fellow, Ferdinand Fernandez? That upstart who knows everything about Roman statuary? Well! He's been excommunicated for plagiarism.' Val is his usual self – blithe and opinionated. It's as if nothing has happened between them. 'It's the talk of the department – has been for days! Don't you remember his cock-sureness, his certainty? All an act. It turns out he's been lifting great swathes of his writing from a lecturer in Heidelberg.'

'A fake, you mean? A man with a made-up past?'

'Exactly that, Don.'

'A beautiful, intricate fiction?'

'The very thing!'

Don notices the German in Val's voice – it's there in every clipped syllable; stronger than in the past.

'Did you know Michael Ross is a homosexual?' he asks.

'I can't hear you – the line is breaking up.'

'Did you know that Michael is a homosexual?

'What a question to ask! I was telling you something far more important. Really, Don, what do you even mean?'

'You knew, didn't you? Of course you did. Anyway, I have photographs – proof. Damning proof.'

'I don't know what you're talking about,' Val says tersely. 'Proof of what?'

'I see you're not denying it. He's gay, Val; the man is as gay as you are.'

'Oh Don, for heaven's sake. You know I never use that term. I'm just an old poof. As for young Michael—'

'He's gay, damn you. I have pictures—'

'Michael is no concern of yours any longer,' Val interrupts.

'But he's a concern of yours, isn't he? He has been all along.'

Val's voice becomes sharp. 'This isn't like you – this new desire for knowledge. When did it start? When did you decide to open your eyes?' Then his voice changes again – reverts to type, as if he is restoring a mask that shouldn't have slipped. 'I simply wanted to tell you that Ferdinand Fernandez is a plagiarist. If Cambridge affairs are of such little interest to you, then it won't hurt you to know that I am to become Master of Peterhouse. Council voted me in last night, unanimously. There really was no other suitable candidate. To think, you were once tipped for the role yourself . . .'

Don finds himself laughing. A silent, mirthless laugh. 'You knew all of this was going to happen,' he says.

'Really, Don,' Val says in a reasoning voice. 'You credit me with more power than I have.'

'Not just the election to the Mastership. I mean everything.'

Everything means the end of his Cambridge life, the move to Dulwich, the spiralling embarrassments and crises. It means *SICK BED*, that strange creation of a split self, still radiating its malign power from the front court of Peterhouse – even as a charred ruin. Don has played his role, but Val has been observing and orchestrating. They, too, have been like the two halves of a split self.

It all started on a summer afternoon in Cambridge – the beginning of a long, patient, determined refusal to forgive.

Don feels a flicker of triumph at the thought of his strange, eventful summer – of perfidious Ben (did part of him, at least, belong to Don?), and then Paul. He reminds himself that lovers never last, at least not in myth. They turn into other things, like flowers. Narcissus became a narcissus. The blood of Adonis gave birth to the anemone. Paul became a hollyhock, and Ben . . . he looks across the room at *Tiepolo Blue*. He still has that.

'Really, Don,' says Val again. 'It saddens me to see you come to this. If only I could help – do something. If only.'

'If only,' Don repeats. 'Why didn't you tell me that you're ill, Val?'

'Ill?' Val waits, as if for dramatic effect, and laughs drily. 'A little local difficulty. *What is else not to be overcome?*'

Val's old rallying cry. And yet, at the end of the sentence, his voice is faint and reedy.

Don lies back with the phone to his ear and forgets for a few seconds that Val is there. Through the window, he hears a car door slamming on the road outside. Then he wonders if he can hear, on the other end of the line, the chapel bell of Peterhouse striking the three-quarter hour.

In the end, Val speaks in a tone of voice that seems to come from the distant past.

'Oh, Don. What a terrible thing.'

The line goes dead.

At midday, he stops by the Crown and Greyhound. He still feels strange – as if his whole body is made of immiscible elements: a chiaroscuro compound.

The pub is empty, large and bright. As he stands at the bar and wonders what to order, his eyes return to the framed photographs covering the walls. They land on the black and white picture of the two women laughing – blonde and dark; younger and older. He comes closer. There is something scribbled in pencil on the mount of the photograph: *Ina Stables and Mariam Schwarz, Belles of the House Beautiful.*

Ina and Mariam – *Mamma*, rhyming with *hammer*. Don's mind spasms through a chain of deductions. They're lovers, not mother and daughter. Mamma is Mariam Schwarz, the inspiration behind Angela Cannon's *SICK BED* – a pioneer of the found object. How could he not have realised? He thinks of the gradual revelation of Venus in the garden: it was a creative act, an example of her late style. Once she was the wife of the art historian Hubert Schwarz – a society couple, renowned bohemians . . . and Val's adoptive parents. The House Beautiful is hers.

He stares at the picture, bringing his eyes close. The relationship with Ina must have flourished in later years, after the great scholar's death. Perhaps the two women were regulars at this place once. Today they're recluses, exiled to a small, ugly extremity of Mariam's house – Val's doing, no doubt – but a quarter of a century ago they were the laughing *belles* in the photograph.

He turns away from the bar. The pub – and beyond it, Dulwich Village – feels so oppressively empty, so languid and still, that all he wants to do is get out. He has seen enough pictures.

In Brockwell Park, the leaves on the trees are browning at the edges, developing the crisp periphery of an egg too long in the pan. But everything else – from the sky, flecked by clouds, down to the swaying blades of grass – is bright and steeped in colour, an insistent reminder that summer hasn't died.

He walks past the duck pond. The water is still. A yellow haze of gnats hovers above. He passes the miniature railway, and the train passes him in the opposite direction, a long bricolage of chimney, engine, carriages and – at the back – a scowling child.

Since he went to The Sphinx, he has been experiencing a strange, intermittent sensation, entirely different from a hangover. It comes in violent rushes – surges of perception during which colour and sound are enhanced to an almost impossible degree. The feeling is inseparable from the memory of those photographs scattered on the toilet floor.

He stumbles across the grass towards the lido. Green is becoming an indigestible colour. A pigment that was once so natural and so lovely seems now to lie on the surface of things like paint – smeared across the grass and the leaves of the trees: excessive, garish green that has been poured and slathered. The slopes are saturated with it. The trees are clots of thick impasto. When the sun shines, the effect is grotesque.

He reaches the lido. There is no one around. The turnstile that leads into the complex won't move. He ignores the printed signs with their apologies and explanations, and rattles the turnstile against its lock before noticing that a staff gate is ajar. He wanders through.

The lido is deserted and blindingly bright. The pool sides are a desert of concrete. Through squinting eyes, he sees that the pool is empty – a vast, hollow sarcophagus – and that its turquoise sides and bottom are peeling and cracked. A plastic chair lies on the dry bed of the deep end. Everything is perfectly quiet and still.

But not quite silent. A gentle murmuring – he thinks at first that it is a plane overhead – comes from the far end of the lido. He wanders along the edge of the blue basin. It is the sound of a radio turned low, not properly tuned – and it seems to be coming from a window in the far corner of the enclosure, a section of the outbuildings not open to the public.

Next to the window is a half-open door. He approaches and peers in. As his eyes adjust to the gloom, he sees a storeroom strewn with rubbish – glasses, bottles, crushed beer cans, a high-rise stack of pizza boxes, a rolled-up carpet, a fridge turned at a strange angle to reveal its grilled rear. A stereo spattered with paint is whistling garbled transmissions. The place is airless, stale and boiling hot.

At the centre of the room are two bodies – a man and woman, pale and emaciated and half covered by a stained sleeping bag which does nothing to hide the man's genitals – a limp cock and glassy balls, translucent and marbled by blood vessels. They look dead, both of them, lying there amid the junk, but Don sees that their bodies are heaving in unison, straining to oxygenate. The woman's hair, blonde and tangled, is smeared across her shoulders and neck.

The inertia of the scene breaks abruptly. The woman sits bolt upright – her body moving ninety degrees. She sees Don at once through the shard of the open door and sets her glare on him. Then – and it seems almost instantaneous with her waking – she begins to howl abuse. The words pour out like an incantation.

'Homo! Fist-fucker! Raving iron!'

She accelerates through the insults, tripping over her words in the effort to expel them, and rolls onto her knees.

'Teapot!' She rises to her feet and moves unsteadily towards him. Her scrawny body glows yellow.

The man turns over and snores horribly.

Teapot. He wonders if he heard correctly. He steps back into the light of the lido. It seems as if she will follow him out, but then the door slams closed in his face. He hears the rant continue within and feels a strange emptiness – an absence of alarm – checked only by vague curiosity at the energy that erupted from that sickened, wasted body and then – equally strange – the pointed nature of her abuse.

He makes his way down Tulse Hill, towards the train station. It is a quarter past three when he arrives – seven minutes until the next train to London. He looks around. He hasn't been to

the station before. A pair of tracks run between two long plat-
forms, both deserted.

He walks sluggishly along the platform and sits on a bench,
running his hands across the undulating sheet of red-painted
steel, gridded with holes. It is hot and tacky in the afternoon
heat. He feels an overpowering desire to doze.

He jolts awake. There are two men on the opposite platform.
They have appeared from nowhere. He hears them before he
sees them. Threats, furious shouts. Then he sees two bodies
locking and unlocking, a flurry of punches and kicks, a jacket
torn off, a head slammed against a pillar. For a second, he
catches sight of a face.

'Ben!'

The shout dies in his throat. He watches, motionless. For a
fleeting moment, Ben is as clear as day, hypnotisingly clear,
before he becomes snarled up again with his opponent, subdued
by a headlock, staggering as the other man drags him in a circle
and rains punches on his head.

The sight is sickening. Don sinks to his knees and crawls to
the edge of the platform, watching them as they spin, a dynamo
of kicks and punches, across the opposite platform, on the other
side of the tracks.

His head and heart are agonisingly heavy, but his limbs are
light – they seem to have disappeared. Only a wincing pain in
one shoulder, and the heat that rises from the concrete slabs
beneath him, into his hands, remind him that he is there – a
body, a man. He tries to keep sight of the two men on the other
side. A child is crying somewhere. He looks around for something to throw.

'Mind that man,' he hears a woman say.

The heat is overwhelming. His head droops. His eyelids weigh
heavily. Curtains of red encroach on his view.

Kneeling at the edge of the platform, he peers groggily at the
train tracks. The rails are crystal-bright: they scorch the vitreous

contents of his eyeballs, sending a stack of white bars through the red void of his inner vision, onto the roof of his brain – blazing stripes like a stave drawn in neon. As he grips the concrete precipice, he knows that he must look exactly like Caravaggio's *Narcissus*, hanging on the wall of the Octagon – yes, just like that, gazing over the bank of the pool at his own reflection, leaning in as far as he can.

But where is Ben? He tries to raise his head.

'Please stand back from the platform edge. The next train is not scheduled to stop at this station.'

The voice is resonant and official, like the announcer of a Pathé newsreel.

Don searches through squinting eyes but his sight is playing tricks. The fighting men are bodies tumbling in space. They flash in and out of view, blocked every so often by silken clouds. The distant platform tilts like a listing ship, finding a new axis. Down on the tracks, empty beer bottles are scattered across the sleepers. The rails glint and the bottles flash. *SICK BED*.

Someone is shouting like a maniac.

He opens his eyes and sees – framed like a photograph in the train driver's window – a heavy-set man beside a woman with a mass of red hair, bare-breasted in the sunlight. Then the black disk of a buffer, a strip of yellow paint, and a corona of light. There is a long, searing screech – just the sound, he supposes, that a Fury would make. He closes his eyes and the noise fills his head. He feels his heart stop with a single thud beneath the velvet lapel of his jacket.

The men on the other side of the tracks didn't see the accident. As the train hit, they were already walking up the path leading from the platform to the main road (a sloping walkway overhung by trees), laughing about something. Above their heads and around their feet, autumn leaves were beginning to fall.

Acknowledgements

I would like to thank Samuel Hodder, my agent, for his belief in this novel and for his friendship. And I would like to thank Juliet Brooke at Sceptre for making the book a reality, providing guidance and inspiration in equal measure.

Thank you also to Louise Court, Helen Flood and everyone at Sceptre for being champions of the book. I am especially grateful to Richard Shone, who read an early draft and responded with wit and wisdom – as well as to Jonathan Cox, who listened to various offhand rehearsals of the novel's episodes. Amber Burlinson gave the text a masterly close read, aided by memories of Dulwich and knowledge of Peterhouse. For his constant support, thank you to Matt Mavridoglou. For their insight and encouragement at different moments, thank you to Donato Esposito, Matt Ingleby, Maggi Hambling, Hugh Monk, Lee Pearce and Iain Ross. I have a debt of gratitude to my doctoral supervisor, Caroline Vout, and my undergraduate tutor, Robert Douglas-Fairhurst, that extends across most of what I write.

Thank you above all to my husband Alexander, to my mother Frances, to my brothers Tom and Patrick, and *in memoriam*, my father Joe.